SCENES FROM THE ENLIGHTENMENT

T0152500

Originally published in Korean
as *Taeha* by Inmunsa, 1939
Translation copyright ©2013
by Charles La Shure

Library of Korean Literature

Library of Congress Cataloging-in-Publication Data
Kim, Nam-ch'on, 1911-1953.
[Taeha. English]
Scenes from the enlightenment : a novel of manners / Kim Namcheon ;
translated by Charles La Shure. -- First edition.
pages cm
ISBN 978-1-62897-068-5 (pbk. : alk. paper)
I. La Shure, Charles, translator. II. Title.
PL991.415.N3T3413 2014
895.73'3--dc23
2014016365

Partially funded by the Illinois Arts Council, a state agency
Published in collaboration with the Literature Translation
Institute of Korea

www.dalkeyarchive.com

Cover: design and composition by Mikhail Iliatov
Printed on permanent/durable acid-free paper

KIM NAMCHEON

SCENES FROM THE ENLIGHTENMENT

A NOVEL OF MANNERS TRANSLATED FROM THE KOREAN BY **CHARLES LA SHURE**

DALKEY ARCHIVE PRESS
Champaign / London / Dublin

INTRODUCTION

Kim Namcheon was born Kim Hyosik on March 6, 1911, in Seong-cheon, South Pyeongan Province, northeast of Pyeongyang in modern-day North Korea. As Korea had just been annexed as a colony of Japan the previous year, Kim spent most of his life as a citizen of the Japanese Empire, a native of a land that no longer existed.

He was active as a writer from a young age, founding a literary magazine with a small group of his high school classmates. Later, as a student at Hosei University in Japan, he joined the Tokyo branch of the Korean Artists Proletarian Federation (KAPF), an organization that had been founded to "work toward the establishment of the culture of the dawning proletariat." His socialist ideology informed not only his writing but his actions as well: in 1930 he participated directly in the proletarian movement by joining a strike by Pyeongyang rubber factory workers, writing and distributing a manifesto supporting their cause. In the fall of 1931 he was one of many KAPF members arrested by the Japanese. In the spring of 1935, the Japanese once again arrested en masse the members of KAPF, ultimately disbanding the group.

After the KAPF was disbanded of, Kim went to work for *The Korea Central Daily* newspaper, and for several years he published no fiction. However, in addition to being a writer, he was also a literary critic, and he continued to publish his theories in an attempt to blaze a new trail for fiction beyond the proletarian movement. The years from 1937 to 1943 saw an increase in his literary production, and it was during this time that he published the present work. In 1945, Japan was defeated, and Korea was liberated at last. Sometime in late 1947, Kim decided to return to his home in the north of the peninsula, where he served as a delegate to the Supreme People's Assembly and as secretary-general of the General Federation of Korean Literature and Arts Union. At the conclusion of the Korean War in 1953, though, the political tide turned, and Kim Namcheon, along with some other former KAPF members, was "purged" (that is, executed) by the government.

Scenes from the Enlightenment was published by the Inmunsa publishing company in 1939, under the title *Taeha*, meaning "great river"—likely a dual reference to the Biryu River, which features prominently in the work, and to the author's desire to produce a family chronicle of grand scope, not unlike a roman-fleuve. In fact, this novel was intended to be the first part of a two-part work. Kim did later write two short stories that depicted events after the end of this novel—one of which was the inspiration for the title of this English translation—but the second part remained unfinished.

The convention at the time was to serialize full-length novels first, publishing periodic episodes in newspapers, and then, if the book managed to garner a measure of commercial success, to publish the book as a whole. *Enlightenment*, however, was a bold enterprise by Kim Namcheon and Choe Jaeseo (the head of Inmunsa), as it was not serialized but published as a complete work. This was a conscious effort to overcome what they saw as the limitations of serialized novels—choosing popular and commercial appeal at the expense of artistry—and restore the novel to its original position as literature rather than commodity.

In the spring of 1938, Kim traveled to his hometown of Seongcheon (the "certain village" mentioned in the first line of *Enlightenment*), where he spent one month researching and gathering material for his novel; he began writing on June 13, 1938. Korea had been under Japanese colonial rule for 28 years at that point, and hostilities in Asia were well under way. Although World War II is generally considered in the West to have begun in September 1939, Japanese aggression began on September 18, 1931, when the Japanese detonated an explosion on their own railway in Manchuria as a pretext for invading this region of China. The summer of 1937 marked the beginning of open war between Japan and China, and Japan moved onto a total war footing. This included measures to mobilize Koreans to fight for the Japanese Empire; the National Mobilization Law was passed in 1938, and allowed Koreans to "volunteer" for the Japanese army. Japan also clamped down culturally, and the traditional Korean folk games and pastimes depicted in *Enlightenment* would have been forbidden.

The story itself, though, was set nearly thirty years earlier, at the beginning of the Japanese colonial period. Bak Seonggwon is introduced as having "just turned forty this year" (p. 16), and it is mentioned shortly thereafter that he had been "a hot-blooded youth of twenty-three or twenty-four" during the Revolt of 1894, making the year 1910 or 1911. This was a critical time in Korean history. Japan had long had its eye on the Korean peninsula, and after victories over China (1895) and Russia (1905), the Japanese Empire coerced Korea into signing the Protectorate Treaty in 1905. This ostensibly allowed Korea to maintain internal autonomy, but it handed the nation's diplomatic sovereignty to Japan, which established a resident-general on the peninsula. A further treaty was signed in 1907, which abolished internal autonomy as well, subordinating the government of Korea to the Japanese Resident-General. Finally, in 1910, Japan annexed Korea, and Korea ceased to exist as a sovereign state.

However, the transitional character of the time period in which *Enlightenment* is setgoes beyond the geopolitical transition of Korea from sovereign state to protectorate to colony. It was also a time of great social and ideological change, when the old feudal system was being challenged—and slowly but inexorably defeated—by the new modern order. As the strict Confucian hierarchy collapsed, the promise (if not yet the full reality) of equality was rising from the rubble. While lineage and status had once been the ruling principles, now it was economic might that ruled. Those who had no place in the traditional hierarchy began to push back, with varying degrees of success.

In addition to the temporal setting, the novel's spatial setting also serves as a physical manifestation of the many transitions Korea was undergoing. Kim's hometown of Seongcheon was, though relatively small, an important location. It was a gateway to Pyeongyang and a place where significant Protestant activity led to a clash between old and new ideologies, and in *Enlightenment* it functions as a metaphor for this conflict and transition. Bak Rigyun and his brother, representing the old guard, live just inside Visiting Immortal Gate, and the monument that is the only pride of their family lies just outside the gate.

The monument erected in her memory was just outside Visiting Immortal Gate, on the left-hand side, beneath the shabbiest in the long row of monument pavilions. When weeds grew in the furrows between the roof tiles and sparrows nested in the corners of the eaves, the Bak brothers would uproot the weeds and clear away the nests with their own hands. But the roof began to sag and the pavilion began to lean to the right. It would take no small amount of money to repair or rebuild it. They propped it up by putting a single pillar on the right side and, although it was still an eyesore, they managed to keep it standing. It was a forlorn sight as it stood there awaiting its own demise—just like their hollow boasting that they were yangban. (pp. 15-16)

As if the imagery itself were not hint enough, Kim spells out the connection at the end of this paragraph. Bak Rigyun and his brother, though of aristocratic lineage, have accomplished nothing on their own, and so cling desperately to the achievements of their ancestors.

Bak Seonggwon, who stands in sharp contrast to Bak Rigyun and his brother, makes his home "at the highest point in the village," near Nine Dragons Bridge. This is the beating heart of commerce in Seongcheon, where merchants such as Nakanishi, Yi Chilseong, and Kim Yonggu sell their wares. Nakanishi is a Japanese who runs a general store where the most wondrous of items are introduced to the people of Seongcheon. Chilseong travels regularly to Pyeongyang to buy produce for his grocery, and Yonggu runs a smaller operation selling candy and cookies, taking to the streets as a peddler during the Dano Festival to earn even more money. The residents of the neighborhood of Nine Dragons Bridge are all characterized by this motivation to turn a profit; they have embraced the new ideology of capitalism and are determined to be at the forefront of the social changes it will bring. In this way the neighborhoods of Visiting Immortal Gate and Nine Dragons Bridge are a microcosm of the changing of the guard that was occurring in Korean society at that time.

One of Kim Namcheon's theories of fiction saw folkways,

not simply as interesting customs and pastimes, but also as a means through which to understand history, and *Enlightenment* is Kim's attempt to put this theory into practice. The lengthy description of Hyeongseon's wedding in the second chapter is fascinating for what it tells us about Korean customs, but Bak Seonggwon's decision to have the traditional Schoolmaster Gu lead the groom's procession and the "enlightened" Choe Gwansul serve as the groom's escort can also be seen as an attempt to achieve legitimacy by bringing together the old traditions and the new culture. The sight generates more mirth than respect among the onlookers, though, and thus this attempt can be considered a failure. But Bak Seonggwon later obtains this long-desired legitimacy thanks to another folkway element of the text: his appointment as vice-president of the athletics meet held during the Dano Festival period.

History is again reflected in this Dano Festival, first and foremost in the contrast between the Dano Festival and the concomitant school athletics meet.

> The games played by the women who went up into the hills . . . were held separately from the men's wrestling, but an order was issued that no other meetings were to be held on the day the athletics meet began. Wrestling was the men's sport, and there were no women spectators, but the athletics meet was an enlightened gathering and thought to be different from something like wrestling, so even if young girls, maidens, and newly married women could not attend, the day was chosen and widely advertised so that at least married women over the age of thirty in their hooded coats, as well as old women and gisaeng, could attend. (p. 231)

The Dano Festival, which represents the traditions of Korea handed down from generation to generation, remains steeped in Confucian ideology, specifically the principle of the separation of men and women. The athletics meet, though, is the product of the external influences of a new culture and civilization. Although it is not possible to do away entirely with the separation of men and women, this enlightened space does allow some limited mingling of the sexes. It is also in this space that Hyeonggeol competes in both the footrace and the mock cavalry battle. Although he is frustrated in his various quests for women throughout the story, first by his step-brothers and later by his father, here at the athletics meet he is able to shine. Despite his heroic performances, though, he does not win either event in which he participates; in the footrace, for example, he places second behind a student from Pyeongyang. Although his decision to leave Seongcheon at the end of the story is a direct result of his frustrations in love, we can perhaps see in his heroic losses at the athletic meet the seeds of the realization that Seongcheon is too poor a stage for the drama he hopes his life will become.

Critics have, however, pointed out that Kim's understanding of history is rather narrow in its scope. For example, Seongcheon is primarily a farming village, but little mention is made of the lives and hardships of the farmers who live there. On a larger scale, there is little overt mention of the loss of sovereignty and the difficulties of life under Japanese colonial rule. It could be said that the "strange and wondrous" goods Nakanishi introduces to the village at the be-ginning of the twelfth chapter, for example, are a metaphor for the fact that the Japanese are the sole conduit for the transmission of Western civilization in Korea. This, however, is merely dispassion-ate commentary on reality and not criticism of Japanese colonial-ism. Criticism, albeit subtle, may be found in the treatment of the surveyors who appear in the next chapter, beating up a helpless vil-lager before being vanquished by Hyeonggeol. These are not simply uncouth and domineering outsiders; they traveled around from vil-lage to village, drawing lines on maps. Korean farmers, who rarely farmed land with officially defined borders, generally found them-selves on the short end of these land distribution policies. In a word, surveyors were a mechanism of oppression by the Japanese, and it is unlikely that Kim Namcheon chose this occupation for these two despicable villains by chance.

That being said, it is true that very little criticism of the co-lonial reality can be found in *Enlightenment*. Of course, censorhip made overt criticism impossible, but many scholars have found fault with Kim for completely abandoning his proletarian ideology and not offering a critical view of history. It is only natural that such a prominent literary critic should be held to the high standards that he had established; Kim himself admitted that *Enlightenment* did not live up to the lofty goals of his theories, so it is no surprise that other critics should feel the same.

Yet this does not diminish the importance of the novel. As a literary work and a glimpse into Korean life and traditions, it achieves much. The care and detail that Kim puts into his descriptions of everyday items and events bring to life a Korea that has not existed for over a century, and the fluid prose draws the reader into the story of one family in one village during a critical time in Korea's history. Although its original title, as mentioned above, would seem to indicate the author's desire to present the sweeping flow of history, *Enlightenment* is probably better understood as a fine-grained depiction of a narrower slice of life—a detailed drawing rather than a panoramic landscape. In that regard, *Enlightenment* plays an important role in the history of Korean literature. It is hoped that this English translation will play an equally important role in fostering understanding of this critical time in Korea's history and culture.

Charles La Shure, 2014

SCENES FROM THE ENLIGHTENMENT

In a certain village lived two families from the Miryang Bak clan. There was Bak Rigyun, whose family had called this village home for five generations, and who made his living selling noodles behind Mr. Gil's smithy, which was next to the herbal medicine shop just inside the Gate of the Visiting Immortal. His younger brother, Seonggyun, ran an inn and stable five houses up. Their children were as numerous as a litter of piglets, but they had nothing in the way of property except the pitiful thatched-roof houses where they lived. Even though they made their livings running a noodle shop and an inn, and even though they had not even a patch of land to their names, they went around calling themselves yangban aristocrats. None of their ancestors had held the post of prime minister, and the family had never produced a high-ranking minister, a renowned statesman, or a famed general. The head of the second generation of their family, after they moved to this village, had been a petty official, who died at a young age; his wife, Lady Seong, had hung herself so that she could follow in her husband's footsteps, earning herself the title "virtuous woman" but leaving behind her their son. This had been recorded in the village chronicle, and when the Bak brothers were in their cups they would recite the Chinese characters of the citation or mumble its Korean translation as if it were a Buddhist chant.

"Lady Seong was the wife of Bak Gwiseong and eldest daughter of Seong Nonsan. When her husband Bak Gwiseong died, she hung herself in devotion to him, and the people of the village buried her body with her husband in a single burial mound. Lady Seong was twenty-three years old at the time."

The monument erected in her memory was just outside Visiting Immortal Gate, on the left-hand side, beneath the shabbiest in the long row of monument pavilions. When weeds grew in the furrows between the roof tiles and sparrows nested in the corners of the eaves, the Bak brothers would uproot the weeds and clear away the nests with their own hands. But the roof began to sag and the pavilion began to lean to the right. It would take no small amount of money to repair or rebuild it. They propped it up by putting a single pillar on the right side and, although it was still an eyesore, they managed to keep it standing. It was a forlorn sight as it stood there awaiting its own demise — just like their hollow boasting that they were yangban.

Bak Rigyun took aside a customer coming in for noodles and complained, "Who does that Bak Seonggwon think he is? He says he's a Miryang Bak but all he does is ruin my reputation, and who knows what Bak family he's from anyway? That vagabond goes around stealing whatever he can get his hands on, saying that he's a Miryang Bak . . ."

There was indeed another family from the Miryang Bak clan living in this village. The head of this family had built a large house at the highest point in the village; it towered above a dozen or so houses, about halfway between the Pavilion of the Descending Immortal and Visiting Immortal Gate, right about where Nine Dragons Bridge was. The master of the house had just turned forty this year, and his name was Bak Seonggwon.

Bak Rigyun may have wondered "what Bak family" Bak Seonggwon was from, but he was, in fact, also from the Miryang Bak clan. It was just that no one knew whether one of his ancestors had been anything more than a petty official. Seeing that his family had no monuments to a filial son or a virtuous woman, he certainly didn't seem to have anything to boast of, unlike Bak Rigyun's family.

He was not originally from this village. He'd moved here some twenty years ago from Eunsan. His grandfather had been a petty official who had schemed his way into some rice from the government storehouse. He'd earned a fortune by lending against rice stipends or buying them up when they were cheap and then selling them again in the spring or summer, when rice prices had risen. Of course, when the people ran out, he distributed his own rice or the rice he used as collateral and then demanded it back at the harvest at exorbitant interest, and it was with this money that he would have bought his land. At any rate, Seonggwon made a good amount of money, but his father had squandered it all with his gambling, his drinking, his frequent visits to Pyeongyang in his later years, and even his smoking of opium, which had just been introduced from abroad. When he died an untimely death, there was little left of his estate.

Not long after Bak Seonggwon had finished his three years of mourning for his father, the revolt of 1894 broke out. At the time, he was a hot-blooded youth of twenty-three or twenty-four. When everyone else fled to the mountains of Gangwon Province, he deemed that it was truly the time for a brave man to take action, and he stayed behind, entrusting his wife and children to relatives who were leaving the village. He traveled back and forth from Jasan to Suncheon, Pyeongyang, Junghwa, and even Hwanghae Province, selling to the soldiers there. Many daring peasant soldiers who had left their farmlands helped transport military supplies, and most of them were paid in silver coins. Seonggwon used brass coins to buy as many of these silver coins as possible and then buried them in the ground in secret.

When the war was over and everyone returned from their place of refuge, Bak Seonggwon took his wife, concubine, and children from Eunsan and came to this village, looking for a place to settle down. What caused him to leave Eunsan and settle here? According to rumors that made the rounds later, he had poor relatives in Eunsan, and if they found out he had come into money, he would have had to spend it all helping them; so he claimed that he had never had anything but his two red fists and quietly left to seek his fortune, finally settling down in this village.

Seeing that he built a small house in the Dumutgol neighborhood just after he first arrived, that story seemed likely enough. He put up his wife and concubine in that small house with its few rooms, and he split up his three children between their mothers. But a year later, when everyone who had fled the village returned and sold their houses because they were broke, he bought dirt cheap the street-side house near the marketplace where he now lived, and he redecorated and expanded the small house where he used to live and kept his concubine and her son there.

Until Bak Seonggwon moved to the marketplace, few people had seen his wife and concubine. So the village was abuzz with all sorts of rumors: that some strange fellow claiming to be from the Miryang Bak clan was living in Dumutgol, that he was a brazen young fellow like no other, that he had three sons and was impudent enough to have two wives, that he had money, or that he didn't have money — there were even rumors about the truth of the other rumors.

The first to become curious about him, of course, were Bak Rigyun and his brother. That fellow claimed to be a member of the Miryang Bak clan, but was it really true? Their wives, for their part, were dying to catch a glimpse of his wife and concubine. Yet during holidays they didn't go into the hills with the other women, nor did they appear beneath the swings, nor did they come out to jump on the seesaws.

But when this Bak Seonggwon promptly bought the best house in the village and split up his wife and his concubine, vague hearsay went out the window, and new rumors spread around the village like the measles — the only thing certain was that he came from Eunsan: some of his cousins and second cousins lived there. But one question remained unanswered by these rumors: where did this fellow — who had not fled with the rest of the village, but had stayed behind to make money, yet was, nevertheless, a good-for-nothing who'd left his hometown behind and set out as a vagabond — where did he suddenly get all this money, this house, and this livelihood?

So Bak Rigyun and his brother used their businesses, asking those who came to eat noodles, those who came to sleep at the inn, and those peddlers and traveling merchants who went from village to village in Pyeongan Province like a millstone spins round, and they learned that Bak Seonggwon had earned a great sum while everyone was off taking refuge during the war.

Bak Rigyun and his brother, who had been ready to look down their noses at Bak Seonggwon, were not only embarrassed, losing their taste for ridicule, they secretly began to fear that he might be more than he seemed. Yet between themselves they said that he could never be a yangban because he was from a different part of the Miryang Bak clan, and whenever they drank, as always, they continued to repeat their mantra: "Lady Seong was the wife of Bak Gwiseong and eldest daughter of Seong Nonsan."

Yet their wives were also curious. Through the open kitchen

door or the cracks in the sorghum stalk fence, they saw Bak Seong-gwon going to and fro in his dress clothes, strong of body and uncommon in countenance; and they had seen his son, the one who would be five or six this year, in his rainbow-striped coat and with his hair tied with thick, Chinese silk ribbons, following along behind a domestic or hired hand; but they had seen nothing of the faces of the two women. What did his wife look like, was his concubine pretty? — they say his wife is the daughter of a family in the Jeonju Choe clan that lived in Gaenggoji, about ten li from here — so where did he get his concubine, and where did a young man still wet behind the ears get a concubine anyway? — he would have been destitute and poor back then. The more they thought about it, the more they were dying to see the concubine's face.

One day, the women got together and, with an old woman who lived next door and was famous for her backbiting, set out for the shrine on the hill behind Dumutgol. The old woman and Rigyun's wife wore large bamboo hats, while Seonggyun's wife, who was still a young woman, not yet thirty, wrapped herself in a plain cotton hooded gown, and they walked down a narrow back alley toward Dumutgol. After hesitating by the shrine, they followed their original plan and went as swift as an arrow to the house of Bak Seonggwon's concubine. They already knew that, although he often slept here, Bak Seonggwon returned to his own home directly after eating breakfast.

The old woman went in first and said, "We would like a drink of water. We've come from the shrine and we're thirsty . . ."

The three of them sat in the house for some time, studying the etiquette of the household and the concubine's appearance, and only left when they'd had their fill.

While the three of them were in near-perfect agreement in their opinions of how the house was kept and of the decorum of the household, they were of two minds when it came to the concubine's appearance. The backbiting old woman and Seonggyun's wife both claimed that no part of her face was without flaw, while the elder sister-in-law — that is, Rigyun's wife — proclaimed that she was a stunning beauty. She said that the old woman was originally a backbiter, so naturally she would say something like that, and her younger sister-in-law finding flaws in the other woman's face could be explained by the fact that she was still young and spoke out of jealousy; everything that she herself said was, however, true to the mark.

The old woman, in her own fashion, spread yet another rumor. All she had discovered was that the concubine had married at seventeen and borne her first child at eighteen, but from this the old woman managed to spin a slanderous tale: that, in the prime of his youth, Bak Seonggwon had won her from her newly-wed husband in a card game. This tale was preposterous, but such fabrications are always fascinating, and it spread as if it were the truth. The sisters-in-law also lied and said they had heard it straight from the woman's mouth. This rumor made the rounds in the village for a long time.

Yet there was not a single person who knew that in Bak Seonggwon's storehouse — a small space as dim as a cave, bounded by walls as hard as stone and half dug into the earth — were three large jars. There were, in fact, two servants who had dug this cellar with their own hands, but not even they knew its purpose. Naturally, then, no one knew that the jars were filled to the brim with Japanese silver coins. Bak Seonggwon had hoarded these silver coins, the coins for which he had exchanged Korean brass coins during the revolt of 1894. According to those in the family, and to the servants and hired hands, that dugout cellar was a shrine for special spirits. And it was true that there were a few pieces of white paper with the names of guardian spirits on them on a shelf in one corner. But this rumor was spread by Bak Seonggwon himself as a scheme to prevent thievery.

Whenever a good wet or dry field became available, if the price of silver was high, he sold a few of the valuable silver coins and then used the proceeds to buy the land without attracting attention.

He was also a fearsome and ruthless moneylender. If a borrower missed the appointed day, he would confiscate houses and land. Houses were fairly worthless, so he generally took the land. In the case of families who were still well off and had land, he would pile interest upon interest over the course of a year, so within two or three years it would grow to many times the original sum. His assets piled up like snow. And yet there were still few in that neighborhood who knew him as a rich man.

It was not long before there was no one left who called him by his name. No one knew who started it, but everyone called him by the respectful title of Assistant Curator Bak. It may have been a title made up by the flatterers who frequented his house, but if you asked Bak Rigyun about it, he would say: "Now look here! People are calling him Assistant Curator, and it seems like a right proper position, but Assistant Curator is just an empty title bought with money, a bought title!" Then he would whip out his pipe from behind his back and puff away at his tobacco to calm his thunderous wrath.

At any rate, he was Assistant Curator Bak. Before he turned forty, at the age of thirty-seven, in fact, he was already the father of five children. Up until that time, he had called his eldest son "Big Boy," his son who had been born in Eunsan "Eunsan Boy," and the rest by their birth order, but he decided to give them new names appropriate to their places in the family in order to establish the proper decorum. His father was Bak Sunil, and he was Bak Seonggwon, so there was clearly already a custom of naming children in each generation according to the principles of metal, water, wood, fire, and earth; but when his eldest son was born, Bak Sunil was intoxicated with liquor and opium and so had not given his grandchild a proper name before he died, just "Big Boy" and "Big Grandson." Bak Seonggwon — no, let us also follow the custom of the people, and from now on call him Assistant Curator Bak — this Assistant Curator Bak was twenty at the time, and he had no particular interest in his children until he passed the age of thirty. Sons had been common in his family since he was a young man, so he was not worried about preserving his line, and there was little opportunity for him to grow fond of his wife or children when he was engaged in various money-making ventures designed to reverse the decline in his family's fortunes. So it was only when he was thirty-seven that he came to name his sons. The character for "Sun" in his father's name contained the character for water, and the character for "Gwon" in his own name contained the character for wood, so all he needed to do was think of a character with fire in it. After all, water bears wood and wood bears fire. After spending an entire day flipping through this book and that, he decided upon "Hyeong," which means "bright," and thus contains the character for fire. He himself shared the second character of his name with his brothers, so, according to custom, his sons would have to share the first character of their names. The names he thus created were as follows.

Hyeongjun, Hyeongseon, Hyeonggeol, and Hyeongsik; he had one daughter, whom he had called "Harvest Girl" because he had "sold" her to the harvest deity, but he did not follow the naming custom and instead renamed her Bopae. Hyeongseon and Hyeonggeol had been born in the same year, but Hyeongseon had been born a month earlier. Hyeonggeol was the child of the concubine and thus not part of the direct line of descent, so he was not called the third child; Hyeongsik, who was two years old that year, was called the third child instead. Up until then, to distinguish them, Hyeonggeol had been called "Jasan Boy," since his mother had given birth to him in Jasan and then brought him to Eunsan, and Hyeongseon was called "Eunsan Boy." Big Boy, or Big Grandson, became Hyeongjun, Eunsan Boy became Hyeongseon, Jasan Boy became Hyeonggeol, Third Child became Hyeongsik, and Harvest Girl became Bopae.

Once he had decided upon the names, Assistant Curator Bak called his three eldest sons before him and made the announcement. Although he did not show it, the happiest of the three was Jasan Boy, or Hyeonggeol, who had always been displeased that the young Hyeongsik was called Third Child when that place was actually his. Of the discrimination he suffered as the child of a concubine, he had always hated most the insult in his name, which was there for everyone to hear. The others, as well, had always found being called "this boy" and "that boy" rather grating on the ear, so they all seemed pretty happy.

"And I also change Harvest Girl's name to Bopae. That's the 'bo' character for 'treasure' and the 'pae' character for 'shellfish,' so call her 'Bopae.' I will tell the whole family, our domestics, our hired hands, our tenant farmers, and our servants — so call each other by your new names."

After sending his three sons out he called his wife and told her, and then he ordered her to tell the domestics.

The eldest son, Hyeongjun, was nineteen at the time and had a room of his own and a wife.

He lay down early that night and stared vacantly at his young wife as she spun yarn in the lamplight. Whir, whir, clack . . . whir, whir, clack . . . the repetitive sound of the spinning wheel mingled with the sputtering of the oil lamp and drifted to his ears like a lullaby. He felt sleepy, so with a grunt he rolled over and lit his pipe. When the bobbin grew full and bulged out, his wife took it off the spindle and replaced it with a new one. She used a wooden stick to oil the spot where the belt touched the spindle and glanced out of the corner of her eye toward her husband. He had finished smoking his pipe and was staring at his wife's side when he caught his wife's glance and grinned at her. She blushed and spun the spinning wheel faster than before. Every time she lifted her left hand to raise the belt, her high sash was pulled up and the white skin next to her breast could be seen. He watched this for a while and then said, "That makes quite a racket. Put it aside and let's go to sleep."

He dropped his head down onto his pillow. They were still at the stage where they were too shy to talk to each other in a bright room. The young woman understood what her husband meant, and although she was shy about immediately getting up, putting out the light, and undoing her clothes, it was an order from her husband, so she admonished herself that she should not dare disobey him and stopped spinning. She took the belt off the spinning wheel, pursed her lips, and then blew out a puff of air to put out the lamp. It was a dark night. The rustling of clothes being taken off could be heard. First she took off her jacket, then her skirt, and then she felt around on the folding screen at the opposite side of the room and hung her clothes next to her husband's. Then she sat down again and unraveled the hand-stitched quilted sash from around her breasts and waist, and then she took off her coarse hemp bloomers.

Hyeongjun waited impatiently for each and every article of clothing to leave his wife's body, and he let out the low sigh he had been holding in. His wife at last took off her long socks and, wearing only a single cotton undergarment, silently lifted up her end of the blanket. She laid her head down on one side of the long 'lovebird's pillow'—the pillow she had made and brought with her when they were married—unraveled her carefully braided hair, and then turned her back toward her husband and lay on her side.

"My name changed today."

She almost laughed at her husband's sudden announcement. She had heard the news from her mother-in-law earlier that day. She said nothing, but in the darkness she opened her mouth for the first time and smiled broadly.

After a while he turned toward his wife, wrapping his leg around her calf, and said, "My name is Hyeongjun. Bright "hyeong" and hero "jun." Hyeongjun. From now on, call me that."

Then he rubbed his face against his wife's back. This time what he said was truly laughable. How on earth could she ever call her husband by name? They had been married for two years, but she had called her husband "Dear" maybe once or twice. So he must be playing some ridiculous prank on her, telling her to call him Hyeongjun. She knew that "Big Grandson" or "Big Boy" were names that others might call him, and she knew that it was not a name for his wife to call him aloud. It tickled when he rubbed his face on her back, and shivers ran through her whole body, so she spun around.

"The second son's name is Hyeongseon, Jasan Boy in Dumutgol is Hyeonggeol, the baby's name is Hyeongsik, and Harvest Girl's name is Bopae."

Once more he said, "My name is Bak Hyeongjun," and then he put an arm around his wife and drew her head toward him. She was overwhelmed and let out the long breath she had been holding in.

"From this summer I will be calling you the father of my child."

She barely managed to say this and then reached out and put her left hand on her husband's back without even realizing it. Hyeongjun thought about becoming a father for the first time five months from now and put his hand on his wife's slightly bulging belly.

Just like that, three years passed. Assistant Curator Bak Seonggwon had just turned forty. There was no one who called his sons by their childhood names anymore. Only Bopae, who turned twelve that year, was still called Harvest Girl by mostly everyone, though there were a few who called her Bopae. Yet there was no problem with calling daughters by just about any name. Bak Hyeongjun, the eldest, already had a son and a daughter. Assistant Curator Bak's grandson was nearly three years old. And there was the granddaughter who had been born just this year. The grandson's name was Seonggi.

Even at the age of forty, Assistant Curator Bak's hot-tempered and stubborn nature had not abated. The prime of life begins at forty, so he was more vigorous than ever. Lady Choe was forty-two, and she occasionally spent the night with her husband, but after Hyeongsik she seemed to have stopped bearing children. Hyeonggeol's mother—that is, Assistant Curator Bak's concubine Lady Yun—was thirty-seven and thus still in her prime, but even though her son, Hyeonggeol, was nineteen this year, for some reason, after giving birth to him in Jasan at the age of eighteen, there had never been any news of another child, so it would seem that it been long since she had stopped bearing children as well. It was for this reason, and because she had always been pretty, that, even though she was thirty-seven, Lady Yun still looked like a young woman without a wrinkle on her face. In the backyard of the house in Dumutgol she built a stone tower to the seven deities and fervently prayed that she would bear more children, and she rubbed her hands raw praying every day to the deity in the cellar, desperately hoping that Bak Seonggwon would not take a younger concubine.

Perhaps it was because of these prayers that Assistant Curator Bak seemed to show little interest in taking another woman. Instead he was terribly fond of his drink, though not so much as to be a cause for worry. Whether he was with his wife or his concubine, he asked for liquor at odd hours, so those in the women's quarters always had liquor and side dishes prepared. Strips of dried meat, pollack, fruit, dried yellow corvina—the cupboard was never bare of these, and there was never a shortage of good meat. They hired an old man from Pyeongyang who was a skilled fisherman, put him up in a room in the rear of the men's quarters, and had him catch fish; and in the winter they had the young people take falcons out to hunt quail. Perhaps it was because he had been a good drinker in his youth, but Assistant Curator Bak did not drink as much as he had in his younger days — yet there were still few days that he did not have a drink. He brewed his own liquor, sometimes adding pear and ginger, sometimes improving the taste with apricots, and he even occasionally put asps or other serpents in jars of liquor and drank these as tonics. While it is true that the drinking gave him problems with his stomach and bowels, he had always been a man of such a strong spirit, never bowing his head to anything, that these did not concern him in the least.

Even when he was drunk, he did not forget his money, his fields, his household etiquette, or his children. He had never consulted with anyone on anything, but when he was well into his cups he would lie alone in his room and mull over one thing or another. His was an obstinate character, and once he made a decision he would see it through. His stubborn and unbending personality, confident and quiet, was made ever more so by the self-assurance that came from never having once been proved wrong. He also had keen foresight, and he was convinced more than anyone of the power of money. He knew that the world still turned on pedigree and family standing, but he was certain that the day was not far off when all this would kneel before his wealth. More than anything else, his confidence was boosted by the quiet belief that the silver coins he had amassed twenty years ago would now begin to hold sway.

He sent his eldest son to the village school to study classical Chinese, but after that he did not send him on to a new-style school. As the eldest son and heir to the estate, he had done all the studying he needed. Money lending, harvesting, overseeing all the family affairs, and managing people were all the skills he would require. Hyeongjun himself showed no inclination to follow his younger brothers when they left the village school for the new Christian school that had opened, and he made no effort to study the new learning when this school closed down after three years and the county magistrate used his influence to found Dongmyeong School. Then again, his younger brothers would soon be third-year students in elementary school, and the following year they would be first-year students in high school, so it was probably no idle rumor that he decided not to go because he would be embarrassed at being a mere first-year student.*

Assistant Curator Bak thought hard about finding suitable brides for his sons. His eldest, Hyeongjun, was already married to the daughter of the Sangmyeong Kim family from Gyeongju and had given his father a grandson and a granddaughter, and their family decorum seemed proper enough — his daughter-in-law was gentle in nature and skilled at working with her hands, so she was the ideal eldest daughter-in-law.

His second son, Hyeongseon, was arranged to be married to the daughter of the Yeonil Jeong family, who lived behind Descending Immortal Pavilion in the upper part of town, and they had already sent letters and the wedding silks. Before long the wedding day would be here. The Jeong family lived in the same village, so he knew their affairs like the back of his hand. The head of the family had held a high government position, from which he had retired, and his estate was considerable.

If there was a concern, it was that Hyeonggeol, who was the same age as Hyeongseon, would be something of a problem. Being the son of a concubine, it would be difficult to find a proper bride for him, but there were other women besides those of eminent families, and why shouldn't he find a bride, Bak thought, so he didn't trouble himself too much over this, either. Hyeonggeol was rather rowdy, and he was much taller than his brother, Hyeongseon, though the latter was a month older; he was even a half-inch taller than his eldest brother, which did not please his father at all. Of course, Hyeonggeol had no control over how tall he grew, but Assistant Curator Bak was also irked by his son's nasty temper. Even when he was young, there were not a few times when he caused trouble at the village and regular schools by beating other children until they bled.

His mother treasured and spoiled him, but that was not

*The modern schooling system established in 1895 consisted of two separate curricula, an "elementary" curriculum and a "high" curriculum, the first lasting for three years and the second lasting for two or three years. Both of these curricula together were what would today be called primary or elementary school. (The distinction between the curricula was eliminated in 1905, and the period of schooling was shortened to four years.) According to official regulations, the students were to be between eight and fifteen years of age, but these regulations were not followed strictly in the smaller villages.

all. Every time Hyeonggeol got in trouble, Assistant Curator Bak thought about how he himself had been such a hot-tempered troublemaker in his youth, and he could not help smiling.

Whatever the case, Assistant Curator Bak Seonggwon's family was as fortunate as it could be. Not only was he himself content, but so was his whole family, and, at least on the surface, his domestics, his servants, his hired hands, and his tenant farmers all seemed content as well. On occasion he went out into the backyard and looked with satisfaction on the waters of the Biryu River, a tributary of the Daedong River, as they flowed leisurely beneath the twelve mountain peaks. For nearly twenty years that river has been with me, he thought, washing away in an instant all my labors and fears and joys, never stopping as it flows, today as it did thousands of years ago, to the Daedong River and then on to the Yellow Sea.

2

When it came to luck or fortune, there was no one in this village who had it better than Assistant Curator Bak. He was wealthy, he had three sons and a daughter — none of whom had fallen victim to epidemics — and his grandson and granddaughter were healthy as well. His family were sated with all sorts of delicacies and wrapped in the finest silks, the rooms were filled with male and female servants, and the outer rooms bustled with hired hands and domestics, and he had more than a few cows and horses, so it would be hard to name another who was more fortunate than he. And yet when it came time for his children to marry, he himself could not step forward to take charge of affairs. So he called for Schoolmaster Gu, who was adept at raising children, and had him put Hyeonggeol's hair up in a topknot and dress him in ceremonial garb.

It was the day that Assistant Curator Bak's second son, Hyeongseon, was to marry the daughter of the Jeong family, who lived behind Descending Immortal Pavilion.

Assistant Curator Bak had slept in his own room the night before, along with his brother-in-law, Choe Gwansul. Choe Gwansul had traveled the ten li or so from Gaenggoji the night before in order to act as an escort in Hyeongseon's wedding. He was only barely past his thirtieth year, and yet the long, white whiskers of his handlebar mustache stuck out from above his mouth, and his hair was cropped fashionably close. A family that strictly observed the old customs would have many reasons not to send Choe Gwansul, who was steeped in Eastern Learning,* but as chance would have it, talk was going around that Jeong Bongseok, the bride's father, had started to believe in Jesus and was therefore interested in enlighten- ment thinking, so Assistant Curator Bak had decided to appoint his brother-in-law, the only one in this village who visited Seoul often, as Hyeongseon's escort. When it came to the new style, he thought there was no one better than Choe Gwansul.

They both got up early. Assistant Curator Bak lifted his head slightly from his bed, tucked a few strands of hair into his topknot, and coughed so loudly that it could be heard in his wife's room. This cough was not simply to loosen the phlegm in his throat upon waking up but also intended as a sign to his servants and wife that he had risen. He gargled with the water beside his bed to rinse his mouth, hitched up his pants, took out his pipe, and tapped it in the wooden ashtray with a loud clang.

Choe Gwansul quickly got up from the bedding he had laid out in the upper, colder part of the room, felt around in his vest pockets, and produced a pack of cigarettes.

"I just happen to have two cigarettes left," he said, "Please, have one." He put one in his mouth and held the other out, and with his other hand he crumpled up the pack and tossed it aside.

"Yes, a cigarette," Bak mumbled, put down the leaf tobac- co he was about to tamp into his pipe, and took the cigarette from Gwansul. He puckered his lips around it and took a flint and steel from his pocket, which he struck to send sparks flying, but Gwan- sul said, "No, use these matches . . . that, that's noisy." He took a long wood shaving from the table. On the tip of the shaving, yellow phosphorous sparkled like sulfur.

---

* Eastern Learning was a movement that began in the second half of the 19th century as a reaction against the influence of Christianity and other Western ideologies, calling for a return to the basics of Confucian- ism. It developed into a religion of its own and later became the religion known today as Cheondogyo, or "the Religion of the Way of Heaven."

"I'm fine. Those are a waste of money when this serves just as well."

With the tips of his fingers, Assistant Curator Bak took the now-burning tinder and put it to the end of his cigarette. After three or four puffs, the cigarette lit. Gwansul furtively tied up the matches again, like a bunch of bananas, and borrowed Assistant Curator Bak's cigarette to light his own.

"I wish these were stronger . . . they taste like stale spirits."

"You've only ever smoked straight tobacco, so they must taste like dried mulberry leaves."

Bak's wife came out from her room and said, "That schoolmaster hasn't come yet, has he?" She began to fold up the bedding.

Gwansul said, "Leave my bedding, Sister. I'll fold it up."

But Bak's wife replied, "No, I'll fold it." Then she asked again, "Should we send someone?"

"Don't worry. I sent someone last night, so why wouldn't he come? He can't be that busy, and it's not like he's traveling a hundred li. It's the same village, after all. Bring Clerk Choe some water to wash up with."

His wife opened the single door that led into the house and yelled, "Bring some water for washing to the master's room!" Then, with the door still open, she said, "Would you like to have a drink before breakfast?"

She looked back and forth between her husband and her brother.

"Please, Sister. Do you think I would get drunk in the morning before going to someone else's house?" Gwansul said, but Assistant Curator Bak pretended not to hear him and only said in a low voice, "When Schoolmaster Gu arrives . . ."

Just then, Schoolmaster Gu coughed a few times to announce his arrival.

"Come in. We were just about to send someone for you."

In a white overcoat and proper horsehair hat, the fifty-year-old Schoolmaster Gu came in rubbing his hands, and Gwansul lifted himself off the ground slightly and sat back down again, while Bak's wife quietly went out the back door.

"It's still cold at dawn."

Bak stroked his beard with his right hand and said, "It hasn't been long since the ice broke up, so of course it's still cold."

At this, Gu rubbed his hands together again and sat down comfortably.

The water for washing came, and then the liquor. Yet none of them drank more than three glasses, aware of the weighty responsibility that lay before them. The liquor was soon cleared away and breakfast was brought in.

After eating breakfast, they took Schoolmaster Gu into Bak's wife's room. In here, Hyeongseon would take his once-braided hair and tie it up in a topknot and then change into his wedding clothes.

When they opened the door, the room was empty.

"Have Hyeongseon come in, and bring in some water in a washbasin and a coarse comb."

Having recited this order toward the kitchen and the room across the way, Bak said, "Now, please come in and have a seat, Schoolmaster Gu. Clerk Choe, too. I will go out and make sure that the packhorse drivers and peddlers have all eaten breakfast."

Bak put his hands and the pipe he held in them behind his back and rushed out through the inner gate and into the yard. The pouch, tobacco pouch, and magnifying glass tied to his belt swung back and forth with each step he took.

With his loose hair hanging down to his neck, Hyeongseon came out into the courtyard with Hyeongjun and they stood on the wooden ledge outside the room. Hyeongjun smiled broadly, but Hyeongseon stared at the floor and blushed a deep red.

"I was wondering why you hadn't cut your hair, but now I see it was so you could put it up in a topknot for your bride when you got married," said their uncle Choe Gwansul, coming out of the room with a grin, but the groom-to-be just smiled back gently and didn't say a word.

"What, are you excited?" Gwansul laughed heartily, and as he was about to cross the threshold back into the room, he looked at the boy's broad frame and said, "Ah, that lad, look at his shoulders! In days gone by we would have said that he should have had three sons already."

In truth, marrying at the age of nineteen was quite late. Choe

Gwansul himself, with his close-cropped hair, the cigarette between his lips, and his frequent visits to Seoul, had married at fourteen, and back then people said he was marrying late and made a fuss about him losing two sons.

"Your bride must be so nervous now, wondering how hideously deformed you must be that you've reached nineteen without marrying; I bet she wasn't able to eat breakfast!" he teased once again, as Bak's wife came out from the room across the way, carrying the clothing that the bride's family had sent for the groom the day before.

"The bride is nineteen, too. These days that's what civilized people are supposed to do," she interjected. She gave the bundle of clothes to her brother, who had come to the door but still stood where he was on the wooden ledge outside the room, and said, "Well go on in, why are you just standing there?"

Only then did Gwansul take the bundle of clothes, enter the room, and shut the door tight.

The hair that had once hung down was pulled up tight, gathered into a topknot, and then wound tightly with string, causing Hyeongseon to furrow his brow in pain as he knelt.

"Does it hurt? That's nothing, if you expect to manage another family's young maiden, you'll have to bear that much pain. Say, pull that a little tighter, would you?"

"Uncle, you're just talking nonsense," Hyeongseon said, opening his mouth for the first time.

"What's gotten into you? Just ask your brother. Ask him whether I'm talking nonsense or not. Anyway, have you ever even seen the bride?"

At this, Hyeongjun laughed. "He must have seen her—he was so excited at the talk of the wedding that he hasn't eaten all day."

But Hyeongseon snorted. "What do you mean I haven't eaten, I ate one more bowl than I usually do. I don't eat when I'm sad."

"That's right. Well spoken. You can be happy about finally getting married, but there is no way you would be sad enough to not eat."

By then, the topknot was finished. Schoolmaster Gu stuck a piece of red coral into the end of the topknot and said, "You can wash up now." He bent down and peeked at Hyeongseon's cleanly scrubbed face.

His skin where his hair had hung down and blocked the sun was exceptionally white. There was not much hair at the base of his skull, just some soft short hairs, and even Hyeongseon felt that a weight had been lifted off the nape of his neck. With his thick hair lifted up, his gentle face looked slender and that much more comely. The fine hairs of his mustache were still soft, as befitted a young man. But when he took off his shirt and bent over to wash his face, it was clear that his arms, shoulders, and chest were as strong as any adult's.

"With those arms, that chest, those shoulders . . ."

Hyeongjun stood behind his younger brother, looking down at him absentmindedly, and smiled broadly to himself as he thought of the day he had gotten married. Though he would never again revisit those years, even now it remained in his memories a day when emotions rolled over him in waves. Back when the basic arrangements for Hyeongseon's marriage had been made, his mother, his father's concubine from Dumutgol, and Hyeongjun's wife had gone to the house of Jeong Bongseok to meet the bride. The marriage had already been more or less decided, so it was nothing more than a formality, but when they returned they all praised the purity of her character. That night, when Hyeongjun asked his wife about her, she said that the girl's face was full like a half moon, her eyes were slender, the ridge of her nose was high but not sharp, and more than anything else her lips were small and lovely. Her figure was shapely, and her hair swung down below her buttocks.

He asked her quietly, "Is she prettier than you were when you were a maiden?"

And she replied, "Don't be silly." She poked him lightly in the side and gave a quick smile. "What is so special about a country maiden like me?"

"But you're still the prettiest to me," he teased her, and she feigned annoyance.

"You're talking about an old woman with two children . . ." she said and then gave a low sigh.

How could she be so crestfallen at the age of only twenty-three? He patted her on the back. But even Hyeongjun could not deny that her body was not as firm and supple as it had been in days gone by.

The next day, he had grabbed Hyeongseon as he was on his way home from school and took him behind the mule mill.

"You've hit the jackpot!"

But Hyeongseon had no idea what he was talking about. "What, have I been gambling or something?"

Hyeongjun clapped him on the shoulders. "Come on, are jackpots only to be found in gambling? This is an even bigger wind-fall than that. Your bride-to-be, Head Clerk Jeong's daughter, is even more beautiful than Yang Guifei!"*

His brother shook off his arms and ran away in a flash.

"Nonsense!" he said, but his mouth broke open like a split sack.

As Hyeongjun pondered these trivial thoughts, Hyeongseon was brushing his teeth with salt, and then he washed his face with hot water. Once finished, he opened the bundle of clothes and put on a pair of white silk pants and a jade-colored jacket, over which he wore a silk vest brocaded with peach blossom designs, and finally he pulled on a pair of thick hemp socks and tied a pair of jade-colored ankle bands tightly around them. He jumped up, tossed aside the belt that had been woven from string bought at the general store, leaving it coiled on the floor, and loosely tied his trousers with a new belt that was as broad as an ironing board. He pulled down his waistband to loosen his trousers and blouse them out around the calves and then, embarrassed by the gazes of the three who stood silently watching him dress, turned away slightly and threw on his overcoat. And yet he couldn't help laughing. He could not fathom why this giggling bubbled up from his restless heart.

After putting on his overcoat, he wrapped himself in his blue cloak, put on his black silk hat, and tied on his sash. Now all he had to do was take his silk fan in his hand and climb up into the saddle.

But they did not leave immediately. After getting fully

---

* A consort of the Tang Chinese emperor Xuanzong, Yang Guifei was purported to be so beautiful that her name became a synonym for beauty not only in China but throughout East Asia.

dressed, he had to greet his father and mother and then take off his overcoat again before he could finally fill his empty belly with breakfast. But even that did not go down easily.

The ice that had been frozen solid beneath the twelve peaks had slowly become riddled with coin-sized holes, like a steamed sticky rice cake, and when these holes began to crack open the meltwater flowed for four days without ceasing. After the clear meltwater, the river grew especially murky and rose conspicuously. Now, with the water running clear again and the level back to normal, a gentle breeze blew in the sunny places below the twelve peaks, and the sap ran through every branch as the buds began to push forth like cottonseeds. It was cold in the morning and evening, but during the day, when the sunshine poured down, it was warm and mild. It was the time when the day's long sun lulled one into a lazy drowsiness. This is what the weather was like on that day.

Not long before noon, Hyeongseon, surrounded by many but aided by none, promptly climbed into his saddle.

Across the street from Assistant Curator Bak's house was Yi Chilseong's house, up the street was Nakanishi's store, and down the street was the house of Kim Yonggu, a candy seller who sold sesame toffee and walnut toffee, as well as ice cream and ice pops — what he called "real candy" — from a wooden box. Men and boys all came outside, and the old women stood in front of the reed fences by their kitchens. The white shadows glimpsed in between the cracks in the fences were the young married girls and girls of marrying age, who could not stand out by the road, peeking out from their hiding places. At Nakanishi's house, Nakanishi himself lived as a widower, so there was no one there to come out to watch. Nakanishi had first come to this village as a postman, and he later ran errands when the provincial army was disbanded and a garrison was stationed here, earning quite a profit in his first year, but now he ran a rather large general store.

Up and down the street, people gathered as they only did when there was a wedding between rich families. Those who had close dealings with the family stood by Assistant Curator Bak's side, while those who did not deal as frequently with him formed groups of twos and threes, whispering to each other as they watched the horses in the street.

The white horse that bore the groom and stood second in the procession, the stocky and sturdy brown mule to be ridden by the escort, and the small donkey in the front ridden by the one carrying the goose, had all been raised by Assistant Curator Bak. He had fed them all with his own hand: the white horse to ride on long trips, the donkey to ride to the threshing ground during harvest, and the mule to turn the mill. Standing in the middle of the road, they must have known that all eyes were upon them, for they raised their hooves, blinked their great eyes, and awaited those who would ride them.

Three rolls of white cotton fabric, which were to be given to the packhorse drivers after the wedding, were rolled out one by one; stretching from the tips of the beasts' noses to their saddles and tails, they were an opulent sight. The horse drivers stuck their horsehair whips into the back of their belts and grasped the reins tightly, and one of them stood there silently stroking his horse's head. Two heralds took their places, standing in front of the donkey ridden by Schoolmaster Gu, who was holding the goose, and carefully watched Assistant Curator Bak, waiting for the moment when their shouts would shake the streets like loud chanting, the horses' bells would ring, and the horse drivers' whips would crack down grandly on the horses' backs.

Everything was in place, but Assistant Curator Bak and Choe Gwansul, the latter serving as the groom's escort, were whispering about something inside the front gate. All eyes were fixed on them. Schoolmaster Gu and the groom, who had already mounted their animals and been waiting for some time, looked their way curiously, one holding the goose and the other holding a fan.

What they were doing was arguing about whether Choe Gwansul should take off the flat cap he was wearing and exchange it for a horsehair hat. But Choe Gwansul had no intention of listening to Assistant Curator Bak.

Up until then, there were only two types of new-style, civilized hats being worn in this village. There was the hat worn by those who were students and the flat cap worn by those who weren't. Of course, not many people wore these flat caps. But Choe Gwansul perched a pair of gold-rimmed, new-style glasses on his nose, wore a pair of high-laced shoes with his black silk overcoat, and atop his close-cropped hair sat the flat cap. He'd even taken a piece of boxwood, stripped it of its rough bark, burned off the knots, and called it a new-style cane.

Never mind the rest, but if he would only take off that flat cap, or whatever it was called, sitting atop his roughly cut hair like some silly rice dish cover, and wear a respectable horsehair hat, like Schoolmaster Gu, then Assistant Curator Bak thought he might be able to ignore the new-style glasses that rubbed his nose sore or the new-style cane he liked to carry around.

At first, Assistant Curator Bak thought he would just turn a blind eye to his brother-in-law's appearance, since his purpose was to send a new-style person to the bride's family, but now that the horses had gone out and he saw how his brother-in-law looked amidst all the people who had gathered, he was so plagued by unease and doubt that he simply couldn't bear it.

But the individual in question just wouldn't budge, and Bak couldn't just stand here and quarrel. When he told Gwansul to do as he wished, Gwansul twirled his mustache once and then strode out to the mule, twirling his new-style cane. He couldn't carry his new-style cane while riding the mule, so he stood by the mule and swung it futilely a few times, then quickly placed it across the mule's back in front of the saddle. At last he leaped up into the saddle, and the sunlight glinted off his new-style glasses.

"Very well, let's go," he said, jabbing his heels into the mule's sides twice.

No sooner had he said the words than the anxious heralds raised their voices and shouted, "Ah — Ah-ha —!"

The donkey began to move forward with its short, plodding steps, while the white horse ridden by the groom swished its tail twice and began to prance ahead. The groom-to-be covered his face with his fan and stared entranced at the undulating road far ahead. The mule ridden by the escort promptly stomped its hooves a few times, then let out a noisy bray before following the horse. The animals moved forward toward Descending Immortal Pavilion, and Schoolmaster Gu's horsehair hat, the groom's black silk hat, and the escort's flat cap all danced up in down in time with the herald's cries and the ringing bells.

A child who had been on the lookout in front of Descending Immortal Pavilion, upon hearing the distant cries of the heralds and seeing the animals and people moving, spun around like a tiny millstone and raced off toward Head Clerk Jeong's house. When he saw the front gate of Head Clerk Jeong's house and the many people gathered there, he waved his right hand.

"The groom is coming! They're past Nine Dragons Bridge now!" he shouted, exaggerating a little, as the party wasn't anywhere near Nine Dragons Bridge yet. A few of those who had been loitering outside the front gate, ready to handle small errands, heard him and rushed into the yard.

"The groom is long past Nine Dragons Bridge now," they cried. "Prepare the table quickly!" These words flew through the yard, the storehouses, the great wooden-floored room, the kitchen, and the cellar.

In the room where the food was being prepared, those in charge of the big table passed mountains of assorted rice cookies back and forth, fussing as they said, "Let's be quick! The groom is outside the front gate!"

A hired hand spread out a mat in the inner room where the groom would sit at the big table and then laid atop that a tiger-striped blanket, and, as he backed out of the room onto the wooden ledge, he glanced at the folding screen in the back of the room with a landscape painting on it and tripped, tumbling head over heels into the yard. Everyone else, completely oblivious to his pain, laughed loudly, while he brushed off the seat of his pants and, not being too hurt, grinned broadly in spite of himself. He turned around when Head Clerk Jeong, hearing the ruckus in the yard, opened the door to make sure that no one had been hurt.

"Take care and don't be hasty," said the head clerk in a low voice and then closed the door again.

Seeing this from the kitchen, a servant known as Yongne's Mother, who had been boiling the broth for the noodles, ran to the mistress of the house, who was brushing the rice cakes with sesame oil in the backyard.

"Someone fell in the yard and hurt their leg! The groom is outside the front gate, and someone has gone and dislocated or broken their leg and is hobbling about, unable to even walk properly!"

Hearing that someone had been hurt, the mistress of the house set aside her rice cake bowl and ran out to the kitchen, but when she looked into the inner yard, nothing of the sort seemed to have happened. Everyone was going back and forth, carrying food to and from the preparation area, and there was not a single person who seemed to be hurt.

"Did someone carry him into the men's quarters?" she asked, and Yongne's Mother headed off toward the yard to check, as a woman making dumplings for the dumpling soup said, "Hurt? No one's been hurt, she's just making a fuss over nothing."

After looking back and forth at the faces of all those present, the mistress of the house quickly realized that Yongne's mother had been full of nonsense and immediately went back to her rice cake bowl in the yard.

In the men's quarters, friends, family, and servants who had been awaiting the groom all put on their coats and hats and quietly got up to go outside.

"I can't hear the heralds yet, so they must not even be at Descending Immortal Pavilion. What point is there in going out too early?" said Head Clerk Jeong, but he too got up and put on his horsehair hat and white overcoat.

Once past Descending Immortal Pavilion, the loud cry of the heralds drifted in, "Ah— Ah-ha—!" and then the donkey carrying Schoolmaster Gu plodded into sight. They could see the white horse carrying the groom, Choe Gwansul's flat cap behind him, and the crowd of children following on either side and at the rear.

"The one holding the goose is Schoolmaster Gu, and the escort is Clerk Choe from Gaenggoji," said some of the young people with good eyes, and Head Clerk Jeong stood beneath the front gate and watched from afar as the company drew near.

With news of the arrival of the groom, even those who had been working put their tasks aside and poured out the front gate. The ladies of the house, though, paced back and forth in the kitchen, trying to forget their frustration. Only the women of lower standing squeezed in among the men, laughing and chattering as they watched the groom on his horse and then laughing again at the sight of Clerk Choe on his mule. He wore leather shoes the likes of which had never been seen in this neighborhood, and on his head sat some strange thing. They had certainly never expected anything like this and found it both surprising and comical.

Many hands helped the groom down from his horse, and two young men in blue silk overcoats led him through the front gate, while servants led his escorts to the men's quarters.

"Clerk Choe, thank you for taking the time to join us," said Head Clerk Jeong.

Choe Gwansul came forward, spinning his new-style cane, which he had somehow found the time to take off the mule, and with his right hand he doffed his flat cap and greeted Head Clerk Jeong, whom he already knew. "Say nothing of it. You yourself must be terribly busy."

"And your father is well, I hope?" asked Head Clerk Jeong.

"He is in good health," replied Choe. "Thank you for asking."

They went into the men's quarters. The children who had been watching by the roadside stared as Choe Gwansul, for quite some time, stood bending over outside, untying his shoe laces, and then they exclaimed in surprise when out of his shoes came not white Korean socks but black Western ones.

"Look at those! They're shoe socks. They're made of leather, and they must cost over a hundred nyang," said one of the children, who apparently knew something of such things.

Not even Nakanishi's general store sold shoe socks. Choe Gwansul had only one pair of these shoe socks made of leather, and when the heels had worn through he had patched them with pieces of thick hemp cloth. But he proudly propped his new-style cane on the wooden floor outside the room and went inside, his new-style glasses glittering.

The big table was just then being taken in to the inner room in the women's quarters. The table at which the groom was to sit was in the center, and on either side were tables for the two young men in blue silk overcoats accompanying him. Flat rice cakes, fermented rice cakes, rice cakes dusted with soybean flour, rice cakes made from glutinous millet, and steamed rice cakes were piled high like pillars on five wooden dishes, then there was a wooden dish each of white fruit and of red, a wooden dish with honeyed cakes rising up like a tower, along with sesame teacakes, soybean teacakes, skewered meats and vegetables, battered and fried meats, apples, round Korean pears, raw chestnuts, jujubes, and anything else you could imagine in great mounds. And on top of each of these mounds was fixed a colorful reed flower. In front of these three tables side by side was a smaller table with bowls for the noodles, glasses for liquor, and silver chopsticks and spoons.

The young men from Schoolmaster Gu's village school, who had spent all night copying down Chinese characters, as ordered by the schoolmaster, sat in a group on the wooden floor outside and set up camp in the yard, and prepared to test the groom's learning. They wrote down ten pages worth of riddles and word puzzles, and one of the young men gave a page to someone to take in.

In the kitchen, the bride's mother could not catch even a glimpse of her new son-in-law's face, but the eldest daughter stood quietly behind the men and took a look at him.

"The groom is quite handsome and well-mannered," she said when she returned, and the mistress of the house let her already-curling lips break into a smile.

Yongne's Mother came in with hands waving once again and, not knowing that the eldest daughter was there, said, "Your first son-in-law doesn't stand a chance! He's quite a handsome young man. You've done quite well. Drat! If only I had met a groom like that."

She laughed for no reason, and then seeing the eldest daughter standing there with her mouth shut tight, said, "You've given birth to such fine daughters, and you have lovely sons-in-law as well. With an elder son-in-law as handsome as yours, who would have thought the younger son-in-law would be so handsome as well?" Then she ran out into the yard.

Hyeongseon glanced at the Chinese character test when it

was brought in but didn't take the brush held out for him, and instead said in a low voice to the person next to him, "Please send it back."

This caused not a little disappointment. He had studied long at the village school and had attended both the Christian school and Dongmyeong School, so they had thought he would breeze through ten or so pages of Chinese characters, and they were put out when he didn't even give the test a second glance. But there was nothing to be done. They couldn't say that they wouldn't bring out the table or tell him to turn around and leave without another word. Instead, someone next to him dashed off the character for "retire."

Upon hearing of this in the kitchen, the groom's mother-in-law shouted outside, "We'll have a separate table for the test, so leave the big tables as they are." Then she changed her mind, "Wait, our distinguished guests are waiting, so we really should get them their food."

But before the big tables could be removed from the room, a round table was brought in. It held only dumpling soup and white rice. At the insistence of the bride's family and friends, the groom picked up his spoon and had a few dumplings.

"They say you have to eat three dumplings if you want your first child to be a son," teased an old woman, and everyone laughed loudly. But Hyeongseon ate only one dumpling. In the men's quarters, the drinking was in full swing.

3

Bobu spent the night at the house of Jeong Yeonggeun, her older cousin, in front of Descending Immortal Pavilion. Her cousin slept in the upper room with his eldest son, and her sister-in-law slept in the lower room, near the warm spot on the floor, with the middle son and the newborn baby. Even though it was her cousin's house, it was still the first time Bobu had slept anywhere but her own home. Jeong Yeonggeun had been an officer in the provincial army, but after the army was disbanded he became an athletics instructor at the school. When he rose before dawn he would wake his seven-year-old son, go down to the Biryu River to wash his face, and then walk along the riverbank playing his trumpet. He taught the students the trumpet as well.

Suddenly waking from sleep, curled up in her blanket, Bobu found that everyone else in the lower room was still fast asleep. First she looked at the ceiling, then she looked around at what was hanging on the walls, and she thought, this is not my house, it is the lower room of my cousin's house, and in the same instant she remembered coming here with her sister-in-law the night before, past the alley leading to the Temple of Merciful Blessings, behind Descending Immortal Pavilion and along the riverbank road. At first she had no idea how she had managed to sleep through the night in a house that was not her own for the first time in her life. But then she remembered how she had been offered the warm spot on the floor but declined it; how the lights had gone out and all had gone to bed, the sound of their breathing growing louder and then turning to snoring as they fell asleep; how she had lain there with eyes wide open, unable to sleep, her thoughts drifting like clouds; how these thoughts had brought great turmoil to her heart, and how, if she happened to start drifting off to sleep, she would be haunted by dreams and unable to move, at last stirring in her blankets as she pondered all these things; and it was only then that she became aware of the fact that this brightly dawning day was the most important day of her life. Today, the nineteen-year-old maiden Jeong Bobu would tie up the long, thick tresses of hair of which she had been so proud, put on a red skirt and a light-green jacket trimmed in splendid colors, and unlock the door to the vast wilderness of life that spread out before her with a strange young man whom she had never even seen before. The happiness of the rest of her life depended on whether or not she could tightly grasp the keys being brought to her by the god of fate tonight. Her heart beat in her chest and seemed to shake the blanket that covered her, and her head weighed so heavily on her shoulders that she could not even look at what was right in front of her; this was completely natural for a mind and body that had to be pure for this tense, anxious, and important moment. Curiosity, anxiety, and unfathomable joy, deep, stirring emotions and excitement, all flowed together like the swollen

Biryu River in the rainy season, and, after these, a single trickle of weighty dread rushed over her strong yet supple body, clear as jade and hard as stone.

What sort of person is he? This thought already had sprung to mind from time to time. She believed that her mother, father, and elders would indeed choose well for her, but the more she thought of it the more she wondered about the countenance and bearing of the man who would become her husband. No matter how she tried not to think of it — knowing full well that her curiosity was not part of her duty as a child, nor was it for the sake of him with whom she was to grow old for a hundred years — the broadly smiling face of a man kept passing through her mind like a dream.

Of course, there was no way of knowing whether the face she saw was without a doubt that of Bak Hyeongseon, the second son of Bak Seonggwon, Assistant Curator Bak; for it was neither a photograph nor a painting, but just a phantom that appeared and then disappeared again like a cloud, so there was no way she could ask anyone about it.

One evening, when she was about to go out to the road to throw away some dishwater that had been sitting inside the sorghum stalk fence outside the kitchen door, her cousin Yeonggeun and another young man had been walking up the road with trumpets under their arms. They must have been on their way to practice the trumpet by Pear Blossom Pavilion or Cheonju Peak. The young man following Yeonggeun wore a black coat and a student's cap, from under which his braided hair hung down; he had a strong nose and large eyes, and when he laughed he showed perfect teeth, like white jade. He waved his arms as he said something to Yeonggeun, and by chance they happened to pass near Bobu, looking straight ahead. Of course, from outside no one would be able to tell whether the person behind the tightly woven sorghum stalk fence was young or old, or even if this person was a man or woman, but the young maiden's heart was burdened as if by some sin, and she took the earthenware bowl and fled back into the kitchen. Her chest pattered like the heart of a startled pigeon. Ashamed, she left the kitchen work to a servant and went to her mother's room. Not long after, from up the riverbank, the clear sound of twin trumpets rang through the mountains and reached her ears.

She drew close to her mother's knees as she mended the soles of some thick hemp socks, but the tumult of her heart, caused by the wandering call of a trumpet, did not abate. Is that the sound of my cousin's trumpet, or of the young man's trumpet? The one that played first, in time and unhesitating as if setting an example, would be her cousin's trumpet. Then the trumpet that played next, somewhat awkwardly and occasionally blaring out a wrong note, would be the trumpet of the young man brimming with vigor. Then the two trumpets played together again and resounded off the mountains across the river, and she could no longer tell which was which, knowing only that her chest was strangely pounding. At times the sound of the trumpets would cease and give way to silence. Are they finished already — she thought, and just then Yeonggeun's sister came in without even a hooded coat on.

"Your brother just went by with someone, both of them carrying their trumpets," she said, a question in her voice.

"Yes, that's Assistant Curator Bak's younger son," answered Bobu's sister-in-law, "They must be going to play their trumpets."

Thus Bobu learned that the tall young man she had seen, the one with large eyes and who showed his white teeth when he laughed, was Assistant Curator Bak's younger son, and from time to time his face would suddenly appear before her.

Some time after, when the proposal of marriage between Assistant Curator Bak's second son and Bobu became official, she would lie awake at night after everyone else was asleep and think to herself of the young man's face, but that face, which had always come to her when she least expected it, glimmered only in her mind and would not let itself be seen. She had no idea what had happened. It flickered briefly but was then gone again, like a mist scattered by the wind. It was as if she were bewitched by a spirit, and there had been times when she had lain awake all night in frustration; but at other times when she was doing something else and not thinking of him, the face would appear again, perhaps in the cloth she was cutting to make clothing or in the shining flames in the fireplace. She was certain that Assistant Curator Bak's second son, Bak Hyeongseon, whom she was to marry, was that young man she had seen. Judging by his age and his grade in school, there was no doubt it was him. She was quietly pleased.

And so it was, on the day that the groom came to the bride's house, because the maiden who was to be the bride could not be at home, she had spent the night at her cousin's and now greeted the morning — this glorious morning that would never come again — from under her blanket and, amidst a flurry of excitement and deep stirrings in her heart, felt there was no doubt that the young man she often pictured, the strong-looking one with the trumpet under his arm who had laughed as he walked by with her cousin, was the one. She had once heard something about Assistant Curator Bak having another son of the same age, one the child of his wife and one the child of his concubine, but now there was no time to consider the possibility that the young man she had seen was born of the concubine, and, in fact, at that moment she did not even remember having heard such a thing.

So she had no idea, having cherished this vision in her heart, that, after she powdered her face, put on her red skirt and green jacket, and set on her head a headdress decorated with seven types of gemstones, she might go into the groom's room to await him with lowered eyes, only to be shocked upon seeing his face, as if he had changed into a different person, and faint away. But fate was not so cruel to her. It did not suddenly shatter her dream and cast it aside, bruised and beaten, but instead gave her a tiny hint at what was to come, pulling at the thread that would unravel her tightly bound heart.

As noon approached, the groom's party passed by Yeong-geun's house with the shouting of the heralds and the ringing of bells, and Bobu poked a small hole in the paper window to secretly look out toward the road, but she found out nothing new. With trembling hands she had done this, encouraged by the fact that no one else was in the room, but, mistaking the sound of a puppy barking for the sound of footfalls, she sat down on the warm spot on the floor in spite of herself and cradled her head in her hands: in the instant that she had poked the hole with her finger and closed one eye to peek outside, the groom had already passed beyond the wall so that only his back was visible, and all she could see was the strange sight of a man of about thirty with a mustache, wearing a pair of new-style eyeglasses and one of those flat caps that her cousin sometimes wore. So there was no reason for her to wonder anew about the groom's face. Only when the day grew long and an old servant came in from the kitchen to bring her lunch, giving her a detailed report as she did so, did Bobu begin to speculate.

"The groom must be handsome, mustn't he? They're all talking about how he has a small figure, a pleasant face, and smallish, smiling eyes, and how he's quite gentle and kindhearted. The daughters of this family are so fortunate to have such well-mannered husbands chosen for them. Now, relax and eat some of your dumpling soup and rice. Someone will be coming soon to get you ready for your makeup."

How much better it would have been had these words simply passed her by, leaving her bewildered; but she was alert, with eyes wide as shooting stars, and heard every last word, for better or for worse.

A small figure, a pleasant face, and smallish, smiling eyes— the old woman's words could not be taken for truth, of course, but the description was so contrary to what Bobu had thought. No matter how old the woman's eyes were, how much she might have seen things differently, there was no way they could be that different. She took a few spoonfuls of her soup, and when the old woman fussed and urged her to eat more, she sent her away, saying, "Go and ask my cousin to come." After the old woman had left, she sat there alone in the room, lost in her thoughts as she compared the face of the young man she remembered with what the old servant had said. No matter how long she ruminated, she could not make any sense of it. Was that mischievous old woman just making up nonsense to tease me? Perhaps she was deliberately trying to fool me into thinking that the groom looked the opposite of his true appearance, so that I would be struck dumb with surprise in his room tonight. That must be it. That old woman is up to some mischief just to get the better of me, she thought; but just as she was about to laugh it away, the thought came to her like a flash of lightning: she seemed to have once heard that Assistant Curator Bak had two sons who were about the same age— that they were, in fact, the same age, one the son of his wife and the other the son of his concubine — and that they grew up as twins but were only a month apart, and when she thought about it she even remembered hearing that the younger brother was much taller and stronger than the older one. Oh my, how could she have completely forgotten about that?

The young man she had been picturing in her mind, the one who had appeared before her eyes, the one she had cherished in her heart in secret, the tall one holding a trumpet, with large eyes and perfect teeth that gleamed white when he smiled, was not the one who would become her husband, who tonight would soothe her beating heart and fumble with her as they searched for the key to the next hundred years of their lives together, but was the one who so cruelly would become her brother-in-law! Could anything be more cruel than cherishing, instead of her husband, not some stranger but the one who would become her brother-in-law?

A wave of shame rushed over her. How on earth could she have suffered such misfortune? Even though she did not yet know the truth of the matter, Bobu was certain that she had most definitely been thinking of the wrong person. No, she had no choice but to be certain. No longer could she keep on this way, picturing that strong young man with the trumpet, and be both glad and anxious in her heart. That would be unforgivable. She would have to crush this spiteful vision into dust, blow away that dust like a mist, and then quickly create a new vision to cling to. Until now she had thought of that young man's face as one most becoming of a man, but right here and now she had to admonish herself, even if it was against her own will, telling herself that it was, in fact, a repulsive, loathsome, disgraceful, monstrous, and despicable face. She could not see him with her eyes. She could not think of him in her mind. And she could especially not hide him in her heart. When he laughed she would have to spit, when he came near she would have to shove him away and hector him, if his lips quivered as if he were on the verge of saying something, she would have to strike him on the cheek with her clenched fist or claw at his nose and lips.

But what sort of new vision should she create to replace that spiteful young man? The old servant said that he was short. No, she said he had a small figure, which is different from short. She said he had smallish eyes, too. And that his face was pleasant — but she had no skill to conjure a countenance from only these things. Would she have to wait until tonight? How then would she keep her mind as clean as a sheet of white paper, pretending that nothing was amiss, in the hours that were left until nightfall? Had not this day been so special, she could have waited a year or two without thinking of anyone. But in order to root out the image of that young man that had planted itself in a corner of her heart, she had to have something new to take its place. Didn't one need the Bible and Jesus to cast out evil spirits? Bobu could not keep her heart steady.

In truth, her thoughts, which had flashed like lightning so far forward, had brought nothing more than shame creeping up into her face and cheeks, but when suddenly their unfathomable and confusing mix poured into her mind, her heart trembled like a boiling kettle and roared like a waterfall, and for a time she could not calm herself.

But still, what she felt could, in a word, be called shame. Yet beneath it she felt that she had wronged her father and mother, that she had wronged the one who was to become her husband, and she was discouraged in the way that people always feel when something like this happens, and certainly there was also a faint regret at having lost the man she had treasured in her heart, accompanied by a feeling akin to disappointment, and finally there were thoughts of disgrace that this man was none other than he who was to be her brother-in-law. In the midst of this muddle of feelings she realized that, even if no one could ever know, even if no one ever saw, and no one ever overheard, it would still be true that she had long cherished him, and so she could not resist the strong guilt and remorse that crawled down her spine, as if she had committed adultery.

She pulled her knees up to her chest and buried her face in them for a long time. Tears began to flow from her eyes, down her cheeks and nose, and through the fingers that covered them. What these tears were, or where they had come from, not even Bobu herself could fathom.

Yet not long after, her heart and mind were light again, as if nothing had ever happened. It was as if the clouds had passed and the sun was shining brightly on her heart. The tears, like the last sentiments of a maiden, had washed her heart clean of all impurities, making her ready for the most important and glorious moment of her life.

Thankfully, just then her sister-in-law brought in an old woman to get her ready for her makeup.

"It will soon be evening, so hurry up and wash yourself and get ready for your makeup." She had bathed the night before at home, so there was no need to bathe now, not to mention no time.

Her sister-in-law gave her baby to her other child and shooed them outside, and then she went to the kitchen to boil water. With her outer garment off and wearing only her inner jacket, her breasts swelled like hillocks, pushing aside the flaps of the jacket. She shoved these flaps into her sash, but when she bent over her white breasts bulged out of the sides of her garment, and even though there were only women there it was embarrassing.

The old woman who got Bobu ready for her makeup had once been a gisaeng. People had always called her "Pyeongyang Aunt." She took out her cosmetics case, powder cases, and powder puffs, and then she took out a pair of tweezers and a ball of thread and laid them out in front of the washbasin. She rolled out the thin silk thread, and with this she plucked out the soft hairs that were still on Bobu's face. When she twisted and rubbed the thread against Bobu's cheeks, pressing it hard and then quickly pulling it away, the stinging made the tears flow. Bobu could stand most of it, but when the old woman did the areas around her temples and the nape of her neck, she could not stand the sweat that poured down her face. She clenched her teeth and stiffened her legs. When Pyeongyang Aunt finally lowered her hands, Bobu unknowingly let out a long sigh.

"Does it sting? Did you think it would be easy to go from being a maiden to being a bride?" the old woman teased, and she continued to roughly pull out the hairs. Bobu's face burned like she had been drinking. When that was over, the old woman took the tweezers and plucked her eyebrows. This stung, too, and it must have stimulated the tear ducts, because tears flowed from her eyes and mucous from her nose, but it didn't hurt as much as before. After doing this, Pyeongyang Aunt left. They would do the actual makeup once she had eaten dinner and returned home, before she went into the groom's room.

In the meantime, the sun had set on the long, early spring day. A cool, refreshing breeze teased calm ripples from the still water. Branches with their buds just beginning to open quivered whenever the wind blew. Above Hwaju Peak, one of the twelve peaks, hung a pale moon as sharp as a sickle.

It was now most certainly night. She went up the Merciful Blessings Temple alley with her sister and crept in through the back door of her house, but their dog rushed out and played at their feet.

"Shoo, shoo," said her sister as she pushed the dog away with her light blue shoes, but Bobu waved her hands as she followed her sister, softly calling the dog by name, "Weol, Weol!"

The dog was just happy to see her again, since she had been gone all day. Perhaps he thought it strange and wondered why Bobu had left and only come back after the sun had set and the cold winds had begun to blow, even though there had been a great feast at home. They went into the kitchen, but everyone had gone into the large room, and there was only a single lamp to light the wide space, casting lazy, flickering shadows on the fireplace, the cupboard, the stone counter, and the dirty dishes on the bare earthen floor.

Bobu followed her sister-in-law into the small room next to the kitchen. Inside were only her mother, her older sister, and the old gisaeng from Pyeongyang. They all looked at her and beamed, grinned, and giggled, but Bobu quickly cast her eyes down and turned her face away from them. She was excited yet troubled. The clothes that she was to wear and the accessories that would go with them and that would adorn her hair were arrayed at her feet, some wrapped in bundles and others stored in boxes.

She took off her clothes again and washed herself with hot water, rinsing her neck, chest, armpits, and face. Now the real makeup would begin.

First, the Pyeongyang aunt powdered Bobu's face white and applied a little rouge to her cheeks and lips. It was the first time in her life she had ever had her face powdered, but Bobu had naturally fair skin, so the powder puff barely touched her here and there: first her nose, then her cheeks, then between her eyebrows and her forehead, and with that her face was as clean and soft as white jade glistening with mist. The rouge gave her a pretty blushing look. Her lips had always been as red as cherries. Her eyebrows were as thin as threads, arching upward and trailing off toward her temples. Her lustrous hair dripped with fragrant, glistening camellia oil and shone like black satin. This hair was braided tight and put up, fastened with small and large hairpins. The hairpin ornament, depicting two phoenixes kissing with their wings spread, shone in dazzling gold. The Pyeongyang aunt lightly set the seven-gem headpiece on her neatly parted hair and then stepped back to view it from farther away; even in the dim light the gold, silver, glass, agate, crystal, pearls, and other precious stones glittered clear and bright, as if a piece of the heavens had been taken down and set on her brow.

No one said anything. The Pyeongyang aunt looked at Bobu, enraptured, and then clucked her tongue. Even though she said nothing, her expression was one of wonder, as if to say, 'Could even a celestial being come down from heaven look so beautiful?' Her mother, her older sister, and her sister-in-law could only stare dumbly at Bobu's decorated face, thinking that for one woman to have been born so beautiful, she must have been blessed by a divine spirit, and wondering if they too had been as beautiful when they were young maidens. The Pyeongyang aunt then put two earrings, their orbs as red as strawberries and large as chestnuts, and embroidered with gold and silver thread, in the lobes of Bobu's ears, which were even whiter than her face. At even the slightest turning of her head, the earrings shuddered softly and prettily like wind chimes.

The high, prominent ridge of her nose curved gently downward into a round tip, while her nostrils flared slightly, and her pretty eyelids ended in long, unmoving lashes like fingernails. Finally a gentle, satisfied smile promised to spread across her lips, her round, charming face held on to it. And then she turned her head, as if to look at the bundle of clothing at her feet, so no one saw this smile. She hastily swallowed it and then carefully rose to change her clothes. Beneath her light green jacket, brocaded with a peach blossom pattern, she wore a skirt as red as the sunset, which hung down to the floor. Where the front hem of the jacket met the skirt a variety of ornaments were hung — an ornamental knife, a tiny needle case, a tiger claw, and other trinkets.

How gloomy was the night. In the groom's room, where the groom now sat near the warm spot on the floor, a red flame danced and flickered atop the candlestick that had been set in a bowl of white rice. He had taken off his black silk hat and cloak, and he had even taken off his overcoat and hung it over the folding screen behind him. The friends who had come to talk with him had all eaten dinner and gone home. The outer room, the yard, the men's quarters, the room across the way, and the kitchen were all bustling, but the room in which Hyeongseon sat alone, bored but not a little anxious as well, had long been wrapped in a strangely silent air.

Suddenly, there was a commotion outside, and the groom realized that the time was fast approaching. He wondered whether he should get up and put on his clothes, but then he had the sudden thought that it might be amusing to pretend not to notice. He tried to stay calm. Someone crossed the yard and chirped in a soft but clearly audible voice, "The bride is being brought in." Then came the sound of doors being opened in every room. Each door spilled light into the once-dim yard, making it as bright as the dawning sky. Someone approached the room and leaned against the window. Hyeongseon heard the sound of someone poking a hole in the paper window, followed by, "The groom is sitting upright on the warm spot on the floor."

"Is he wearing his overcoat?"

"He's just sitting there without it."

Goodness, they must be telling him to put on his overcoat, that, whether he was a man or not, it just wasn't proper for him to not be wearing his overcoat when seeing the bride for the first time, and he shouldn't go against etiquette. He realized that his legs were restless and unable to hold still, and he leaped up and took his overcoat from over the folding screen.

As he stood there with the coat in his hand, however, there came the distinctive sound of silk sweeping across the wooden ledge outside the room, and then the door slid softly open. The flame of the candle shuddered once and then writhed like a snake. With no chance to put on the overcoat, he just stared dumbly at those coming through the door: first an old woman, then a set of brilliant and dazzling clothes quietly moved into the center of the room.

"What does it matter if you put that on now? Just leave it off." The old woman laughed kindly, took the overcoat from his hands, and hung it over the folding screen again. The bride sat down with one knee raised and faced the candle, showing her profile to the groom. Only then did Hyeongseon see her. The red skirt was wrapped around the lower part of her body and held the beautiful, decorated girl like a vase held a flower. It was a pretty flower vase. Her oiled hair was tied up and her cheeks were smoothed, the hairs having been plucked by the silken thread, and only now did he realize how soft was the line of her face as it curved down from her cheeks to her jawline and throat. He was pleased. The light-green silk brocaded with peach blossoms reflected the red candlelight, and he stared dumbly at the face of his bride, which shone gently with the colors of the rainbow.

The woman who had brought her in — she must have been a relative of the family, a woman blessed and fortunate — moved the folding screens to one side of the room, and then she took out the mats and blankets that had been prepared and laid them out over the warm spot on the floor. Only when she carried the blankets past the groom did he realize that he had been gazing at the bride's face like a starving man at food, and he turned his eyes toward the other side of the room and began fidgeting.

"Now, you must be very tired today, so you should go to bed. I've brought you some apples and pears and chestnuts from the banquet table, but even if you don't eat anything else, at least share this one apple between you. They say that you have to share an apple if you want to bear sons and daughters and live happily together. Now, as for you . . ." She turned toward the bride. "You are no longer strangers, so don't just sit there. I'll be leaving now, so have a good time."

She looked behind the folding screens once again. After making sure there was nothing there but the thick wall, she looked back at the two young people — one standing next to the bedding, and the other still sitting there motionless, looking at the candle — and took a few steps backward before gently opening the door and leaving the room. There must have been many people gathered around the door, quietly listening for voices inside, for when the old woman opened it and went outside there was a murmuring of many indistinct voices. The sound soon died down, but every now and then a giggle or deep breath could be heard, so apparently no one had left yet.

The two people inside the room knew that it was customary for the people outside not to leave for some time. No one knows how this custom of watching the newlyweds' room started, but they did as curiosity commanded, staying even after the lights were snuffed to entertain themselves by poking holes in the paper doors and windows and listening in or spying on what was happening inside.

The bride and groom stayed motionless for some time, like a couple waiting for their photograph to be taken. They weren't sure who should speak first, or even if they should speak at all.

After remaining like that for a tediously long time, the groom, aware that he was still distant in his heart from the one who remained seated, strutted past the bride, as if he had made a sudden resolution. Then he stood straight before the candle and looked down at her vacantly, as if he were going to say something.

"Why don't you get undressed?" said someone from outside. It might have been someone who had been watching through a hole in the door and grown impatient, or it might be someone teasing them, but, emboldened by these words, the groom lifted his right hand ever so slightly . . . but he couldn't reach out to the bride, so he instead brought his hand to the still-flickering candle and snuffed out the flame at the base of the wick. The room grew dark. The bride, thinking that the groom was about to touch her, felt anxious at first, and when the light suddenly went out she felt a chill like cold water down her spine. She let out a low sigh in the dark, suffocating air.

Carefully, the groom walked past her. He didn't so much fear that he would accidentally touch the bride's foot or hand, but that he might step on her skirt, or swing his arms and hit her headpiece, hairpin, or earrings.

He went to the warm spot on the floor and sat down with a thud, then undid his ankle bands and unfastened the buttons on his vest. There was no way they could see anything in the darkness, but those outside must have been able to tell from the rustling of silk, and some women chattered, "The new groom is undoing his own clothes, that's no fun. What is the bride, a sack of barley?"

Then someone else's voice, perhaps that of the bride's mother or some other relative, said from out in the yard, "That's enough peeking — the young people need some room to breathe, so leave them be."

"We were about to leave anyway. This is no fun. The bride and groom aren't children, after all, so they should at least talk to each other or something," said a few voices from by the doorpost. "What's the point of watching this?"

Then came a farewell: "I bid you good night. I am going to retire."

Now there would be no more onlookers. Even if there were a few persistent people still watching, the groom thought that he should do his duty as a man and then get some rest, but he was still unable to say anything, so he reached out his arm and fumbled around for the bride's wrist. It was warm and soft. But it was also still, and she did not react at all to his grasping it. He gently pulled her to him, and she lifted up her body and then leaned toward him. She had been still, but she had also been ready to move at the slightest effort on his part.

From the time her aunt had first brought her into the groom's room until the moment that the light went out, Bobu had kept her eyes downcast, staring at the ground without ever once looking anywhere else — at least this was how she appeared to her aunt, to the groom, and to those looking in through the holes in the paper doors. Yet unbeknownst to anyone, she had cleverly managed — just once — to glance at the groom. Was he handsome or ugly, where were his eyes on his face, where did his nose jut out . . . it was not to learn these things that she stole a glance at the groom's face. Tomorrow morning, when the doors and windows grew bright, she would easily be able to look at the sleeping face right beside hers, and even if she did look at him, no matter how he happened to look, she had already shared his bed, and this after the ceremony that had announced them to the world, so there was nothing to be done about it. Their parents had planned it, it had been announced to all, and today it had been recognized and blessed by everyone. Bobu knew very well that even if he were a cripple she would have to live with him, even if he were missing an eye she would have to wait on him, and even if he were a hunchback she would have to serve him. Nor was she so impatient that she was prepared to risk drawing attention to herself by shifting her gaze to see what her husband looked like.

And yet she could not but carefully, without anyone realizing, look at his face. She could not stand to not see it. When her aunt took the bedding to the warm spot on the floor, at the moment she felt the groom's burning gaze shift away from her, her lowered eyelids flicked upward and she caught a quick glimpse of his face. Even though she had not looked directly at him, she could roughly judge by his shadow how tall the man standing before her was, so for a moment she was able to ponder the fact that he was not tall: the man she now saw only briefly with her own eyes was, as she expected, not the young man with her cousin who had been carrying his trumpet along the road toward Pear Blossom Pavilion when she had gone outside to throw out some dishwater. She was not the least bit surprised. She thought, resignedly, 'So it's not him, just as I thought,' and even though she, of course, felt a faint disappointment inside, she did not feel even the slightest hint of foreboding about now having to live with some unavoidable misfortune. So, with nothing to give her any idea of what he looked like — in fact, all she had done was to intuitively determine whether he was the man with the trumpet and did not have any clear impression of his actual appearance — when the man reached out his hand, fumbled for hers, and then drew him toward her, she felt at ease enough to allow herself to be pulled close.

'From this day forward I belong to this person. I have devoted myself wholly, body and mind, to this person. More than that, I have given everything I am to this man.' Thus that vision of the tall young man with the trumpet that had haunted a corner of her heart — the man who was to become her brother-in-law, whoever he might be — had been nothing more than an evil apparition. The dreams of the young man she had harbored in her heart until now she considered wicked thoughts planted by this evil spirit, and even as she felt more like a sinner than ever, in her contrition she tried to turn these thoughts into a deep affection for her husband.

The man's hand was fumbling with her long hairpin as he pulled it out. She stayed calm, but his warm breath brushed by her ear and made her heart flutter. The hand seemed to tremble a little, but it made no mistake as it pulled the hairpin from her hair. He tried to take off her headpiece. As the man's hands hung above her forehead, as if tickling her, the bride took them in her own and they took off the headpiece together. He put it on the table at the other end of the room and then sat there for a while without a word. She had helped him take off the headpiece, so maybe now he wanted her to undo her own clothes. She might be able to take off her headpiece and pull out her hairpins, but how could she undo her own clothes with her own hands? How could she so boldly, so rudely reveal with her own hands the chest, stomach, and legs that had been wrapped in her undergarments, wound in her sash, and hidden from all eyes in her inner jacket and vest, bloomers, and skirt? If the man just left her here like this and lay down in bed by himself, then she would sit here, alone and pitiful, without even blinking an eye until the eastern sky grew bright and the sun rose in the window. This is what she thought to herself; but the man was, of course, not so unkind.

He undid the ties of her skirt. They had been tied in a number of knots, to be playful, and he undid them one knot at a time. She felt sorry for him, so she finished untying them herself. Then the man began untying the strings of her jacket.

He untied everything that needed to be untied. He had helped untie the ties for her skirt and the belt full of ornaments, but she could take care of the ties for her bloomers or undergarments herself. He untied the strings of her jacket, so it was up to her to take it off or not. Then Hyeongseon just cast off his own clothes and climbed into bed. As a man, how could he do anything more than that, short of impudently, doggedly grabbing her hand, or actually saying something to her? So he laid his head down on the pillow and waited there quietly in the darkness for the bride to do something. All was silent for a moment. Hyeongseon heard his heart beating.

Bobu neatly folded the clothes that the man had taken off. Then she quietly pushed them up against the folding screen at the other end of the room. For some time she sat still, not knowing what to do. Actually, she knew quite well what to do, and how to do it, but she couldn't find the courage to see it through. All the groom had to do was say something to her, or even just tug at the legs of her bloomers—he didn't even have to pull at her wrist, like before—she thought she would have been able to find courage in this, but he had made things awkward and didn't move a muscle as he lay in bed, cruelly leaving her there by herself.

Yet Hyeongseon was not really that mischievous. Neither was he so heartless, unfeeling, or foolish not to realize that if he didn't do something, the bride might spend the entire night sitting there next to the bedding in her undone clothes. He desperately wanted to leap up, cast off her jacket, unwrap her skirt from around her, and promptly take her by the arm and lay her head down on the other side of the long pillow. But he could not act so crudely, so instead he gave her a brief chance to act. He groaned and, as if stretching out, clasped the blanket between his legs and turned over. Hearing the sound of the blankets rustling, along with the sound of the man's groan and the sound of him turning his heavy body over, the bride caught on quickly and took off only her skirt and outer jacket before quietly moving over to the bed. But she only made as if to lie down and, concerned that her skin might touch the man, or that her face might touch the pillow, she curled up and lay there uncomfortably.

It was only then that the jaguar's blood welled up inside the chest of the young groom. Only then did he twist his body like a raging beast, lay the bride down on the pillow and pull the blanket over her.

And then it was all over. It was very hot under the blanket, but all they had to do now was go to sleep.

But, oh dear, they had forgotten one thing. The apple that had been placed on the big table, and which the woman had earnestly begged them to eat—it may have been Hyeongseon who thought of it first, but it was Bobu who got up and brought the apple back from the bowl. What a predicament they would have found themselves in if the man had forgotten this and just gone to sleep. She hadn't even realized that she was genuinely hoping that they would be happy and prosperous, give birth to a first son, and live well. She picked up the apple, brought it back with her, and lay down in bed. Then she worked up the courage to slowly hold the apple above the man's face. The man took it, bit a chunk out of it, and then handed it back to the bride as he chewed on it.

Only then in the darkness did the bride allow herself a soft, satisfied smile, and only then did she feel intoxicated by the scent of the man under the covers, and she brought the apple he had taken a bite of to her mouth.

It was then. It was just then. There was a thud on the wooden ledge outside and a large stone smashed into the door post. She was startled. The bride didn't drop the apple, but she buried her face in the man's chest out of fright.

"Who's there?"

This was followed by the sound of doors opening, one, two, and three — the doors to the outer room, the room across the way, and the master's room opened all at the same time. But there was no other sound. Then a dog barked.

It was too much for a prank — Bobu was not the only one who thought this. There was a bustle out in the yard. Someone must have come up onto the wooden ledge and picked up the stone that had been thrown.

"What is this stone? It's quite big. What bastard did this?"

Someone else must have chased them through the front gate and returned.

"He's already gone down by the river; I have no idea who it is, but he seemed pretty tall."

Bobu was struck with fright at these words. A tall person — who could it have been? If it had not been simply a prank or a joke, then it would be clear to all that this was the act of someone who was displeased or irked by their marriage. Perhaps this is why, after the front gate had been shut again, they heard from out in the yard,

"Someone takes their pranks quite seriously."

After these last words from Head Clerk Jeong, spoken so loudly that they must have been intended for the groom to hear, everyone returned to their rooms and it grew quiet again. Everyone must have immediately suspected that this was the act of another man who loved his daughter, and everyone must have also realized that if word spread of this incident, it would cause no small problem.

Bobu was afraid that her parents or her new husband would get the wrong idea about her. In truth, there was no one: she had never even raised a finger to or cast a glance at anyone, and never had any man done anything of the kind to her. She had thought that the young man with the trumpet, the one who would become her brother-in-law, was to be the husband who was now lying beside her, but even that young man himself had no idea of this, and though she couldn't say that she had never cherished him in her heart, there was no one who knew of her feelings. Of course, it wasn't even a question of anyone else knowing or not knowing. For this reason, after the upset caused by the thrown stone, when she heard that a tall fellow had fled toward the water's edge, Bobu could not deny that she felt something tap lightly on her heart. There must be many tall fellows. But hearing that this tall fellow had fled to the water's edge, and with that light rapping on her heart, she thought that it couldn't be anyone but the young man with the trumpet, her brother-in-law who was no more than a month younger than her husband.

In truth, though, it might not have been him — this thought occurred to her so suddenly that she herself found it strange. If it really had been him, how could he have committed such an outrage here, in the room where his own brother and his bride lay? There was no way that he could have longed for her . . . though it may have been true that, for her part, she had thought of him, was it not also true that he could not have thought of her in the same way? If this were so, then he would never try to hinder her happiness or show his displeasure, and there was no way he would ever commit such an outrage. Thus it could not have been him. But who on earth could it have been? She had no idea.

What was her husband thinking? If her husband chose to doubt her, then this incident was more than enough to support those doubts. What should she do about this curious situation? She could only wait for him to act, her face shamelessly buried in his chest and her breathing unsteady. What explanation could she give, what at all was there for her to say about the incident, which she herself could not even begin to fathom? If she were to be whipped, then she would be whipped, and if she were to be punished, then she would be punished. She kept her face buried in her husband's chest as she thought these things, but then, "Finish eating the apple now."

The man's strong arm wrapped around her chest. It was the first time she had heard his voice, and the first time he had embraced her. No, it was the first time since she had left her mother's embrace and grown up that the arm of any other person had touched the body she had guarded so carefully.

It was true, there was no one like a husband. She was touched that a single phrase and a single strong embrace from him could smooth everything over. She must serve this husband no matter what happened. She thought of him as a being so great that even if she were to grind her body into dust to serve him, it would still not be enough. She did not even try to hold back the tears that gushed out from within her, and she took a bite of the half-eaten apple while lying in his embrace. Her tears must have fallen on the apple, for it tasted salty. She took one bite, then two, and chewed them noisily. Her tears fell onto the man's chest.

4

Hyeonggeol slept late, which was unusual for him. On any other day he would have been playing his trumpet in the pine forest behind the school or down by the river or exercising on the horizontal bar in the school's playground, all before even eating breakfast, but today he was sleeping late.

But he was not unaware that the window had grown bright, nor had he thrown the covers over his head or slipped off the pillow to lie drooling on the floor; he was lying flat and still on top of his covers, his eyes wide open, without getting up. At first, he could not understand what was so different about this day or why he should be so loath to get up from his bed. Was it because there was no one around to scold him if he got up late, as his father had slept at the main house the night before? Yet his father never particularly cared whether he got up early or late. Even if his father had been sitting in his room, banging his pipe on the ashtray, or coughing especially loudly, or receiving his breakfast, he might have asked his concubine sitting at the corner of the table, "Has that boy Hyeonggeol not gotten up yet? He must have been out late last night." But he wouldn't have gone any further than that.

Of course, if he woke up late, his mother would come to his room and stand next to his bed, smiling widely as she looked down at her son's face and said, "The sun has already risen an arm's span in the sky and you're still sleeping!" or, "Aren't you going to go out and play your trumpet today?"

It had already been quite some time since she had opened his door today. But when she saw her son lying there, his eyes blank, she closed the door she had just quietly opened. Although Hyeonggeol was not paying attention to her, he did wonder why she said nothing today, why she had changed into her best clothes and left the house early in the morning, and where she was going without even having eaten breakfast.

Then again, perhaps it was because he knew the reason for all of these things that he lay there on top of the covers, not sleeping but not tossing and turning either, until the sun had risen an arm's span into the sky — or, as someone given to exaggeration might say, until midday.

In fact, Hyeonggeol himself was well aware of these things. He knew why he was lying here and loath to get up, and why his mother had not said anything. It was the morning of the day that Hyeongseon, his respectable brother, no more than a month older than him, a brother who was treated better than him because he was the son of his father's wife, was marrying the daughter of Head Clerk Jeong.

Thus his father had not returned to Dumutgol last night but had gone straight to the main house and slept there (of course, it wasn't as if his father always slept here in Dumutgol); his mother had changed into new clothes, gone to the main house before dawn broke, and before she went had quietly opened the door to his room and then closed it again, unable to say anything even as she saw her son lying there.

Some time after his mother had gone, a messenger boy arrived from the main house, and the servant boy, Samnam, opened the door and relayed the message: "Someone has come from the main house to ask you to come out and go eat breakfast there."

Although it would have been enough simply to say they wanted him to eat breakfast at the main house, the young boy was far too careful, so his words sounded ridiculous, and this displeased Hyeonggeol so he said nothing. The young boy, even though he clearly knew that Hyeonggeol had heard him and was just not answering, yelled again, "Go out and eat breakfast!" Hyeonggeol realized that, if he did not answer, the young sharecropper's boy would stand there all day shouting at him, and even though rage boiled up from inside him, at the same time he felt sorry for the lad.

"I'm eating—" he shouted in an angry voice, then calmed himself and said softly, "Tell them I'll be eating here."

Samnam, with absolutely no expression on his face that might betray any concern over whether Hyeonggeol spoke angrily or softly, closed the door and said, "Tell them he said he will be eating here."

Hyeonggeol lay there in his room as he listened to the boys talk, but then, when he heard the sound of little footsteps disappearing toward the front gate of the house, he sat straight up.

The children had acted in quite a displeasing manner, but the sight of him lying there since morning must have been rather boring as well.

"Our young students must be brave, cheerful, generous, and ready to sacrifice." He heard these words over and over again from his arithmetic teacher, his history teacher, during geography class, and during gymnastics.

He picked up his clothes and put them on and then opened the door leading out into the yard to let in some fresh air. He got up to fold his bedding, but a middle-aged servant came in from the kitchen and, although she didn't ask him what was going on, practically grabbed the bedding from him with an odd expression on her face, somewhere between awe and fear.

He said nothing and went out. The rays of the spring morning sun were warm. He stared at the sun until he was blinded and then washed his face. As soon as he went back into his room, the breakfast table was brought in. He knew that a servant from the main house had just brought a large wooden platter with his breakfast on it. Yet he ate his breakfast and prepared to go to school, as he had always done. Knowing that he might be late, he hurriedly threw on his overcoat, pulled the braided hair that ran down his spine out from within the overcoat, and then stopped to think. 'This braid'— he pulled it forward and looked at it for a while. 'This braid'— plaited sleek and smooth from three strands and tied at the bottom with a black ribbon.

'Humph, today I must cut off this blasted braid, no matter what.'

Then he flung it over his shoulder again with his right hand, like a gymnast, his firm resolve evident.

After putting on his student's cap, he stepped into the leather shoes outside his door and left the house. It was not far to the school. Once across the stepping stones in the Dumutgol stream, he would walk for some way along a narrow path, like a levee between rice paddies, and arrive at the school playground. There was a Confucian shrine halfway up the pine-covered hill, and next to it was a lecture hall. This was the classroom.

Once outside the front gate of the house and past the large willow tree, the well, and the zelkova tree, he could clearly see the school playground. There were students jumping straw ropes while still wearing their black overcoats, and there were other students who had hung up their overcoats and were hanging from the horizontal bars. It seemed that there was still some time left before school. He looked at the sun: it wasn't nearly as high in the sky as he had thought it was. It was only just above the pine forest on the hill behind the school. He did not run but marched along smartly like a soldier, and he felt very satisfied as he held his bundle of books in his right hand. His braid waved back and forth across his back, and this morning the feeling of the ribbon brushing his buttocks was particularly annoying. It seemed to make a loud slapping sound as well. He thought that only chopping the thing off entirely, and doing it today, would bring him any relief, and this thought pleased him, as if he were planning revenge on an old enemy.

Hyeonggeol was in the first year of high school. So when the elementary school students saw him they would stop in their tracks, bring their legs together, and bow to him. On the other hand, when he saw a second- or third-year high school student, he had to bow to them. It was pleasant enough bowing and being bowed to, but he was even more grateful that there were no upperclassmen who were younger than him. Some of the students would bow and then pretend to play a fanfare using their hands. Son Daebong was one of them. It was said that his mother had prayed diligently to the mountain spirit of Mount Daebong, behind the hot springs in Yangdeok, and had then bathed in the hot springs, and by the grace of the mountains and the water she had become pregnant with him, so they named him Daebong. Even though his parents refused to allow him to cut his hair, saying that the blood of monks would flow like a river if he did so, he rolled up his sleeves and fought for anything that was new-style. When he saw upperclassmen he greeted them with the faux fanfare, and when he saw lowerclassmen he made them greet him the same way.

Hyeonggeol passed beneath the sign that read "Dongmyeong School" and hung from the front gate at the entrance to the playground, and saw Son Daebong skipping toward him around the track that ran along the outside of the playground. Wearing only his vest, he had cast off his student's cap and tied up his hair in a knot to keep it from getting in his way. He wasn't running very fast, and he rhythmically skipped in big strides, so it looked like he was practicing for the three-legged race that was to be held during the athletics meet. He was looking far off into the distance, and it wasn't until he was right in front of Hyeonggeol that he saw him; he stopped suddenly, almost falling over, and bowed to him without even putting his legs together. Hyeonggeol stopped walking and acknowledged him, and Daebong, even though he was gasping for breath, rolled up his left hand, put it to his mouth, and blew a fanfare: "Tantara!!"

Son Daebong was a third-year elementary school student, and after he went to the athletics meet in Pyeongyang the year before, he always played a trumpet fanfare after bowing. The number of students who imitated him was growing, but there were some students among those who had gone to Pyeongyang who disparaged him, saying that what he did was just pointless fakery and that there wasn't a single student in Pyeongyang's Daeseong School or anywhere else who pretended to play the trumpet like that. Yet Daebong was unshaken and had kept up the practice.

Some time ago, one student had asked their gymnastics teacher, Jeong Yeonggeun, if it wasn't improper to pretend to play the trumpet after bowing, but the teacher said that there was no harm in it. Mr. Jeong knew very well that the student was talking about Son Daebong. Daebong blew his trumpet after bowing not only to upperclassmen but also to his teachers. When Mr. Jeong first received this treatment from Son Daebong, he laughed a little and didn't quite know what to do. But it was true that he was more than a little pleased, as Daebong's bearing was militarily strict.

"You were late today because of Hyeongseon's wedding!" Daebong was serious only when bowing, but when that was done they were close friends who teased each other.

"Why should I be late when someone else is getting married? Just because a maiden gets married, it doesn't mean that the young man next door will hang himself." Yet even as he joked, Hyeonggeol was not in the most pleasant of moods. He was not too late, but it was true that he was later than usual, and he could not deny the fact that Hyeongseon's wedding did have something to do with it. "Anyway, I've resolved to do something, so we should do it together."

"What have you resolved to do this time? And whether you've made a resolution or not, why should I have to do what you do? Am I your wife, or one of your family's servants?"

"Is that all you can think of, wives and servants? Just come with me." Hyeonggeol dragged Daebong toward the shade of a large ginko tree. "Let's cut these off," he said, smiling as he touched his braid.

"If I cut mine off now there will be hell to pay." As usual, Daebong's face betrayed his reluctance.

"I've let mine be because of my mother, too, but today I am

resolved. There is no reason to carry around such a useless thing, nor to keep something that just gets in the way all the time, and it swarms with lice besides. I'm cutting it off."

"We young students need to be brave. Hang it, I'm cutting mine, too."

The two of them laughed heartily and went up to the school office. Hyeonggeol held his braid in one hand and fingered it as he walked, while Daebong took the hair that had been tied up on his head and wiped the sweat on his brow and head with the ribbon. Then he took the old braid, which wasn't too long, and twirled it around, singing,

> "Steel-boned, stone-muscled
> Young man,
> Do not forget
> The spirit of civilization!
> Let us pursue virtue
> And nurture wisdom,
> And thus become
> The leaders of civilization!"

The two of them kept time as they marched up the hill. They made an unconscious effort to avoid any stray thoughts, so that they would not shrink from their decision. If they thought about what might happen after they cut their hair, they might waver in their resolve. So they immediately called the school errand boy and asked him to bring out the barber's clippers.

"They'll soon be blowing the trumpet to announce the start of school," he said as he reluctantly came out with the clippers.

To this, Hyeonggeol replied, "I'll be blowing the trumpet. Cut Daebong's hair first."

Daebong, for his part, climbed up onto the stone wall next to the hill and shouted toward the playground and classroom, "First-year high school student Bak Hyeonggeol and third-year elementary school student Son Daebong are cutting their hair!"

They knew that their teachers wouldn't scold them that much if they were late because they were cutting their hair. All of the students poured up the hill to watch them. They gathered in a circle next to the trash can beneath the poplar tree. Daebong turned down the collar of his outer vest and stood hunched over in their midst.

Someone mumbled, "Hyeonggeol and Daebong are cutting their hair, so the sun is probably going to rise in the west tomorrow."

Gilson, who had cut his own hair quite some time ago, stepped forward. "Let me hold your braid," he said, and he took the ribbon and lifted it up.

"When the clippers touch my hair, sing a song for me," Daebong said, but instead of sounding like a jest, it sounded almost tragic, so Hyeonggeol took the lead and began singing,

> "It's come, it's come,
> Spring has come."

Then all the students echoed him,

> "It's come, it's come,
> Spring has come."

And then everyone sang together,

> "Spring has come at dawn
> To these mountains and streams.
> All things in their season
> Shine with light,
> So blessings abound
> On this lovely spring day."

As the sound of singing rang out, the clippers, with their few missing teeth, clattered and began cutting Daebong's hair from the bottom up. The errand boy began at the hairline and worked his way up towards the crown, where he stopped clipping. Gilson tugged at the ribbon with his right hand; only about a fistful of hair was still attached to his head.

"OK, I'm cutting the rest of it." The errand boy was a little nervous, so he grabbed the clippers with both hands and shoved them into the hair. Everyone was quiet. As the errand boy's hands moved, the sound of the clippers grew particularly loud. When he pushed the clippers through one last time and then drew them back, the braid tied up with the ribbon fell away from Daebong's head. Gilson held it up and shouted, "Long live Son Daebong!" Then he put it in the trash can. Daebong smiled broadly as he brushed off his head, but when he stood up it was difficult to tell whether he was laughing or crying.

Then it was Hyeonggeol's turn. He put his bundle of books and his student's cap on the stone wall and then took off his overcoat and put it on top of them. As he unhesitatingly rolled up his sleeves, someone teased him, "Well, Hyeonggeol's gone and done it now."

But just at that moment, the trumpet announcing the start of school sounded. Hearing this, the errand boy said, "Let's cut your hair after the first class or at lunchtime."

"That won't do," objected the students who had gathered round. "Then you might not be able to cut it at all." So Hyeonggeol decided to cut his hair then, and the students who had gathered round all went to their classrooms.

"I'll talk to the teacher," said Daebong, and he walked off with his arms around his classmates' shoulders, looking more lively than before. Hyeonggeol waved at them and then sat down. The errand boy cleaned the clippers once with a brush. He unfastened the screws and brushed out the hair, and then he took out a dropper of oil and squeezed some onto the parts where the metal pieces rubbed against one another. He tightened the screws again, held the clippers by his ear, and then squeezed the handles. He was listening to hear if they sounded loose or tight. It was just over a year since they had been purchased, and there were only two of their kind in this village, used to cut the hair of nearly ten people a day, so there was no way they could be in good condition. Green rust tinged the edges, and a few teeth were missing, so sometimes they would just grab the hair and get stuck. But everyone knew that the clippers always plucked at the hair and hurt, so they didn't mind.

The cool steel touched the back of Hyeonggeol's head. Then, with a continuous clatter, the cold metal went up and over his head once. The wind that blew on his head was suddenly cold, and a chill went down his spine. His braid brushed past his ears and then flopped to the black earth before his eyes. Yet the clippers were still just going up and down, trying to tame his hair. With his hair swept away by a brush, he felt refreshed beyond compare, but on the other hand, he could not help but feel a strange regret swelling up in his heart. He slowly touched his head with his right hand. On any other day it would have been slick with his oiled hair, but now the stubble pricked his palms and his hands faltered. It was as if he were touching a head that did not belong to him.

"Well done," he said. He brushed his clothes as he got up and then tossed the long, black braid into the trash can, but then it made him think of his mother's forlorn face. He quickly put on his overcoat and student's cap, as if trying to drive his mother's face away from his eyes. The hat fell all the way down to his ears, and his scalp beneath the hat was chilled. He picked up his bundle of books and ran straight toward the classroom.

At lunchtime, Hyeonggeol did not go home but went to Gilson's house, which was located near the Confucian school, and ate lunch with him. For some reason he did not want to go home. His mother wouldn't have come back yet, so he needn't have worried about her discovering that he had cut his hair, but it was something he was going to have to face sooner or later. Avoiding his mother's gaze wasn't the only reason, though, it was just that there was a lot going on inside his head and for some reason he didn't want to go home. After their afternoon classes, the entire school body of nearly one hundred students took off their overcoats and tied straps around their shoes, and then they practiced group gymnastics under Mr. Jeong's guidance in preparation for the athletics meet. When this was finished, Hyeonggeol had to go home. He wanted to just go into the mountains or down to the river and play his trumpet, but he had to drop off his books at home, and even if he took his books with him or slung them over his shoulder like a soldier carrying his leather sack, his trumpet was still at home. So he stepped out of the school gate, thought for a while, and then went into the mountains alone. He wanted to find a warm, sunny place to take a nap.

He went into the pine forest behind the shrine of Confucius and arrived at the hill before Three Pines Pavilion. The warm spring sunshine drenched the winter's dry, yellow grass, but no green shoots had sprouted yet. He lay down flat, with his bundle of books as a pillow and his hat covering his face.

Even when he closed his eyes, though, he couldn't help thinking of his newly cut hair and his mother. She was going to be surprised when she saw his shaven head. Every time Hyeonggeol had tried to cut his hair, his mother had adamantly opposed it, telling him to wait until after his coming-of-age ceremony, and now that he had done it, she would think there was some connection with Hyeongseon's wedding. She would no doubt think that he had cut his hair because he was unhappy that Hyeongseon had gotten married. Even though Lady Yun was not the first wife of her husband, it still hurt her to see her only son treated as the child of a concubine, so Hyeonggeol's action would be no small upset for her. Hyeonggeol had never before seen Bobu, the second daughter of Head Clerk Jeong and the bride to whom Hyeongseon had today been married. Yet Lady Yun had at first asked around, intending to arrange a marriage between Hyeonggeol and Bobu, and she had shared her thoughts with her husband. Assistant Curator Bak thought the marriage appropriate and had heard that the young lady was excellent in character and all other respects, but he could not escape the thought that Head Clerk Jeong would find fault with the fact that Hyeonggeol was the son of a concubine. So as soon as the words left Lady Yun's mouth, he lied and said that they were now discussing a marriage between the Jeong family daughter and Hyeongseon, and even if there was only a month's time between their weddings, wasn't it proper to marry off Hyeongseon first before it was Hyeonggeol's turn?

Although she knew that her husband did not make that much of a distinction between his wife's child and hers, she could not defy him, no matter how much she wanted to. So that was how Hyeongseon came to be married to the Jeong family daughter. Hyeonggeol did not know any of this in detail, but his mother had once told him that the Jeong family had an excellent daughter and asked him what he thought. After that, he had asked his friends about her, making sure that they would not suspect anything, and learned that she was a beauty beyond compare, that she had studied both Chinese characters and the Korean alphabet from her father, and that she could sew well. But his mother never mentioned the matter again, and shortly thereafter her marriage was arranged with Hyeongseon.

This was why his mother could not say anything about Hyeonggeol's behavior that morning, and, for his part, Hyeonggeol was not unaware of what was on his mother's mind. But he also had no way of dealing with the frustration that welled up in his heart, but that was directed at no one in particular. No one could say that suppressing that frustration by shaving his head was not a completely reasonable action.

He had cut off his hair. No matter what happened, he had cut off his hair. In truth, it wouldn't have mattered if he had cut his hair or tied it up in a topknot when he got married. Couldn't he do without the black silk hat, the blue cloak, the bone belt, and the boots, and just wear his student's cap and his overcoat? A wedding might take who knows how long, and it would soon be the Dano festival in May, when they would have the school athletics meet, where many students from all over would gather, and nothing would be more shameful than having to wear that bothersome braid at that event. Even if that were the case, though, what was he to think of his mother's sorrow?

Thoughts kept spinning around inside his head. He tried to sleep so that he couldn't think of anything, but his eyes refused to close. So he did what he always did when he couldn't sleep: he held his breath until he grew dizzy. If he kept this up for a little, his head would grow lighter and feel as if it were filling up with gas, until it finally reached a state of near vacuum. While he did this, he would carefully count one, two . . . and by the time he reached one hundred he would fall asleep. After some time, his head felt light, and as he counted eighty-six his eyelids grew heavy. He didn't reach eighty-seven. He finally fell asleep.

He did not know how long he had been asleep when someone crept up like a cat and lifted the cap from his face. When he opened his eyes he saw a young woman who wasn't even wearing a hooded coat. The sun had already set, and a chill wind had begun to blow all around. The sound of the wind through the pine forest was like a flowing stream.

What woman would be on the mountain, not even wearing a hooded coat, and so rudely and impertinently waking a young man from another family ... but when he looked closer he saw that it was Ssangne, the wife of Duchil, his father's hired hand.

Even if there was no chance of her wearing a hooded coat, what was Ssangne doing in a place like this after sunset? He wondered if Duchil had gone out to collect firewood and she had gone out to meet him, found a young man lying on the cold earth, unaware that the sun had set, and then discovered that it was the son of her master and decided to wake him, but even when he looked straight at her she just stood there with her head lowered and said not a word.

Hyeonggeol quietly sat up. "Are you on your way to meet Duchil?"

She said nothing in reply to his question but just stood there with her hands clasped in front of her. Hyeonggeol slowly grew angry. So he leaped up to face her, but the face that stared back at him was ever so beautiful.

She was twenty-two, that is, three years older than Hyeonggeol. It was only then that he discovered that standing before him was not a female servant who had been sold to his family when she was young and grown up with them, nor the wife of the hired hand Duchil, but a beautiful, mature woman. Her plump red lips jutted out, and it seemed there was a faint shadow over her deep, round eyes. Her hair was somewhat disheveled, and the edges of a black ribbon hung down behind her white kerchief. The ties of her jacket strained to hold in her bulging breasts. He looked at her hands and arms. The backs of her hands were ruddy and swollen from being soaked in cold water, but these were met by the white skin that flowed out from inside her sleeves and which must have flowed back upward to form gentle hills around her shoulders and chest.

How could he have been so blind to such a beautiful and attractive woman—as he stood staring at her in rapture, intoxicated by these thoughts, he suddenly grabbed her hand. The woman's face flushed red. Her ears grew even redder than her face. Her lowered face and the silky hair that fluttered down from her neck danced before Hyeonggeol's eyes. He wanted to say something, but he must have been struck speechless, for his throat was stuck shut. Night was already wrapping the mountain in darkness. He followed the passion that swelled in his heart and turned toward the pine forest, leading the woman by the hand.

The woman he had thought would meekly follow him like a cow as he led her away instead stood her ground and did not budge. "I am the wife of another."

But these words now had no power to check Hyeonggeol's actions. Even Ssangne herself knew this. What did Duchil matter, and what did it mean to be his wife? He was still a domestic when he turned thirty, and it was only last year that he managed to make Ssangne his wife, wasn't it? If the master had not given him Ssangne as his wife, he would now be living a dreary life as an old bachelor with unkempt hair, and Ssangne would also be an old servant bent with age. She had said, "I am the wife of another," as if they were a respectable couple, but they were still nothing more than servants in the house of Assistant Curator Bak. Her master's son was leading her away, so what sort of nonsense was "I am the wife of another"— but there was no need to think of such pathetic things.

Like a raging tiger, Hyeonggeol turned and drew Ssangne's body to him, then, holding onto her, turned back around and rushed into the dark pine forest.

The woman kicked and struggled for a while, but then went limp, leaning against Hyeonggeol and wrapping her arms around his neck. Her hot breath poured out on the back of his neck, but the words that followed were quite unexpected.

"Doesn't even a servant deserve more respect than this?"

Her next words surprised him even more. She suddenly changed to a familiar tone of voice and said, "Aren't you yourself scorned because you are the son of a concubine?"

It just couldn't be Ssangne's voice. Hyeonggeol wondered if she wanted to dig her own grave by saying such nonsense to him, but when he looked down at her, he saw that it was not the Ssangne he had just grabbed. It was a new bride wearing a red skirt and green jacket, with her hair done up in a ceremonial headpiece, and he was startled to see that it was really the second daughter of Head Clerk Jeong...

There was a loud noise in his ears. He awoke to find that it had been a dream, and Son Daebong stood next to him with a trumpet in his hands. "What are you doing napping in the mountains. Do you want to be possessed by a ghost? Don't you know the old saying, that if you sleep in the mountains you'll be bewitched by a fox?"

He couldn't clearly hear what Daebong was saying. He still had not fully awoken from his dream. His heart pounded and his head felt light, and the sound of the trumpet rang in his ears. The sun on this long, spring day was still high above Hwaju Peak.

"What, were you really having a dream?"

Daebong had dropped down beside him, and Hyeonggeol spun around, pinned him to the ground, and pressed down on his throat. Daebong was caught unawares by the abrupt attack and fell flat to the ground beneath Hyeonggeol, but then he flung the trumpet onto the dry grass and grabbed one of Hyeonggeol's hands with his right hand and twisted. Their legs locked together and they rolled over, tumbling down the hill together.

They rolled, they struggled, and they tumbled until finally they snagged on a low pine tree and came to a stop. Hyeonggeol was now on the bottom, and Daebong was on top.

They were grabbing at each other's throats, mumbling "you jerk," when their eyes met. Hyeonggeol looked up and cracked a broad smile. Daebong looked down and smiled, too. Then they began to laugh. Finally they got up and brushed off their hands.

Gilson's mother, who had come out to the well to draw water, had seen Mr. Son's son Daebong walk by, run into some young man in front of Three Pines Pavilion, and begin to wrestle and struggle with him, so she left her bucket by the well and ran back into the house.

She found Gilson sawing some wood and cried, "Go quickly to Mr. Son's house and let them know! Something terrible has happened, terrible I tell you! Their son has run into someone — knives are flashing; by now he might be passed out, lying in a pool of blood! Go quickly to Mr. Son's house and let them know. Whatever should we do? Their precious son, born out of prayer and devotion; have the heavens no pity?"

Gilson rushed out to find two young men standing side by side on the hill. One was Daebong and the other was Hyeonggeol. His mother was still carrying on as she came out of the front gate of the house, and he looked at her and said doubtfully, "What do you mean they're fighting?"

"Your eyes must have rotted, don't you see them, there, on the Three Pines Pavilion hill?" she said, and pointed to the pavilion, but even his clouded eyes saw nothing but two young men standing side by side. Ah, what on earth could be going on, he thought, and he rubbed his eyes and looked again.

"You've gone senile, I say, senile!" he scolded his old mother. "Now go fetch the water."

At last the sound of a trumpet was heard from the mountains. Gilson's mother still stood at the edge of the yard, looking toward Three Pines Pavilion, bemoaning her lot and thinking that she was not long for this world.

When Lady Yun returned to the Dumutgol house and asked the servant about Hyeonggeol, the servant said that he had eaten the breakfast that had been brought from the main house and gone to school on time, without incident. Hearing that the school trumpet had sounded quite some time after he had left the house, she could tell that he hadn't woken up that late. But she also heard that he hadn't come home for lunch, for some reason.

Perhaps something had come up, or perhaps he had not been hungry after eating such a big breakfast, she thought, and she shared these thoughts with the concerned servant, but Lady Yun could not help but be worried by the fact that he did not come home even after school was finished. She told Samnam and a servant to look for him at the school or by the river, but they returned and told her that the school was empty and there was no sign of anyone by the river.

But just as the sun was about to set, he walked in through the front gate with Mr. Son's son. Hyeonggeol, with his hat pushed down low on his head, went straight into his room, while Son Daebong strode purposefully into the inner yard; when he saw Lady Yun, who had opened the sliding door of her room, he took off his cap and bowed to her.

"Have you been well?"

"I haven't seen you in quite some time, Daebong. But what happened to your hair?"

Daebong stroked his head once with his right hand and said, "It was such a burden and always getting caught everywhere, so I cut it off today. And they told us to cut it off at school."

Then he smiled broadly. But Lady Yun did not smile, and she asked, "Have you seen your mother and father?"

"I saw them earlier."

"And they told you that you had done well?"

"What, is it such a big deal to cut one's hair?"

"How can you cut your hair before you get married? I can't imagine why you would, whether they told you to do so at school or not."

"They say that cutting your hair helps you do arithmetic better."

"Then no one has ever passed the civil service examination before, or the literary licentiate examination?"

"Studying at the public school and studying at the private village school are different. They don't know about the new-style education at the village schools."

Lady Yun said nothing and drew on her long pipe. Daebong finally walked away toward Hyeonggeol's room. He took off his hat and shoes on the stone step and then winked as he stepped into the room, and Hyeonggeol stuck his tongue out a little at him.

Lady Yun watched Daebong go into Hyeonggeol's room before shutting her door. There was something about the way the two boys were acting that made her uncomfortable. Daebong had always greeted her whenever he came over, but the way he came into the yard and bowed deeply to her, as if to show her his shaved head, or how he kept talking back to her, or how Hyeonggeol just went straight into his room without even glancing in her direction, there was something strange about it all. So Lady Yun put down her pipe, went out into the yard, put on her shoes, and crossed into the outer yard. She pulled opened the door to her son's room and asked, "What did you do for lunch?"

Daebong was sitting there with his legs out and his cap off, polishing his trumpet, but when he heard the door open he pulled his legs in and sat up straight, while Hyeonggeol sat upright with his cap pulled down to his ears. He looked up at his mother and said, "I was busy, so I ate at Gilson's house."

"You shouldn't get into the habit of eating at other people's houses," she said and looked at his face around his ears. His skin where his sideburns had been was white, bare of even a single hair. Her heart sank.

Hyeonggeol saw his mother's expression suddenly change, and he hurriedly lowered his head. His mother said nothing. She stood there like that for a while then closed the door and went back to her room. She couldn't even begin to think of what to say.

When Hyeonggeol saw that, upon seeing his shaved head, his mother left without saying anything, although he might have felt differently from her, he was still upset. He did not feel even the slightest bit of regret at having shaved his head. He had simply done what had to be done. If this caused his mother grief or made her angry, he could just ignore her, the way Son Daebong had done. But this was not the only problem that shaving his head would cause.

There was still a small part of him that wanted to throw himself to the ground and vent his anger until he was spent. He wanted to beat someone to his heart's content, or to be beaten by someone until he fell down. That would make him feel much better, he thought, and everything pent up inside him would be released. But whom could he beat, or who could beat him? He couldn't think of anyone in particular, and it ate at him.

After Daebong left, he ate a quick dinner and then lay flat on the floor in his room, but then he left his room so his mother wouldn't see his shaved head. He thought he would feel a little better if he got some fresh air down by the river.

The small stream that flowed through Dumutgol passed under Nine Dragons Bridge and flowed into the Biryu River. He followed the small road that ran along this stream until he came to the main street. The night was already dark. The wind gently passed through the bare trees. The moon was as thin as a thread.

He passed by River View Pavilion and gazed at the large, frightful silhouette of Ganseon Pavilion in the distance as he walked upriver toward Cheonju Peak. He began to whistle. He thought it might make him feel better. He sharply whistled the melody to a song encouraging students to study. The sound of his whistling was cold and drifted up into the quiet night sky. He thought he heard footsteps behind him. He stopped whistling and turned around to see the shadows of two women enter the Merciful Blessings Temple alley behind Descending Immortal Pavilion. They soon disappeared behind the stone wall. The sound of the swift water beneath the Bridge of the Ascending Immortal came afresh to his ears. Sometimes it was like the sound of a rain shower, and other times it was like the sound of a light drizzle. He went down the embankment and made his way through the dry weeds to the river's edge. It was even darker by the water. Only in the places where the river reflected the sky did the crescent moon hang there backward, casting a dim light. He sat down. The cool mist from the surface of the river chilled his head. He put his hands in the water. It was as cold as ice. He wet his head with the water.

But suddenly a thought came to him. Were the two women entering the pagoda alley from Head Clerk Jeong's house? It was on that alley. Had the bride been hiding someplace to be made up before going to the groom's room and was now on her way back with one of her relatives?

He looked back and saw the large silhouette of Descending Immortal Pavilion, and behind that the tall pagoda of Merciful Blessings Temple, but beyond that it was too dark for him to tell if anyone was there. He thought that it must have been the daughter of Head Clerk Jeong, Hyeongseon's bride, and he got up and shook the water from his hands.

All of a sudden, the dream he had dreamt on the mountain came back to him. The image of Head Clerk Jeong's daughter with her red skirt, green jacket, and ceremonial headdress and the voluptuous body of Duchil's wife Ssangne, together set his heart boiling like a kettle, and he felt something well up inside him. Hot steam shot out of his nose as he breathed out. He stood there in a daze for some time, trying to cool his desire, and then he slowly moved his legs and climbed back up to the road.

Some time later he found himself walking up the alley behind Merciful Blessings Temple. He hesitated, but he did not stop fumbling his way up that road.

5

At the end of the long main street, just outside of Visiting Immortal Gate, there stand five or six old monument pavilions, including the one for Bak Rigyun's grandmother Lady Seong, and beyond those pavilions are two or three more monuments standing there bareheaded and uncovered, their faces splotched and stained. Before them is a wide field, and, as can be guessed by the stakes sticking out of the ground here and there, this is where the cattle market is held once every six days. This field is commonly called Soujeon. At a corner of this field is a small path that leads to the public cemetery and Sonu Stream, and at the opposite corner of the field is another path that stretches out a good way, lined with a half dozen poplar trees, before joining the newly built road to Pyeongyang and Wonsan at Fealty Bridge.

There is also a road as thin as a belt that forks into two, a shortcut to the newly built road, with one fork crossing Dolchani Hill and heading on toward Pyeongyang, and the other heading up toward Fealty Hill and picking its way across streams and through mountains toward Wonsan.

One warm day, late in the waning afternoon, while the green buds of the poplar trees were sprouting into light-green leaves, the grass below was pushing forth soft green shoots, and a single cluster of azaleas, which someone had secretly planted there, was blooming with pink blossoms, a lone white horse galloped out of Visiting Immortal Gate with a thunder of hooves, circled the field of Soujeon once, leaned toward the earth as it twisted through the poplar-lined path that led to the newly built road, and then galloped off toward Fealty Bridge, leaving a fine white dust in its wake.

The horse galloped freely, as if flying among the clouds. The road that was left behind stared impassively at the horse and its young rider, galloping away faintly in the distance, wrapped in white dust and the pounding of hooves.

The white horse rushed over the empty road as if on wings. It took the road to Wonsan that wound left across Fealty Bridge, and in no time at all it flew up the pass of Mount Fealty like an arrow from a bow. It had climbed more than halfway up the pass. But then something happened. The horse suddenly snorted and reared back, its front hooves flailing in the air. The rider was lifted from the saddle, but he clung to the horse's neck and skillfully brought the beast to a stop. The horse had been galloping at a frightful pace, but the rider had pulled on the reins to stop the horse in the middle of the road. The horse had reared its front hooves in the air and nearly flipped over backward, but with a great bellow and snort it settled down again and came to a sudden halt, just as its rider had commanded. Still trembling from the speed of its gallop, the horse trotted in circles. The young rider, lightly dressed and with a student's cap sitting back on his head and strapped around his chin, took the whip and reins in his left hand and patted the horse's back with his right, wiping down the heavy sweat with a towel. The horse welcomed the caress of its master and blinked slowly as it finally stood still. At last, the rider on his horse looked down. There, a sturdy young man of around thirty was driving cattle along a shortcut and up onto the road.

"That was close!" The sturdy young man had a towel wrapped tightly around his head, and he smiled widely; it was Duchil. The young man on the horse made no reply. It was, of course, Hyeonggeol.

"You ride very well."

Hyeonggeol did not reply to this either, but instead waited for Duchil and the cows to climb up onto the road. "Where are you going?" he said at last.

"To the hemp field to load up some wood."

"The hemp field? That must be thirty li, why are you leaving so late?"

"The moon will be out, so it won't matter too much if I am late."

Hyeonggeol watched the cows and Duchil picking their way up the pass, and at last he said, "Well, have a good trip." He spoke more politely than usual.

At this, Duchil turned quickly and said, "Thank you, and take care."

Hyeonggeol waited until Duchil had disappeared over the pass, then he turned his horse toward the shortcut. The horse bent down and followed the narrow, winding path. Hyeonggeol held the reins loosely and leaned back in the saddle, swaying with the slow walk of the horse.

Sitting on his horse, Hyeonggeol was thinking that it wouldn't be until late at night that Duchil would return home. The moon would soon be full, and so its soft, clear, bright light would reveal the mountains and fields and houses and river. A night when forsythia and azalea and weigela would be in full bloom, when every tree branch would be dotted with new shoots and early willows would waft their green fragrance, and when the green grass would sprout up whispering beneath the dew flowing down from the moon. On this night, Hyeongseon would share the passion of youth with the daughter of Clerk Jeong he had brought home not long ago, and when Duchil's wife, Ssangne, unable to control her ripe and ready body, free after so long, would toss and turn all alone in that small room facing the river in the main house. What would she think of when she was alone? Would she be waiting for her husband, who had gone off for wood, to return? Or might she be thinking of nothing, fast asleep, entrusting her full, round bosoms to the moonlight that stole in across the windowsill?

The horse walked over flat land. It plodded along monotonously, not letting its eyes stray from the road. Only then did Hyeonggeol look up and see Sachang Pond in the distance, its waters swollen, and next to it the old ravens' nests in the branches of the two poplars, and across the field behind them, the schoolyard. He shook off these thoughts, raised his right hand high, and slapped the horse on the rear with his whip. The horse leaped and broke into a gallop. The whip came down once again, and the horse stretched out its legs and began to fly over the road. The horse did not pick its way through the byways between the fields and pass through Visiting Immortal Gate but dashed straight up the hillside and arrived at the schoolyard in an instant.

In the schoolyard were Hyeongseon, Gilson, and Daebong. There were three or four others beside. They had shed their overcoats and hats, fastened their hemp sandals tight to their feet, and were practicing their sprinting. They had drawn a line beneath the pull-up bar with chalk and were each toeing that line with their right feet. Their toes waited tensely for the signal as they rested on the chalk. Gilson stood to one side to give the starting signal, while four others prepared to run. Yi Taeseok, who had been exercising on the pull-up bar, rubbed his hands together and watched the scene.

"One!" Gilson shouted out vigorously. "Two, three!"

At the count of three, the four began to run. Gilson stood on the white line and watched the racers from behind as they ran. Hyeonggeol got down off his horse. He tied the horse to a tree and crossed over to the schoolyard.

The race was to the poplar tree at the end of the schoolyard and back. Falling behind and then racing ahead, jostling for position, the four runners each swiped at the poplar tree with their hands before sprinting back. Hyeongseon was in the lead. Behind him was Daebong. The other two were each a stride or two behind. But then, as they approached the finish line, Daebong passed Hyeongseon, and though Hyeongseon pressed his lips together and did his best, he crossed the line a step behind.

"Hyeongseon's been using up all of his energy these days, ha ha ha!" laughed Taeseok.

Hyeongseon, who had collapsed onto the grass and was panting for breath, sprung up and said, "Ah, go to hell! I let you win."

Daebong winked at Hyeonggeol and said, "Yeah, thanks to you I've finally won once."

Hyeonggeol said nothing and just put his hands down on the grass and did a few somersaults. Then he pushed back his sleeves and did a few pull-ups on the pull-up bar.

"I wonder if there will be wrestling at the athletics meet," said Taeseok as he sat on the grass, and Hyeonggeol came over and flopped to the ground next to him.

"Won't they have wrestling at the Dano Festival?"

"Well, with the athletics meet going on, where would they have it?" said Hyeongseon as he came and sat down beside them as well. He had cut his hair soon after he got married. Daebong had cut his hair for the second time only a few days before, so his scalp was still bare, but it had been well over a month since Hyeonggeol and Hyeongseon had cut their hair, so it had grown back quite a bit. Only three days after getting married, Hyeongseon had cut his hair and come to school. It wasn't until a month later that he brought along his wife. In all truth, after school finished and he was hanging around with his friends like this, he was actually beside himself with thoughts of his wife. Thus Taeseok had not been far from the mark when he teased Hyeongseon for fading at the last moment and losing to Daebong, whom he had always beaten.

Hyeonggeol listened to Hyeongseon and then offered a detailed explanation of his idea. "Can't we just have the athletics meet for one day? So on the first day we wrestle in the field of Soujeon, outside Visiting Immortal Gate, on the next day the women can play on the swings in the hills by the pine forest, and on the third day we can have the athletics meet here, can't we?"

"Well, we might be able to do that, but if we start wrestling I don't think we'll be able to finish it all in a day." Hyeongseon was not trying to correct his brother, he was just trying to establish his opinion again.

"Well, if not, then the men can wrestle on the day the women go up into the hills."

No one had much to say to that. Hyeonggeol glanced toward the horse as if he had suddenly thought of something. At that, everyone looked at the horse. With no grass on which to graze, the horse just stood there blinking anxiously.

"Do they know which schools will be coming to the athletics meet yet?" Gilson said, fingering something in his vest pocket.

Daebong, who had been looking at the horse, said, "Most of the students who went to Pyeongyang last year will come. So, firstly, Pyeongyang." Then he held up his hands and began to count on his fingers. "Plus Suncheon, Eunsan, Jasan, Yeongyu, Gangseo, and Nonggang makes seven schools at the least. And they will be coming from Daeduri as well and probably also from Gichang. I wonder if the yokels from Gangdong and Yangdeok will come as well. They might not even have schools there yet."

Gilson counted along with Daebong on the fingers that were still in his vest pocket, and as soon as Daebong finished talking he said, "Hey, that's quite a lot . . . eleven schools if they all come! This is going to be quite a gathering." He held out ten fingers and then stuck up a single thumb.

"Then what about the essay contest on Buddha's birthday?"

Hyeongseon was worried again, but Hyeonggeol waved away his concerns. "Who cares if we don't do so well in the essay contest? The athletics meet will be here in a month, so we should do our best then." He spoke as if he had everything figured out.

"Floating the lanterns on the Biryu River is more fun to watch on Buddha's birthday than the essay contest," interjected Taeseok. "The essay contest is all a sham, anyway."

They all sat in silence for a while. The evening sun was slowly sinking behind Hwaju Peak. The young men, sitting in a circle, were all lost in their own thoughts and staring off into the distance.

— Hyeongseon thought at first about Buddha's birthday, but then he soon began to think of his wife. Now that evening is getting on she will be waiting, I should go soon, but if I get up first everyone will tease me . . .

— Hyeonggeol suddenly thought of Duchil's wife, Ssangne: would she be busy in the kitchen of the main house now, or would she be in the mule mill, or going to draw water, or perhaps she had rolled up the legs of her pants and was washing laundry in the water; but then he started thinking about the athletics meet again, whether she might be able to come to the wrestling grounds to watch, and his mind wandered . . .

—Daebong thought back to the athletics meet in Pyeong-yang the previous year, thinking about what that grand spectacle would look like if it were moved to this small village . . .

While they were each absorbed in their own thoughts, Gilson must have been thinking about wrestling. "Before we go," he said, quickly brushing off his pants as he stood up, "we should wrestle each other."

Shaken from their sweet thoughts, they all rose to their feet at once, and from the looks on their faces they must have thought it wouldn't be a bad idea to wrestle after all.

At times like these, Hyeonggeol was the first to step forward amiably. "Alright then, let's have a bout, and I'll roll you around like a log." He tossed his cap onto the ground, knelt down on the short grass, and braced himself with his arms.

"Let's have a go, then," said Taeseok, the oldest of the group, and he tightened his belt around his waist and stepped forward. Gilson took off his own belt and tied it into a thigh band, then tossed it to where the two boys sat facing each other, and another student took off his belt and gave it to Hyeonggeol.

They each grabbed the bands around the others' thigh, locked themselves into position, and began to slowly straighten up. With one hand Hyeonggeol grabbed Taeseok's thigh band, and with the other he patted him on the rear.

"Is it your wife who has been making you this fat?" he said, and Taeseok replied, "How rude! Who would say such a boorish thing!" He struggled to get up.

"Well, if you want to see rude . . ." Hyeonggeol said, and then he nimbly leaped up and shouted, "Let's go!"

He attempted to lift and throw Taeseok, but Taeseok planted his feet and stuck out his rear, not letting Hyeonggeol pull him close . . . but then Hyeonggeol leaned back, lifted his opponent off the ground, and threw him hard.

"You can tell your wife later that I'm sorry," he said, brushing off his hands and freeing his legs as he looked down at Taeseok, who had one hand on the ground. Taeseok looked up at Hyeonggeol with a grin on his face, and then he put both hands on the ground and crouched there.

"Right, now let's see the brothers go at it," said Daebong as he grabbed Hyeongseon's hand and pulled him forward, but Hyeong-seon grimaced and shook off his grasp. "Eh, who wants to wrestle anyway?"

Hyeonggeol saw what Hyeongseon was thinking and quick-ly put on his cap. "Let's go have dinner," he said, and ran toward the road. Since Hyeongseon was heading straight home, ideally he would have left the horse with him and gone straight to the Du-mutgol house, but Hyeongseon was always careful and never rode by himself.

So Hyeonggeol left them behind and leaped up onto the horse's back. Gilson went up onto the road by himself in front of the Confucian school, and the rest of them walked in single file on the path that led to the road, talking noisily about something as they went.

Turning away from the sound of their murmuring, Hyeong-geol whipped the horse once on its rear. The horse stretched out its four legs and began to trot. The red sun like a clot of blood was passing behind the twelve peaks, the sky and the mountains were dyed pink with the sunset, and the fresh greenery on the trees before the Biryu River looked thick and black. Hyeonggeol looked on this scenery from a distance and let the horse go where it would. Not long after, the horse passed by the well. But then, for some reason, it slowed its clopping stride and snorted once. Startled by the sound, Hyeonggeol looked at the road ahead and saw Duchil's wife Ssangne approach him and then turn onto the small path toward Dumutgol, carrying something in a large basin. The horse must have snorted in gladness at the sight of Ssangne, who fed him three times a day. At first Hyeonggeol was startled to meet Ssangne so unexpectedly, and in such an unexpected place, but his surprise soon gave way to gladness. Ssangne seemed happy that the horse had recognized her, and she smiled broadly at the animal, but then she glanced up at Hyeonggeol on the horse's back, hastily wiped the smile from her face, and quickly turned onto the small path.

The horse galloped off down the road. Hyeonggeol just sat atop the horse and thought about Ssangne's figure as she scuttled off with the basin in her arms, about how she had smiled broadly at the horse but then wiped that smile off her face when her eyes met his, about the skin barely visible beneath the old, white towel she had wrapped around her head, the skin that had not been darkened by the sun, and how white and soft it must be. The horse turned onto the main road. Hyeonggeol did not want to take the horse directly to the stable and tie it up there, instead wanting to cross Ascending Immortal Bridge over the Biryu River before heading home, but he found himself suddenly lost in thought and let the horse have its head. The horse found its way back to its stable.

He tied up the horse in the stable and passed before the men's quarters; as he passed by the inner yard beyond the central gate, he caught a glimpse of Hyeongseon's wife, Bobu, going into the backyard. Hyeonggeol hesitated for a moment and stood there watching her as she went, but then he slipped quietly through the men's quarters yard to avoid drawing his father's attention and went back out onto the road. On the road to the Confucian school, he met Hyeongseon, Daebong and the others coming the other way, said goodbye to them, and turned by the well onto the narrow path toward Dumutgol. The sun set, and a black veil of darkness was suddenly drawn over the fields, leaving the faintest of lights in the east. Hyeonggeol sank to the ground on the lonely road, trying to collect his thoughts. But it did not take long for him to realize that he sat there on the road, with no thought of eating dinner, because he was waiting for Ssangne, who had gone to Dumutgol, to return.

He was startled. Do I really have feelings for Ssangne? Faced with such a direct question, Hyeonggeol felt rather embarrassed and confused, for a number of reasons. So far, every time he had caught even a glimpse of the question in his mind, he had turned tail and fled far away. It was difficult for him even to determine if he was truly attracted to Duchil's wife, Ssangne. How could she ever hope to match Bobu in beauty, or cleanliness, or purity ... but the latter was already his sister-in-law. He had seen her only for an instant, and from afar at that, yet he still felt a faint jealousy creep up on him, wondering how Hyeonseon could be so lucky to get such a pretty and admirable wife. But these thoughts were overshadowed by the round, innocent face of Ssangne. He could make no sense of his heart, whether he truly longed for Bobu or whether he was more drawn to Ssangne. And as he could make no sense of these feelings, his reaction was to try to cover them up and put them out of his mind.

He sat on the road, trying not to think about it all. Duchil's wife was already Duchil's wife. She was the wife of another. On the other hand, though, she had been a servant in his household, and even now she was only a hired hand. There was something that he could do, but that would be shameful. He sat there dumb for some time, only vaguely aware of these various problems scattered on the lonely road in the darkness as he waited for Ssangne.

Actually, he was thinking about something other than these things. In truth, he was thinking about her eyes, her nose, her lips, her back, and her bosom, her plump bosom hidden beneath her jacket; he pondered all these things as they flashed into his mind.

In the distance a faint shape appeared. Even the thought that this shape was approaching him was enough to set his heart pounding; he wondered if his heart had ever throbbed so before, and when he saw clearly that the approaching shape was Ssangne, he wondered if he had ever hidden on the road and waited so anxiously for someone to approach, the wife of another — no, a servant in his household, one who had carried him on her back when he was younger, a young servant girl he had grabbed by the hair and struck — had he ever imagined that a day would come when he would wait for her, unable to control himself, unable to make any sense of how he felt? But there was no more than a brief moment in which to think these thoughts. He pushed down the fluttering in his heart and, led by a powerful force that drove all of his emotions, suddenly stood up.

Duchil's wife, Ssangne, was walking along with her short, quick steps, holding her empty basin and wrapped up in her innocent thoughts — had the horses been fed, or were they waiting desperately for her to return, having gotten nothing to eat? — when she was faced with this sudden and unexpected man rising from the street, and she stopped short and nearly let out a startled gasp, so great was her surprise. But when she saw that the man standing on the road was none other than the young master of her household, the young master of the Dumutgol house where she had just delivered the special dish of steamed rice cakes in her basin, she was startled yet again.

The light had long since faded, and the darkness hid their faces, so she could not see that he was blushing a bright red, but when he made to say something, hesitated, and then let out a sigh, she could easily tell how feverishly hot his breath was. Of course, she could not see that his eyes were bloodshot. And yet a strange flame flickered like a torch in the eyes of this man as he looked sidelong at her, so she quickly lowered her gaze from his. She instinctively knew what intentions such an expression on the face of a man conveyed. As if quietly waiting for some unexpected word or some action to befall her body, Ssangne stood there before Hyeonggeol with her head bowed.

"Where have you been?" he asked her in a formal way.

Hyeonggeol struggled greatly to suppress his emotions and say these few words, words that were far too trivial and bland to express what was in his heart at that moment.

And yet both of them felt, at the same time, a strange nuance in these words because of Hyeonggeol's unintended use of polite language. For Ssangne, it was the first time in her life she had heard anyone take care when speaking to her. Hyeonggeol, on the other hand, had no idea how those words had come out of his mouth; they were so strange that they did not even seem to have been spoken by him.

Then, as if he had only barely managed to come to his senses, he said, "You went to Dumutgol?" He turned his eyes away from Ssangne, who stood there speechless, not knowing what was happening. A long, soft sigh escaped his lips, and, like boiling water settles when removed from the heat, he found himself regaining his composure in the stillness between them. To give her some space, he took a step back from where he had been, standing face-to-face with her. When he looked down at her again, she lifted up her head.

With a look of relief on her face she said, "They said that you are late for dinner at the Dumutgol house, and that they are waiting for you." Then she looked down at her feet again. She longed to quickly remove herself and flee from this unfathomable place, if only he would make way.

But Hyeonggeol ignored what she had said and replied, "Duchil is off in the hemp fields. He will probably be late." Then he looked straight into Ssangne's eyes. With dusk now turned to dark, he opened his large eyes wide to stare deep into hers.

Only then did Ssangne seem to realize the meaning of Hyeonggeol's strange behavior, and she felt truly ashamed. For a moment she forgot her status as a servant, thinking of herself only as a pure young girl. But then she was Duchil's wife, and Duchil was the hired hand of the young master that stood before her, so thinking again of how she was this man's servant girl, she said nothing in reply. She drew on the last of her courage and, as if asking him to make way, took one step forward with her head bowed and made for the creek to her right, but Hyeonggeol threw his large arms around her and held her fast.

"What if someone sees us like this?" Her words were quiet, but she struggled valiantly to break free from his grasp. Of course, the strength in her arms was no match for Hyeonggeol's arms and chest as he held her tight.

Then, from Hyeonggeol's lips fell strange words like pebbles: "At night, when the moon has gone down." His lips found hers as she turned her face away and his hot breath poured from them, and at last she let the basin drop as if her arms had lost all strength, and he brought the face of the girl crushed in his embrace up to his eyes.

Then, as if the thought had suddenly occurred to her, Ssangne said, "Let me go," and she squirmed in his grasp. Only after caressing her face once more and stealing her lips again did he finally take his arms from her. With her head hung low she freed herself from his grasp, picked up the basin with one hand, and ran off down the path in silence. Hyeonggeol's voice as he said "Before Duchil comes back" was ringing in her ears as she turned onto the broad road.

The moon, which gave off a dim red light, one side draped in darkness, must have been passing behind a thin cloud, as the road was bathed in a soft white light. Ssangne did not wipe away the tears that flowed down her face and, unable to tell whether these tears would bring her happiness, ran quickly down the road with her short steps.

Hyeonggeol stood there idly until he could no longer see Ssangne. When she turned off the main road into the alley that ran by the Confucian school and so was lost from his sight, he looked up at the moon, and then he slowly turned his steps toward Dumutgol.

6

Ssangne had been sold as a servant to Assistant Curator Bak's household thirty years ago, when she was nine years old. She had been born the third daughter of a poor farmer in the small village of Seochang, which stood on a sandy hill some thirty li to the west of this village, across two rivers.

Ssangne's two older sisters had both already been sold to another farm, and Ssangne had two younger brothers as well. In the year that she was sold, there was an epidemic after the monsoons, and her mother passed away, along with many other people in the neighborhood. The previous year there had been a drought, and the entire region was suffering from a poor harvest, so when the monsoons came and the epidemic followed, though it died out that autumn, there was nothing to harvest in the fields. The roads were choked with vagrants from every village who had left their farmlands, and the streams of villagers moving toward Hamgyeong or Hwanghae Provinces, the men with their burdens on their backs and the women with their burdens held to their bosoms, did not slow until early winter. Ssangne's family had been among them.

Her father gathered the few dishes they owned, packed up their belongings, put his four-year-old son on top of the baggage, took his six-year-old son and Ssangne by the hand, and left Seochang late in the morning on a brisk, cloudy day in late autumn, to head into town. They rested a night in Bak Seonggyun's inn inside Visiting Immortal Gate, and from there they intended to leave on the four-hundred-li road to Wonsan, where things were said to be good.

Even with his four-year-old son on top of the baggage, for his six-year-old son and Ssangne to travel four hundred li without stopping — and on a treacherous road, as the new road had not yet been built — could take anywhere from ten days to two weeks. At a time when every day counted in the race to settle down before winter fell upon them, he didn't even have enough money left in his pocket for a ten-day journey. He wanted to buy a horse or donkey somewhere to bear his children, but, of course, there was no way he could come up with the money for that. After spending a sleepless night with these thoughts, he was left with only one option — the measure that everyone else was taking.

The only way to both reduce his load and secure the money for his journey was to sell Ssangne as a servant. Nearly fifty by now, he had desperately hoped to avoid this measure, and indeed he had avoided it up until the day they left their home. But now that he had walked thirty li and spent his first night on the road, he was faced with the realization that such a long and distant journey with three children was nearly impossible.

After talking it over with a packhorse driver who shared their room, he could come up with no better idea. At first he burned with anger, but when not a single person he talked to could think of any other way, he had no choice but to make this decision.

He asked Bak Rigyun to help him find someone to buy Ssangne as a servant, but there didn't seem to be anyone in that town who might be able to spend a lump sum of money to buy someone in that lean year, beside Assistant Curator Bak Seonggwon, who was in the midst of expanding his property and his influence. But Bak Seonggyun told Ssangne's father to not even bother looking into it, carrying on about Assistant Curator Bak not needing another blasted servant, but in the end it was determined to leave her with that family. Assistant Curator Bak's family already had one fully grown servant for each household, so they didn't need another hand, but they could buy her dirt cheap, and when Assistant Curator Bak discovered that the ill-natured Bak Rigyun and his brother were advising against it, he quickly decided to bring Ssangne into the household. Her price was two hundred nyang. Her father haggled, saying that she was worth three hundred nyang, even if it was a lean year, but when Assistant Curator Bak said that if he didn't want two hundred nyang for a girl who was barely nine years old, that was the end of it, her father was obliged to settle on that price.

Her father put his youngest son on his back and his baggage and oldest son on the donkey and then reluctantly set off on the road outside Visiting Immortal Gate, and from that day forward Ssangne became the property of Assistant Curator Bak's family.

Assistant Curator Bak's young wife, who had just passed the age of thirty, at first comforted and consoled Ssangne as she sat there crying, then admonished her in a high and haughty tone, and finally instructed her to call Assistant Curator Bak "Master," herself "Mistress," her sons "Young Master," and the fully-grown servants either "Sister" or "Mother," depending on their age.

"Since you are still a child not yet ten years of age, I will teach you matters of etiquette both great and small, the first being obedience, the second being respect, and the third being to carry out the work you are entrusted with; you must not forget these things, and you must take care in your conduct," she emphasized once again. From then on, Ssangne could not even cry when she wanted to. Happening to shed a few tears when in the toilet or alone in her quarters, if she heard someone outside she would immediately wipe them away, stand up, and fix her expression as if she were drawing it on her face.

Duchil arrived as a domestic three years after Ssangne, which would make it ten years ago. At the time, Duchil was a fully-grown bachelor of twenty-one.

Duchil was born the third son of Kim Bau, a tenant farmer under Assistant Curator Bak's father-in-law, a member of the Jeonju Choe clan of Gaenggoji; one of many children in a poor family, Duchil failed to marry as he grew older, so, hard-pressed by the repeated poor harvests and household difficulties, he finally left his family to become a servant. His parents were respectable, so leaving his home to become a domestic was a bitter pill to swallow, but when he looked back on it later, not only could he see no other way to get married, but his family of over ten brothers and sisters had been in such dire straights at the time that, had he not sacrificed himself, they would have been unable to farm that season and even would have soon been faced with starvation. So Kim Bau had gone to Mr. Choe, Assistant Curator Bak's father-in-law, and explained the situation, begging him to allow Duchil to live as a domestic in Assistant Curator Bak's household.

For Assistant Curator Bak's part, because of the soaring number of people giving up their farmlands due to the continued poor harvests and the epidemic, he had been able to buy at a giveaway price a plot of land large enough that it would take a single ox a month to plow; but the tenant farmers were moving around quite a bit and it was tiresome and troublesome to find a proper tenant, so he was already planning to hire a few more domestics and try his own hand at farming this year. Thus it was his good fortune that a strong young man like Duchil came crawling to him of his own accord; yet still Bak feigned reluctance. "Well, my father-in-law is so insistent on this, so I'll have to give it some thought, but I already have enough help to go around, and as you know grain prices are steep . . ."

He went on like this for a while, then he tapped out his pipe and cast an uninterested glance at Bau and Duchil, who knelt there before him bowing repeatedly, before going on. "At any rate, even if I plan on doing the farming myself, it is not proper to turn away someone who has come to me. Considering your situation, and as long as you are diligent in your work, it won't do any harm in the days to come to have some extra help. This is a lean time of year in the farmhouses, so why don't you take about ten bushels of millet?" And in this way the deal was concluded.

So Duchil's family received ten bushels of millet, and they were able to survive on that for the year.

From the next year, they agreed on the sum of thirty nyang per year. In addition to this, at Assistant Curator Bak's house, Duchil received three meals a day, a set of winter clothes without an overcoat, a blue, single-knit jacket and trousers in early spring, a white, single-knit jacket and trousers around the Dano festival, a hemp jacket in summer, and a quilted jacket and trousers in autumn — with these clothes he got two pairs of wrappings for his feet and three towels with which to wrap his head, and that was all.

One way or another, he managed to pass three years, but his prospects seemed dim, and idling away his time doing the work of others at the age of twenty-two or twenty-three seemed rather pointless when he thought about it, so he considered giving up his life as a domestic and returning to Gaenggoji to help out with the farming—something that even his family had subtly suggested—but when his fourth year as a domestic came around, Duchil made no move to leave the dim servants' quarters at Assistant Curator Bak's house. Instead he wordlessly continued his life as a domestic, seeing to his work like an ox. Of course, it turned out that he had something else in mind: Duchil secretly coveted sixteen-year-old Ssangne, who was just coming into bloom.

Yet even though Ssangne may have been a lowly girl, her heart was that of a budding maiden, so there was not a chance she would give any thought to the likes of Duchil. There was the young master Hyeongjun, who was the same age as her, and below him, though they were three years younger than she was, were Hyeongseon and Hyeonggeol. As a servant, she could not dare to set her heart on one of the young masters, but her two round, clear eyes had looked on them for so long that she knew little else—there was no way that her heart could ever be swayed or drawn by a man whose face was red with pimple marks, whose hair had never seen a comb and was braided and coiled haphazardly on the top of his head, then wrapped in a cotton cloth, and whose cotton clothes were stained with dirt and sweat.

In her youth she had always brought out his meals, but as she got older she did not look directly at his face, and she left the bringing out of meals to the older servants and cleverly avoided even getting close to Duchil.

But Ssangne continued to grow. A flower never forgets to bloom: when she turned eighteen, even though she was weighed down by the arduous work and her poor food and clothing, the fine hair that had covered her face gave way to alabaster skin, and her cheeks blossomed red. Her lips may have been chapped, but they grew particularly red in color, and her bosom swelled noticeably beneath her summer jacket. Beneath her skirt, her hip bones were wrapped in ample, supple flesh. In the eyes of all, her body was now that of a woman, a maiden in the bloom of her youth who had grown without shame.

Duchil's carnal desire, which had grown almost too great to resist as he got older, reached a frightening peak at the age of twenty-seven. Late one summer evening, having returned from weeding a broad patch of the millet field, Duchil received his supper in his room. It so happened that day that the older servants were all off on errands, and it was Ssangne who brought him his meal.

She wrapped a rough cotton skirt around her waist, and the hemp jacket had ridden up to reveal her white skin. As she bent to set down the table, Duchil, who was paying no attention to the table at all, stared at the part on Ssangne's bent head, and with his two hands he suddenly grabbed Ssangne's as they grasped the edges of the table. She managed to place the table more or less safely on the floor, but Duchil knocked the cold pickled radish soup with his knee as he got up and overturned the bowl. As he reached to grab her jacket with both of his arms, like some wild animal, Ssangne braced her foot against the doorsill and tried to shake off the grasp of this leech of a man. The tops of Duchil's feet were soaked by the soup, and the spoon clanged loudly against the bowl, but he did not even hear it. With a frightening strength he tried to drag Ssangne kicking into the room, but there was a sound outside. Duchil released his grip and Ssangne fell backward into the yard, while Duchil lay on the floor in the dark room, panting as if he had just run ten li.

"Ssange, what's the matter with you?"

When Duchil was certain that this was the voice of one of the old servants, he was somewhat relieved. The servant must have known what had transpired, as there was no word from the courtyard. Ssangne's shoulders heaved as she walked slowly toward the kitchen with the old servant.

After this had happened, Ssangne took such great pains to avoid appearing in front of Duchil that it was obvious to everyone. Once he went out to Visiting Immortal Gate with three or four workers to thresh the wheat, and Ssangne was told to bring them their lunch in a basket, but even though this order came from her mistress, she hesitated for some time in the kitchen. The old servant took pity on Ssangne and said that she would take it, so nothing much came of the incident, but Assistant Curator Bak's wife could not help but take an interest in Ssangne's shunning of Duchil.

Assistant Curator Bak had long since guessed that the reason Duchil had not complained about the hard work and labored as faithfully as an ox for six or seven long years was because he had his heart set on the blooming Ssangne. So when his wife, Lady Choe, said, "That Duchil fellow must have played some prank on Ssangne because she doesn't even want to take him his lunch in the fields," he took the pipe that had been clenched in his teeth out of his mouth and simply replied, "Duchil will be thirty before long."

Then he put the pipe back in his mouth, and his wife stared at his profile as he puffed smoke, blushing slightly when she imagined that her husband, though he would not say it aloud, might also be thinking, 'And Ssangne will be twenty soon,' and picturing Ssangne's newly round buttocks. But she said nothing and retired to her room.

Yet there was another small incident that caught Bak's wife's attention. On the day her eldest son Hyeongjun married a girl from the Jeonju Kim Clan in Sangmyeong, Ssangne did not eat her breakfast, and late that night she sat dumbly in front of the beehive in the backyard, crying and sighing in vexation.

Hyeongjun brought his wife home as soon as they were married and, as they were not on bad terms, no matter what pointless thoughts Ssangne may have harbored in her heart, there was no chance of there being any trouble between them; yet after a year had passed and she turned nineteen, when Assistant Curator Bak's wife took a close look at her, she realized that Ssange was growing more and more conspicuously beautiful, and that there was no small danger of her causing trouble.

Even if nothing happened with her eldest son, Hyeongseon and Hyeonggeol were coming of age, and even her husband, who, while he seemed to be too busy making money to think of anything but his concubine—well, to put it bluntly, there was no telling what he might do. Once her thoughts brought her this far, she suddenly began to think that she would have to do something as soon as possible, lest her sons or husband end up going astray. So after carefully considering the matter by herself, she arrived at a fine idea.

One day, when her younger brother Choe Gwansul was visiting in the men's quarters, she quietly called him into the women's quarters. Gwansul had just started believing in something called "Eastern Learning" and was traveling to Seoul regularly, and his path took him often to the men's quarters of their house, where he proposed to teach his brother-in-law, Assistant Curator Bak, enlightenment thought and this Eastern Learning.

"I wanted to discuss with you the idea of marrying Duchil and our Ssangne; what do you think?" she asked him, and Gwansul, who had shaved his head and was wearing Western eyeglasses, although he still went around wearing a horsehair hat, absentmindedly touched his hat strings and his beard and replied politely to his sister, "Enlightenment thought, and of course Western Learning and Eastern Learning, all argue for the freeing of servants, both male and female. So as long as you have no thought of making any girls that Ssangne might bear servants later on, then it is only proper that you should take this course of action. I do not know, however, how your husband will take this."

"Well, my husband knows that Duchil has his heart set on Ssangne and that he has worked hard in this house for nearly ten years without a word." This is what she said aloud, but Gwansul's elder sister, Lady Choe, thought to herself: 'Whether he opposes it or not, we need to marry Duchil and Ssangne quickly to put my mind at ease about everything. If anyone opposes this plan, it will surely be from suspicious motives, so no matter what I must say to convince them, this must be handled according to my wishes. By the look of things, there is no doubt that Ssangne had her heart set on Hyeongjun, and though she will not have had time to harbor any untoward thoughts so soon after his marriage, the heart of a girl is as fickle and fey as a cat, so if I let things run their course, our household might suffer a hundred years of misfortune, or, as Ssangne appears to be rather shrewd and sly for a girl, there is a chance she might act inappropriately toward Hyeongseon or Hyeonggeol in the future — whatever the case, I will have to convince my husband by whatever means necessary and see this plan through.'

In fact, Assistant Curator Bak agreed with Lady Choe at once, before she even had the chance to lay out her carefully considered plan, and this made her somewhat leery. There was no way he should have agreed so gladly, no rhyme or reason behind such a greedy man so easily giving away property he had bought for a considerable sum; did he perhaps have some other hidden motive? No matter how long she ruminated on it, though, she could not think of anything at all.

"They say all enlightened civilizations do this, so we should keep with the times, and the children are getting older and reaching maturity as well, so I'm worried that they might make some mistake in the future. When all of these things are taken into account, this course of action seems best, and that's why I proposed it." After she stated her case like this again, they discussed in detail what to do next.

Assistant Curator Bak and his wife were agreed on the matter, and not long after he chose a day on which Duchil was off and called him into the men's quarters.

"Next year you will be twenty-nine years of age, and it won't be long before you are thirty. It has been eight years since you came to us, so you are of the age when it is time to establish your own family. You may have forgotten, but the first thing I said to you when I saw you was that if you did your work diligently, it would do you no harm for the future. So, what do you think . . . if you are willing, Ssangne is now all grown up . . ."

Here he stopped for a moment and examined Duchil's face, which was filled with joy and a smile that stretched from ear to ear, and all he could do was bow his head low and say, "What could I possibly have to say about something my master has decided?"

Bak noted the unbridled happiness spreading across Duchil's face and said, "To say a few words about the girl who is to become your wife, she was entrusted to me when she was nine years old by her father as he left for Wonsan, and at that time I placed in his hands a considerable sum of money, when I had little to spare. Thinking about it now, if you consider the interest, that sum would now be quite large. However, I have no intention of being so cruel to you. (At this, Duchil, who had been a little nervous, looked relieved, and once again he bowed at the waist and pressed his hands together in his lap.) But there is something I must say to you, and that is that, according to a custom handed down long ago, any daughters born to the girl would normally be bound to my household, but I have something different in mind: I intend to do away with this custom in the future, so whether you have sons or daughters, you may raise them as you see fit. We will pass the rest of the year as now, and next year, after the harvest, you can put up Ssangne's hair and live in the servants' quarters by the water."

When Bak finished speaking, Duchil bowed low and touched his nose to the ground, and then he returned to his room. It was no great joy to go from being a domestic to being a hired hand. His joy was in the fact that Ssangne, who all could see was a beauty, was going to be his.

But, unlike Duchil, the Ssangne who left the men's quarters in the evening of the next day ran straight to the outhouse with tears brimming in her eyes. In the toilet, with no one else around, she had a long cry. What use was it to cry? Whether she liked it or not, next autumn she would end up as Duchil's wife. Unless she fled to a distant place, or threw herself into the river and took her own life, or took arsenic and caused her flesh to rot, no matter how she cried or struggled, she was going to become Duchil's wife.

If she had an agreeable husband, what bitterness would remain even though she lived her whole life as a servant? What did it matter if that husband was a domestic, and why should she hold a grudge if the daughters their marriage produced lived as servants for generation after generation? Furthermore, how much better it was to be the wife of a hired hand than it was to be a female servant, and how superior was a hired hand to a domestic? Yet these things meant nothing to Ssangne. Even if she became a hired hand, would she not do the same things and suffer the same things? If that was her lot, her one desire was to at least share this life with a man who pleased her. Saying that it had to be a man who pleased her did not mean that she had someone in mind. It was just that Duchil was so boorish and slovenly that she was not drawn to him in the least.

But if she were to bemoan her lot in life, then had not all these things been set in motion the day that her father first sold her as a servant? Now that she was at this point, arguing this way or that and trying to split hairs was nothing but foolishness. It was not that Ssangne was unaware of this fact. It was precisely because she was aware of it that she had listened to Assistant Curator Bak's words with her head hung low and then had left his room without saying a word.

Things, cruelly, went according to plan. And so it was that, in the autumn of the following year, Ssangne became Duchil's wife and the pitiful victim of Duchil's long-harbored carnal desires in the servant's quarters by the water at Assistant Curator Bak's main house.

The dim light of the moon shone in the window. Duchil's wife Ssangne lay alone, flat on the bare floor of the servant's quarters, which faced the Biryu River.

On her way back from the Dumutgol house, where she had dropped off some steamed rice cakes, she had met Hyeonggeol on the road and suffered unexpected shame, and for some time she walked with quick steps, not bothering to wipe away the tears that flowed down her face, until she reached the main road. She went in through the rear gate facing the water, passed by her room, and then walked through the inner yard and into the kitchen.

"What took you so long?" asked the old servant.

Ssangne had calmed down enough by then to lie and say that she had briefly helped wind the yarn around the warp beam at the Dumutgol house.

Lady Choe, who heard this from within her room, silently scolded the concubine. 'How can you put to work someone who was sent on an errand?' When Ssangne asked what had happened to the feed for the horses, mules, donkeys, and cattle, the old servant said that it had all been delivered. So Ssangne took a plate of rice cakes, along with some rice, pumpkin stew, and some kimchi that she was told to give to Duchil when he returned, and went into her room. No matter how much she thought of dinner, she couldn't seem to muster any sort of appetite. Her heart pounded at that moment, and she wondered if what had happened to her on the road had been a dream, or if she had gone insane and been bewitched by some spirit, but in the next moment she realized that it had indeed happened just as she remembered, and her heart sank, and then the blood drained from her face and even made her feel a little faint. In truth, she had never experienced anything like that, even in her dreams. On the day when Hyeongjun, who was the same age as her, was married to the girl from Sangmyeong, she did not eat at all and sighed before the beehive in the backyard when night came, something that later became gossip on the lips of all the old servants and wives of tenant farmers, but it was not out of longing for the young master that she had done so. Unlike other families, this family had a custom of not marrying their sons before the age of eighteen, and though others may have argued the virtues of this custom, Ssangne, who had wondered if she would ever get to ride the wedding palanquin, took no small comfort from this, thinking, 'Even the Master's sons have given no thought to marriage yet.' But that comfort was shattered with Hyeongjun's marriage, and she was already at an age when her heart was vexed, so she could do nothing to stop the sighs and tears from pouring out. It had been ten years since her father and younger siblings had abandoned her here in this town and gone off toward Wonsan to find a way to make a living, but they had not once sent word about whether they were even still alive, and so she wondered where they were and how they were making a living, or if they had died and turned to earth, or if they had become ghosts and were floating through the air like kites that had broken their strings. But more than simply wondering about them, she longed for them, and more than longing, she felt sadness, and more than sadness, her heart welled up, but she felt these things only after her face was wet with tears. How could they have driven me into this pit? — with such resentment added to her tumult of emotions, she even grew so cold as to think that it would be better to take her own life than to live out that life in such a world as this. By the time she had managed to quell such thoughts and come to her senses, she had missed breakfast, and when night fell she sat absentmindedly by herself beside the beehive in the backyard. Now, in the room she shared with Duchil, she wondered how could she ever hold her head up to the heavens and be so impertinent as to dream of being held in a young master's arms? And yet just before, not in a dream but in her waking hours, such a thing had happened right there on the open road, with the most handsome and dashing of the young masters, so it was no wonder she had thought she might have been bewitched by a spirit. Yet, no matter how hard she thought about it, she knew it was no spell. She opened her eyes wide and looked at the window. The gaps in the latticework were distinct, and through them she could clearly see the nearly full moon, high in the sky, shedding moonlight like streams of water, so it was unreasonable to think she had been bewitched by a spirit. She stuck out her tongue and sucked her lips. The sweet taste of the young master from Dumutgol was still there. The passion she felt when his lips, hotter than fire, searched her cheeks and then the skin beneath her nose and then finally found her lips, was still in her body. It had definitely been no dream. She thought of the words he had forced out with his hot breath: "When the moon has gone down." She suddenly got up, opened the door leading to the water, and went out. Before reaching the main gate there was a low bramble hedge, and in it was another, small gate. If the young master came, he would definitely go around by the water, pass the mulberry grove, and come in through this gate in the hedge. Duchil had not yet come back with his load of wood, so the main gate to the outside was still open, but if he came in through that gate he would have to pass through the yard in front of the men's quarters and then walk by the stables and come around by the path behind the toilet to reach this place, so she was certain that the best way to reach her room without anyone knowing was to come round by the water and pass through this hedge. There was a small gate that led into the yard, but he would have to pass the kitchen in order to enter the outer yard if he went that way.

She ran out in stockinged feet and undid the latch on the hedge gate so that it could be easily opened by pushing on it from the outside. She looked up at the moon and saw that it still hung two arms' spans above the twelve peaks. When that moon sets, Duchil will return, she thought suddenly, and then she wondered if she was really waiting for the young master to come for her.

She went back into her room, closed the door, and then lay flat on the warmest part of the floor without putting down any bedding. She thought of Duchil. She wondered if Duchil's daily badgering, no matter how fatigued he might be, had not already prepared her heart to receive the young master. No matter how lowly she might be, and whether or not she had any affection for Duchil, was she not still the wife of another? When she thought about it, just having her lips stolen by some young man and falling into his arms should have made her feel guilt and regret, and here she had opened the gate herself to wait for another man who was not her husband to come to her.

And yet she did not make any effort to get up and bar the gate again. What if her husband were to have some unexpected encounter on the road and not return until dawn? No, what if he were to spend the night in a hut by the hemp fields and not return until the eastern sky was bright? — in a corner of her heart she quietly wished for these things, it was true. She tried her hardest not to think any idle, burdensome, or filthy thoughts. But the scene where she met the young master on the road and then parted from him, this she played over and over again in her mind.

How she had walked slowly down the narrow path unaware, with a basin in her hands, how she had been startled by the pale, white shape that had shot up suddenly in the middle of the street, how she had been taken aback once again to see that the shape was, unexpectedly, the young master from Dumutgol, how she had been ready to scream sharply but then felt ashamed, for some reason — all of these things she quickly passed over in her mind; but the events afterwards she drew out as slowly as she could and dwelt on each detail, savoring everything, from the part when the young master had spoken to her in polite language to the part when she had pulled herself away after the kiss and shed inexplicable tears as she walked quickly down the road bathed in the dim light of the moon behind the clouds. She played this over and over in her mind, and if she heard the young master's footsteps passing by the mulberry grove before she grew sick of it, then she thought it wouldn't matter whether or not Duchil came driving the cattle. She had shared Duchil's bed countless times, and she had even had a miscarriage only six months after she had put up her hair, but when she imagined the young master's caress it felt as if she had never given herself to anyone before, as if she were a virgin who had been sheltered so that no one had ever dared lay a finger on her. In truth, in the year and a half she had been married, she wondered if even once she had ever given herself up to passion.

She lifted her hands and pressed them down on her bosom. She wrapped her arms around herself. But she could not feel any of the overwhelming, throbbing, indescribable emotion that had welled up when the young master embraced her as she held the basin with one hand. She let out a sigh and turned over.

Before long the window grew dark. Unable to calm her pounding heart, she looked toward it to find that the moon had nearly disappeared behind the twelve peaks. She covered her face with her arms and nearly screamed with agony, wondering what she was going to do. Whether it was a fit of fear that the young master would appear once the moon set, or whether it was a sign of her fanciful urge to grab the moon and stop it from setting, she could not tell.

But then, oh dear, she heard the sound of the great gate by the men's quarters swing wide open, and then what was clearly Duchil's voice as he drove the cattle, hiya, hiya!, and finally even the clear sound of him leaning a load of wood against the gatepost.

Duchil was back. The young master had not come and Duchil had come back — as this thought imprinted itself distinctly in her mind, Ssangne took her hands from her head, whispered "Thank goodness" as if waking from a dream, and then let out a long, thin sigh. Even though Duchil had driven the cattle a distance of some sixty li, he took the time to pile the wood in the yard of the men's quarters.

Ssangne quietly got up and stood for a moment in the middle of the darkened room. She clutched her dizzy head with both hands and mumbled once, aloud, "It's good that he came back early."

7

After the first-year high school students studied arithmetic under Mun Useong, the teacher who had been appointed a month before, their studies for the day were over. But after class ended every day, the students all still had to practice their group gymnastics for the athletics meet, under the guidance of Jeong Yeonggeun. So Hyeonggeol grabbed his book bundle and, with nearly twenty other students, left the classroom and headed down to the schoolyard. There were five or six first-year high school students who had not yet cut their hair, but only two of them still had topknots, which they wore under their straw hats. Among the upperclassmen, though, were many older, newly married boys, and these wore horsehair or straw hats.

The school had, of course, encouraged those boys who wore their hair in braids, and the grown students who wore their hair in topknots, to cut their hair, and they had lectured the students, telling them that the entire student body should have their hair cut by the athletics meet, but there were still quite a few students who had left their hair as it was. These students were reluctant to participate in the group gymnastics. In fact, most of these students were young men approaching the age of thirty who had studied quite a bit of classical Chinese in their villages, dozens of li from the town. When they had finished their studies they either stayed in the classroom to avoid the group gymnastics or went off into the mountains if the weather was nice.

Mr. Jeong had argued that the school had to be most strict in disciplining these students, but concerns were expressed that, if these students were treated too harshly, they would flee the already small school; so in the end the school had adopted a policy of tolerance.

On the way from the classroom to the schoolyard, Hyeonggeol met Son Daebong and three or four students coming from Three Pines Pavilion. They had finished class an hour earlier and had gone into the mountains to pass the time, and now they were heading down to the schoolyard to take part in the group gymnastics practice. Seeing Hyeonggeol, Daebong skipped forward a few steps to walk beside him. He put his arm around Hyeonggeol's shoulder and said, "Let's go take a look at the bicycle on the way home."

Across the street from Hyeonggeol's family's main house — that is, Assistant Curator Bak's house on the main street — was the house of Yi Chilseong. It did not take even a day for the rumor that he had bought a bicycle in Pyeongyang some days before to spread through the whole town. So, until the day before yesterday, people had bustled and children had gathered in front of his house, just like they would have had there been a traveling troupe of performers or a banquet. Living near Assistant Curator Bak as he did, Chilseong had always benefited from the acquaintance, so the day after he brought back the bike, he pushed it into the yard of the men's quarters and showed it to Bak's whole family. Hyeonggeol was there at the time, and the women had, of course, closed the inner gate, but they looked through the cracks in the door to see the amazing sight of the bicycle.

When Daebong first heard that Chilseong's family had gotten a bicycle, he talked loudly about how everyone gathered like flies to see such a trivial thing and how he had seen people riding bicycles like monkeys swing through the trees when he had visited Pyeongyang the year before, so what was so great about Chilseong and his bicycle, which he had only now barely learned to ride? After a few days, though, he grew anxious to see the bicycle up close, as he had only ever seen them from afar, and briefly at that, and he was itching to touch the shiny, complex gears and mechanisms he had seen in Pyeongyang. But there was something else that had whet his appetite. He just might be able to get another look at the wife Chilseong had brought back from Pyeongyang not long ago, so thus he would be able to kill two birds with one stone.

But rumor had it that Chilseong had closed the front gate to his house yesterday morning and was now not showing anyone the bicycle. When people first bustled around the house to get a good look, they would constantly rap on the seat, ring the bell, spin the pedals round and round, and, unable to control their glee, climb onto the thing and take it for a wobbly ride down the road, but after three or four days of this, Chilseong grew tired of the clamor. He had made his living as a peddler of wares, and when he was young he had gone around with boxes or a pack on his back, later buying a donkey after he saved up some money so he could travel around to the markets held in a few of the villages in the region and sell his wares there, and about a year ago he had settled down in the market here and began to make frequent trips to Pyeongyang, bringing back fine dried fish, dried seaweed, and sacks of rice to sell at his grocery. According to Chilseong, he had bought the bicycle so that he could get quickly to and from Pyeongyang, especially now that the new road had been built, but after a few days of rushing around and being unable to sell his wares because of the contraption, he realized that it was useless, and from then on he decided to not let anyone look at it. He would be sitting there with his notebook open to do some bookkeeping, counting up sums on his fingers, when some children would come by and say, "Let's see the bicycle!" Even when he sat down to a delicious dinner with his wife, licking his chops at the pickled radishes and mackerel on the table, these fellows would come by and pester him: "Show us the bicycle!" This got to be such a bother that he even thought of doing as some suggested and charging money to see the bicycle, but then he realized, "I'll never be able to use the bicycle," and he lied and said it was broken, and he stowed it away in his storehouse. So Daebong had no way to see that blasted bicycle, as he did not know Chilseong well, nor did he have any influence of his own. Hyeongseon was his best chance, but Daebong was not on particularly good terms with him, so his friend Hyeonggeol would have to do.

"I've seen him ride, and he has a long way to go. If you've seen people in Pyeongyang ride bicycles like monkeys swing through trees, the way Chilseong rides will make you sick to your stomach," said Hyeonggeol, teasing Daebong.

"It's not that I must see it or anything, but Gilson or someone else said that it doesn't look like a new one at all but like an old, used one. So I want to see if that is true, and while we're at it, wouldn't it be great if we could take it out and learn how to ride it?"

"And he said he was going to lend it to you? I bet if you were to give him a choice between his woman and his bicycle, and ask him which he would lend out, he would sooner hand over his woman than that bicycle."

But Hyeonggeol had also been tempted by the talk of taking the bicycle out and learning how to ride it. Rushing along on horseback was a thrill, so sitting right down on the metal machine with two wheels and flying down the road like a swallow would have to be breathtaking. So he was walking along, trying to think of some clever way they could get their hands on that bicycle, as Daebong had suggested, and Daebong followed behind, mumbling, "Well, if he doesn't want to lend out that bicycle, I'd be fine with his woman."

But they were already in the middle of the schoolyard, and then they heard the sound of a trumpet, and when Mr. Jeong ran out with his riding crop they were busy lining up according to year.

Even as they were all busy bustling around, trying to find their places in formation at the sound of the command "Fall in!" Daebong and Hyeonggeol were still each obsessed with thoughts of the bicycle.

They made short work of "ATTENTION ... dress right, DRESS ... ready, FRONT ... sound off ... by the right flank, MARCH," then they repeated the maneuver of switching from marching in columns of four to marching in rows of four; when they had circled the schoolyard like this for about a half hour, the drill practice for the day ended, and they quickly ran off to Chilseong's place.

Daebong waited outside while Hyeonggeol, who was close to the family, walked right in and asked most politely, "Is Chilseong at home?"

"He's gone into the countryside," came his wife's voice from inside, and then she greeted him: "Welcome."

Hearing this conversation in the yard, Daebong thought that he should stop loitering about outside and go in, even though it might be impertinent to do so; he sauntered in and stood right behind Hyeonggeol. Chilseong's young wife slid open the door to her room, and she stood with one foot on the threshold and her left hand on the doorpost, about to talk with Hyeonggeol, but then she shrank back at this strange young man who had wandered in, only showing her face again when Hyeonggeol asked, "Ah, so Chilseong is not at home?" so she could reply "He went to town." She did not hide her face again after that.

"Then it looks like we are out of luck," said Daebong, and he winked at Hyeonggeol.

"Hmm," replied Hyeonggeol, and then the two young men looked toward the mistress's room and grinned widely. Chilseong's wife also looked as if she were about to smile in return, but then she moved her lips, as if she thought to ask them why they had come.

Hyeonggeol saw this and said, "Ma'am, it is nothing like that," and he took a step farther into the yard. "It's just that I saw Chilseong riding the bike in the yard of the men's quarters in our house, so I don't really need to see it again, but Son Daebong, here, I'm not sure if you know him or not, but he is the son of Mr. Son, who lives down the hill. So this fellow asked me if I would show him the bicycle, and that's why we came here together, but since Chilseong isn't home, well, it looks like everything has gone sour." Then he looked back at Daebong and said, "Anyway, it looks like you have some pretty bad luck. You haven't come to visit in days, and then you come on the day when Chilseong isn't home, what sort of rotten luck is that?" And after this jest he turned back and asked Chilseong's wife, "So, did he leave on a very long trip?"

On the one hand, Daebong was amazed to see Hyeonggeol chatter like this, but, on the other, he was also a little jealous of how well Hyeonggeol was doing all by himself, so before he knew it he was standing next to Hyeonggeol and staring right at the face of Chilseong's wife.

He thought to himself, 'This is more fun than riding a bicycle ten times. How nice it would be if we could sit next to each other on the wooden floor and chat . . .'

But then Chilseong's wife said, "He left for Alme this morning, and he has business there to take care of, so he should be back by tomorrow evening or so. At any rate, the bicycle's owner doesn't have to be here for you to take a look at it, does he? It is sitting in that shed, covered with a cloth, so wait here."

She turned and went down toward the kitchen, apparently to get her shoes before coming outside. Daebong looked at Hyeonggeol and stuck his tongue out. "That's quite fine."

But Hyeonggeol couldn't figure out whether he meant it was quite fine that they would get to see the bicycle or that Chilseong's wife looked quite fine. For his part, Hyeonggeol thought briefly about Duchil's wife, Ssangne. At any rate, they would not get to ride the bicycle. Babbling idly with another man's wife as they touched the bicycle was not that appealing, and he would much rather get one more look at the face of Ssangne, whom he had not seen even a glimpse of for a month, not since their simple embrace on the road. So before Chilseong's wife even came out of the kitchen, he said in a low voice, "I'm not going to ride the bicycle. I'm going."

Daebong winked again. "I prefer women to bicycles."

Chilseong's wife came out of the kitchen into the yard, wearing on her bare, white feet a pair of yellowed hemp sandals with the heels pressed down, and said, "Hmph. He takes care of this bicycle or whatever it is as if it were the spirit tablet of one of his ancestors . . ." She flared her nostrils. It seemed to be a sign than she truly bore no ill will toward the young men.

"I'm sorry to inconvenience you like this," said Daebong, cutting in, but she shook her head — her hair was braided with a red ribbon and brought up around her forehead, without even a headscarf to cover it — opened the door to the shed without a word and went in. From within the shed, the smell of salt, the smell of seaweed, and the odor of dried fish all assaulted their noses at once, but Daebong stood close behind the woman, staring at her buttocks. Hyeonggeol, who had stayed behind in the middle of the yard, stared blankly at the woman's underwear hanging on the laundry line and then said, "Take your time with the bicycle, I'll go home and get the horse . . ." and ran off by himself to the front gate.

Daebong replied, "Ah, wait for me, where are you going?" pretending to be flustered and in haste, but he was secretly pleased, thinking, 'All for the better. He knows when three is a crowd.' Which is not to say, of course, that Daebong had any thought of misbehaving or doing anything untoward with another man's wife in this empty shed with no one else around.

Daebong was one of two children, and his older sister had already married, so in a way he was Mr. Son's only child. Mr. Son doted on his only son far more than was common in other families, but as he was not all that rich he was not able to find that magnificent a bride for Daebong. He had decided to marry Daebong to the Miryang Bak clan, specifically the nineteen-year-old Geumne, the eldest daughter of Bak Seonggyun, the owner of a stable and inn, and the younger brother of Bak Rigyun, who at least held himself to be a yangban. His family had already sent the customary gifts to the bride's family, and they were set to be married come early summer, but, at eighteen this year, Daebong was not that enthusiastic about marrying her. He was not too pleased that her family was a clan of layabouts with no substance other than empty claims of being yangban, but, more than that, he did not like Geumne herself. They lived in the same neighborhood, so he had seen seen quite a lot of her until only a few years ago. There was a rumor that she was a skilled weaver, and, perhaps because her family ran an inn, many extolled her amazing cooking, but such things were not attractive to Daebong. She might weave fine cotton or silk clothing, or spin thread on a spinning wheel, but if she had known how to read a bit . . . no, even more than that, if she had just been a buxom girl with a pleasant face, then he would have had no complaints.

She was nineteen this year and at the peak of her beauty, and she would, of course, have changed from two or three years ago. But Daebong still vividly remembered that last glimpse he had caught of Geumne, in the kitchen of Bak Rigyun's noodle shop two years ago.

From what he had seen then she was thin and scrawny, and her face was pale but peppered all over with tiny, dark pimples. He wondered who would want a girl like that and pitied in his heart the man who would be her husband, but the man who would be her husband turned out to be Daebong himself.

When the matchmaker had first visited, he had tried to sway his mother, saying, "I'm not going to get married," but she scolded him at once, asking him what kind of talk that was, him being late for marriage as it was. If only he had spoken more carefully and confessed his reasons — "There is no way I will marry that girl with a face like a toad's back!" — but simply trying to convince his mother that he wasn't going to get married was doomed from the start.

His mother went to see the girl for herself, and when she came back she said to herself: "A girl with flesh on her cheeks is naturally foolish. Her neck should be fair and long and her face thin, then she will be kind and clever, and she will know how to respect her elders. Furthermore, she has a proper figure, is not untidy, and is a superb weaver and cook, so it will be impossible to find a better bride than her. It seems that we continue to be blessed by the spirit of Mount Daebong." Then she even said that, when the new grain came in after they held the ceremony in autumn, she would have to prepare a half bushel of rice cakes as an offering for the mountain spirit, who dwelled in the mountains behind the hot springs of Yangdeok.

There were times that Daebong craved a woman and did not mind too much the idea of getting married, but when he saw fair maidens or the pretty wives of others, he despaired at the thought of living with Geumne for the rest of his life. He also hated how, when he passed by Visiting Immortal Gate, Bak Rigyun would call him into the shop to have a bowl of pressed noodles for lunch, since Daebong was going to be his nephew-in-law. Once, he reluctantly went inside, only to find Bak Rigyun gossiping about Assistant Curator Bak, repeating his mantra of "Lady Seong was the wife of Bak Gwiseong and eldest daughter of Seong Nonsan" and boasting about his family, and finally even boasting about his niece, Geumne, when he really shouldn't have, and Daebong was desperate to escape. So, from then on, he avoided that house and passed by along the water's edge, and on the rare occasions that he was spotted he would lie and say that he had just eaten lunch and was on his way back from a walk to clear his head after drinking.

At any rate, he did not want to marry Geumne, but neither could he come right out and say that he didn't want to, so whenever he saw a woman who was naturally pretty he felt like teasing her or playing a prank on her.

When Chilseong's wife pulled back the cloth that had been covering the bicycle, he looked it up and down and said, "That is one odd-looking contraption." He gave the seat a few pats, then touched the handlebars with his fingers and said, "This must be the bell," as he looked this way and that at a round, flat piece of shiny metal. At this the woman stood there satisfied, with a pleased look on her face, and then, realizing that the young man did not know how to ring the bell, reached out with her right hand and gave it a ring. Daebong pretended to be surprised and said, "Gosh, what is that sound? Well, my, that is quite a clamor, isn't it? So you get up on this seat, ride this fellow out into the street, and when you see a dog or a person you give this thing a ring, no? Ha ha, that's something."

Then he looked down at the pedals and the chain, and he gave the tire a squeeze with his fingers. "Chilseong must ride this well, no?" he said, looking at the woman's face.

"Well, he's just gotten it, so when would he have learned to ride it well?" she said, grinning.

"If he went to Alme this morning, I wonder why he didn't ride this bike. Ah, that's right, the road is rough."

"It sure is. The road is rough, and just think what could happen on a dangerous road if he made a mistake, not being a skilled rider. So he only rides the bicycle when he goes to Pyeongyang."

Having come this far, it didn't seem that there was that much left to say. Daebong could either thank her for letting him look at the bike and take his leave, or he could come right out and shamelessly ask if he could take the bike for a ride, even if it meant being turned down, so he made a show of carefully looking over the bicycle once more and asked, "They say your family is from Pyeongyang . . . where exactly in Pyeongyang?"

"Sachang Market."

"Sachang Market? Well, that's right across from Seolsudang Village, isn't it?" he said, repeating the few bits and pieces of information he had heard.

"Have you been to Pyeongyang?" asked Chilseong's wife, surprised but also pleased.

"Well, last year we went up for the athletics meet. We saw bikes then."

At this, Chilseong's wife covered her mouth with her hand and laughed. "How embarrassing," she said. "I thought you didn't know how to ring the bell."

"Well, we did see them but we didn't actually get to touch them," Daebong said, laughing as well. "Why, Chilseong is no ordinary fellow." Then he grumbled as if to himself, "First he brings home a woman from Pyeongyang and now he has bought a bike. Well, Chilseong is always first in these things here in this village."

Chilseong's wife blushed a little at this. "What a thing to say. Why would he bring back someone like me from Pyeongyang? I would just give Pyeongyang a bad name."

"What are you talking about? I've been there myself, and there is no one better than you in all of Pyeongyang."

Even though she realized that this young man was teasing her, deep inside she wasn't displeased by it, and she sighed, "And here I am, wasting away in this country village."

In the meantime, Hyeonggeol, who had left Daebong at Chilseong's house, crossed the main street and passed through the front gate of the Bak family's main house to see the old fisherman from Pyeongyang mending his nets at the heated end of his father's room, and his father sitting by the stationery chest at the other end, working an abacus and flipping through his account book; Hyeonggeol then passed through the central gate and went into the mule mill. Inside, the mule stood there, chewing on dry fodder after having turned the mill, the blindfold having been removed from its eyes, and it flared its nostrils. The person who had been driving the mule and hulling the rice was nowhere to be seen. The rice had been abandoned in front of the winnower, still on the straw mat or in the wooden pan, and the winnowing fan and the sieve were laid carelessly on the floor, so it was clear that, until a moment ago, someone had been working there and then had given the beast some dry feed and gone off to the kitchen to get some water, or perhaps gone to relieve herself. Should he stand there until Ssangne returned? But he didn't want it to seem as if he had deliberately come to see her. It would seem more natural if he went round to the horse stable and then stopped here by chance on the way back from seeing the horses. So he turned and was about to head to the horse stables when he heard footsteps behind him. He turned around, thinking it would be Ssangne, and found his twelve-year-old sister, Bopae.

"What are you doing standing here, Brother?"

He was abashed, as it seemed she knew what he was thinking, but he said, "I was on my way to the horse stables," and then continued on his way. In the stables there was no donkey, just the white horse standing all by itself. Hyeonggeol stood there for a while and stared at the horse. Ssangne must have returned to the mill at last, as he heard her chatting with Bopae. He turned on his heels and went back to the mill.

"What happened to the donkey?" he asked, to no one in particular.

"Duchil took it out for a ride," replied Bopae, standing next to Ssangne.

"Did he go far?" he asked in return. Having asked this, he looked at Ssangne, but she was blushing and fidgeting with the straw mat on which millet had been spread out. Hyeonggeol also hesitated for moment, realizing the meaning hidden in his question. So he changed the subject and asked another question: "Where is Hyeongseon?"

"I don't know, he is doing something in his room."

"And his wife?" he said, asking about Bobu, even if it was somewhat of a non sequitur.

"She . . ." Bopae swept off the millstone with the broom she was holding and then continued, "She's probably reading her Bible or sewing, or something like that."

"Her Bible?"

"Yes, the Jesus book. Not the hymnal, but, you know, that other, thick book."

Hyeonggeol stood there silently for a moment. "Why, does she believe in Jesus?" he asked after a while, and Bopae put down the broom, sat down on the edge of the straw mat, and began toying with the grains.

"I asked her once, and she said that she didn't believe. She said that believers did not marry Gentiles." Bopae seemed ready to talk about it in detail.

Hyeonggeol attended a Christian school and knew a little about Christian doctrine, but he wanted to hear what Bopae had to say and asked, "What is a Gentile?"

"You don't know what a Gentile is? It's someone who doesn't believe in Jesus ... you know, Gentiles; how can you not know that?" said Bopae with a smile.

"If she had believed in Jesus she would not have married into our family, so they had a marriage of Gentiles."

At this, Ssangne grinned for the first time.

"So what is our eldest brother doing?"

"He is taking a nap, and his wife is feeding the baby."

Everyone is so carefree, Hyeonggeol thought, but, of course, he didn't say so aloud.

"Little Brother didn't say anything to you today?" he asked.

"What would he say, go to school? Father would know, but how would I?" Then, as if she had just realized something, Bopae suddenly got up. "Well, I had better go with Tansil from next door before the sun sets," she said, and ran out through the central gate.

"Where are you going?" he called after her, but Bopae did not answer, her skirt swirling as she ran off.

Moving the millet from the mat to the wooden pan, Ssangne picked up Bopae's end of the conversation and began to say, "She asked me to go with her to pick wild greens, but I was too busy. . ." but then she trailed off at the end, so it didn't seem as if she were even talking to Hyeonggeol. She had started speaking with the idea of answering him but suddenly grew nervous when she realized that it was just the two of them.

But Hyeonggeol was just as nervous. Since the brief emotion that they had shared on the road a month earlier, they had seen each other a few times, but this was the first time they had spoken alone.

The two of them were silent for a while, aware of the strange mood they shared in both body and mind.

Ssangne should have scooped up the pounded rice, moved

it to the winnower, and then scooped up the millet, but her cheeks burned under Hyeonggeol's gaze and she could not budge. She crouched there with the wooden pan in her hands, gathering the rice and then scattering it again. After a long while, Hyeonggeol coughed. Ssangne listened to hear what he would say, and she heard his slightly trembling voice: "Where did Duchil go?"

"Quite a way off, a two-day trip." No sooner had she answered than they heard a murmuring from the yard of the men's quarters.

Hyeonggeol realized that it was Son Daebong, speaking with his father, standing before the wooden ledge outside his room. Ssangne also heard Daebong's voice, saying, "Well, I will head off to the stable now." At this, she stood up at once, brought the mule to its feet, and then took the broom and a basket and went behind the millstone.

"What are you doing, standing here?" Daebong asked Hyeonggeol, standing behind him with a smile on his face.

"The mule is turning the millstone, the donkey is off to another village, and there is only the white horse left here . . . so, did you get to ride the bike?" Hyeonggeol regained his senses and turned to face Daebong.

"The bike, how could I ride the bike? Let's take the horse out to Visiting Immortal Gate. Let's at least ride him."

Hyeonggeol and Daebong finally went to the stable. Hyeonggeol entered the stable, untied the horse, and gave the reins to Daebong, and then he took down the saddle and put it on the horse's back. He tightened the girth around the horse's belly and took back the reins, and then Daebong said, in a low voice, "Hey, let's go back to Chilseong's house tonight. Chilseong's wife seemed to be a bit lonely, so I told her that we would be visiting her tonight."

Daebong was so dogged and affable it was absurd, and Hyeonggeol looked at his grinning face for a while before he finally said, "I don't want to. I'm not going."

"Why, is something going on? Do you have someone waiting for you tonight?"

Hyeonggeol just led the white horse out into the yard without a reply.

8

Leisure, if it goes on too long, becomes tedium. In the prime of youth, when a young man feels he could defeat even a tiger, he might spend a long day or two loafing about the house if he is not charged with a specific task, but if that time stretches without end into months and years, it becomes an unavoidable ennui that ensnares his youthful flesh.

When Hyeongjun was in his prime, two years past his twentieth birthday, he had nothing to do.

He would, on occasion, ride his horse around the fields, follow the threshers around at harvest time, accompany the old man from Pyeongyang, and go fishing from time to time, and, if he felt like it, take a turn at falconry in the winter, but this was all he did for the entire year.

Yet, going to the farmers' huts at harvest time to distribute the threshed grain or touring the fields after the rainy season were not his full-time jobs. Others were hired to take care of these things. So when work was busy and hands were few, he would go out if he felt like it, as one might go on a picnic.

As he could not oversee even such trivial things as these, it was only natural that he could not involve himself in any other household task. Work that he could do if he pleased or just as easily let be, work that he did simply to pass the time . . . these things did not have the power to tame his youthful vigor.

If only he could take charge of one area of the household, whether it be land, money, business, or whatever, there had to be some task for which he could take responsibility, but Assistant Curator Bak had not yet given his consent to his eldest son. When he thought back to his own youth, it wasn't as if Hyeongjun was still too young, but there was just something youthful about him that made him seem weak and unreliable, and Assistant Curator Bak himself was still too young to entrust his son with his business. He was now only just forty, and no matter how much he took on, he still had vigor and wit to spare, so there was no need for him to rely on his childish son.

Assistant Curator Bak had taken charge of the household before the age of twenty, and his success at righting the listing family ship at such a young age was due in no small part to the era and also to Bak's personality, but his father, Bak Sunil, had long since abandoned his responsibilities to the household, spent his time away from home, and devoted all of his energies to wasting the family fortune, so, from a young age, Assistant Curator Bak had already mastered all tasks great and small.

Yet Hyeongjun had always been different in character from his father, and his environment and circumstances were completely different from his father's as well. He had had no jobs other than the trivial tasks his father had left him, which he undertook simply to pass the time, and even in those tasks he had numerous menials, servants, and hired hands beneath him, so there was absolutely nothing at all for him to do.

If Hyeongjun had not been the eldest son, if he had not been the heir who was responsible for inheriting the household, then he could have been given some farmland and founded his own household, or he could have been charged with some other task and made his living that way, but this was his lot, and his destiny was tied to this house.

On top of that, Hyeongjun could not spend money freely. Because he had no business of his own in which to earn or spend money, every penny that he spent had to come from his father or mother. He lacked nothing in food or clothes, and he did not live on his own, nor was there anything that he needed to buy from the outside world, so he had no particular need of spending money. In addition, he had never taken up drinking or any sort of hobby, so he had never really needed any money.

Born the eldest son of a well-to-do family, he had not fallen into drinking, women, or gambling, even at such an advanced age as twenty, in part because his affection for his wife had not yet begun to wane, but also because there was no one fit to be his companion in these activities. As his father was still in his forties, those who were just a little older than Hyeongjun were his father's friends, while those just a little younger than him were Hyeongseon or Hyeonggeol's friends. If there had been a companion the same age as him, they certainly would have gotten along and gone around together, but unfortunately there had been no such fellow as of yet. No matter how wearisome and lonely the night grew, he gave no thought at all to leaving the house.

But it had already been four or five years since he had gained a wife, and the sweet dreams he had had around the time of his marriage had already faded, as his wife, who was now the mother of a son and a daughter, was inevitably lacking in numerous yet subtle ways as the object of this man's unchanging passion or attraction. Her once-firm muscles had lost their suppleness, and her breasts, which had always hung low like two melons, had sagged even further while she raised their two children and, like her lower belly, had lost their buxom smoothness and were now splotched and wrinkled with fat. Her eyebrows and hair had grown especially thin, and her teeth seemed to poke through her gaunt cheeks. In addition, she had to play the role of eldest daughter-in-law, she was pestered incessantly, and when night came she fell asleep after only a few turns of the spinning wheel. Even her husband's affection must have been a nuisance to her, as she never seemed to be satisfied. Hyeongjun got the sense that his feelings toward her were definitely changing with the coming of spring. He grew agitated over nothing in particular, he was restless to no end, and at times he even vaguely felt cruelty and violence welling up from deep in his heart.

Unsure of what exactly it was that these feelings of his demanded, he had discussed in detail with his father opening up a large general store, one that would bring together a number of shops, shops like Nakanishi's store, Chilseong's grocery, and Yong-gu's cookie store, but his father did not give his approval, saying that it was too early for something like that. For a long while, Hyeongjun just crouched there, unsure of what his father meant, whether he meant that it was too early to run a business as one's vocation or that it was too early for Hyeongjun himself to try his hand at something like that.

"I don't think that running a business is beneath us. But all things considered, it is still too early to open up a shop alongside

Chilseong across the street or Nakanishi. Also, I have lent some money to Chilseong, so I think it would be best for now to wait and see what happens."

Assistant Curator Bak thought that the wisest policy was to limit his business to money lending. As long as he lent money, he believed that, when he needed them, fields, houses, and businesses would all be his. So he thought of Chilseong's business as his own. Chilseong might even expand his business into a general store in the future, but Bak thought it would be worth watching to see just how long his store would last in the face of the rapidly multiplying interest. He could have his fill of the interest and then take over the store, or he could leave the store as it was, collect the interest, and be Chilseong's savior. There was a reason, after all, that he thought there was no need to bow to others and start a business himself.

After his father had eaten and gone off to the Dumutgol house, Hyeongjun lit the lamps in his father's room and sat idly on the cushion where his father had been sitting. The stationery chest and closet had been locked. Assistant Curator Bak mostly left his documents in this closet and stationery chest in the main house, while he kept his cash hidden deep in a small room in the Dumutgol house. But when he left his room in the main house, no matter where he was, he always locked everything.

Hyeongjun sat there for a while, until he heard the sound of the large front gate being locked out in the yard.

"Who is there?" he asked in a dignified voice.

"It's me," Ssangne's quiet voice answered. After the sound of the door closing, for some time there was no sound at all from outside. She was standing there for a moment, waiting with her hand still on the door handle, to see if there would be some order or command. But no other sound came from the men's quarters. Only the light of the lamp was red in the rice paper window.

After some time, Hyeongjun heard the loud thud of someone stepping down onto the stone step, followed by shoes shuffling across the yard. The steps grew more and more distant until they could finally be heard no more. Ssangne had gone behind the outhouse, past the water's edge, and returned to her room.

Hyeongjun sat for a while longer on the cushion. He vaguely realized that Ssangne had locked the front gate and thought, 'There will be no one else coming into my house tonight.'

'Duchil has gone on a trip to Hoechang to collect money.' He thought back on Duchil's trip. It was just yesterday evening, at around this time, after Assistant Curator Bak had pushed back the dinner table, that he called Duchil and told him to make a trip to Hoechang. "I've written down twenty nyang as traveling expenses. The road is long and the donkey has had nothing to do, so ride him and leave early. You must bring back the money this time, so bring the donkey into his house and set up camp there until he pays you. What a despicable fellow! To put me off like that. Who lends money at four percent interest these days . . . doesn't he know I showed him kindness?"

With these words he told Duchil that he absolutely had to bring back the money this time, even if it meant ruining the man's house. On the following day — that is, that morning — Ssangne had gone out with the donkey's feed at sunrise, and, as the sun rose, Duchil rode the donkey out of the great front gate and left for Hoechang.

'It might take two, or even three or four days.'

Hyeongjun shot up, locked all of the doors, and put out the lights. He went to the room of the old man from Pyeongyang and found him tying his nets, mumbling that he was going to go out early in the morning to cast them.

"Let's play a game of janggi," said Hyeongjun, and the old man, with his bent back and topknot nearly white as a cocoon on his head, put down his net and took out the janggi board and the bag with the pieces inside.

But they had not even played half a match when Hyeongjun grew tired of the game. He had not even started the game because he had wanted to play. It had been awkward sitting all by himself in the empty men's quarters, but there was not really anywhere else for him to get some air, so he had decided to go back to his room and turn in early. Yet his heart was restless, so he ended up not doing that. He vaguely felt, deep down inside, that something he had only thought about for a long time might happen tonight. So he had to somehow pass the time until that moment came. He thought about helping the old man from Pyeongyang with his nets, but then he had seen the janggi board and idly thought about playing a game, and so he chose to go with the janggi.

But the same was not true for the old man from Pyeong-yang. Tonight he had planned to fix his nets and go to bed early so that he could go out to the river before dawn, and he was working as quickly as he could when the young master came in and stood there blankly for a while before proposing a game of janggi. At first the old man thought about how busy he was, and about games of janggi played beneath the shade of trees by people who were at lei-sure to complain about their lot in life — he started playing out of a sense of obligation, not really wanting to take part, but as he was now past fifty, nearing sixty, in fact, and had no real hobbies but for playing janggi, once they began he found himself with an appetite for the game. He squinted at the janggi board in the dim lamplight; the movements of the horses, the straight lines of the chariots, the jumping cannons, the elephants and their L-shaped moves, and the little guards and soldiers following at close quarters . . . yet for some reason the young master moved his pieces to the most obvious spots and let them be captured.

The board was in complete disarray. The young master would move his horse directly in front of his opponent's chariot or put his cannon in a position from which it would have to retreat the very next move, something he would have seen if he had just been think-ing a single move ahead.

The old man would say, "Check," and, without any thought for what came next, the young master would hastily block this and say, "Escape." A game so lopsided was no fun at all, so he even tried to give the young master some advice. "But that's right in the path of my chariot."

"Ah, this just isn't working. Let's stop." The young master swept the many pieces still left off the board and then leaned back with his hands on the straw floor mat.

"Are you not having fun?" asked the old man from Pyeongyang with a smile. He put each of the pieces back inside the bag, hung the bag in its place, propped the janggi board up against the rear wall, and then went back to mending his nets. He must not have given another thought to the young master as he lay there, staring up at the rafters jutting out like ribs from the ceiling plastered with fine gray loam, because he did not even glance at him. Instead, he sat there fixing the net knots as if he had completely forgotten that he had stopped his work to play janggi with the young master. His hair was white, but his face was tanned dark from years in the sun. An old, red chest sat alone by itself against the loam-plastered wall, and atop that rested the old man's thin bedding and blanket, along with the sweat-stained wooden pillow and the stuffed pillow. The only other objects in the room were four or five nets that hung on the wall, and a single bamboo hat for summer use; the old man sat as tranquil as a picture in their midst, with the net frame in front of him. Hyeongjun could not lie there long in that sort of air or that sort of atmosphere. The scent of an old man mingled with the scent of a widower and, on top of that, the smell of water and the reek of fish. An anxious young heart lying amidst this scenery only felt more suffocated and oppressed.

Hyeongjun left the old man's room and returned to his own. Before he entered his room, he stopped and listened, cocking an ear toward the room across from his, where Hyeongseon and his wife sat with the light on, Hyeongseon reading a book and his wife perhaps mending socks, or maybe the two of them were both reading books, as he heard low voices chatting now and then, and finally he turned to look toward his mother's large room. Hyeongsik and Bo-pae must have fallen asleep, but the light still shone red. The whirring sound of the spinning wheel must be the old servant, but then he heard a soft coughing from his mother, so she must have been spinning silk thread or sewing something.

The night was still young.

He opened the door to his room and went inside. His wife must have fallen asleep, holding their daughter in her arms in the warm part of the room, with the light still lit. Next to them was his son, Seonggi, and Hyeongjun's bedding had been laid out at the other end of the room.

His wife opened her sleepy eyes when he entered, and she squinted at her husband as he stood in the center of the room, but then she rubbed her eyes a few times and turned back to her daughter. This was because the child had started whimpering when her mother's breast had suddenly been plucked from her mouth. She soothed the baby by mumbling something to her and went back to sleep herself.

Hyeongjun sat down in his place and watched his wife as she slept. He was bored just sitting there, so he put his pipe in his mouth. He had only taken a few puffs when Seonggi, who had been sleeping between them, began to cough harshly. So he put out the pipe and quietly opened the door to let the smoke out.

He lay down with his clothes still on. The sound of the spinning wheel from the room across the way had stopped. The sound of chatting voices from Hyeongseon's room had faded as well. He heard only the sound of his children breathing, mingled with the snores of his wife.

Hyeongjun put out the light. It was dark. The yard was black as well. Everyone must have put out the lights in their rooms and gone to bed. As he lay there in the darkness, all the things that had been just vague thoughts played out before his eyes — Duchil's wife Ssangne, her face, her breasts, her buttocks.

Hyeongjun sat up like a bolt in his bed and opened the door to the room without a sound. He went out, closed the door, and stood there outside for some time, and only after he heard the sound of breathing and snoring from inside the room did he step down into the yard.

The black dog that had been sleeping beneath the wooden ledge crawled out, shook itself, and then stood in front of Hyeongjun, wagging its tail.

"Shoo," he scolded softly, and the dog backed away from him, but then it bounded off breathlessly toward the central gate. Hyeongjun feared that anyone not fast asleep would be startled awake by the sound, so when he passed the other rooms he made a low coughing sound.

He went to the central gate and lifted the bar, without making a sound, and then he opened the door just wide enough for a single body to pass through; he knew that if he opened it just a little wider it would make an ear-piercing creak. The dog understood its master's intentions, squeezed through the door, and ran out into the yard of the men's quarters before running back to Hyeongjun and sniffing around quietly.

"Shoo. Shoo!" After scolding and thus quieting the dog, he went around behind the toilet, passed by the stables, and headed for the rear gate by the water's edge.

The sky was pale, with stars here and there studding the darkness, which stretched down to the undulating crags of the twelve peaks. He put his hand on the millet-stalk fence and stood there for a moment. A short way off was the tightly shut rear gate, and next to that the kitchen of the humble annex where Duchil lived. He thought about Ssangne, lying fast asleep right now in that room.

At last, Hyeongjun realized that there was no reason for him to hesitate here, grasping the fence. He strode bravely forward, as if he had thoroughly steeled himself. But as he drew closer to the room, the sound of his footfalls grew softer and his steps grew slower.

He finally stood in front of the kitchen door. Now all he had to do was put his hand on the latch, pull it back, go inside, and then open the inner door. But such a simple and straightforward action was not as easy as he thought it would be. He hesitated, putting his hand on the latch and then taking it off again, and then he tensed his arm and pulled, but surprisingly the door was locked from the inside.

Damn. He took his hand away and then stood there for a moment to calm himself. His heart had already boiled over and the froth had since settled back down, while the blood had drained from his face.

Why was the door locked? But when he thought about it, he realized that they might always go to sleep with the door locked from the inside. Even if they did not always lock the door like this, as Duchil was not home, she might have gone inside, hastily shut the door behind her, and lowered the floor bolt into the stone sill. Thus there was no need to think it strange that the door was locked, and all he had to do was shake the door a few times and give a soft command: "Open the kitchen door." Then, no matter how deeply asleep she may have been, she would open her sleep-filled eyes, and though at first she might wonder who wanted her to open the door in the middle of the night, she would then realize that the rattling sound was coming from the kitchen door, that the one who spoke the command was from her master's house, and that, judging by his voice, he was the eldest son. As she tied up her jacket, wrapped her skirt around her, touched up her hair, and otherwise bustled about, he would once more urge, "Open the door quickly," and she would fall over herself to open the door. Then he would follow her into the kitchen, grasp her wrist and lead her into the room, and then one thing would lead to another and that would be that. As he thought about all these things and was about to reach out to rattle the door, he thought he heard the sound of murmured voices.

Hyeongjun stopped for a moment, thinking at first that he might have been startled by the beating of his own heart, but no, the pounding of his pulse in his chest was as it had been all along. What, then? Might not Ssangne be mumbling in her sleep? He strained to listen again, but the voices had already stopped.

Out of nowhere, the black dog sniffed around his toes. He pushed it away with his heel and put his hand on the latch, but this time he definitely heard a man's voice come from inside the room. He didn't know what was being said, but the words were short, and it was clearly the voice of a man. But whose voice was it? There was no doubt that it wasn't Duchil's.

But if it wasn't Duchil, who on earth was the man lying there with Ssangne in the darkness, with not a single light lit?

Hyeongjun stood still for a moment, then he came to a different decision than the one that had first brought him to stand in front of this room. He backed away a few steps and then, deliberately stepping loudly, went back to the rear gate, lifted the bar, and went into the yard by way of the riverside path. He cleared his throat and made as if to shout at Ssangne, but then the door opened and a young man suddenly emerged from the darkness.

9

Assistant Curator Bak was able to have an extraordinarily enjoyable morning. This was because the day had finally come for Bak Rigyun and his brother—who had interfered in all of Assistant Curator Bak's matters, both big and small, and who had opposed him to his face and behind his back for the twenty years since he had first come to this village—to completely submit to him.

Hyeonggeol's mother, Lady Yun, had left her husband's room in the Dumutgol house early and was now in the women's quarters there, cooking fish that had been caught by the old man from Pyeongyang—she had seasoned the fish with soy sauce, and when the soy sauce boiled, she told a servant to bring the sweet black syrup that had been put in the storehouse—while Assistant Curator Bak was still asleep, alone in his bed.

But then, from the main gate came a voice: "Has Assistant Curator Bak woken yet?" It was clearly either Bak Rigyun or his younger brother, as the intermediary, Mr. Kim, had reached a rough agreement with the assistant curator last night in the men's quarters, saying that he would send either Bak Rigyun or Bak Seonggyun in person the next morning.

Assistant Curator Bak heard the voice but, even though he guessed who it was, did not get up from his bed and instead lay there with his head on his pillow until the servant boy Samnam went out to the main gate and came back with the message.

He got up with some effort, threw on his clothes, folded his bedding in half and pushed it to the back of the room, and then he opened the door of the room to let in some fresh air.

"Tell him to come in." With this, he coughed twice, as was his habit, and then he rinsed his mouth out with the rice water by his bedside and spat it out into the spittoon. He sat down on the cushion in the warm part of the room and picked up his pipe, and he was about to pack it with finely cut tobacco when Bak Rigyun came in, saying, "My apologies for coming so early." He was over fifty now, and his hair was peppered with white beneath his plain sheer cap, while his long, thin face, which showed signs of paucity and want, looked rather foolish with its fine lines and yellowed beard.

Assistant Curator Bak thought to himself that it would be quite a sight to see this face red with liquor and endlessly repeating "Lady Seong was the wife of Bak Gwiseong and eldest daughter of Seong Nonsan," but he said, "Please come in. Well, you've got quite a grand plan this time, and anyway it's a good thing to keep up with the times and make your move before everyone else. Let's have a smoke."

Bak Rigyun rustled around, feeling the pockets of his overcoat, clearly looking for the deed to the house, so Assistant Curator Bak again said, "Here, have a smoke," and pushed forward his jade tobacco chest. Bak Rigyun took his hands out of his pockets and packed some tobacco into his pipe. Then he pushed the tobacco chest back, lit his pipe in the brass brazier, and sucked in a few puffs of smoke.

"I heard the gist of things last night from Mr. Kim, so I guess there is not much more to say, is there?" Assistant Curator Bak opened with these words as he leaned on the armrest next to the stationery chest, his pipe in his mouth. He continued, "For the deeds to both houses, four hundred nyang, at six percent interest."

As he cut to the chase like this, Bak Rigyun pulled his pipe from his mouth so suddenly it made a smacking sound, and he forced a laugh out from behind his yellowed, unkempt beard. "That is precisely it, of course," he said, and he quickly bowed his head to Assistant Curator Bak, though the man was ten or so years younger than himself.

Assistant Curator Bak picked up a key and got up to open the rear closet, and Bak Rigyun took from his pocket the two house deeds and the promissory note he had written and fingered them as he sat there.

After looking over the deeds and the check, Assistant Curator Bak placed four hundred nyang in front of Bak Rigyun. "You will have to fix up the houses if they are to be used for the Dano Festival. And let's fix the monument pavilion by Visiting Immortal Gate while we're at it."

He expected these last words to disturb Bak Rigyun, but the man unexpectedly replied, "I thought the same at first, but after giving it some more thought, I have to fix up my house, and there are many things to fix at my brother's house as well, so I don't think there will be enough money. So we'll fix the monument pavilion next time. After all, we have to take care of the dozen or so people living in the two houses first, right?" He was completely humbling himself in order to curry favor with Assistant Curator Bak.

"Of course, what you say is the truth. The monument pavilion doesn't feed and clothe you, does it? At any rate, I think you have made the right decision. From here on out, the inn must follow the new ways as well; you may have been able to attract pack-horse drivers with the stable, but how could you bring in respectable customers? The new road has been built, and the way from Pyeong-yang to Wonsan will be opened soon, so a lot of respectable customers will stop by, and you'll have all of these new gentlemen, like surveyors, stopping by your large inn."

It may have been rather unpleasant to be forced to send Mr. Kim here to negotiate over money, but since it had come to this, there was not much Bak Rigyun could do. He could only leave with a smile on his face, if not in his heart, at least for the sake of his future affairs.

Of course, when the brothers had agreed to borrow money, use the athletics meet to be held during the Dano Festival as an opportunity to fix up Bak Rigyun's house, open up a new-style inn, and repair the dilapidated parts of Seonggyun's ramshackle old house so that they could open a stable and noodle house there, Assistant Curator Bak was not their first thought. Even though none of the many places they visited would give them money, with the houses as collateral, they thought that, without a doubt, they would be able to get some money from Nakanishi, but he turned them down as well, saying that he did not have enough (perhaps because he intended to expand his general store before the athletics meet), and so, in the end, they had no choice but to send someone to Assistant Curator Bak's house.

For his part, Assistant Curator Bak had his own plan. It was clear that both inns and general stores would be successful in the future, but he felt that it was too early for him to open one himself. However, it was also a plain truth that he who made the first move in these things would win in the end, so having others do the hard work while he wielded the real power behind the scenes seemed to be a clever scheme, no matter which way you looked at it.

Thus it was Assistant Curator Bak's plan to come forward when someone said they wanted to open an inn and lend this person an amount of money that would not hurt him, and the ones who ended up flying to him, like moths to a flame, were the Bak brothers.

So now he held the title deeds to both houses, and, with the agreement that one of the houses would be fixed up before the Dano Festival, he had agreed to hand over the four hundred nyang requested by the other party, without shaving off a single penny. If the inn succeeded, he would be busy collecting that much interest, and if the inn was not as successful as he thought it would be, they would lose the house and be carrying beggar's bowls before the year was out. Whatever happened, Assistant Curator Bak was waiting for his chance to bring Bak Rigyun and his brother to their knees.

After he had sent Bak Rigyun away, he ate breakfast, quite satisfied with himself, and there was good reason for this. But, as is often the case in life, after an unexpected stroke of good fortune there sometimes comes an unexpected stroke of ill luck.

After eating breakfast, Assistant Curator Bak sat for some time in his room in the Dumutgol house, putting the documents in order and stacking his checks in a neat pile, then soothing his stomach with honey water to wash away the last of the liquor he had drunk with Mr. Kim the night before, and after this he thought about taking a gill net out in this thoroughly hot weather and perhaps rowing out on the river with the old man from Pyeongyang—it was with these pleasant thoughts in mind that he left Dumutgol and went to the men's quarters of the main house, wearing only his plain sheer cap.

He entered the yard, and the old man from Pyeongyang was hanging up his nets by the corners. "How have you been?" he said in greeting.

"I thought maybe we could go out onto the river today." Assistant Curator Bak had been quite courteous to the old man in recent days, to keep his spirits up.

"Well, Master, how would you like to cast the nets and catch some mandarin fish with me? If I could dive, I would spear the mandarin fish myself, but I'm too old for that now, so why don't we try catching them with little minnows as bait." No doubt, it was a happy occasion for the old man from Pyeongyang to see Assistant Curator Bak in good spirits.

With his pipe in his mouth, Bak took a quick tour around the yard. He went to the mule mill, then to the earthen cellar filled with grain, then to the stable, where he looked at the horses for a while, and next he turned back the other way and looked out beyond the fence onto the vegetable patch that had been planted there and the fruit trees with their green leaves, before finally going all the way to the back gate and at last coming back to the yard of the men's quarters. Everything was peaceful. The cow was out plowing the fields, the mule was hulling rice in the mill, and Duchil's wife, Ssangne, was working next to the winnower with a towel on her head and covered in husks and dust — and since he was in such a pleasant mood, he passed through the central gate and looked around the inner yard as well. His daughters-in-law greeted him. His first wife greeted him as well. His grandson ran out into the yard. Bak was not the type to readily hug children. But today was somehow different, and when Seonggi came walking out, he picked him up at once, went through the large gate, and passed out into the backyard. There was a large apricot tree by the bramble hedge, beneath the tree was a bundle of straw decorated with white paper for the god of the house, the god of the earth, or some such spirit, and all around that irises were in full bloom. A laundry line woven from hair was supported by posts along its length, and it ran from the eaves on one side to the eaves on the other side, like a crossbeam. In the distance, he could see the green buds of the peonies and magnolias ready to bloom. The light of the sun in these days between late spring and early summer poured down, brilliant and full, into the yard.

"How much have you been eating, little fellow? . . . Baba baba bababa."

Bak mumbled at his grandson and then went back into the central yard.

"Oof. He's too heavy for me to carry," he said and put Seong-gi down on the stone step.

"Seonggi, you're living in luxury today. You got carried around by Grandpa!" His grandmother, who had leaned Hyeongsik down against the doorsill, waved her hand at the child, while Hyeongjun's wife stood in the kitchen door. They stood there like that until Bak walked out through the central gate.

After taking a walk around the house, both inside and out, and seeing with his own eyes that all was calm and content, Assistant Curator Bak was even more pleased, and he thought that he would take the punt out on the river, catch some fish, and have a drink with some red pepper paste stew; he saw to his stationery chest, bookshelves, and the closet, and he was just about to change into more comfortable clothes. Just then, though, his eldest son, Hyeongjun, appeared in his room and knelt before him, saying that he had something to tell him in private.

Bak had untied his ankle bands and was changing his socks. "Very well, what is it you want to say?"

To himself, he thought, 'I wonder if he is going to tell me that he plans on opening a general store, as he mentioned not too long ago. If he does, I will tell him in detail how Bak Rigyun put up his house as collateral to borrow some money, and even how he plans to open a large traveler's inn instead of the inn and stable, and then I will admonish him to continue to look after our household affairs for another few years.'

But, to his surprise, Hyeongjun opened by asking, "How are things going with Hyeonggeol's marriage?"

'It is only right for the eldest brother to worry about the marriage of a brother who has no wife at his age. I wonder if he has found a suitable woman somewhere,' thought Bak to himself, and he replied, "We are still looking into it."

"Is it because there are no women from suitable families?"

"Well, in a word, that is not far from the truth. Why, do you have a proper family in mind?"

"No. I'm just concerned that you might miss the proper time or be brought to some disgrace, if you spend too much time choosing the right woman."

"It's not that we are choosing the right woman, just that it is only reasonable to avoid too lowly a woman." Bak then lowered his voice. "His situation is different from yours, you know. There don't seem to be any families worth marrying that will take us, only families that look on us from afar, and we have to think of our good name and so cannot just go around begging. So we are still looking around here and there."

Even after hearing his father's explanation, Hyeongjun did not leave but sat there without moving for quite some time. Assistant Curator Bak wanted to get up and go to the women's quarters, where he would let them know that he was going fishing and that they should prepare lunch and bring it out to the punt, but when he caught a glimpse of Hyeongjun's face, he saw that he was mumbling to himself as if there was something more he wanted to say. So Bak straightened up again and looked at his son.

"It's just that Hyeonggeol will bring us shame if we don't take care of him. Late last night, I was taking a walk around the yard, and I saw Hyeonggeol come out of Duchil's room." Having tattled on his brother in a single breath, Hyeongjun lowered his head for a moment. He could not help thinking that "a walk around the yard" was a simple enough explanation, but in that one phrase there were actually more complications than he dared to mention.

Of course, Assistant Curator Bak was not a little startled by this news. Even without an explanation, it was clear what Hyeongjun meant when he said that he saw Hyeonggeol come out of Ssangne's room in the middle of the night, when Duchil was not there. Bak said nothing for a while.

Hyeongjun must have been encouraged by his father's reaction, for he went on to say, "So I grabbed him and told him that talk of marriage was flooding in from all directions, and I asked him what he thought would happen if he behaved himself like this, and he just stood there quietly and then asked what business it was of mine. So I told him it was late and that he should go to bed, and I thought of scolding Duchil's wife, but then I figured that covering it up would make it less shameful, so I just left it alone."

Bak listened to his son quietly, and as soon as Hyeongjun finished talking, he said, "Very well. Now go look after your own affairs." Then he turned his head toward the door to the inner yard.

Having started his tale, Hyeongjun had been about to continue talking, but, at his father's words, he felt ashamed and simply replied with a soft, "Yes," and then he slid the door to the inner yard open and went out.

After Hyeongjun left, Assistant Curator Bak sat in stunned silence for a moment and then changed back into the clothes he had just changed out of.

The old man from Pyeongyang came up onto the wooden ledge and opened the door, as if to urge him to hurry, but Bak said, "Something has suddenly come up, so I don't think I will be able to go. Let's go tomorrow."

Bak was not a little displeased about what had just happened. The old man from Pyeongyang had come in with a smile on his face to see about going out in the punt, but, having been rejected and not having any idea why, he was a little embarrassed and shut the door again. As he was carrying his nets and pole out to where the punt was, he saw Assistant Curator Bak hurry out of the main gate wearing only his plain sheer cap, and he thought that, indeed, something had come up.

Bak plucked his pipe from his mouth and waved it about, then he turned down the alley leading to the Confucian school, took the side road by the dry fields, and arrived at Dumutgol at once. It was, of course, after Hyeonggeol had gone to school.

But Bak had not come back to the Dumutgol house to call Hyeonggeol and rebuke him, nor did he want to find out the truth of what had happened or anything like that. So it didn't matter whether Hyeonggeol was there or not.

But when he came in through the front gate and realized that he had come all the way back to Dumutgol, he realized that his behavior had been rather unbecoming. He had canceled a fishing trip and rushed over to Dumutgol all because of this matter, and when he thought about it he could not help but feel embarrassed. That his son had entered the room of a menial — even if it was true, as Hyeongjun had said — was no reason for him to hurry about as if some great disaster had occurred.

And, for that matter, he did not want to go straight into his room. In truth, he had run here to hastily discuss with his concubine all matters relating to Hyeonggeol's marriage, but that sort of thing would not work out just because he rushed it, and there wasn't really that much of a hurry anyway.

In truth, the motivation behind his strange behavior, which even he himself could not make sense of, was his anger at having a pleasant morning suddenly ruined. He had listened to Hyeongjun, and his son's concern that they were being too particular about Hyeonggeol's wife sounded like nothing more than an impertinent criticism of his taking a concubine, and that did not sit right with him. But it would have been too awkward to criticize Hyeongjun for speaking his mind, and his aimless fury had sought some sort of outlet and thus had naturally caused him to run hastily down the road to Dumutgol.

So he walked about the yard as if he were searching for something he had lost, and after poking his head in here and there, he went straight back out the main gate. Then, in case any one saw him, he puffed away at his pipe, clamped his left hand into a fist and put it behind his back, and then passed by the stream next to Nine Dragons Bridge and walked back onto the main road, as if he had just eaten breakfast at Dumutgol and was now on his way to the main house.

This was after the old man from Pyeongyang had gone out to the river. So he told his servants to send out lunch in a basket, absentmindedly picked up a net and went toward the rear gate by the water's edge. Before he reached the rear gate, though, he met Duchil's wife, Ssangne, as she came out of her room and into the yard. It was the second time he had seen her that day, but after hearing what Hyeongjun had to say, she somehow appeared different from before. And for some reason she turned red and bowed her head lower than usual as she made way for him.

"You should have lunch ready by now, so bring it out to where the punt is," he said, as if everything were normal.

Ssangne replied, "Yes," but when she disappeared around the corner, Bak pondered on how he had spoken as usual but hesitated a little inside.

'At first she was a servant girl, then she lived as the wife of a hired hand, and now . . . yes, now she is my third son's mistress,' he thought, but strangely enough he did not attribute this turn of events to Hyeonggeol's misbehavior. He did not suddenly feel any displeasure toward Hyeonggeol, the source of this trouble. As he went down to the river's edge, Bak strove to clear his mind of these distracting, troublesome thoughts, and he shaded his eyes and looked down from the embankment to where the punt was and yelled, "Old man, bring the punt in for a moment! I want to go, too!"

The punt had left the bank and was just about to enter the rapids where the fishing grounds were. The old man turned his head and the bamboo hat atop it in the direction of the voice, and when he saw that it was Assistant Curator Bak, he wordlessly turned the boat around and rowed toward the stake on the riverbank. Bak watched this and then came down from the embankment and slowly walked to meet the punt at Cheongpa Hill.

"So, did you take care of your affairs?" asked the old man, grinning as he grasped the pole with one hand and greeted Assistant Curator Bak, but Bak put his net in the boat without replying and then climbed in himself. Only then did he say, "I've seen to them," and he went into the center of the boat. When he saw the old man about to push off again, he said, "Wait a moment. I've told them to give us some liquor and something to make soup, and someone is coming down now."

He saw Ssangne descending from the embankment toward them, carrying something in a basket.

The sun was hot, but the wind, as it swept across the Biryu River while they fished, was cool.

Bak boiled some mandarin fish soup on the spot and ate it with his liquor, and he returned to Dumutgol feeling rather tipsy. It was an early summer night, long after darkness had fallen, but the weather had grown cloudy in the evening, and the air was sultry and stifling, as if it might rain during the night.

He went into the men's quarters to find his concubine, Lady Yun, waiting there with the lamp lit, having already laid out the bedding.

"What did you have for dinner?"

"We boiled some of the mandarin fish that we caught. Say, did they bring back any of the other fish?"

"I boiled two mandarin fish with some young catfish and gave that to Hyeonggeol, and I boiled some goby minnows and long-nosed barbels in soy sauce."

Bak took off his socks, and then he picked up his glass of water and began gulping it down. "If you're thirsty, I can bring some omija tea or honey water," suggested his wife.

Bak drank for some time and then asked, "Is Hyeonggeol at home?"

"A little while ago he said he was going out to get some air."

"He went out again?" A somewhat displeased look passed over Bak's face. Then he backtracked and asked, "What time did he come in last night?"

"I'm not sure. Probably before midnight."

Bak said nothing in response to Lady Yun's reply and sat there looking blankly at the lamplight for some time. Not yet forty, Lady Yun still had a young and beautiful figure and eyes. She could not understand why her husband was displeased today, but she said, "Let's go to sleep. Here, take off this cap and lie down." She took off the cap and placed it on the stationery chest, then she undid his vest and untied his belt for him. "The sun must have been hot. You've burned."

But Assistant Curator Bak sat there and gave no thought to lying down or to answering Lady Yun, and then he abruptly asked about Hyeonggeol again. "You have no idea where Hyeonggeol goes out at night?"

"I don't know. He's probably out with his classmates in the mountains or maybe at his teacher's house."

Bak lay down in bed. But then he sat back up and took a drink of water. Lady Yun asked, "Shall I light your pipe?" But he did not answer, instead asking, "Is there any news from that family in Cheongsiul?"

"Before the sun went down today a matchmaker came by, and she said that she hadn't said anything to the family yet but that there was a good chance, although I don't like either the family or the girl."

"Why, what's wrong with this family?"

"What do you mean, what's wrong? It is a family that has suffered ill fortune and is in decline."

"Whether they have ill fortune or are declining, all that matters is if the girl is a good fit. We're not planning on living off the family, are we?"

"Well, it's easy to say that all that matters is the girl, regardless of the state of the family, but if her family is too poor we will have all sorts of difficulties, won't we? In any case, I don't know if the girl is mild-mannered, but I hear that she has no skill at weaving and isn't all that clever, and the fortune-teller says they aren't compatible anyway."

"They aren't compatible? Then the marriage is no good."

That she couldn't weave or that she did not look too clever, these were problems he could work around, and he could point out that the family's declining fortunes were no more than a trifling matter, but, though he did not know the details himself, if they were not compatible then there was nothing even Assistant Curator Bak could do. So he inquired in more detail, "How exactly are they not compatible?"

"Their birth years are rabbit and snake, so they will not be drawn to each other, and when you bring the five elements into it things get even worse."

Bak listened as he took a few puffs of the pipe Lady Yun had given him, and then he handed back the pipe and lay down in bed. Lady Yun covered him lightly with the quilted blanket and asked, "Shall I turn off the light?"

"If Hyeonggeol comes home tonight, tell him that he is not to leave the house again at night," Bak answered and closed his eyes.

"Why? Has he been going someplace he shouldn't?" Lady Yun turned a little pale as she asked this question. Bak wanted to leave it at that, not really wanting to tell her the truth, and he wavered for a while before he said, "He's been seeing Duchil's wife . . . why her, of all the women out there?"

Before he had even finished talking, Lady Yun said in surprise, "What are you talking about? Hyeonggeol is going out to see the wife of a hired hand? Where did you hear such slander? He would never do a thing like that! Do you know it to be true?"

"It's true, that's all you need to know. There's no need to bandy words over it."

Assistant Curator Bak turned over and let out a long sigh that smelled of liquor. Lady Yun sat there beside him, moving her lips as if to say something.

10

Not long after Assistant Curator Bak had brought his family from Eunsan to Dumutgol, bought a large house by the main road, and set up two households — one for his wife and one for his concubine — Bak Rigyun's wife, his sister-in-law, and the gossipy old woman from next door stopped by the Dumutgol house on their way back from the shrine to the village god to see what Assistant Curator Bak's concubine, Lady Yun, looked like. The gossipy old woman, after looking Lady Yun up and down, came back having discovered two facts: namely, that she had been married at the age of seventeen and that she had borne her first son at the age of eighteen, and to this the old woman added all sorts of nonsense, going around spreading rumors that, when Assistant Curator Bak Seonggwon was in his prime, he won her in a game of cards, stealing another man's new bride.

At the time, the people of this village said that this was not a very reliable tale, being the prattling of an old woman famous for her gossip, and yet, out of jealousy, they ultimately ended up accepting it is as the truth. If someone had later looked into his history, they could have related something that was somewhat closer to the truth, but over the course of ten or fifteen years his children grew up and Assistant Curator Bak himself became a native of this village, so people's curiosity faded and no one sought to find out anything about Lady Yun's history.

Lady Yun — her name as a child had been Tansil — had, in fact, been married to a man in the town of Suncheon at the age of sixteen. Her family was part of the Papyeong Yun Clan, located in a small village about five li from the town of Jasan. They were, at first, a fine, well-to-do family, which wielded some influence, but in later years their fortunes declined, the family suddenly fell on hard times, and, with the changing political situation, they were worse off than ever. Perhaps it was because of her family's ill fortune at that time, but not even a half-year after she was married, her husband, during the rainy season, went out onto the waters by Changmal to catch fish with a scoop net and was drowned in the strong currents. She had never gotten along with her mother-in-law to begin with, and after this occurred her mother-in-law mocked her, saying that she had brought the ghost of King Suro into their family, and with the entire family tormenting her she had no choice but to pack up her things and move from Suncheon back to her family near Jasan.

At her parents' home lived her old parents, her sister-in-law, and their two children, but her brother had taken ill several years ago and died suddenly. Some said that some old spirit or the spirit of a deceased king had been awakened, so they slaughtered a large pig, held a shamanic ritual, and even faithfully carried the newly spun thread on the first day of the rabbit in the new year to ward off ill fortune, but the household never recovered and things just gradually grew worse. Her parents' hope rested entirely on their only son, a ten-year-old boy, and their two grandchildren, but they did not want to see their eldest daughter-in-law grow old as a woman widowed in her youth, and now their daughter had been widowed as well, bringing great worry to the household.

On the evening of the day their daughter Tansil had packed up her things in Suncheon, climbed into a shabby palanquin, and arrived home through the front gate, her mother simply cried in her room, while her father, known as the scholar Yun, had heard that she was coming and was not even at home, having gone out to spend the entire day drinking.

But with the household in such disarray, the two widowed sisters-in-law did not have a very good relationship. Since they shared the same fate, they should have comforted and helped each other, but whether because of their personalities or their tempers, they did not get along, the one cantankerous, and the other, Tansil—though it is no surprise that at the age of seventeen she was not yet mature—constantly complaining and taking offense at everything, so, especially when the two of them were together in the kitchen, they would clash.

These clashes were not over anything serious; they were just differences of opinion on trivial things, like what to put in stews, how to wipe down the table, how to flip vegetable griddle cakes, or how to sew, and at first they would grumble at each other and then not speak to each other at all, at least until they found something else to find fault with and raised their voices again. When these complaints at last reached their mother's ears there would be a reckoning, and if they somehow reached the ears of the old Yun, there would be such an uproar that the household would be turned upside down.

With Yun already angry and unable to put his mind at ease, the commotion in his household pushed him over the edge, and, on rare occasions, he would let his temper flare and bellow at them, at times even shouting that their world had collapsed around them, so each should leave home and go their separate ways.

In the end, her father would say whatever horrible things came to mind, such as, "How pathetic a bastard would I have to be to put up with hectoring from my daughter-in-law and my daughter?" or, "You nags, if you had done right by this house, do you think you would have killed off your strong young husbands and become wretched young widows?!" After shouting like this for a while, he would go out for a drink somewhere, and her mother would go into her room and rain down imprecations. Half of what she said was wailing. Then her sister-in-law would go into her room, hold her children, and start crying as well, while Tansil herself would go into her room and sniffle away her tears. But this was not the end of the uproar. There was no way there could ever be peace when Yun came home drunk. When he came in through the door, he threw to the ground whatever he could lay his hands on. He meant to destroy the house and kill everyone with his bare hands. When the cries of the children rang within and without, her mother would at last grasp hold of her father to hold him back, and the young women would rub their hands together, begging him to forgive them of the horrible sins.

Then her father would grab her innocent mother and yell loud enough to shake the tiles off the roof: "You old hag, if only you had brought them up properly our household would not have come to this! You doomed this household from the start, having children and then raising them poorly!"

"Yes, it is all my fault. But what can we do? Please calm down. The children have said that they were wrong and that they will behave in the future, so please be patient just for today." Her mother would cringe before the old man and finally get him to lie down.

This was how Tansil became a young widow and lived with her parents, and just when her life had grown wearisome, one day the fresh-faced young Bak Seonggwon came into the men's quarters of their house. Seonggwon's father, Bak Sunil, had lent them three hundred nyang five years before at six percent interest, and Seonggwon had come to settle accounts, saying that none of that amount had been paid.

At the time, Bak Seonggwon was still living in Eunsan. His father, Sunil, had died from opium in Pyeongyang a year before, but before he died he had squandered the family fortune with years of drinking, women, and opium, so when Seonggwon inherited the household when he was just twenty years old, all that was left were some certificates of debt.

People sometimes said that the age of nineteen was an unlucky age, and this was why Bak Seonggwon, who had a bright future still ahead of him, had to see his father, Sunil, die away from home, but for Bak Seonggwon and his family this was actually good fortune, for Sunil had left this world without having caused too many problems for his family. Seeing how relieved both Seonggwon and his wife, Lady Choe, were when his father passed away, others might have reproached them, but, in fact, it was difficult to blame them. For, in truth, had his father gone around to visit the few debtors that were left and tidily gathered up their money, he would have had enough to buy more of that black or white powder, and there would have been no money left for even a funeral; the body would have been wrapped in straw without a coffin and the bereaved would have been out on the streets with begging bowls, at least for the time being. They say that even an ox needs stepping stones to climb a hill, and even someone like Bak Seonggwon would have been able to leave no impression at all with just his two bare hands. He brought the body back from Pyeongyang, had it buried, and observed the year-long mourning period, and when this was over he gathered up his documents and went around to see the debtors. Unlike his father, he was vicious and miserly, and he mercilessly took the debtors to task. What his father had not dared to do for the sake of face and honor, Seonggwon did obstinately with no concern for the thoughts of others.

So it was that Bak Seonggwon came to this house of the Papyeong Yun Clan in Jasan. As soon as he entered the men's quarters, he looked down with contempt at Yun, who was even older than his own father had been. "So, someone dies and there is not so much as a word of condolence from you . . . what sort of ignorant behavior is that?"

In truth, Yun had nothing to say in reply. His own household was in disarray, and there was not a day without some disaster, so he had had no time to spare. Bak Sunil's son was still at a tender age, so Yun had calmly thought that the young man would be as meek as his father and not demand payment of his debt, but after hearing the first thing out of Seonggwon's mouth after he had set foot in the house and introduced himself, the already-agitated Yun was quite startled.

"Well, at least let me tell you about my situation," began Yun, but when he saw the displeased look on Bak Seonggwon's face, he changed his tone. "The very year that your father lent me the money, some gold mine or something went right under, wouldn't you know. After that, what a wretched world it was . . . well, it is embarrassing to talk so openly about my household like this, but..." He continued, "First my younger son got a large boil on his back the month he was to be married, and right before the wedding he was struck down, and then misfortune befell my older son, and finally my daughter, who had just been married, lost her husband and moved back into our house ... well, with our household having reached the end of its fortunes like this, how could I even think of showing my face outside the house? So I stayed home and did not go out, and I avoided visitors as best as I could, thus building up a wall between myself and the rest of the world. When I think about your late father and the bonds of loyalty between us, in such a situation I would not have been overstepping my bounds to immediately rush over and take care of the funeral arrangements myself, but I was just out of my mind. To tell you the truth, I have merely been clinging to this pitiful thing I call a life, but I doubt anyone else would even bother to do that were they in my position. So please do not be too upset by this, things are no different than they were when your father was alive..."

Then he forced a smile across his wrinkled face. But Bak Seonggwon, as he sat there in his mourner's horsehair hat, did not look at him as he replied. "As you know, I am not in a position to listen at leisure to explanations about anyone's situation, with my father passing away as he did — do you think I would go around visiting the houses of others dressed like this otherwise? So, whether you came to pay your respects or not, that is nothing more than something mentioned in passing. I have also been placed in charge of a household with failing fortunes, so I, of course, understand the various situations of others. They say only a widow understands a widow's plight. Coming to pay one's respects, well, what sort of good would that do? It was out of my immaturity that I just came out and scolded you for what I thought of as disgraceful behavior. Anyway, I am still in mourning for my father's death, so I cannot stay long at the houses of others, and thus I must ask you to settle your account, even if you have to draw on your stores of grain."

Bak Seonggwon's words to Yun were as cold as an autumn frost. Even considering his acquaintance with his father, Bak had no right to treat his elder this way, and, whether he was a creditor or not, Yun thought his outrageous words and deeds were disgraceful. Yet he had no choice. To be in debt is to be no different from a criminal, so there was nothing else he could do but swallow his anger and fury and appeal to this young fellow's pity and convince him to show mercy.

"Well, I know it may sound like I am just repeating what I said before, but with my circumstances as they are . . . you said just a moment ago that a widow understands a widow's plight, well, maybe if we wait until the bad fortune leaves and things get a little better . . . ah, I'm terribly sorry to ask you this, but perhaps you could see it in your heart . . . please . . ."

Anyone would have been embarrassed to see the obsequious expression on Yun's lips and around his eyes and in the way he kept bowing his half-whitened head. The way he sat there and kept repeating "please" was truly awkward for Bak Seonggwon as well.

Thus he came up with a plan, deciding that he would not look Yun in the eye but instead rattle off a speech that sounded like it had been prepared in advance, and then he would get up from his seat, return to the town of Jasan, and find a man to send back in his stead.

"Well, there is nothing more to be said about it, just pay the amount with six percent interest for four years and seven months — we'll assume that has been extended once a year. As far as I know, you still have your fields and your house — if you were wretches with nothing left at all, it might be different, but as long as you have something, how can you say you cannot pay your debts? So let's settle your accounts cleanly now, and then later, once you get back on your feet, we will be able to help each other if necessary . . . this way everything will go smoothly, no? I have some business in Jasan Town, so tonight I will either send someone or come back myself. I have made the calculations myself already, so please take a look at the documents."

As soon as he said these words, Bak Seonggwon shot up from his seat. Yun had listened to Bak Seonggwon without being able to even raise his head, and then he also stood up, his face white, but he only stood there with his lips trembling, and it was some time before he could speak properly. Only after Bak Seonggwon, in his mourner's hat, had left through the main gate did Yun say to himself, "What a disaster!" Some time later he muttered, "How on earth could something like this happen?" Then he sat down, feeling faint and dizzy, leaned back against the wall, and closed his eyes.

Yun's daughter Tansil knew that there had been a guest wearing a mourner's hat in the men's quarters, but she had no idea what sort of person he was. In days gone by, they would have ordered a domestic or a hired hand to draw water, but these days she or her sister-in-law had to lift the bucket and carry the water jar themselves, and so it was on that day that she had gone out of the front gate of the house and was on her way back from drawing water at the well beneath the large willow tree that stood by the entrance to the road leading into Jasan Town. There was a rear door from the kitchen that led straight to the well, so there was no need for her to pass by the men's quarters and ever show her face to visitors from outside, but she had just picked up the water jar and taken three or four steps on the path from the well when she came face to face with the visitor in his mourner's hat, the hems of his mourner's clothes flapping about as he hurried out of the main gate.

She carried the bucket in one hand and used the other hand to steady the water jar on her head, revealing the white skin under her arm, and in her teeth she gripped the end of the cloth she always coiled up and placed on her head when carrying the water jar there, and it was just then, on the path, that she ran into the visitor who had come out of the men's quarters of her house. Tansil simply lowered her eyes, unsure of how to behave, and stood there motionless on the path. A flurry of thoughts flitted through her mind: had the water from the jar dripped down and caused her hair to stray down to her forehead, were her clothes properly fastened in the front, was her skirt fully wrapped around her bottom . . . with no time to think about every little thing, she had been spotted in this state by the man wearing the mourner's hat.

Bak Seonggwon calmly looked the young woman standing in front of him up and down — judging by her plump cheeks, she didn't seem to be any older than eighteen — and then quietly stepped aside. The water jar nearly brushed his hat as she passed by, and he watched as she went in through the rear gate of Yun's house.

'She's no maiden, so she must be Yun's daughter, the widow who is now living with her parents,' he thought, and then went into town.

Yun sat without a word for quite some time in the men's quarters and then suddenly fainted, falling flat on his back. He had long suffered from dizziness and fainting spells, and now he had lost his senses. The entire household rushed to him and barely managed to bring him round, but he could not say anything of his own will and had become an idiot. Only his eyes and his lips moved; he had lost all function in his hands, his feet, and even in his tongue.

Bak Seonggwon, who had said that he had business to take care of in Jasan, was drinking at the house of Clerk Im that evening and asking in detail about Yun's daughter Tansil, discussing with Clerk Im the possibility of doing something about her, when someone from the kitchen came in and relayed the news that Yun had suddenly been completely paralyzed. Seonggwon was quite shocked. He had not raised a finger, but no one could deny that he was the one who had directly caused Yun to faint and lose his senses, and thus suffer total paralysis.

Clerk Im, an idler in his thirties, had been saying, "Wait, are you telling me that you have fallen for this young widow?" He had laughed heartily and continued, "Don't worry about such a small thing. That household wants to see things settled quickly as well, and that young woman now has no chance of riding a palanquin to a new husband's house, so just leave it to me." When he heard that Yun had been completely paralyzed, though, he was suddenly sober, and he stared at Seonggwon, stunned into silence.

Bak Seonggwon was open-minded enough to consider taking Tansil in exchange for the debt that he coolly claimed was as dear as his own life, and he was also quick-witted enough to adapt to circumstances. He pushed back from the liquor table, left Clerk Im, and ran back to Yun's house by himself.

When he arrived at Yun's room, all of the other family members were sitting there as well, but they soon took their leave, leaving only Yun's wife sitting next to the sick man. Yun's wife knew that this disaster had occurred after this fellow here in the mourner's hat had come and gone, but she also knew that it had happened after a quiet chat, with no raised voices at all (she still did not know what they had talked about, only that neither had raised a finger to the other), so she disliked him, but she was also mildly curious about him, though she could not figure out why. Yun's wife, the rest of his family, and his neighbors all firmly believed that his current state was no doubt due to an evil spirit. So her hatred for anyone was overpowered by her fear of the workings of spirits, be it the spirit of King Suro, the spirit of a lord, the house deity, or even the spirits of the earth.

"I am sorry that this sinner in mourning clothes keeps coming by," said Seonggwon, standing on the wooden ledge outside as if he were reluctant to enter the room. When Yun, lying flat in his bed in the warm part of the room, vaguely saw Seonggwon standing there, the color in his face changed, the muscles began to twitch oddly, his lips began to move, and the next moment his expression changed again like lightning, so it was impossible to tell if he was smiling, if he was angry, if he was vexed, or if he was glad — each person who saw him came to a different conclusion.

"Ah, how could such a disaster have suddenly befallen our esteemed Scholar Yun!" When his enemy said these words with sadness on his face, Yun could no longer look at him and closed his eyes, and then his shoulders began to shake as he cried. His wife thought that something surely must have happened with this young man in the mourner's hat, but Bak Seonggwon did not change the gentle expression on his face and said, "You must have been shocked at this sudden disaster. My name is Bak Seonggwon, I live in Eunsan Town, and my late father was Bak Sunil — the 'sun' character for 'simple' and the 'il' character for 'peaceful'— he passed away last year. In my father's last will and testament it was written that Scholar Yun in Jasan had borrowed a certain amount of money four years ago . . ."

He began his explanation like this, sitting on the edge of the ledge outside, but when he reached this part he stopped and looked back and forth between Yun and his wife.

'Now I know why he fainted. This son of Bak Sunil came to demand payment of the debt, and my husband no doubt suddenly fainted and lost his senses because of some cruel words that were said,' thought Yun's wife, and immediately a whirlwind of sadness, hatred, and bitterness that she could not control flashed across her face.

Seeing these emotions, Bak Seonggwon continued talking. "Before my father died, he sat me down and said, 'For various reasons, Scholar Yun has these days suffered many losses in his fortunes. We also do not live as well these days, and we are not like those who did not have anything to begin with — what can be more pitiful than losing what you once had? So, in the future, even if it should be after I die, it would be one thing if Scholar Yun should once again come into his fortune as in days past, but if he does not, then we cannot press him heartlessly over a few coins, seeing as he is my friend, so if you would just convey the will of your father . . .' It was with these words that he passed away, and your humble servant became the head of our household, and still being in mourning I could not travel far, so it is only today that I have been able to visit your house."

He lifted up his eyes beneath his mourner's hat and looked at Yun's wife. Only then did an expression of relief cross her face, and she realized that the man she had vaguely resented and hated was not at all the sort of person she thought he was, and she even thought that perhaps he might be someone who would help their family in the future. And yet as soon as this person had left, Yun had collapsed on his straw mat, and she didn't know what had happened. Thus there were traces of undispelled doubt still on her brow, but Bak Seonggwon pulled his legs up and sat cross-legged on the ledge, as if to continue speaking.

It was only when he moved that Yun's wife realized her guest was still sitting outside the room. "Oh, my, look at me. Please, do come in. And close the door behind you," she said, getting up from where she sat.

Bak Seonggwon declined her offer several times, saying he was fine where he was, but then he entered the room and sat at the opposite end. After he closed the door, he said, "When I first greeted Scholar Yun, he asked about my father, so I told him everything that had happened, but he seemed rather startled by it all, so since I had business to attend to in Jasan Town I told him that I would take my leave. But he told me this was nonsense and that he could not just let me go no matter how squalid his home might be, and then he grabbed my hand and sat me down again, saying that our two households were too close for me to leave so hastily, and when I said my business was urgent he asked me to stay for just a brief time and talk about our families. I told him how my late father spent his final days before he passed away, wandering away from home, and how one as lowly as I had to become head of the household and find a way to make a living . . . well, fortunately I did not have many family members and so was able to get by, but it was all such an indescribable hardship. Yet I am still young enough to manage somehow, am I not? And then my esteemed elder here said that he was relieved to hear this but that his own situation was unspeakably wretched, and since the failure of his gold mine he had experienced all sorts of political difficulties, calamities, and hardships, and he bemoaned the disasters that had befallen him, growing agitated and pale. But then he said that, be the past as it may, what would he do in the future? — what if he were, for example, to die right now, what would become of his wife, and would his immature little children not be out on the street begging with gourds? — so I tried to comfort him, telling him that this was absurd and I would never allow such a thing to happen as long as I still drew breath. Then he grabbed my hand and said that he could not be more grateful, but he kept talking about some young woman who had been widowed in Suncheon Town and had come back to live here. So I ended our conversation by saying that he should not worry about that and leave it to me, telling him that when I returned from my trip into town we would discuss things in more detail, and then I went into Jasan Town. At the time, he didn't look quite right, but I never imagined that such a disaster would befall him, and now I truly don't know what to say, what with you thinking that this happened because of my visit . . . how can I ever make up for this . . . ?"

He bowed at the waist and then saw a look of gratitude appear on Yun's wife's face, so he pulled at her heartstrings again: "It is my ill luck that these things happen wherever I go."

But Yun's wife said, "Whatever are you talking about? This was all his fate and his destiny. The misfortune that has plagued this house for years seems to have finally run its course. I don't know if we buried our ancestors in the wrong place or if we are paying for the sins of a past life, but this is too harsh a disaster. We have experienced so much that I no longer feel sadness, I no longer shed tears, I no longer want to do anything . . . even serving the high spirits. They say the god of the house has been awakened, the spirits of the earth have been awakened, the spirit of a lord grows angry, or the spirit of King Suro is furious, that some spirit or another is taking its revenge on us, and so we have held shamanic rituals and carried the charmed string, and, for the past few years, the sound of the double-headed drum has not stopped, but every day we spend on this earth is doomed, and things just get worse, and now this disaster happens. I am sick of this now. I don't want to deal with anything, I would rather just take my own life and die, but even though this would be a blessing, I must think of my children, and that is the life I must live . . ."

At this, Yun opened his eyes wide, his face went pale and then grew red in turn, and he trembled violently, and his wife said, "What is the matter? Why are you vexing me as well?" She covered him with the blanket and picked up a bowl of rice gruel, then put that down and picked up a bowl of honey water, and then put even that down and picked up a bowl of medicine in her haste, but none of them must have seemed right, as Yun only twitched the muscles on his face.

"How regrettable! If only you would say a few words, whatever they might be . . . what a disaster!" wailed his wife. Then Yun closed his eyes and tears like raindrops ran down his cheeks.

Bak Seonggwon quietly stood up, walked over to where Yun was lying, and calmly looked down at his face. "Sir, be at ease. If you get upset like that you will only make things worse. Don't worry about anything . . . I will honor the request you made of me if it is the last thing I do, so don't worry about anything, just put your mind at ease so you can get better. I have already told Mother here everything, so don't worry, just relax and recover quickly." He spoke in a solemn, comforting tone, and Yun, perhaps understanding his words, perhaps not, simply shed more tears.

His wife, sitting next to him, was also sobbing as she said,

"My dear, I heard everything in detail from this young man. I will do as you wish, so don't worry about anything, please just get better soon."

"Well, I will now head back into town and finish taking care of my business, and I will stop by again on my way home." Bak Seonggwon did not say this to anyone in particular but just so that Yun and his wife could hear, and then he backed away and passed over the threshold of the door to Yun's room.

"Oh, my, I can't even offer you dinner. Oh, goodness, that is just not proper."

Thus Bak Seonggwon left the house of the Scholar Yun, went into Jasan Town, and spent the night there.

Yet when the sun rose the next morning, Yun fainted and did not wake again, and he was no longer of this world.

Having heard news of the death before breakfast, Bak Seonggwon bought most of what would be needed for the funeral in town and then went to the home of the bereaved, and after the four-day funeral he took Tansil as his concubine.

But even after he took Tansil as his concubine, Bak Seonggwon could not immediately bring her home to Eunsan. His family had always been well off, so there was plenty of room in the house, but he had not yet finished the three-year mourning period for his father. So even though Tansil gave birth to Hyeongeol the following year, it wasn't until the year after that, when the three-year mourning period was over, that she left her parents' home in Jasan and went to live in Eunsan.

Not long after this, the Revolt of 1894 broke out, and when the war ended, Bak Seonggwon took his family and moved to this village where they lived now, first settling in at Dumutgol.

Having lived beneath strict parents-in-law at the age of sixteen, then with her parents for nearly three years, and now as a second wife, Lady Yun — that is, Tansil — had never run a proper household of her own, where there were others to order around, but she had also never experienced anything as disheartening or miserable as when she lived at Dumutgol and was pestered by Bak Seonggwon's wife and children. Bak Seonggwon had never been one to pay heed to what either his wife or concubine said or to get involved in fights between them, nor was he one to allow there to be fights in the first place, so Lady Yun and Hyeonggeol alone, treated as a second wife and a child of a concubine, lived lives of misery. Things were different than they are now, and it was the custom of the times to not bow to the concubine of one's father, and from all lips they received nothing but humiliation and scorn, but they could not say even a single word in reply. If life had gone on like this for over a year, she might have made up her mind to somehow better her plight in any way that she could. Her less-than-gentle disposition had been softened considerably after sharing a kitchen with her sister-in-law, but she still had to suppress her desire to have a good row and get everything off her chest, and so not a day went by that her head did not pound.

It was only after Bak Seonggwon bought the house by the main road and moved his wife and her children there, freeing Lady Yun from having to live crammed into one house with them, that she was able to breathe and start keeping house properly.

They expanded the Dumutgol house as well, building a men's quarters with a yard attached, reworking the rooms they used to use into a storehouse and earthen cellar, and expanding the women's quarters to a proper size, so, though it was not as big as the main house by the main road, it was cozy and tidy enough, and she was not inconvenienced in any way.

She got some menials of her own and no longer had to worry about going into the kitchen, and her husband spent nearly half his time at Dumutgol, sleeping and eating breakfast there the next morning, so it never felt as if there was not enough food prepared.

Although Lady Yun was known by the indelicate titles of "second wife" or "concubine," now she was a proper lady with a large house of her own. Bak Seonggwon gave her family still living in Jasan a certain amount of money and then cut ties with them for financial reasons, so she worried less about them. Not long after that, her mother, who was really all that was left of her family, passed away as well, so all that remained was her younger brother, but he had long since moved in with a family that ran an inn in Pyeongyang, so she did not need to worry about her family at all.

At long last, she was able to look on her future with a mind at ease, and the more at ease she was, the more grateful she was for the blessings of the high spirits, so she began to serve all manner of ghosts and spirits, as she had so often seen her parents do at home since her youth. Behind the women's quarters she set up the straw shrine, by the front gate she hung a portrait of the spirit of the gate-keeper general, on the central pillar she hung a symbol of the house god, on all sides of the small pillars she hung symbols of the earth god, in the storehouse she put a jar for the harvest god, and from the ceiling of her room she hung a likeness of the maiden spirit; year-round, she carried the charmed string and, from time to time, held various shamanic rituals, serving more demons than could be named, and she did not forget to hold Buddhist services or pray at the Temple of the Sojourning Immortal.

But for reasons she could not fathom — perhaps Shakyamu-ni Buddha was angry with her — after she gave birth to Hyeong-geol there were no signs of life in her womb, so every year she held a ritual for Shakyamuni, and she erected an altar to the general of the seven stars and nightly drew water as a libation, but it was all to no avail. For the first few years, Bak Seonggwon almost never visit-ed the room of his first wife, and in recent years, he had only shared her room a few times a year, yet she had somehow given birth to a daughter and a son, receiving Bopae and Hyeongsik, while for some reason, Lady Yun was not able to have any children after Hyeong-geol.

But her only child, Hyeonggeol, was at least a son, and that son was quite good-looking, had a friendly disposition, and was quite manly, and this made Lady Yun exceedingly happy. When he was young, he often got into fights with the other children at school or with his step-brothers, Hyeongjun and Hyeongseon, but he nev-er lost. He was thus the cause of much trouble, though she thought this was better than not being able to lift up one's head and walk-ing around beaten and whipped all the time. Furthermore, she was aggravated to no end by the fact that, by age, Hyeonggeol was the third son, but because he was the son of a concubine, he was not counted as a legitimate child and was called "that Jasan boy," while

Hyeongsik was called the third son instead; but at least he never gave ground to the children of Bak Seonggwon's wife, even if it meant coming home with a bloodied nose, and that made Lady Yun feel better.

In Hyeonggeol's younger years, Lady Yun had had no recourse but to fret alone whenever he was treated coldly because he was the son of a concubine, but when he grew older he would take on anyone who even hinted at acting that way toward him. Whenever their offspring caused harm to another, mothers always visited the houses of the wronged to say that they were sorry and make amends, but Assistant Curator Bak hated when there was discord between his concubine and his wife over the fights of children, so even if his wife, Lady Choe, harbored some grudge deep in her heart, she could never voice even a hint of her displeasure. So whenever anything happened with Hyeonggeol, Lady Yun would be inwardly pleased but outwardly pretend not to notice, and if she happened to encounter Lady Choe, she would simply say, "Hyeonggeol's temper is quite distressing. I've never seen such a violent and vicious child."

But when Hyeonggeol passed the age of ten and began to look like a young man, Lady Yun suddenly had another thing to worry about. That concern grew as he reached the age of nineteen, and it was now at its most intense. She was worried about his marriage.

Lady Yun sat alone in her room with the lamp lit, waiting for Hyeonggeol to come home. The weather, which had been cloudy and sultry that evening, turned to rain as night drew near. The raindrops were not large, but there was some wind, and the trees creaked and raindrops spattered on the wooden ledge outside her room. She went out to her husband's room and lit the wick of the lamp there. Her husband was tired from having spent all day out on the river, baking in the sun, and he was also half drunk, so he snored lightly as he slept. She took a look around his bed, checked the front and rear doors, and then put out the lamp and returned to her own room. She had not even put out her bedding, though the servants were all asleep, and she sat there puffing away at her pipe, lost in the thoughts and memories that clouded her mind. She had no way of knowing that Assistant Curator Bak was the vile man behind her father's death; she remembered how she had lost her first husband in

Suncheon, moved back into her parents' house and constantly got into childish fights with her sister-in-law, and then married Assistant Curator Bak and lived first in Eunsan and then in Dumutgol, but in all her recollections she never once suspected Bak Seonggwon. Of course, even if she did learn that secret now, she could not avenge her father on Assistant Curator Bak or leave this house and spend the rest of her life wandering, but it would be something she could use to her advantage to confront her husband with when she was venting her anger against him or grumbling at him. But Clerk Im, who had a vague idea of this secret, disappeared during the war, so the secret became forever Assistant Curator Bak's alone. In the twenty years since she had come to live with Assistant Curator Bak, though there had, of course, been a number of conflicts, and she did have complaints, it was true that he cared for and loved her, and she was satisfied and devoted to him.

Even the troubles with Hyeonggeol's marriage were because she was a concubine, and Hyeonggeol was the son of a concubine and thus a victim of his fate; she knew that it was not because Assistant Curator Bak discriminated between Hyeonggeol and his children by his wife. In fact, her husband was pleased and hopeful because Hyeonggeol was more manly and spirited than other children, not meek like a girl. But these days, when they were busy trying to find a bride for Hyeonggeol, she found this talk of him visiting the room of the hired hand's wife unfathomable. Her husband was quite angry, and he had forbidden Hyeonggeol from going out at night anymore, so she was more concerned about what the immediate future held than about the talk of Hyeonggeol's marriage.

And even if she put that off as something that would happen in the future, she still had to deal with the issue at hand, which was what she would say to Hyeonggeol when he came in and, with these words, hopefully knock on the door of his heart, which had been confused since he cut his hair. Lost in these thoughts, Lady Yun waited for the sound of footsteps at the front gate. The rain slowed for a brief while but then poured down again. But she heard no sign of any footsteps.

She absentmindedly smoked her pipe, though she was not very used to it, so much so that the room was thick with smoke, the lamp looked like the lamp of a fishing vessel gleaming through the fog, and her head spun. She got up and opened the upper window to let some air in. The faint light shone out into the yard, and the raindrops glistened like silken threads. The smoke that wafted out the window drifted off in one direction before being caught up in the wind and rain, and the smoke near the ceiling writhed and billowed as the cold air came in.

When the smell of smoke had left the room, she went to shut the window, but then she heard the sound of the central gate opening. Hyeonggeol was finally coming in. He lowered the bar to lock the door and, seeing the faint lamplight in his mother's room, made straight for his room before glancing in her direction. With no umbrella, wearing only a bamboo hat, he walked along in his leather shoes with the legs of his trousers rolled up.

"Hyeonggeol, you're just coming in?" she said, leaning out with the lamp in her hand.

"Mother, why are you not asleep yet?" He took off his bamboo hat and brushed the raindrops off his clothes.

"You hadn't come in, and it was raining, so I was worried about you and waited up."

"It's just a little rain," he said. "What could happen?" Then he turned to go into his room.

"Come in for a moment. Before you go to bed."

He hesitated, one foot on the stone step, and asked an obvious question: "Me?" Then he lowered his head and, with his bamboo hat in his hand, walked along the stone step.

"You couldn't even borrow an umbrella? Where did you go off to?"

He could not say where and instead said, "An umbrella? Not everyone has one of those," and he stood there fidgeting on the stone step, flicking off the mud stuck to his feet, but not once looking her in the face.

"Why don't you come in?"

"But my feet are wet."

"Use that rag to wipe them off."

Hyeonggeol stepped into the room. Only then did he finally look up at his mother, as if to ask what on earth was going on.

"Have a seat there."

She put down her pipe and brusquely sat down in the warm part of the room. Hyeonggeol sat down at the opposite end.

"Your father is worried about where you are going at night. And he said that you are not to go out at night anymore."

Having said what she wanted to say in one breath, Lady Yun watched the expression on her son's face from across the room. Even in the dim light she could clearly see the color of his face change. But Hyeonggeol said nothing in reply. He only sat there in silence. And it seemed that the look on his face changed a few times. Yet when he finally lifted his head and looked at his mother, he said, "Is that all you wanted to say to me?" There was little emotion in his voice.

She was taken aback for a moment. "Yes. But since when do you refuse to answer when an adult asks you a question?"

She had not intended to rebuke him, but when she finished talking she thought that her tone had been one of reproach, and she realized that she had become somewhat flustered.

Damn it—this was not something she should have said when she was emotional . . . if her son was hurt and got up and left the room, it would be worse than if she had not said anything at all. She was still uneasy about having said this when Hyeonggeol calmly answered, "It seemed as if you already knew where I had been going when you asked, so I did not answer."

Hyeonggeol's calm and respectful reply cut Lady Yun to the quick. She had no idea that he would dare to answer her so directly. If it was true that he had been seeing the wife of a hired hand, he should have turned red, stammered for a bit, and then mumbled a few words to explain himself, and if it was, on the other hand, a barefaced lie, he would have demanded to know what she was talking about and insisted that he had been on his way home from the house of some friend or the house of his teacher, but when he calmly accepted his mother's words and essentially admitted that he had been seeing Duchil's wife, it came as quite a surprise to Lady Yun.

"I asked you because I didn't think it was true," she said, and lowered her head. When Hyeonggeol heard this and sensed the melancholy in her voice, he became upset and lowered his head as well.

"My goodness, how foolish of you to visit her so often that others noticed!" His mother said this without even being able to look him in the face.

"So often? My eldest step-brother had come out for his own purposes, and we ran into each other there."

'What? The eldest . . . Hyeongjun?' But these words Lady Yun only murmured in her mind and did not say them aloud. Then she thought, 'And then he went and confessed this to his father.'

But if she made a fuss over this it would damage the loyalty between the brothers, so she did not speak of it again and sat there quietly for some time. At last she said, "Even though you are a man, you must respect your own body and you must take care in your conduct. No matter how much you may like her, you must think of her status. And with all this talk of your marriage these days, if this rumor were to get out, it would be more than just an embarrassment, it would affect other things as well."

But Hyeonggeol shot up and said, "I am not getting married." Then he threw open the door and went out into the rain.

"What?" Lady Yun got up as well, but she could say no more and only stood there in the middle of the room for some time. When she finally went to the door, Hyeonggeol had long since gone into his own room.

11

The Presbyterian church was a building that used to be the house of Mr. Kim, a low-ranking local official, up the road toward Descending Immortal Pavilion from Nine Dragons Bridge, then around a turn to the left and across the street from River View Pavilion. The house originally had a kitchen in the corner and rooms off two adjacent sides in an L-shape, but the house had been renovated: the earthen floor of the kitchen had been filled in and a high wooden floor erected there to serve as a pulpit, and both interior walls leading to the two wings of the house had been knocked down. The medium-sized room that formed the end of the L next to the road was where the men sat, while the medium-sized room that formed the end of the L on the other side was where the women sat. The roof was left as it was, with only the main gate renovated to support a high flagstone roof, and at the top of this was placed an elegant cross made of wood. Next to this was a stepped belfry of five-or-six levels, covered with straw mats, and in this hung a bell. The room that had been used as a storehouse by Mr. Kim's family was expanded to serve as a home for the family of Reverend Yi from Pyeongyang, and in the room above that boarded Mun Useong, the new teacher at Dongmyeong School. Mr. Mun was a young teacher, not yet thirty, who had attended Ilsin School in Pyeongyang and was a devotee of Christianity, and at the school he taught courses such as mathematics and history.

The peonies were in full blossom, so it was not quite yet time for the Dano Festival in the fifth lunar month. When the tree peony flowers faded and fell, the irises flourished beneath the bramble hedges and on the ridges between the rice paddies, the cattails bloomed in the slopes of the newly built road, and finally the woodland peonies blossomed, then the Dano Festival would arrive.

There was a little more than a fortnight left until then, though.

It was a bright Sunday, clear after the rain that had fallen in the night. Students from Dongmyeong School, including Bak Hyeongseon, Bak Hyeonggeol, Son Daebong, Yi Taeseok, and Kim Gilson, had attended the morning worship service and, with their hymnals tucked under their arms, strolled along after Mr. Mun to gather beneath an apricot tree amidst the blooming peonies.

When a few of these, namely Son Daebong, Hyeonggeol, and Hyeongseon, were young, before Dongmyeong School had been founded, they had stopped attending the Confucian school and begun attending the Christian school, so they were not blank slates when it came to Christianity. So even though they might not have known the true meaning of John 3:16, Hymn 3 in their hymnals, and the Lord's Prayer, they could recite them properly in loud voices. But they gave no thought to keeping the Sabbath, attending worship, or praying before eating and going to sleep, nor did they buy hymnals or Bibles. They attended a Christian school, so they listened to the Scriptures being read as one might listen to old proverbs, and they sang hymns as one might learn simple songs. The stories told by shamans and the prayers offered by priests or pastors, they were all the same, just playthings to be mimicked for a joke and a laugh.

So after the Christian school closed down, they did not even consider going to church, and even at Christmas they might go just to look around, but then again they might not.

Not long after Mr. Mun took up his new post, though, they said that they believed in Jesus and started going to church.

Even after he started his job, though, he did not continuously preach Christianity during class or anything like that. Mr. Mun was said to hail from Gangseo County, west of Pyeongyang, and he was upright in character and learned in the new knowledge, so he captured the hearts of the students as soon as he came to this town. The teacher of classical Chinese at Dongmyeong School was no different from the headmaster of a Confucian school, and even those who taught the new learning were older men who had only a scattered knowledge of their subjects. Even Jeong Yeonggeun, who was popular with the young people because he taught gymnastics and drilling, was too strict and stern to become close to the students. Yet Mun had attended Daeseong School and graduated from Ilsin School, so he knew quite a bit about the new learning and enlightenment thought, and, on top of that, his faith in Jesus gave him the opportunity to fraternize with a good number of Westerners, and he had read all sorts of Western books, so it was a given that the students would be wholly taken with him.

He got the job at the school through the offices of Reverend Yi, and when he arrived he took the room above Reverend Yi's and began his simple life as a bachelor.

When he first arrived all by himself, with no wife and children in tow, his tidy life as a bachelor drew the attention of the villagers. After they learned that he was the child of a noted family in Gangseo, they grew even more curious about his lifestyle. Even the women began to gossip about Mr. Mun, saying that he must not have gotten along with his wife, otherwise he would not have come to this out-of-the-way neighborhood to live by himself and let his youth go to waste. At first, there were rumors that his wife had died or that perhaps he had a concubine he would bring to the village after he knew what the neighborhood was like, but recently some of the women from households that believed in Jesus said that he was the descendant of a strict yangban family, and this family had forbidden him, though he might be taken with enlightenment thought and go around as a teacher, to bring their daughter-in-law with him, so he had come on his own. This rumor must have been fairly plausible, as no new rumors were reported after this.

The only thing the students ended up discussing, though, was the fact that he was a devoted follower of Christianity. There were those students who had been brought up in Confucian families and thus did not like the Western learning, thinking it suspicious and wondering how such a decent teacher could believe in Jesus; but to those students who had grown up here and gone to the Christian school, he was a powerful motivation for them to examine Christianity once again, this time in a completely different light.

Yet each student's direct motivation for following Mr. Mun to church was different.

First of all, there was a reason that Hyeonggeol was closer to Mr. Mun than the other students.

After Mr. Mun had taught mathematics to the first-year high school students for only a few days, at around the time class finished and school ended for the day, he took a survey of the unmarried students. There were a few students who had not been married yet, but of the nearly twenty students in the class, there was only one student who no longer wore children's clothes but hadn't even been engaged yet, and that student was Bak Hyeonggeol.

He was remarkable in appearance, and the clothes that he wore and the way that he carried himself did not suggest that he was a child from a poor family, so Mun thought it odd that he had somehow not yet been sacrificed to the ideology of early marriage. Of course, after the introduction of enlightenment thought, there were quite a few enlightened families that did not want to marry their sons at the age of eleven or twelve, but the fact that he had not even been arranged to marry at the age of nineteen meant that either his family was a very enlightened, new-style household, or that there was some more hidden reason. As Mr. Mun left the classroom, he called Hyeonggeol to him, and he told Hyeonggeol that he could visit him in the evening whenever he had the time, in the room above Reverend Yi's house, located in the church.

After hearing Hyeonggeol's detailed explanation of his situation, as well as the concerns of Hyeonggeol and his mother, Lady Yun, which were part and parcel of that explanation, Mr. Mun taught him in great detail that prejudice based on status and discrimination between legitimate and illegitimate children were the dregs of a bygone era, and he told him that there could be no such discrimination in this civilized era. He went on to teach him about the emancipation of menials, the abolition of superstition, the repudiation of the ideology of early marriage, and the improvement of lifestyle habits, and he said that it was the duty of young men to devote themselves to these things. There were parts of what Mr. Mun said that Hyeonggeol understood, and there were many parts that he just skipped over because he had no idea what his teacher was talking about, but he believed that everything Mr. Mun said was right and simply listened quietly. After this, Hyeonggeol and Mr. Mun had an exceptionally close relationship, and although they did not forget the strict relationship of teacher and student, there was a bond felt by both of them that went beyond that. This was around the time that Hyeonggeol had grown close to Ssangne. But Hyeonggeol kept his lips sealed about his relationship with Ssangne and never discussed it. And he did not tell Mr. Mun that he had resolved to himself that he would never again listen to any talk of marriage. Not long after this, he became a believer who went to church for Sunday and Wednesday evening services.

Hyeongseon took a different path to becoming a churchgoer.

Hyeongseon's new wife, Bobu, proclaimed that she did not believe in Jesus, but he knew that, when she came to him as a new bride, she brought with her in her chest a Bible, a hymnal, a picture of Jesus ascending to Heaven, and a picture of Jesus praying in Gethsemane, and he also knew that, although Head Clerk Jeong did not attend church, he was not opposed to Christianity, either.

"Are you afraid that I will say something if you say you believe in Jesus?"

Actually, Bobu knew of a young woman who, after she married into a family that exalted ghosts and demons as high spirits, was driven out of the house for reciting the Christian scriptures, and although her new husband, Hyeongseon, would never do anything like that, she still did not want to give him the opportunity to make fun of her, so she hid her true feelings: "If I believed, I would say so. I said I don't believe because I don't."

"So why the Bible? And why the painting of that carpenter's son, that long-bearded fellow, going up to Heaven?"

"So what if I read that instead of a book of fairy tales when I am bored? And those paintings, they are just scraps of silk or hemp that I have gathered."

But when Hyeongseon laughed, Bobu laughed along with him, even though she knew what the laughter meant.

After Mun Useong came along, though, and not long after Hyeongseon learned that he was a devoted believer of Jesus, he said to his wife one night, "They say the new teacher, Mr. Mun, believes in Jesus. They say he's very devoted, so I think I'll go to church, too."

Bobu thought that he was still trying to see how she felt about this and so said nothing.

"Give me that hymnal and that Bible."

She finally looked up from her sewing and stared at her husband, as if she were trying to determine whether he was being serious or speaking in jest. He didn't seem to be jesting, so she asked, "What will you do with them?"

"Hyeonggeol from Dumutgol believes as well, and everyone is going, so I thought I would go, too."

"What, you believe just because others believe?"

"You believe, so I thought I would try believing."

Even though she thought he was joking, Bobu grinned and said, "Please, who said I believed?"

But she immediately put the clothing she was sewing back into her sewing box, got up, opened up her clothes chest, and took out the Bible and the hymnal. A happy blush spread across her face. Hyeongseon took the books with one hand, and Bobu opened up a drawer and took out her holy icons. "This painting is a painting of Jesus ascending to Heaven three days after being nailed to the cross, this is a painting of Jesus praying in the garden of Gethsemane, this is a painting of Jesus when he was young, and this is a painting of Jesus' mother, Mary . . . she is quite pretty, isn't she?"

Hyeongseon listened quietly as Bobu explained each of them, then he cocked his head and looked at her with a gentle smile. "You must know more than those big ministers and elders." He was pleased at his wife's extensive knowledge. "I went to a Christian school, so I've heard the Bible, but goodness. Still, I can sing a few verses of hymns. Shall we go this Lord's Day?"

"You go. You are, after all, the son of an enlightened family, so it's much better than serving demons."

Bobu was now openly encouraging him. Hyeongseon thought to himself, 'So it was true,' but he said nothing and instead opened the Bible and flipped through its pages. "But you must want to go quite badly," he said as he leafed idly through the book.

"Can I go just because I want to? A young woman must be careful of the company she keeps, after all."

"I will see to it . . . you should come along."

But it was obvious her husband spoke in jest. So Bobu flashed a grin and said, "When everyone else goes, then I will go, too."

"You think not everyone goes now? A lot of people go."

"Still, I will go later. You should grow strong in your faith. Me, I'll go wearing a hooded coat after I have a baby."

Hyeongseon stared transfixed for some time at his wife's suddenly brightening face and then said, "The night is old now, let's lay down the bedding and put out the light."

Hyeongseon went to church on the very next Sunday.

As for the others, Son Daebong went on Hyeonggeol's advice, and then Kim Gilson and Yi Taeseok began to go to church at the encouragement of Son Daebong or Hyeonggeol. Daebong did not bother explaining what Christianity was, or what its truths were, or that you would go to Heaven when you died.

"Hey, Gilson, let's go to church this Sunday," he blurted out.

His friend retorted, "Why would we go there?"

Daebong immediately replied, "You don't want to go look at

the women and the maidens? We sing hymns together, pray, and call each other Brother and Sister. It's fun!"

When Daebong tried to tempt him like this, he at first said, "Get lost," and then smacked him on the shoulder and walked away laughing, but early Sunday morning he ate breakfast early and then went to Daebong's house, saying, "Is Daebong there?" When Daebong emerged from the front gate, Gilson stood at attention, saluted, played a fanfare through his cupped hands, and then solemnly proclaimed: "Mr. Mun believes."

"Of course he does, that's why we're going," Daebong replied. "What did you think?"

In this way, they each began to go to church.

When the service was over, the men would leave first, and then, some time later, the women would emerge wearing their hooded coats and return to their homes. It just so happened that day that the older men had remained in their seats to discuss something, leaving the young men no place to sit, so Mr. Mun was obliged to lead them here under the apricot tree behind the church.

"As the reverend said, there are now a few villages with worship services that are burning up the demons, and if you would like to attend please come back here after lunch. However, there will be a lot of adults in attendance, so there is no need for our young men to swarm these places, and I think a better way of observing the spirit of the Sabbath would be to form evangelism teams to abolish superstitions on the Lord's Day, to go to the houses of families you are close to and to flawless families, and hand out Bibles and hymnals, and to work to spread the truth of our Lord's word. Using examples from our lives, explain just how much of our hard-earned money has been thrown away on shamanic rituals, charmed threads, shamanic incantations, divination, exorcisms, prayers, and other things done in the service of ghosts and demons, offer detailed comparisons with the excellent lives of enlightened foreigners so that you may enlighten people, and give them hymnals, Bibles, paintings, and other things for them to look at. Once you have done this with a family, you should visit them often, and in everything, no matter how trivial, always speak of the truth of God. At the same time, tell them of the things we talk about every day, such as the improvement of our customs and practices, or the emancipation of menials, and counsel them to leave behind their dark lives and move into the world of light. Finally, you must be on your guard, most of all, against being rude or causing offense. It is important, above all, to become friendly first. Looking into the women's quarters at any time in families with strict household etiquette, for example, may lead to young men being misunderstood, so you must always take care and bear these things in mind."

As he listened, standing next to a cluster of peonies, Hyeong-geol's mind wandered for a moment. "Looking into the women's quarters: these things young men must always bear in mind and refrain from." When he heard this, he suddenly thought of Duchil's wife, Ssangne. He looked up to see Hyeongseon staring directly at him.

'I wonder if Hyeongseon knows as well, having heard from Hyeongjun's lips that I came out of the room of Duchil's wife. If that is so, then his wife, Jeong Bobu, and the whole family might know.'

As he thought these things, his face grew hot and he felt a hatred toward Hyeongjun, and, even if for only a moment, he felt a hatred toward Hyeongseon as he stared straight at him.

He looked quickly at Daebong, who must have been thinking of Chilseong's wife, as he grinned widely at Hyeonggeol.

"Now, divide up into pairs," said Mr. Mun, "each of you taking a Bible, a hymnal, and five paintings, large or small, and depart immediately. When you return for the evening worship service, please report in detail on the results of your evangelism."

He leaned to the side so he could see the women's seats and said, "The women are gone now, so let us take our leave."

Hyeonggeol paired up with Daebong. They walked out in front of River View Pavilion and down to the edge of the Biryu River. Standing on the embankment, Hyeonggeol asked, "Whose houses should we visit?"

"Let us take turns. We will go to one house of your choosing, then I will lead the way to another house."

Hyeonggeol pondered Daebong's reply and said, "You have a place you're thinking of going? I have a place in mind as well."

"Whose house is it? You go first."

"Well, how about the noodle shop by Visiting Immortal Gate, run by that Mr. Bak, either that house or the house of his brother, who runs the inn and stable."

Before Hyeonggeol could even finish speaking, Daebong leaped toward him, "You think you're being funny?" he said, and tried to grab Hyeonggeol by the collar.

Hyeonggeol threw his head back and guffawed, "Alright, alright, I won't do it again!"

The houses that Hyeonggeol had suggested were those of Bak Rigyun and his younger brother Bak Seonggyun, and Hyeonggeol was teasing Daebong because he was going to be married to Bak Seonggyun's daughter Geumne in only a few days.

Even after Daebong calmed down, he looked sour, as if the jest had left a bad taste in his mouth.

"What, did I make you angry?" Hyeonggeol asked.

"Me, angry? Get lost!" Daebong said with a breezy laugh, but when he thought of being married to that abominable Geumne, he was indeed upset and could not help being depressed.

They walked downstream in silence for some time before Daebong said, "The place I am thinking of is in front of Descending Immortal Pavilion . . . shall we go there first? It's a family living in a wing of my relative's house, newly arrived from Pyeongyang."

Hyeonggeol agreed, "Yes, let's go there."

They doubled back, went up the alley next to River View Pavilion and went out onto the main street. Daebong led the way and turned to the right, and he turned again at the well of the government office. After going some way, he said, "It's the rear wing of this house." They had stopped in front of a stone house. He stood there for a little while longer and then explained, "If we go around to the rear, there is a separate house there." Then he whispered into Hyeonggeol's ear: "It's a gisaeng's house . . . do you think it will be OK?"

"I don't know." Hyeonggeol was surprised, and he hesitated there for some time, lost in thought, as he had not expected someplace like this. "We can't have discrimination between high and low, can we? So it shouldn't make a difference, but still, we are only students after all." Hyeonggeol expressed his reluctance.

"Then it will be fine. Isn't the goal of religion to do away with discrimination? Whatever the case, I'll take responsibility for this, you just follow me. I only heard that they moved in, I haven't actually seen them for myself. We can kill two birds with one stone."

Daebong grabbed his arm and led the way. Hyeonggeol did not mind, either. Had there been some reason to back out, had he been able to come up with some fault in the plan . . . but the hearts of the young men could not but be enticed. With their ramie overcoats flapping gently behind them and their books and paintings in their hands, they followed the wall around to the rear gate.

"Is anyone home?" Daebong called at the rear gate. In front of the gate was a vegetable patch. There was no answer from within.

"I said, is anyone home?" he asked again and then winked at Hyeonggeol.

"Who's there?" It was the faint voice of a young woman.

"It is I," he said, answering like a proper adult, and then he looked at Hyeonggeol again.

"Mother, someone has come for a visit. Please go out and see who it is."

Outside the front gate, the two young men stood enchanted by the woman's beautiful voice. At last a woman past the age of fifty, wearing old straw shoes and a hemp skirt, crossed the yard and lifted the bar from the door.

"And where might you be from?" Seeing that the visitors standing before her front gate were two young students still wet behind the ears, the woman was suspicious and glanced back and forth between them.

This time Hyeonggeol spoke. "We have come from down below in the village. Is the master of the house at home?"

"Only the mistress is here. But what brings you?" she stammered, but, from within, the young woman's voice said, "Whoever it is, tell them to come in. They have come to visit, after all."

Hearing this, the older woman suddenly smiled broadly and stepped to one side of the front gate. "Please come in, humble though our home may be."

"Ah, we are fine here," said Daebong, declining her offer, but

Hyeonggeol said, "Well, just for a moment, then," and ducked in through the gate. Daebong followed him in.

In the inner room, behind a beaded curtain, a gisaeng, who appeared to have just put on her makeup, smiled gently, pulled aside the curtain with one hand, and stepped out onto the freshly wiped wooden ledge.

"I apologize for the trouble you took to visit our humble home," she said, and serenely bent one knee in a half-bow. It was customary to use informal language when speaking to a gisaeng, but Hyeonggeol murmured, "It is we who are sorry for paying such an unexpected visit."

"Please, come up. My room is humble, but please come in." The gisaeng at first invited them up onto the wooden ledge outside the room but then invited them into the room itself.

Daebong glanced at Hyeonggeol and said, "Well, let us go in and have a talk," and he took his shoes off on the stone step and stepped up onto the wooden ledge. Then, guided by the gisaeng, they entered the room. The old woman went into the small room on the other side of the kitchen.

The room the gisaeng led them into was wider than it was deep, with fine wicker mats laid over rough straw mats, and at the warm end of the room there was an armrest atop a fancy cushion. In the rear of the room were a wooden chest, a lacquered wardrobe inlaid with mother-of-pearl, and a clothes rack all in a row, and at the end of the warm part of the room was a stationery chest. Next to the clothes rack was a low, folding screen painted with flowers, and next to that was a brass lamp stand. In front of the stationery chest was a white jade tobacco case, and lying on a brass ashtray was a long pipe. The gayageum that stood in front of the folding screen reached up to the shelf below the roof where an image of a maiden spirit was enshrined.

"It's already summer, and the day outside must be hot," said the gisaeng, offering them fans painted with swirls of red, yellow, and blue. She continued, "Please, take off your overcoats and have a seat."

The two of them put down the books and paintings they were holding in their hands, took off their hats, and pushed them back behind the cushion.

Having seated her two young guests on the cushion, the gi-saeng sat in the middle of the room, pulled out the tobacco case, and filled her pipe with tobacco.

"Has it been long since you came from Pyeongyang?" asked Hyeonggeol.

"It's been over a month now. A relative of mine lives nearby and said that the scenery around here was quite beautiful and pic-turesque, so I thought I would take a look, and the famous gisaeng Buyong was born here long ago as well. My name is also Buyong, and there were a lot of things here I wanted to see, so I came for a visit. It's such a new place, I am counting on the love of many men."

She finished tamping down the tobacco in her pipe. It was as fine as yellow cow hair in the bowl of the pipe.

"Why don't you have a smoke to pass the time?"

She held out the long pipe in her thin fingers, adorned with jade and gold rings, and Daebong took it without hesitation and put it to his lips, but then he suddenly remembered that believers in Jesus refrained from drinking and smoking, and he said, "It's hard to turn down something prepared with such care, but I never learned how to smoke." He gently put the pipe back down on the ashtray.

She looked at Hyeonggeol and said, "Then you, Sir?"

But Hyeonggeol answered, "I never learned how to smoke, either." But he was amused that Buyong had called him 'Sir.' (No one ever would have guessed that he was still a bachelor at his age.)

"My, how respectable you both are. Presumptuous though it may be of me to say so." Buyong smiled, showing only the lower row of her small, white teeth.

"It is not that we never started smoking because we are re-spectable, but that we used to smoke and have recently quit," Hyeonggeol laughed.

"What, you quit smoking?" Buyong's smile disappeared and she looked at Hyeonggeol with a straight face.

"Don't misunderstand me. It looks like we will now have to begin our evangelism . . . we have come here as evangelists."

Hyeonggeol looked over at Daebong for a moment and then uncrossed his legs before crossing them again.

"The reason we have come to see you today is the same reason that we have stopped smoking and drinking. To come straight to the point, we have come here to encourage you to believe in Jesus."

A look of confusion passed across Buyong's slender face and appeared in her sparkling eyes.

Believe in Jesus — she could not tell if this was just a passing jest, if he was teasing a lowly girl with idle nonsense, or if perhaps he was alluding to some deep meaning. Buyong also thought that she might have even misheard him.

"You take your jest too far," she murmured quietly, and her beautiful eyes glanced sidelong at Hyeonggeol for a moment before she broke into a small smile.

Hyeonggeol opened his mouth to assure her that this wasn't the case, but he was struck by the smile that parted her lips and stammered for a while, unable to look her in the face.

"We would never do such a thing." This was Daebong, who sat at his side and now took the lead. "Look at these. These are a hymnal and a Bible, are they not? And these paintings as well..."

He chattered as he took out the books and prepared to make his move, but Buyong broke in. "I thank you for thinking of someone like me, but even if I were to believe in Jesus, how could such a woman as I go to church?" Her voice was plaintive, with an undertone of scolding.

"What do you mean? Do you think that Christianity discriminates between people?" Daebong retorted, but to himself Hyeonggeol thought that Buyong's words were closer to the truth.

"Let's say that I was foolish enough to go to church. From that day forward, not a single decent woman would come."

"That is not our concern. This Jesus does not distinguish between high and low."

Daebong was just haphazardly repeating things he had heard, with little thought for the effect his words would have, but Hyeonggeol thought that they had strayed from the path by coming to this place to evangelize. He felt his first flush of excitement fade, yet now that they were here they could not just leave, so he said: "I believe that you are wrong to think this way. Asking you to believe in Jesus is not asking you to simply come to church. Depending on the person, sometimes it is best to just come to church; among those who go to church regularly to pass the time there are those who gradually realize the truth and spirit of Christianity; but there is no need for someone like you to do that. I believe that whether or not one goes to church is not nearly as important as reading the Bible and the hymnal, coming to understand the true spirit of Christianity, and then instilling that spirit into our everyday lives. Just as you have said, if you were to come to church, obstinate people who are still steeped in the old customs might scowl, and some of the women might not come to church anymore. I do not know if it is proper to lose a million false believers to gain one true soul, and though that, in fact, may be right, in the world in which we live, it may create difficulties. So, whatever our true feelings may have been in coming to see you, just think of it as a friendly visit, since we were out evangelizing anyway, and do not mistake our true intentions. We will leave these books here with you, so that you may look at them in your spare time. As far as we are concerned, there is no such thing as high and low among people. We are all the same, and those born fortunate become yangban, while those born unfortunate become commoners, so do not forget the message we have shared with you: do not be ensnared by demons and superstitions, and accept the new civilization in order to live a better life. Ah, well, my preaching has grown long, so let's just leave it at that."

Hyeonggeol grinned widely and looked at Daebong. Buyong, whose face had flushed with excitement as he spoke, said, "Thank you for your wonderful words." She bowed her head, as if she cherished genuine gratitude in her heart.

"Ah, there is no need for that. Well, there are other places we must visit, so we will now take our leave." Hyeonggeol picked up his hat and the other books and stood up.

"What? No, you cannot just leave like this. I was just about to offer you each a glass of sikhye . . ." She stood up and blocked their way to the door. "Mother, please bring us some punch or some sikhye," she shouted toward the room across the way.

"No, please. We will come again to visit. We have spent too long here already. We must now go visit other places."

Daebong had already put on his hat and was brushing the

wrinkles out of his overcoat, and he pushed aside the curtain and stepped out onto the wooden ledge. Buyong could not very well just grab the hand of another woman's husband (though he was, in fact, a bachelor) whom she had only just met, so she was quite anguished, but she was afraid that if she hesitated she would lose the other one as well, so she stepped in front of Hyeonggeol and left him with no place to go.

Hyeonggeol picked up his hat and the bundle of paintings and then, as if he had just thought of something, said, "Ah, here, take a painting as well. This is a painting of Jesus as a child, being cradled by the Holy Mother Mary." He took a painting from the bundle and placed it on top of the stationery chest, and then he glanced out beyond the curtain. Daebong stood in the yard waiting for him.

"Oh, I am indebted to you for all these gifts. But, well, your friend is standing there outside. Please wait here while I go bring him back."

But Hyeonggeol had put on his hat and was straightening his coat strings. "Please, step aside."

She suddenly reached out with both of her hands and grabbed the hand that was about to push aside the curtain, unaware of what she was doing at that moment, shaking her head back and forth as the scent of camellia oil wafted from her neatly combed hair. Hyeonggeol looked down at Buyong's hands holding his, and only then did she blush scarlet. But she could not let go; she just stood there like that for some time. With the curtain drawn, no one could see into the room.

12

A few days before, an entire oxcart of products that had never before been seen in this village had been delivered to Nakanishi's store from Pyeongyang. Until that day, goods transported the one hundred sixty li from Pyeongyang to this village were brought by packhorse drivers or traders on the backs of donkeys or mules, carried by peddlers or A-frame carriers, or, in winter, usually carried by sleigh over the snow and ice. A typical load of goods for moving house or other large cargo such as grains, salt, or seafood, were shipped up the Daedong River and then up the Biryu River on steamers or flatboats. A few dry goods shops might ship silk or linen, and when Chilseong rode his bicycle up to Pyeongyang to buy things, he shipped them back as well, and when Nakanishi brought back crates of bulk merchandise or even when Kim Seongu brought back a few boxes of those lovely cookies, they used these steamers or flatboats.

But then, with the Dano Festival coming, the weather grew dry and the waterline dropped, leading to a delay in shipping, so Nakanishi quickly decided to load up one of the new oxcarts, bring it down the flat, newly constructed road, and transport the cargo from Pyeongyang to this village in one day and one night.

As the ox panted and pulled the cart on its two large, sturdy wheels over Dolchani Hill, past Fealty Bridge, and through Visiting Immortal Gate, not only the young Nakanishi, with his overcoat around his shoulders and his geta on his feet, but also a good number of children and people who had nothing better to do, came out to see the cart. They walked along the street, following the cart, and they watched as each and every piece of cargo was taken down from atop it. When all the cargo was unloaded, the ox was led to Bak Seonggyun's inn and stable to be fed, while the driver went into a room and made short work of three bowls — two don, five pun worth — of noodles. (Since Bak Rigyun was fixing up his house these days, he had moved his noodle shop into the kitchen of Seonggyun's house.)

Some of the children were fascinated, not only by the cart, but also by the fact that the rough-looking cart driver had eaten three bowls of noodles, and they ran back to their friends gathered in front of Nakanishi's house and added a little to the truth, spreading the rumor that the strong young man that had driven the cart here had eaten five bowls of noodles in a row.

But as excited as they were about how many bowls of noodles he ate, the children were even more excited and fascinated by the strange and wondrous things they had never seen before and which were now pouring out of the boxes and straw packing as the cargo was unpacked. Every time an item was brought out, the children jostled for position among the adults, and they laughed and chattered as they tried to figure out what each thing was used for. Nakanishi was puffed up with pride, and even Gochokai Darō, who worked for Nakanishi and was the son of a worker at the government office, was as elated as if he had been offered a government post.

Among the merchandise that had been brought on the cart and was now being set up and stacked in the shop, the ten boxes of kerosene were the most expensive. Each of the wooden boxes stamped with the words " 'Pine Tree' Brand Kerosene, New York, U.S.A."* contained two shiny tins of kerosene. Nine of these boxes were stacked unopened in the yard, and though Nakanishi could have taken his time, he plucked one of the tin cans from a box as everyone watched and, with the claw end of a hammer, punched a hole in it. Then he took a tin pump from its straw packing, put it in the hole, and pulled repeatedly on the metal wire. From the drainlike hole the kerosene flowed out of the can and into a fuel tank, like a newborn baby peeing.

He took a large lantern chimney down from the row of large and small lanterns that hung on the back wall, put a shade on the lantern, inserted a wick, and then, with a match lit, the end of the wick, which hung down into the tank filled with kerosene. He was lighting the lantern before the sun had even set. The villagers standing around him in the street were fascinated by what he was doing, and their mouths hung open. People kept asking him how much the kerosene cost, and someone from the store avoided the questions by saying that they would have to wait and see.

This was not the only new thing that day—the matches that Nakanishi had used to light the lantern were also making their first appearance in this village. Prior to this, they had used the rough matches with yellow phosphorous at their tip because they were more convenient than a flint and steel, but these new matches

---

*There was a pure spirits turpentine product under the "Pine Tree" Brand label manufactured by the Stallworth Pine Products Company in New York in the early 20th century. As turpentine is essentially distilled pine resin, this makes sense—however, it is unlikely that this same brand produced kerosene, which is a distillation of petroleum and has nothing to do with pine trees. Likewise, turpentine is a solvent and could not be used as fuel, so it is possible that the author confused this with kerosene.

could be struck and lit anywhere and were easy to carry around in matchboxes. They looked like toothpicks, or splinters of bamboo, or thin reeds, and it was amazing to see them spring into flame when scraped against a rock, a pillar, or a wall. Someone said that they would be ideal for lighting pipes; someone else said that they would be great for families with children, who constantly had to light and relight lamps at night; and yet someone else said that they would be perfect for going to the outhouse in the middle of the night.

Those gathered were familiar with Western socks, but never before had they seen so many socks tied together in bundles. They had seen Choe Gwansul from Gaenggoji wearing socks in his laced-up shoes, patched heel and toe with bits of hemp cloth, but they had never seen socks tied together in bundles like dried fish. "Clerk Choe from Gaenggoji won't be wearing his patched socks anymore," someone said, and everyone gathered around laughed loudly.

The blue-dyed paper bags with the flames on their labels were candles, the square tins with pictures of a woman standing on them came in all sorts of colors and clearly held paint, and the things that looked like short canes covered in fabric were surely parasols. Large wooden boxes were carefully emptied of their straw packing and wood shavings, and when people looked to see what might be in them, they found milky-white bowls, glass dishes that would show whatever water, rice, or kimchi they held, and splendid chamber pots decorated with flowers that were far too lovely to pee in. They were accustomed to cheap ceramic bowls — large, rough bowls from the earth mines and kilns of Dongchang or Jikdong painted with dark blue lines on a light blue background and decorated with fish or other such designs — so these smooth porcelain and glass dishes looked to them as if they would crack and shatter the moment one put kimchi or soy bean paste soup in them.

Finally, there were two boxes left that were not too big. One of them was clearly cigarettes, judging by the fact that the words "East Asian Tobacco Company" were written on them. From the other, slightly smaller box came a few even smaller boxes made from strawboard. Nakanishi opened one of these boxes without hesitation and took a small paper bag from within, then he opened that paper bag, poured into his hand some small red objects like red beans, and popped them into his mouth. He chewed them with a crunching sound, swallowed, and then let out a big breath, as if he had just eaten hot peppers.

Nakanishi looked at Mr. Kim, who stood in front of him with his mouth open in wonder, asked, "Would you like to try some?" and then picked up three or four of them and dropped them into Mr. Kim's outstretched hand. As everyone watched, Mr. Kim pushed aside his short, bushy moustache, put the candies in his mouth one at a time, and carefully crushed each with his molars.

"Are they tasty?" someone asked, and Mr. Kim let out a rush of breath and nodded his head. "They're good. They're good!"

Hyeongseon had been on his way home from school for lunch when he saw the large crowd of people gathered in front of Nakanishi's shop and, wondering what was going on, did not go through the front gate of his house but drew closer to Nakanishi's house and looked toward the shop over the shoulders of the crowd. After staring for some time at the lit lantern hanging there and the various goods that had just been taken out of their crates and chests, he worried that he might be late and ran home.

His father was in his room, but he went into the women's quarters and said to his mother, "Lantern shades, socks, parasols, and all sorts of things have arrived at Nakanishi's. We should buy four or five lanterns to use in the men's quarters and some of the other rooms."

"We might buy one, but what use would four be? We still have four or five gallons of castor oil left, when are we going to use that?" His mother was realistic and paid no attention to her son's words.

"Well, why don't you buy one and try lighting it. They are as bright as day, so even a large room will be bright as day, too, if you use one."

"Talk to your father about it. Not me."

Hyeongseon had said four or five, but if they were to light lanterns at Dumutgol as well, they would need another four or five, so he thought they would need about ten in total.

"Really, Mother, you are quite pitiful," he said, clucking his tongue, and then he went back to his room.

As he left, Lady Yun mumbled as if to herself, "And how are we supposed to buy this oil? Even without lanterns, I've had no problem sewing your silk jackets and padded socks."

Hyeongseon went into his room and, even after his wife brought out his lunch, went on for some time describing to his wife the lanterns, socks, parasols, and everything else he had seen.

His eldest brother, Hyeongjun, woke up from a nap he was taking in the cool part of his room. He swatted away a few buzzing flies that were already hovering about him. Then he complained to his wife, who was sitting at the warm end of the room suckling the baby, "What is Hyeongseon carrying on about now? Can't a fellow get some sleep?"

"He said that Nakanishi got some lanterns or lantern shades, and he asked Mother to buy some," she muttered, repeating what Hyeongseon had said.

"If he wants to buy them he should buy them, why does he have to make so much noise?"

"Who made any noise? Don't talk nonsense. You'll just sour your relationship with him again."

Hyeongjun said nothing in reply to his wife's scolding, simply turning away and trying to get back to sleep. He had been trying hard to dream a dream. He was hoping to dream about anything, interpret that dream, and then follow the liaison, Mr. Shin, to the back room of Mr. Bak's house, where the master of the dream game sat and waited. But trying to fall asleep in the middle of the day was no easy task, and when he finally did fall asleep the baby would cry, a fly would land on his nose and tickle him, or someone would mumble something out in the yard, and he would wake up again before he could dream anything. With his eyes bloodshot, he tried to think of what he had dreamed, yet he could remember nothing but silly and trivial things.

Just now, he had finally managed to shut his eyes and fall asleep when he was startled awake by Hyeongseon mumbling something to their mother in the women's quarters, and when he tried to get back to sleep his eyes just would not shut. It felt as if he had dreamed something, but when he rummaged through his mind for the pieces, he saw himself running through the woods, coming upon a bog, and hesitating there as he wondered whether he should try to cross it or go around, until he woke up, but then when he thought about it again it seemed as if he had carried a dark scythe into the mountains to cut down trees with some maiden before he woke up, and his anger began to boil over because he could not figure out what had happened.

That rotten bastard going on about his lanterns or whatever it was had ruined his chances of having fortune fall right into his lap, so he was ready to lash out at the first person he saw. But his wife was already in a foul mood because he had rummaged through their chest, taking the money she had brought from her family when they were married, and left the house several days in a row, so if he vented his anger on her over this, he would be in for a headache. In the end, he just swallowed the rage that rumbled like thunder inside him, turned away, and lay down facing the wall.

It had not been long since Hyeongjun had started playing the dream game. Even when, not knowing what to do with his extra energy, he had gone to the room of the hired hand's wife and run into Hyeonggeol there, he'd had no interest in gambling at all. From his youth, he had on occasion played card games for money, but he did not follow these games as they made their rounds and had never bet a large sum on them.

But when he had been unable to let the affection he had felt for Duchil's wife, Ssangne, flow and that affection began to boil over from deep inside, he could not be shut in at home. A trip to some place refreshing, like the mountains or the beach, would have purified his spirit and put his mind at ease, but he did not think of that, and instead, as it was the middle of May and thus peak season for catching perch, he borrowed some nets from the old man from Pyeongyang and went out onto the Biryu River. When he was shut in at home, his heart only grew more restless and he could not even look at his family, so he set out on an outing and hoped to catch some fish.

He put a reed hat on his head, rolled up his pants above his calves, put straw shoes on his bare feet, and then went out the quiet rear gate. He followed the embankment down a short way to Ascending Immortal Bridge, which carried the alley that led to the

Confucian school. He went up onto the bridge, which had no railings, and followed the dim road that ran alongside Hoejindae. The clear river water rushed by swiftly beneath him.

The river first flowed around the twelve peaks and then widened out like a great lake in front of Cheonju Peak, where the waters were so still that the roofs of Descending Immortal Pavilion and Merciful Blessings Temple were mirrored in them, and then the river flowed on like oil until it roiled in the rapids beneath Ascending Immortal Bridge and Drifting Cloud Pavilion, finally smoothing out again as clear as jade beyond that. The wind on the river brushed his cheeks on that early summer morning, and he began to hum and sing a folk song to go along with the sound of the rapids.

> "I catch the clams and put them in my bag,
> And I catch my beloved and put her in my heart."

He sang this verse and then delicately sang the nonsensical chorus of "Hongyara dengyara ang!"

He crossed the bridge and started on the path into the mountains. He was planning to cross over the hill and go to the river on the other side. The Biryu River flowed around the long chain of mountains that stuck out like a peninsula and bent back around to the north. It is said that the Biryu, which literally means "hidden stream," got its name from the fact that the waters hidden in the mountains gushed down into the riverbed on the other side.

He rounded the hill and headed down the riverbank on the other side, singing another verse as he went, and this time he was carried away in his joy and lifted up his voice to sing.

> "My beloved, caught in a squall in her silken summer jacket,
> Look at those breasts like duck eggs!"

He sang this lively verse and then was about to sing the chorus again in a lilting voice when he heard the sound of people from the direction of Soil and Grain Pavilion on the ridge of the mountain. He wondered what this sound could be so early in the morning, and he peeked through the pine trees in the direction of the sound to find a large number of people all in a bustle, and then someone pointed in his direction and they all turned to look at Hyeongjun. He suddenly grew afraid, wondering why there were so many people there away from the eyes of others. So he pretended not to have noticed them and took long steps away from them and down toward the riverbank.

But then, from behind him, he heard someone who seemed to know him: "Isn't that Master Hyeongjun?"

He turned around and saw that it was Mr. Shin. He was dressed lightly, with only a brimless hat on his head, and he came rushing down the mountainside. "Where are you heading off to?" he asked when he drew close, slowing his steps.

"I was bored, so I thought I would go catch some perch," Hyeongjun replied.

Mr. Shin came to stand beside him. "Ah, that's right, it's perch season, isn't it." Then he looked around and quietly asked, "Do you want to try something fun?"

Hyeongjun could guess what he was talking about, but he asked anyway. "Something fun? Well, you wouldn't have been drinking this early in the morning."

Mr. Shin waved his right hand in the air as if to say, 'What are you talking about?' and then said, "Is drinking that much fun?" Then he drew close and whispered into Hyeongjun's ear: "Do you want to try writing out a slip for the dream game?"

"No. How would I know how to do that?" Hyeongjun refused with a serious look on his face.

"Well, there's nothing to it, really. You just dream a dream, interpret it, and then bet on it. You'll be lucky, I think, so why don't you give it a try?"

Mr. Shin seemed intent on dragging Hyeongjun into the dream game. Those who played moved locations every day to avoid the eyes of the patrolmen or their henchmen, and today they had met in the woods behind Soil and Grain Pavilion. They had been careful to keep quiet, but then someone who had bet on "boundless gold" had won. So the gamblers, forgetting where they were, had sent up a cheer of wonder, but when they looked down they saw someone looking up at them, wearing a conical hat and carrying nets down to the river. They were just about to flee before even finishing reading out the results when Mr. Shin said, "That's Assistant Curator Bak's eldest son," and everyone stopped in their tracks. It would just not do for news of this to get out, so they decided to bring Hyeongjun into the game, and Mr. Shin had come down after him.

"We just had someone win with 'boundless gold,' so it looks like everyone is lucky today. The bet was for one hundred nyang, so the master of the game had to pay him three thousand nyang and nearly soiled himself. Why don't you give it a try?" When Hyeongjun still refused to listen, he said, "Don't be so pointlessly stubborn. If you keep refusing, everyone will think you're one of those patrolmen's henchmen, and who knows what they will do then?" It was a thinly veiled threat.

Hyeongjun, who had never been all that strong-willed, reluctantly said, "But I don't have any money."

"I can lend you as much as you need. I mean, who wouldn't lend you money? If you've dreamed a dream, I'll lend you however much you want."

So Hyeongjun reluctantly followed him up the mountain.

When he arrived, there were only a dozen or so people there. Of these, some five or six were gamblers and the rest were the master of the game, the scorekeeper, and the liaisons. The liaisons gathered the slips of paper and bets from decent folk and checked the results for them when the winning sign was revealed. Libertine though he was, the master of the game was ghastly pale as he paid out three thousand nyang. Hyeongjun knew him well. His name was Oh Mandal, a rake of about forty years or so who had a name for being good at cards and had one pale eye. He was now paying money out of a large money bag, the amount calculated by the scorekeeper, and a few gamblers in a wooded hollow behind the pavilion had forgotten where they were and were chatting noisily.

"OK, listen to my dream. So, anyway, I have an entire steamer full of steamed white rice cakes, and I am sitting there talking and laughing with the daughter-in-law of the rice cake shop owner as we ate the rice cakes, and after I have my fill, the girl and I get along quite nicely. So how should I interpret this dream? I think getting along with the girl is more important than eating a lot of rice cakes. So I thought of picking either 'bright bead' or 'invitation from above' from among the Four Ladies, but then I thought old Pale Eye there would not choose one of the Four Ladies. And this is the first game, so I just wrote down 'boundless gold.' And wouldn't you know it, 'boundless gold' is the right one, the right one! How amazing!"

A young man with only a towel wrapped around his top-knot carried on like this, and a man with a pockmarked face sitting across from him said, "Never in my life have I stuffed myself with rice cakes," and then he rattled on about how wonderful it would be to have a dream of eating rice cakes and then win by betting on "boundless gold."

"You're telling me! Last night, I drew water and then prayed until my knees chafed." The master of the game, having handed out all the money and hearing them carrying on about their silly dreams, scowled at them. "Stop your chatter now. You don't want to be dreaming in a prison cell," he scolded them.

Hyeongjun squatted down next to the pavilion and stared blankly at the master, the liaisons, and the gamblers as they chatted. A large piece of paper had been soaked in perilla oil, and on it was drawn in ink the likeness of a human body with thirty-six signs around it, and this had then been laid on a flat spot on the grass. Mr. Shin grabbed the paper and brought it to Hyeongjun. In one hand he carried a carved woodblock, and he spread out the paper on a flat spot on the ground and said, "OK, these are the thirty-six signs. Starting from here this is 'capturing leader,' 'laurel plank,' 'glorious life,' and 'spring of meeting.' "

He stopped, showed him the signs on the woodblock, and then continued: "Next are the Four Ladies, 'stopping jade,' 'bright bead,' 'invitation from above,' and 'union.' You know these, right? If you dream of having a union with a woman, then you choose 'union'—that's how it works. Next are 'three lumps,' 'unified seas,' 'nine officials,' and 'great peace,' by the neck here is 'sun mountain,' things like official attire or a military officer's cap would go under 'fire official' or 'well of advantage,' by the foot here is 'kind nature,' the eyes are 'bright light,' 'advantage' here is also known as 'Old

Man Advantage' and applies to old men, then there is 'river shrine,' 'fortunate descendant,' and so on. You get the idea."

Hyeongjun already had the basic idea, but he listened without a word. Mr. Shin was busy explaining all the signs when the master said, "Let's play another round here." He had just lost three thousand nyang and wanted to make back at least half of that.

But then, from the hollow, came the voice of the pockmarked man. "What are we supposed to do for dreams?" He went back to his seat, displeased.

"Look here, who says we should stop just because I won? All we have to do is close our eyes to dream. Let's go again." The man with the towel on his head rolled up his sleeves and leaped out of the hollow.

So they decided to play another round right there. Mr. Shin took a piece of paper and gave it to Hyeongjun. "If you'd rather not be part of the group, you can go home and write out your sign, and I can bring it back for you."

But Hyeongjun took the piece of paper and made no reply. He was thinking of what he had dreamed the night before.

The master of the game took a piece of paper and a brush and went off somewhere. He was heading into the woods to pick one of the thirty-six signs to write down.

"He's going up to the top of the mountain, so I bet he will write 'earth mountain' or 'mind of the heights,' " came the teasing voice of the pockmarked man from within the hollow.

The master laughed and said, "Since you know me so well, write down whatever you wish," and then he disappeared into the woods.

Hyeongjun was embarrassed to admit it, but the night before he had dreamed about going into Ssangne's room and being caught by a patrolman. He didn't know how it had happened, but he pulled Ssangne to him as she resisted and they rolled back and forth for some time, when suddenly the door flew open and a strong young man rushed in. He was shocked, thinking it might be Duchil or Hyeonggeol, but, to his surprise, it was a patrolman. The patrolman told him that he had clearly entered the house to commit robbery, and, no matter how he tried to explain himself, the patrolman bound his hands, told him to be quiet, and struck him on the shins. The patrolman grabbed him by the neck and shoved him, and he stumbled backward toward the door, caught his heel on the doorsill, and fell on his back, but as luck would have it he opened his eyes and found that it had all been a dream.

For this sort of dream, he could not choose anything like the Four Ladies, or "highest fortune," "highest honor," or "auspicious commodity," so he had no choice but to write something like "capturing leader," but while "capturing leader" might have worked if he himself had been a patrolman, or if he had been at a drinking party with some patrolman, he had instead dreamed about going into the room of a married woman, being accused of being a robber, being bound by a patrolman, and then tripping on the doorsill and falling over backward, so he felt somewhat uncomfortable and displeased about the whole thing. But if he were to write something, he felt that the only thing he could write was "capturing leader," and everyone was waiting for him to write something down.

After some time, the master of the game came out of the woods carrying a bundle. He said, "I'm tying up the thirty-six signs," and he tied up the bundle like an oriole's nest around the end of a bent pine branch.

The scorekeeper held a piece of white paper and the woodblock, and waited for the slips of paper to come in. The liaisons gathered, and then the gamblers slowly gathered as well. They held out their money and the slips of paper on which they had written down their signs to the scorekeeper. Hyeongjun was reluctantly writing down "capturing leader" when Mr. Shin came along and said, "How much are you going to bet? Maybe twenty nyang? It is your first time, after all."

"Yes, let's do that." Hyeongjun handed Mr. Shin his piece of paper. Hyeongjun watched closely as the paper was inspected and his bet was taken.

"OK, I'm opening up the bag."

The master, blinking his pale eye, reached up to the branch and took down the bag. Everyone stared with piercing gazes as he opened it. Pale Eye opened it with practiced ease. "I bet someone will win again this time," he said with a grin.

"Humph. I'll bet that everyone misses this time," groused the pockmarked man, suspicious of the master's smile.

"It's a hit this time, I tell you, a hit. Look, a hit!"

But when he opened the bag, the sign was "certain gain."

"Who got it?"

The only one who had written down "certain gain" was Pockmark. But he must not have been too confident in his dream, as he had not bet that much. After paying out thirty times the bet, the master of the game kept the rest for himself.

After blowing twenty nyang in less than an hour, Hyeongjun, who had no experience with gambling or games of chance, had lost his appetite for the game.

"What sort of dream did you have that you wrote down 'capturing leader'?" Mr. Shin asked.

He left out the part about having gone into Ssangne's room and just said that he had been bound by a patrolman and been roughly treated by him, so that he had caught his heel on the doorsill and fell over.

"Then you interpreted that dream wrong. If you caught your heel, that's 'certain gain,' isn't it? — the dream itself was right, you just got it wrong when you wrote down 'capturing leader.' What an excellent dream indeed. Anyway, you are walking around with a fortune," said Mr. Shin in genuine admiration.

Now that he thought of it, Mr. Shin's explanation seemed quite plausible. He had caught his heel and fallen over backward before waking up, so it was "certain gain"— he realized that he had to ruminate on every aspect of every single dream. Even if he had lost twenty nyang, this gambling wasn't so dull after all, and he thought that he might be lucky or fortunate enough to come into a windfall, just like Mr. Shin said.

That was the end of the game for that day. He went home, got twenty nyang and then brought it over to Mr. Shin's house, and when Mr. Shin took the money he said, "I'll let you know when I hear of some good games, so just dream some good dreams. If you don't want to actually be there, you can just send me a piece of paper. I'll take care of everything for you. You may not know it, but there are quite a few men in this village who sit at home like gentlemen but have gotten a taste for this game through us liaisons. It helps pass the time, and if things go your way you may come into a windfall!"

At that moment, Hyeongjun did not really have any desire to try his hand at the dream game again. But from that day, when he would wake up in the morning, the dreams he had dreamed the night before were so strange and wonderful that he would not even eat his breakfast and instead would have a good time trying to interpret the dream according to the thirty-six signs. If he thought his interpretation was a good one, naturally, he would think of placing a bet on it. So he would eat his breakfast and, figuring he would get some fresh air while he was at it, take about fifty nyang from his wife's chest and go to visit Mr. Shin.

If he had tried it three times and missed all three times, he would have quit, thinking the game was one he had no chance of winning, dream or no dream, but even a blind man stumbles onto the door latch from time to time, and Hyeongjun's sign was picked just once. Having his dream hit the mark whet his appetite, and from then on he began to use all his spare time to play the dream game.

After he ate he made a fuss about going to sleep, and when he went to sleep he was desperate, praying and begging with his hands to his chest that he might dream a dream, and when he awoke he went out of his mind trying to interpret his dreams, sitting there with his eyes glazed over like a madman.

At first, his wife had no idea what was going on with her husband. He often went out, and when he came back home he always went right to sleep. So she thought that he must have a woman somewhere whom he was going to see. And, come to think of it, her husband's attitude toward her was not as gentle as it used to be. So one day she said, "Is there something you need to take care of these days?"

"No, it's nothing, just that someone has a good gold mine, and I've been going to see it."

'A gold mine?' she thought. 'What gold mine could this be that he would not tell his father about it?'

So she asked, "Have you started a gold mine, then?"

"No, I haven't started a mine. I need to find out if it's worth it or not before I start. This is nothing for a woman to get involved in!"

He got angry, so she could not ask any more.

But today Hyeongjun was napping. Mr. Shin told him of a good game where there would be a lot of gamblers, and, since there was the worry of being caught if they always met in the mountains, this time they would place their bets and open up the bag in the back room of Mr. Bak's house. So Hyeongjun was napping in order to dream a new dream, since his dream from the night before had been nothing special. He must have dreamed the dream he wanted as soon as he closed his eyes, for he quickly got up and went out.

He dreamed that he had boarded a large boat and crossed the Biryu River, so he was certain this would be "laurel plank." He hesitated, wondering whether he should bet the thirty nyang he had in hand or if he should get some more from his wife or mother and bet fifty or sixty nyang, but then he just took his thirty nyang and went to Mr. Shin's house. Mr. Shin said that he had been waiting for him, asked him if he had dreamed a good dream, and then said that the room was rather small that night and it would be risky for many people to meet, so Hyeongjun might not want to go in person. Hyeongjun thought that, if that were the case, there was no need to go, so he wrote "laurel plank" on his piece of paper, rolled it up tight, and then handed over the money as well. Mr. Shin told him that they wouldn't open the bag until late at night, so he told Hyeongjun to pick a meeting place and wait there. Hyeongjun thought for a moment and then suggested meeting by the bramble hedge outside the rear gate of his house.

It was already evening. On his way home, he thought about what Hyeongseon had said earlier, and he stopped in at Nakanishi's store. There he looked at all of the new items that had come in before, and then he went home and ate dinner.

Hyeongseon stayed in the women's quarters until late at night. He ate dinner and went back and forth between the men's quarters and the women's quarters, and in the end he bought four lanterns and a tin of kerosene. The big one he hung in his father's room, and he hung the three small lanterns in his mother's room,

Hyeongjun's room, and his own room. The kerosene lanterns were so marvelous that they were all everybody talked about after dinner. In the women's quarters, Bopae put the lantern next to the old oil lamp to compare the two, and they chattered as they lit them and put them out again.

Hyeongjun's wife wanted to make some pretty clothes beneath the bright light, and she sat there sewing a collar on the silk jacket she had brought with her when she got married, but Seonggi and her young daughter climbed up onto her knees and pestered her. "Go see your father," she said, and pushed Seonggi toward Hyeongjun. Hyeongjun was thinking about the dream game and had no thought to spare for the children or anything else. His wife had passed off the children to him without knowing this, and Hyeongjun flew into a fit of anger at her. He said that he did not want to be bothered by the children, and he shot up from where he sat and left the room.

"I won't ask you to watch the children, please don't leave!" she called after him softly, but he paid her no mind and went off somewhere without even a hat on his head. She had been especially careful, thinking that perhaps it was her own inattention that had caused her husband to not want to be at home these days. So she immediately regretted the way she had acted toward her husband. But it was not like her husband to grow angry over something like that. She feared that she might even lose her husband's affection forever if things went on like this. She wanted to act like a child, running out and grabbing her husband's arm or the hem of his clothes, begging him not to leave and promising him she wouldn't do it again, but her mother-in-law and sister-in-law were sitting in her mother-in-law's room, and in the room across the way her brother-in-law and his wife had the light on and were not yet asleep, so she could not act however she pleased. Neither could she take out her anger on her children, so she stuffed the clothes back into her sewing box and, with her lips primly shut, she gathered her children to her and lay down. She was so upset she suddenly wanted to cry.

Hyeongjun stood in the yard of the men's quarters and looked up at the sky. The weather was cloudy. It was near the end of the month so there was no moon yet, and only the big stars shone now and then. The evening breeze was refreshing. The new lantern was not lit in the men's quarters, as Assistant Curator Bak was not there. Hyeongjun went and sat down on the ledge outside the room, but all he could think about was the dream game.

The dream he had dreamed earlier that day had been unusually clear and extraordinary, and even now it all appeared clearly before his eyes: he was crossing the river on a flat-bottomed boat with boatmen pushing the boat along with poles on either side, and on the boat with him were women, each with a bundle of wood at their sides. Yet there was one thing that wasn't clear: what he had gone to the twelve peaks for that he would be coming back on a boat. But the reason he was on the boat probably wasn't all that important. He was on a boat, so it must be "laurel plank." He sat there by himself and thought about it over and over, not realizing that he was like a pipe burning by itself, thinking that this time he would surely hit the mark, when Duchil came out of his room by the path behind the outhouse and greeted Hyeongjun as he crossed the yard on his way to the front gate.

"Where are you going?" Hyeongjun asked.

He stopped and politely replied, "I am going out to get a few workers and also to stop by at a house that is holding ancestral rites."

"Who is holding the ancestral rites?"

"It is a year since Mun Gildeok's father passed," he answered. He hesitated there a moment longer, his feet fixed to the ground, and then he bowed again and went out of the main gate. But then, having only gone a few steps, he came back in, put the bar back down on the main gate, and retraced his steps. It was around the time to lock the front door, so he had closed it himself and made for the rear gate instead.

Hyeongjun, who had been thinking of "laurel plank" in the dream game, trying to wring one last drop out of an already dry dream, suddenly thought of Duchil's wife, Ssangne.

'Hyeonggeol will probably continue to see her whenever he thinks that Duchil is away. Did Father even say anything in reprimand to Hyeonggeol? Would Hyeonggeol still be visiting her if he had been reprimanded?'

These were the thoughts going through Hyeongjun's mind.

The truth, though, was that Hyeonggeol had only visited Ssangne twice. He did not really take to heart the night that he was discovered by Hyeongjun, and the next day he went to Ssangne's room again, but after walking back to his room in the rain and being scolded by his mother, he had not gone back even once. Actually, the day after that second day, Duchil had returned, so he couldn't have gone back even if he had wanted to.

'Duchil will be back late tonight again, and if Hyeonggeol gets wind of that he might come back. This time I will have to give him a proper talking to or let the family know what is happening.' Though these thoughts came to mind, on the other hand, Hyeongjun also thought, 'Shall I have a little fun, threatening Ssangne over her relationship with Hyeonggeol while I wait for Mr. Shin to arrive?'

Hyeongjun himself was well aware that the virility he had forgotten for some time, thanks to the dream game, was now surging up within him again. 'I must do my duty as the elder brother, wherever that might lead. The eldest brother's responsibility is to watch his younger brothers' actions and guard against wrongdoing.'

He reasoned with himself like this on the surface, but deep down he was thinking, 'If I go into Ssangne's room and give her candy with one hand and threaten her with a knife in the other, she will surely fall into my clutches. Then I will feel much better, and when Mr. Shin tells me that I hit the mark in the dream game with "laurel plank," he will hand over a purse full of money, thirty times thirty nyang, and from that I will take a certain amount and give it Mr. Shin for a job well done and split the rest with Ssangne. If she refuses it, I will chide her and tell her that she must accept money from her master's son, and I will give it to her even if she doesn't want it.'

As he pondered these things, he got up from the wooden ledge, went around behind the outhouse, and walked to the rear gate.

Duchil's room was dark. She wouldn't be asleep already — not long ago she had gone from the master's kitchen to feed the animals in the stable and then returned to her own house with a basket of rice, so she would have eaten dinner with Duchil and would only now have finished cleaning up the kitchen and be waiting in her room for her husband to return, sewing even after a hard day's work. Thus putting out the lights this early might be a sign that Duchil was not home and a way to attract Hyeonggeol's attention. But then, beyond the wide-open rear gate, he saw something white fluttering in the darkness.

After eating dinner, Ssangne had taken some linen clothes out to do a rough washing, and now she was hanging out her undergarments next to the bramble hedge outside the rear gate.

Hyeongjun stepped outside the gate and watched her until she finished hanging her laundry, and when she picked up her large basket and turned to go back inside, he grabbed her by the waistband. He took the basket away from her and dropped it on the ground, just lightly enough so that it wouldn't break, and then threw his arms around her waist.

Ssangne was surprised by Hyeongjun's actions. Only a few days ago he had caught the young master from Dumutgol coming out of her room and had reproached him, then the next day he had gone and caused a stir by telling her master, and he had even spread the word so that it had reached the ears of the old servant; so what did he think he was doing now, grabbing her with his own hands? She would have known nothing of his trouble-making had the old servant not called her into the kitchen and told her about it. So she already thought he was contemptible for going around whispering rumors in such an unmanly fashion, and when the young master from Dumutgol came again the second day but then never came back, she despised Hyeongjun even more for his part in that; but, now, grabbing her bodily with his own arms, son of her master or no, this was disgraceful. She straightened up.

"Let me go." She shook off the arms that were wrapped around her waist.

Surprised by Ssangne's unexpectedly cold reaction, he faltered, took a step back, and then stepped forward and said in a threatening tone, "What do you think you are doing?"

"What would you expect me to do, then?" Her next words she did not utter, but she lifted her chin haughtily and thought, 'I may not have been faithful to my husband, but I will not break the rules of morality.'

He spoke again. "Are you really going to be like this?" But Ssangne said nothing in reply and only stared straight at him. "Well, if you are, I will tell Duchil, and I will see to it that the two of you have no place in this household."

He looked at her once again, as if to say, 'Are you fine with that?' Seeing her speechless, he took this as a clear sign of surrender, and he relaxed the expression on his face and held out his right hand once more.

"Do as you wish," she said. "What more can you do but kill me?"

Yet Hyeongjun could tell well enough from her tone that 'Do as you wish' did not mean 'I give my body to you, so take it and play with it as you will,' but 'Kill me if you will, for I will never grant your request.' He slapped Ssangne on the cheek and walked straight out the bramble hedge gate toward the water's edge. He paused on the embankment for a moment to calm himself and saw Mr. Shin approaching from below. When he asked him about the game, he found that the sign had not been "laurel plank" but "blue cloud." He said nothing and went off to Mun Gildeok's house in a huff.

Outside the twig gate, he called in to the bustling yard, "Is Duchil there?"

Duchil rushed out and said, "You asked for me?"

Hyeongjun looked at Duchil standing in front of him and said, "Your wife has behaved crudely and allowed Hyeonggeol from Dumutgol to visit her at night, and if things go on like this the family will come to disgrace, so you must pack up and leave."

Duchil had no idea what this sudden outburst meant, and he stood there for some time without a clue.

13

Just as Hyeongjun was snitching on Hyeonggeol and Ssangne to Duchil at Mun Gildeok's house, having been unable to have his way with Ssangne and losing at the dream game on top of that, Hyeonggeol was walking past the government office well in front of Descending Immortal Pavilion, dressed in light clothes.

After his mother had scolded him for seeing Duchil's wife, Hyeonggeol did as she commanded and did not visit Ssangne's room again, but he cleanly ignored the admonition not to go out at night at all. He didn't go out for about two days, but then he went to the Wednesday evening church service, and, after this, though there may have been days when he stayed home, if something came up he did not hesitate to leave the house. Assistant Curator Bak and Lady Yun each told him not to go out once, but not only was there no way they could keep a young man like that cooped up, they also felt guilty about telling their grown son that he couldn't go out. So, even though he had crossly blurted out that he wasn't going to get married, they set out to find a proper woman for him as quickly as possible, thinking that it was their duty as parents to plan Hyeonggeol's marriage.

Hyeonggeol had eaten dinner, and, seeing the overcast weather and not really feeling like opening his books to study, he left the house with the idea of visiting Mr. Mun's house. But as he stepped out of the front gate and headed toward Nine Dragons Bridge, he thought he might end up being a nuisance if he visited Mr. Mun's house too often. He had gone last night, and if he went again tonight, though Mr. Mun might always greet him warmly with no sign of displeasure on his face, he must have studies of his own to attend to, and Hyeonggeol had to think about keeping up appearances. Since he was out, he went to Daebong's house, but Daebong was already out somewhere else. Hyeonggeol was certain that Daebong had realized Yi Chilseong was off somewhere and had gone over to Chilseong's wife, perhaps to play cards. Chilseong's wife was the daughter of a family that ran a noodle shop in Pyeongyang's Sachang Market, and though she had gone through a bit of a wanton phase when she was younger, she was later married to a man in Sangwon County or thereabouts. She felt this husband was too young for her, though, so she left him and returned to her family. Chilseong had often visited Pyeongyang, from the time he was a peddler, but around the time when he found a place in the market to sell his groceries, he spent as much time at the Sachang Market noodle shop as he did in his own home. He caught the eye of the family's daughter, who was living at home because she didn't like her husband, and the two of them ran off to start a family. And though they did indeed start a family, just as they say you can't teach an old dog new tricks, when Chilseong traveled to other areas to sell his wares, his wife was so bored that she couldn't stand it. She even tried playing card games by herself once or twice. Chilseong was not some husband she had been married to against her will, so she was happy enough when he was there, but when he traveled elsewhere she was so lonely in this provincial town she thought she might die. Thus Daebong, who had come to look at the bicycle, became a good friend to talk to, and although she had nothing else in mind when she invited him over to her house, as the days went by and they grew closer . . . well, he was a fully grown bachelor, so there was no telling what might have happened by now.

Hyeonggeol could thus guess at Daebong's whereabouts. So he did not even think about going to Chilseong's house to look for him. If it were just Daebong there by himself that was one thing, but if he should happen to run into Chilseong instead, there would be no end to his shame. Hyeonggeol did think briefly of Ssangne, but Duchil would be home, and even if he weren't he did not really have any desire to go see her.

So he wondered if he should just go home and go to bed, but then he suddenly thought of Buyong, whom they had visited under the pretext of evangelism. He had gone in at Daebong's urging and spouted all sorts of nonsense before leaving, but the gisaeng was courteous and carried herself in a dignified way, and, more than anything else, he could not forget how she had grabbed his hand by the beaded curtain and then blushed, not knowing what to do, so before he knew it he had walked up the street toward Descending Immortal Pavilion and was now passing by the government office well.

Without even whistling, he slowly put one foot in front of the other, thinking all sorts of things about Buyong as he went.

What would she be doing now? Even if she wasn't widely known, being a gisaeng only recently come from Pyeongyang, judging by her appearance, her figure, and the way she treated people, anyone who laid eyes on her would want to spend time with her, and on dark nights like this with few stars in the sky, even those who were not libertines or rakes would surely visit her house and spend the night tastefully, having a drink and listening to her play the gayageum. On moonlit nights, light entertainment by which to enjoy the light of the moon might be nice, but on days like today, when the weather made the spirit heavy, a more elegant person might prefer to lift the liquor glass and share moments to make the heart brim. Thus there was no way that a young student of nearly twenty who had visited once as a Christian evangelist would ever see his turn come to peek into a gisaeng's house, and even if his turn did come, what gisaeng would ever be glad to see him? Realizing that what he was looking for was ultimately empty vanity, he grew even more melancholic. But he did not want to just turn around and go back. He wanted to loiter about outside the walls of the house and simply listen to the sound of the gayageum from within. And he wanted to hear that clear and beautiful voice floating out every now and then.

He walked along slowly thinking these things, but when he had just about reached the front gate of Daebong's relative's house, two drunk young men came around the corner of the walls of Buyong's house and stepped out into the street, spouting unrepeatable curses.

"These boorish yokels, it serves them right to get what's coming to them, jerking us around like that."

They were mumbling about someone as they approached, and Hyeonggeol saw that they each wore flat caps, black Western suit jackets, and tabi boots, and their calves above their boots were wrapped tightly with strips of cloth. They had towels around their necks, and as they came out they tossed away cigarettes they hadn't even smoked halfway — they were no doubt the surveyors who had shown up in this village a few days ago. Behind them, though, staggered a man who looked to be in his forties, helped along by others as he let out quiet cries of pain. His clothes were a mess and he was not even able to stand up straight, and as soon as he cleared the wall he went off in the other direction.

The surveyors walked right past Hyeonggeol. Their shoulders were still full of the strength they had used to beat the other man, and they bumped Hyeonggeol aside, paying no attention to someone like him, and spat on the street. "We'll beat to a pulp anyone who stands up to us," they said, their tone suggesting that they would beat even the child they had just shouldered out of the way.

Hyeonggeol felt something boil up from inside him. He turned his head. "You there, you two are that good at beating people, eh?"

It wasn't that he was angry at being looked down on, but when he realized that the fight that had just happened had taken place at Buyong's house he was furious.

"Why, do you want a taste?"

The flat caps turned around at once, and the men looked as if they were ready to strike at that moment. Hyeonggeol stood there calmly and looked them up and down. "You two, you're still wet behind the ears."

The man they had thought was just a child stood there, his two feet planted firmly on the ground and his arms coolly folded across his chest. Impudent bastard — even as they thought this and even as the fury began to spread like wildfire through their liquor-addled minds, Hyeonggeol's two hands suddenly grabbed each of them by the throat. He had prevented them from headbutting him. They twisted their heads, but when they realized that they could not overcome the strength in Hyeonggeol's arms, which were jammed under their chins like pillars, the one held by Hyeonggeol's right hand quickly began kicking, but Hyeonggeol pulled him by the throat and cracked him in the head with his forehead, and the young man went limp and collapsed. Now it was one-on-one. But before Hyeonggeol had even a moment to catch his breath, two hands hard as stone came flying at his left arm. Using his hands like a blacksmith's tongs, the young man pried open Hyeonggeol's fist, and with all his might he grabbed Hyeonggeol's forearm and pulled it toward his belly. Now all he had to do was strike Hyeonggeol with his leg and he would go down. Hyeonggeol drove his head straight into his opponent's chest like a bull, and, with his left arm still locked, he again grabbed the man's throat. His hand slipped up and touched the man's lips, and the wide mouth with the scraggly beard opened and bit down on the back of Hyeonggeol's hand with his sharp front teeth. The pain that suddenly flooded through Hyeonggeol's entire body was rather a stimulant that caused him to summon up the last of his strength. He didn't care if his hand was torn. He pushed his opponent with all his might, drove him against the wall of the house across the way, and began to beat him furiously about the stomach and chest until the young man was spent, all the strength leaving his mouth and his arms, and he swayed there for a moment before sinking to the ground with his back against the wall. Hyeonggeol disentangled himself and then aimed a kick at his head with his leather shoe, and the flat cap fell from the young man's head and rolled across the ground, while the young man himself was knocked out cold. Hyeonggeol grabbed his bleeding hand and went back out onto the street, but in the dark night shadows of people were talking noisily.

"Who was beaten, and who did the beating?"

Hyeonggeol did not want to deal with whatever consequences there might be, so he ran off down the road. He had done nothing wrong, but he was worried that there might be a fuss if a patrolman arrived. He ran off toward the river and stopped to catch his breath, when he heard someone coming up behind him. He thought about jumping beneath the embankment to hide before the shadow drew close, but the footsteps that came down the alley after him were not rough, and he stood there for a moment, leaning ever so slightly forward. If the hand on his shoulder meant him harm, he could drag his attacker down the embankment and into the water. But then even those light footsteps faded and the river's edge was as quiet as it had been before. He could hear the sound of the rapids beneath Ascending Immortal Bridge in the distance. He turned his head.

There, well within his reach, unexpectedly stood a young woman.

"Who is it?" he asked. She was clearly someone who had followed him from the scene of the fight, but he knew of no woman in this upper part of the neighborhood who would approach him from behind and then stand there without a word.

"It's me," she answered, and the voice was that of a woman still resplendent in his memory.

"Buyong," Hyeonggeol mumbled softly. This is how unexpected and also how glad a meeting it was. He had guessed that the two surveyors that had gone down at his hand had been on their way out of Buyong's house after making a ruckus there, but he never imagined that Buyong would be among the spectators to the fight, and he never would have dreamed that the footsteps following along behind him after he ran off to avoid dealing with the aftermath would be hers.

Hyeonggeol took a step back on the road. Buyong was there. He could not clearly see her face. He slowly walked to her side. The fragrance of aromatic oil wafted through the air. Buyong said nothing. Hyeonggeol said nothing. They stood side by side until Hyeonggeol took one step up the street, and from beside him came the sound of light, dry leather shoes.

They silently walked toward Pear Blossom Pavilion, up the shore of the Biryu River.

The faint sound of frogs croaking in the river could be heard. The frogs were croaking desperately, trying to hatch their eggs in the dark, starless night.

In all her eighteen years, Buyong had never been struck speechless like this in front of someone. Ever since she was young, people had doted on her, praising her for being so courteous and sociable. It was the first time she had ever just walked silently next to a man without being able to say a single proper word of greeting or give a single compliment. She struggled to speak the words that filled her heart to the brim. But the words that would come out if she opened her mouth seemed so inadequate to convey what she felt.

Buyong had entertained a guest who appeared to be some sort of scholar and, after preparing liquor for this guest, became so absorbed in talking about the poetry of her namesake, the famous gisaeng Kim Buyong, that she lost track of the time. But when the night grew late, two rude outsiders rushed in like fish into a weir and began to raise a ruckus. She spoke to them politely, telling them that she already had a guest, but they refused to listen, and they insisted on picking on this guest until they at last impertinently lashed out in violence against him. Not long after the servants who had brought the guest had finally managed to escort him out, again there came the clamor of fighting. She rushed out, thinking that perhaps those two fellows had again lashed out in violence against the guest, who had left without even being able to straighten his clothes, but there was no sign of him, and instead there was a scuffle near the street. Four or five onlookers had already gathered round, and though it was so dark that nothing could be seen clearly, two of the three in the scuffle were definitely the outsiders who had just left her room. One of them had fallen to the ground and was writhing and moaning like a toad, while the other was grappling with some young man in light clothes. Thinking that, surely, these two fellows had begun fighting with this young man after leaving her house, Buyong squeezed between the dozen onlookers that had by then gathered and craned her neck to see who it was that was fighting these two. But there was no way she could see the face of the young man who drove his opponent into the wall and then rammed his head into his belly. The two were locked together and wrestled for some time, threatening each other, kicking at each other, and striking each other continuously. After some time, one of the two must have been pinched or bitten somewhere, for she heard a scream amidst the gasping, and Buyong felt that she had heard that voice somewhere before and so tried even harder to get closer to him, when suddenly a face she knew passed before her. The face of that young man — the young man who drove his opponent hard into the wall and dropped him like a sack of rice before nimbly freeing himself and running off — it was clearly the face of that young student who had visited Buyong's house on Sunday and told her to believe in Jesus.

That student — she did not know his first name or his family name, but she had held in her own hands the fierce pulse that beat in his wrists.

He had struck down those two outsiders as strong as oxen, but he must have been so tired after that long fight that he let out that scream. Buyong, caught up in the excitement and without even realizing it, had run down the alley after the student, who had freed himself in a flash, crossed the street, and run off down to the river's edge.

But as she walked along the tranquil riverbank in silence next to this young student, Buyong felt something in her heart like a tightly wound cotton ball coming undone. It filled her heart like a vapor and then spread up to her face through her throat and her nose. It was only when it had spread through her entire body that Buyong realized she was wrapped up in happiness.

"Let us sit here."

Pear Blossom Pavilion stood somber on the hill above, but in the night as black as ink even it could not be seen. They knew that they had arrived at a weeping willow when they felt the willow branches tickling the tops of their heads.

They groped around for the trunk of the willow and found two spots where they could sit side by side. Hyeonggeol held out his uninjured hand in the darkness. It felt as if his fingertips brushed her skirt, but then her warm, delicate hand found his. He sat down first and then led Buyong to sit down next to him. The scent of the woman wafted round the willow tree. Cheonju Peak could be seen faintly against the night sky, but beneath it nothing else was visible, not the river, nor the pavilion. A fisherman's fire flickered sleepily above Ascending Immortal Bridge like a star. Even the croaking of the frogs had grown distant.

"Do you know who I am?" Hyeonggeol asked softly.

"What woman would be indiscreet enough to follow someone she does not know on a starless night?"

Hyeonggeol clasped Buyong's two hands in his. Her rings were cool and refreshing on her warm fingers. Only when her hand was in his did Buyong think of the man's right hand. And she thought back to the single cry that had rung out during the fight.

"Is your right hand hurt?"

"It is not serious, but it looks like he bit me."

"Those rude, disgraceful fellows." Buyong rebuked them aloud and then gently took her hand from Hyeonggeol's to take out a handkerchief, but she had forgotten to bring even that when she hastily ran out of her house. She silently tore off a skirt string. "Let us bind it with this."

"The bleeding seems to have stopped, so it should be fine as it is."

"No. Let us bind it with this." In the darkness, Buyong bound his swollen right hand. She held his hand in hers and stroked it gently. "Doesn't it ache?"

"He bit me when he was drunk, so what poison could there have been? It will heal as it is."

They did not want to talk about the fight anymore. On such a beautiful and lovely night, they did not want to think such vulgar thoughts.

"Do you like this town?"

Buyong had no ready reply to this question and smiled quietly instead. She wanted to say that the mountains and waters were lovely, and she liked them even more because of him, but she did not dare say the words. After a long while, she finally replied, "The mountains are green and the waters are deep and even the people are few, so how can this not be paradise?"

Hyeonggeol realized that Buyong was referring to an old poem that sang of the twelve peaks of Mount Mu, the Biryu River, and Descending Immortal Pavilion, and he thought of the lines. It was a poem by Jang Munbo, and the original went like this:

"Mountains green, waters deep, and folk seldom seen,
I ask, is this place not then paradise?"

He mouthed the lines to himself and than asked Buyong, "Buyong, have you heard the famous poem of Descending Immortal Pavilion?"

"I have not been here long, so I have not yet heard it. I asked a scholar about it, but he said that he did not know it, either."

"It has not been long since I heard it myself, and even the one who taught it to me did not know the name of the poet." He stopped talking for a moment and then began reciting.

"I am deep in thought and the clouds are damp,
The flowers do not want the rain to stop.
I hope to see him just before dawn,
And for ten days ascend nine times to the pavilion."

"I don't think it is that well written, but it seems to have been based on the name of the pavilion, Pavilion of the Descending Immortal."

Buyong recited the words to herself and then asked, "How did the end of it go again?"

Hyeonggeol recited the Chinese characters and then added the interpretation: "I hope to see him just before dawn, and for ten days ascend nine times to the pavilion."

The wind whistled through the trees. The rustling of the willow branches reached their ears. Then the wind seemed to subside and fat rain drops fell.

"Is it raining?" Hyeonggeol held out his hand. A raindrop fell on his outstretched palm. "It's raining, let us go before we get wet."

Hyeonggeol got up, but Buyong stayed where she was. "So what if we get a little wet?" she teased him, but when Hyeonggeol didn't budge from where he stood, she reluctantly got up as well. "Since it's raining, why don't you stop at my house before you go," she urged, standing next to him.

"I live with my parents, so I must be home early."

"But it's raining."

"Right. It's raining, so I need to go before I get wet."

They talked quietly as they slowly walked up the way they had come down.

"You can stop by my place for an umbrella before you go, can't you?"

Hyeonggeol said nothing.

"The last time you came you left in a hurry as well, and I don't even know your name. Tell me at least that."

"Well, it doesn't really matter if you know my name, and I could tell you it right here easily enough."

Yet he did not tell her his name as they walked, and even as they went up the alley in front of Descending Immortal Pavilion and turned onto the main street, he made no attempt to free his hand from Buyong's as she led him along. When they reached the spot where the fight had been, there was no sign of anyone. By that time the rain had died down quite a bit.

Hyeonggeol followed behind Buyong as she led him through

the front gate of the house. She put the bar back down across the gate and then went into her room, and she held out a towel to Hyeonggeol, who was milling about on the wooden ledge. She parted the beaded curtain, looked at him, and said, "Please come in. The rain might get in."

The room, which Hyeonggeol had visited with Daebong in the middle of the day the last time, somehow looked like a completely different room, one that he was seeing for the first time. He quietly entered through the open door.

"Dear me, Mother has already laid out the bedding, how hasty she is," Buyong mumbled to herself, folded up the cotton indigo blanket with the red band sewn around the edges, pushed it into a corner, and then put down some fancy cushions. "You must be cold from the rain," she said, smiling. "Come sit down here at the warm end."

"The rain was nothing, I am just sorry for being so uncouth as not to even be properly dressed." Hyeonggeol grinned sheepishly as he wiped his face with his still-wet hand.

"Oh, don't worry about that. Please, don't concern yourself and come down to this end. And do not think too poorly of me because of this shabby room."

Once in her room, with the brass oil lamp lit and burning bright, and her skirts swaying lightly back and forth, Buyong's words were far more intimate than they had been outside. There was no formality to them, and she spoke freely, as if to a man to whom she had given her heart. Hyeonggeol was grateful that Buyong treated him with such intimacy, and so he accepted her offer, crossed over to the warm side of the room, and sat down with his legs crossed.

After seating the young man, Buyong quietly looked at his face again. His forehead, nose, eyes, mouth, ears — Buyong was pleased with what she saw and lowered her head to look at his chest and knees. But when her eyes settled on the hand resting on his knee, she was startled and stood up. From the wardrobe she pulled out cotton like a pile of snow and poured onto it some kerosene that she had bought not long ago.

"My goodness!" She unwound the bandage and was startled once again when she saw the wound. The teeth marks were vivid on the back of his swollen hand. She wiped his hand with the kerosene and then pulled it closer to blow on it a few times. "Should I light cotton and sear the wound?"

"Let it be. The more you touch it, the longer it will take to heal," said Hyeonggeol with a laugh.

But Buyong, rather than searing the wound, took out a white squid bone from a drawer in her stationery chest, ground it down with a knife, and then sprinkled the powder on the wound.

Hyeonggeol felt a strange thrill as Buyong took care of him. If he went home like this, his mother would look at him with wide eyes, ask him where he got this wound, and then hurry to sear the wound and apply medicine, and once done with that she would make a fuss and have the boy servant Samnam or another servant fetch the doctor, devoting herself to the care of her son, but his mother's caresses were nothing like the thrill he felt from Buyong's touch. When he received his mother's love, he thought that the giver of that love was happier than he was as the receiver, but now for the first time he was subtly intoxicated by the bliss of one receiving love. It was not Buyong, who caressed his wound, but Hyeonggeol himself, who sat there at ease and let her take care of him, only occasionally refusing her attentions, who looked infinitely happy. He imagined for a moment that his wound would take a long time to heal and that Buyong and her warm, delicate hands would not leave his side that whole time. He vaguely thought that it would be a beautiful, blissful, and brilliant life.

"What are you thinking about?"

Her voice was so lovely and beautiful as she asked this, Hyeonggeol could not help grinning. "I was just lost in my whimsy."

Before he had even finished saying these words, his left hand climbed up Buyong's back.

"My body stands at the door, but my heart follows you on the road," he recited.

At last he touched Buyong's hair and then stopped, and he

turned his head and looked at the oil lamp at the cool end of the room. The lamp light danced red next to the folding screen.

He was referring to an old poem:

"I stand leaning against the door frame,
But my spirit follows the beautiful woman."

Yet Buyong, unlike her namesake, Kim Buyong, could not reply with:

"The donkey struggles
And I did not know why,
But my longing for you
Made the load this heavy."

Buyong could not imagine that the heart of the gisaeng Kim Buyong could be filled with love for a man when she teased him so sharply as this. It was something that had happened over two hundred years before and thus was hard for Buyong to imagine, but the Buyong of today thought that the words of the Buyong from long ago, in response to the poem of some scholar, were clever and witty, but also that they could not have come from a heart intoxicated by the fragrance of love. So she could not reply to the verses Hyeonggeol had recited with the verses written by Buyong from long ago. This was how grateful she was that Hyeonggeol had given her his heart, and in her warm happiness she did not even notice the night growing later. Just then, though, she wondered what would happen when Hyeonggeol lifted his silken folding fan and prepared to go, leaving her with little hope of seeing him again, and she thought of a famous love poem by the Buyong of long ago. She called to mind one passage — "Your fine silken headscarf is wet with tears, but there is no promise to meet again" — and she quietly recited the verses in a coquettish voice, then she lifted her head and looked at the young man. She reached out her right hand, took up the brush on top of her stationery chest, and wrote these verses on a piece of paper.

Hyeonggeol waited for her to put down the brush and then wrapped his left arm around her waist. "Is this truly how you feel?"

But Buyong said nothing. She held her head up and gazed into Hyeonggeol's eyes, as if trying to catch a glimpse of the passion of a young man who had been given the heart of a young woman. Their eyes met. But their lips opened even more quickly … Hyeonggeol let go of the arm he had been holding and stroked Buyong's hand. Her slender, jade-like hands were flushed red as peach blossoms.

He murmured: "On Buyong's arm is inscribed someone's name, and the inked letters are clear on her white skin."

Buyong immediately brought out a needle with a long thread and an inkstone and replied, "The waters of the Biryu River shall dry up before I forget my promise to you."

She stared at him for some time before grinding up the ink, and then she pulled up the sleeve on her left arm. Hyeonggeol took the inked needle in his wrapped right hand.

"What shall I write?"

"Write your name."

Only then did he realize that Buyong did not even know his name. Yet he did not want to inscribe his full name on Buyong's arm. "Let us be stars. Not the sun, not the moon, but stars that shine alone in the dark night."

Hyeonggeol brought the tip of the needle to Buyong's arm. The sharp point pierced her white flesh. Buyong smiled, satisfied, as the ink was inscribed clearly on her arm. Then she pricked a black tattoo on Hyeonggeol's arm, and the two of them listened in silence to the sound of the sputtering lamp. Even after the first rooster crowed, Hyeonggeol did not leave Buyong's house.

14

Duchil did not wait for the ancestral rites at Mun Gildeok's house to finish and went back home as the rain was falling in large drops.

When he first heard the words of his master's first son, Hyeongjun, he wanted to return home at once. He thought he would only feel better if he confronted his wife and, if she replied vaguely or ambiguously, beat her furiously. But he needed some more time by himself to figure out what had happened, and so he just went back into the room with his friends as if nothing had happened and sat there for some time, lost in thought.

Of course, the command to leave at once was not something to take too seriously. Eldest son or not, until the day he took charge of the affairs of the household or until Assistant Curator Bak passed away, Duchil knew well that Hyeongjun was in no position to order him to come or go. Even if Hyeongjun spoke to Assistant Curator Bak, and then his master came to him and ordered him to do something, he surmised that he would not be in any trouble if he did not leave his home on the word of Hyeongjun alone. If Assistant Curator Bak felt the same way as his son, he would summon Duchil at some point and issue a command. Thus Hyeongjun's order to leave home immediately was not something to be too afraid of.

Yet when he looked at the facts, even if he was truly being ordered to leave home, this in and of itself was not all that painful. He did not think it would be all that difficult to feed just the two of them, whether they left their farmland and followed the newly constructed road, traveled around with a surveyor's pole, or carried burdens for others. Although he worked all day until his very bones were tired, and he often thought that he would be able to get by somewhere else, he persuaded himself that to just run away without any command from his master, Assistant Curator Bak, who had given him Ssangne as a wife and raised his status from domestic to hired hand, would be the most ungrateful thing he could do.

So, it was one thing if Assistant Curator Bak himself came to him and, after listing his reasons, said to him, leave my house and go live somewhere else, but until that happened it made no sense to pack his belongings on the word of Hyeongjun alone.

The one thing that Duchil's thoughts continued to stray toward and dwell on, however, was the question of what sort of relationship there was between his wife's "behavior" and the young master from Dumutgol.

Duchil knew, of course, that his wife was not that pleased to be with him. This had been the case when he was still working as a domestic, long before he tied his hair up in a topknot, and he was at least aware enough to know that, even after he became Ssangne's proper husband, she never really served him with all her heart. Yet she never rebelled against him, argued pointlessly with him, scolded him, or anything like that, and he had been secretly waiting, thinking that time would pass, that they would have a child, and they would naturally become a harmonious family. He was terribly disappointed when she did get pregnant but then had a miscarriage, but he did not sink into despair because of it. His wife was still beautiful, and though she said little and some might call her standoffish, she had never brought him any sadness. He had thought that she was not coquettish or affectionate or caring, like the wives or concubines of the rich, but, as befitted a poor wife, she was healthy and diligent and simple. He had trusted her. If anything, his love for his wife had only increased since his days as a domestic, and it had not wavered a bit. Even as he worked hard every day for ten years, thoughts of his wife brought him joy, and when he unwrapped his feet after a long day, received his dinner, and gazed on his wife's face, the thought of leaving his house with hoe in hand the next day did not seem that distressing. As long as he had Ssangne by his side, he felt that he could do anything, and as long as she took his hand and followed him, he felt that there was no place too fearsome for him to go. That was what Ssangne — what his wife — was to him.

When he first heard that his wife was deceiving him and having an affair with someone else, for quite some time he naturally had no idea what Hyeongjun was talking about. It couldn't be, it can't be, he told himself hundreds of times, shaking his head, but then, when he lifted his head again, his master's eldest son still stood there with the same expression on his face. He felt sadness before he felt rage. Hyeongjun walked away quickly, like an angry person who had said what he wanted to say.

That the man seeing his wife was none other than the young master from Dumutgol . . . if that was so, then why on earth would the eldest son come to him himself and tell on Hyeonggeol — he wanted to ask these things, but Hyeongjun had already left.

Duchil got up from where he sat and left Gildeok's house as if he were going to the outhouse.

"Where are you going? The drinks and snacks are about to come out," Gildeok said.

He replied, "I'm just going out for a moment." The rain was falling in large drops as he stepped out of the front gate.

As he walked quickly, the cold raindrops landing on his face and head, he began to grow even more anxious. He went around by the river and arrived at the bramble hedge, and, when he saw his house, for the first time in his life he felt a terrible passion writhe in his chest like a flame. It felt as if, after flinging open the door and going inside, he would grab the first thing he found and begin swinging it about. He scared himself. Left to his own devices, there was no telling what he might do — he might race about like a raging horse. He reached out his hand, opened the fence gate, went into the backyard, and then opened the door to his house. The inside of the room was dark. At the sound of him opening the door, there should have been the sound of someone stirring inside, but there was nothing.

"Are you there?"

There was no answer. He took an ashen pole standing by the door and swung it around the inside of the room. He touched on nothing but the sewing box. The room was completely empty.

'Has she gone somewhere? Was what Master Hyeongjun said really true?'

Duchil did not even think about going inside but sat there on the threshold facing the yard, where the rain had begun to fall more steadily.

He had been sitting there for a while when he heard the sound of footsteps from the mulberry grove, and finally Ssangne opened the gate in the bramble hedge and came in out of the rain. She came up onto the earthen floor before the door and took off the corner of some old sack she had been wearing as a hat, and then she leaned against the doorpost and brushed against her husband's shin with her knee.

"Oh!" She gave out a low, startled cry.

The scent of his wife's flesh wet from the rain filled his nostrils. He did not move from where he sat as he asked, "Where did you go?"

His wife hesitated for a moment and then blurted out, "I went over to Little One's house to see if I could be of help..."

Then, without even finishing, she slipped by her husband and into the room. Her damp skirt brushed Duchil's cheek as she passed.

Once in the room, Ssangne calmly began to put out the bedding. She had been emboldened by that one lie she had just blurted out. After almost falling victim to Hyeongjun, for some time she had been at her wit's end, but at last she had gone to see an old woman famed for her skill at telling fortunes. When she sat quietly across from the old woman and began, "I must be possessed by a cursed spirit, for something horrible has happened to me," she felt no shame — or indeed anything at all.

"How old are you?" the old woman had said.

"Twenty-two."

A flame as small as a bean rose up from the oil in the soot-blackened lamp. Beneath the lamp, like a withered gourd, the wrinkled old fortune-teller sat at the small, dog-legged table, unmoving and resolute, her legs crossed and holding a long string of coins and some loose coins in her hands.

"How old is your husband?"

"I think he is thirty-one."

"Thirty-one?" Her eyes as thin as worms opened wide. "Well, then, tell me your story."

Ssangne lowered her eyes for a while and thought. She had come because she had not been able to think, but now that it came to spilling everything and talking about her situation, she was quite ashamed. She lifted up her head and looked around the small room once.

"No one else is here, so tell me what is on your mind," the old woman urged her.

Ssangne wrung her hands, hesitating as she went, but at last let everything come gushing out. "It was when the flowers fell, about a month and a half ago. My husband had gone on a journey of about two days, and my master's third son, who had always acted oddly toward me, came into my room at night, so what was I to do? I thought I would go along with it as the mischief of a young heart, but things quickly grew serious, and after he visited a second time I could not get him out of my head. Then my husband returned home, so there was no way I could see the young master again, but things took a turn for the worse when the eldest son took a liking to me and began pestering me. He knew what I had done with my master's youngest son. My husband will surely find out about this tonight, and if it comes to that, I think it might be better for me to just make a clean break from him rather than spend the rest of my life being treated ill. But even if I don't, my world will be turned up-side down, and I have no idea what I will do from here on. So please divine my fortune so that everything may be clear, and ask the spir-its if it is, in fact, my destiny to live without a husband I never loved in the first place, and if the young master truly has feelings for me or if it was just a lark for him."

The old woman nodded her head of streaked-white hair. She gestured at Ssangne's hands with her chin, and Ssangne quietly put the white copper coins she had been grasping in her right hand on the table. Only after the fortune-teller saw the money did she hold up the coins that were in her hands and begin to mumble. After mumbling for some time she tossed the string of coins onto the ta-ble.

"Your ties with your husband are not your destiny, I see."

When she heard this, Ssangne thought for a moment that she felt relieved. "Please toss them again to see if this is really true." Her voice trembled slightly as she spoke. 'Just as I thought . . . he is not my destiny — that Duchil I detested so when I was a maiden; that Duchil, for whom I felt no thrill at all well up inside me when I lay down next to him against my will. Losing his seed that was growing inside me before it could be brought into the world, that, too, must have been so that there would be no bond between us in the future. It is clear that all of this is the blessing of the exalted high spirits.'

As she gazed blankly at the coins scattered on the dog-legged table, no two coins touching each other, Ssangne was thinking once again that it was her destiny to leave Duchil.

Yet even as she thought this, she was also worried and fearful at the thought of what it would take to leave him. And she could not hide from the fact that she also felt pity for Duchil. Ssangne knew well the fervor with which Duchil loved her. This was why she had asked the old woman to throw the coins again, just to make sure that this divination was correct. But Grandmother Bosal shook her head slowly. And then she said, as if chanting, "If we fuss over things two or three times, the high spirits will grow angry," and denied Ssangne's request.

Ssangne had no choice but to ask whether her relationship with the third young master, the young master from Dumutgol, was her destiny. As the old woman bobbed her head and took up the string of coins in her right hand, Ssangne was desperately nervous. She thought that her fate would be decided by the way the coins fell when the fortune-teller tossed them.

'Young Master, Young Master of Dumutgol, tall, neat, manly, and excellent Young Master! How can this lowly servant serve such a noble person as yourself? It is not my destiny. Please treat me as a rock you kicked at on the road.'

Ssangne prayed, moving her lips silently. Yet her deepest desire was quite different, and she knew this because she was happy enough to cry when she saw two of the coins tossed by the fortune-teller finally come to rest touching each other. Did not the scattered string of coins on the table reveal that the young master of Dumutgol and Ssangne were a match made in Heaven, a tie that had been blessed by the high spirits?

Ssangne left the house of the old fortune-teller. It was raining. She wanted to walk in the rain, soaked to the skin. But she borrowed a sewn-up corner of a sack and put it on her head as a hat, and then she walked along, lost in thought. She knew clearly what she had to do, but how she would achieve it was no small problem. Whatever will be, will be. He is my spouse determined by the heavens—when she thought of it this way, it seemed only proper that she should roll up her sleeves, cut off her relationship with Duchil at once, like slicing a knife through bean curd, and then run off to a place far away with the young master from Dumutgol. But then she reconsidered—I should wait beneath the tree with open mouth until the fruit ripens and falls from the branch, since this relationship has already been blessed by the high spirits, and Duchil will leave of his own accord, and the young master will fall into my arms like a ripened piece of fruit — and thought that it would be reasonable to say nothing and wait calmly with steeled heart until that day came. These thoughts circled around in her head, and before she could reach a conclusion, she had arrived at her home. The line that she had visited Little One and borrowed a corner of a sack as a hat was a complete lie she had made up on the spot.

Ssangne put out the bedding in the dark room as if nothing had happened, then she took off her skirt and lay down beneath the blanket.

"Go draw a bowl of cold water," Duchil ordered from where he sat on the threshold. But Ssangne held her breath and lay there in silence.

"Are you deaf?"

Duchil was not the sort of man to repeat himself. The request to bring him cold water didn't seem like something that would come out of his mouth, either. If he wanted a drink, he got up himself, went into the kitchen, took out a bowl with his own hands, and scooped up some water to drink. Even if he had asked her to fetch him some water, if there was no answer he would have normally said to himself, "She must already be asleep." But today, Duchil yelled at her with annoyance in his voice. She thought that some talk must have reached Duchil's ears.

"You're still not going to get up?"

Before he had finished speaking, Ssangne pulled back the blanket with a rustle and got up. Her husband's voice sent a chill down her spine like a knife. Only then did she truly realize the strength of the man. This strength — a strength armed with an explosive power sheathed in terror on this dark, rainy night; a strength that seemed as if it would overturn the entire Universe like a flash of lightning if she touched even a corner of it — flickered before Ssangne's eyes. She drew cold water in a large bowl and crept carefully to where her husband sat.

Duchil took the bowl of water Ssangne had drawn for him, and, for a moment, he felt the urge to throw it in his wife's face. But he brought his trembling arms under control and noisily gulped down the water. It was still raining. He shook out the bowl he had just drained dry and then he handed it back to his wife.

"Shall I go get more?" she asked, but Duchil could not answer. As she asked this, Ssangne could not help feel a sudden pity for her husband well up in her heart. But it was ultimately not born of any affection for him. When she realized that it was not, in fact, love, sadness filled her heart.

Duchil quietly got up from the threshold. He stepped into the room and stood next to his wife without a word. The sound of the rain falling and water dripping from the eaves was loud in his ears, and he put his left hand around his wife's shoulder. With a terrifying strength, he embraced his wife. He swallowed back the tears that glistened in his eyes and said, "Let us go live in a place far off." He buried his face between her breasts and said, "Let us go live in a place far off, just the two of us."

Ssangne could not hold back the tears that gushed up from inside, but when she realized the meaning of Duchil's words, she trembled from head to toe in fright.

Although Duchil ate breakfast early the next morning, he gave no thought to going out to the fields, even when the sun rose an arm's span in the sky.

Ssangne could not be at ease, but she did the work that she was charged with in the kitchen of her master's house out of habit. Yet she was confused by her husband's strange attitude and worried about what trouble he might cause in the future, so much so that she could not concentrate on the task at hand. As she came back from hulling rice in the mule mill, she saw Duchil loitering about before the wooden ledge outside the master's room, and she put down the bowl with the rice husks, hid in the shadows, and watched to see what her husband would do. Judging by the white leather shoes outside the door, Assistant Curator Bak must have eaten breakfast at Dumutgol and just come in.

"Master, it is Duchil." He stood there with his hands clasped and, after hearing a sound from inside, said, "I have come because there is something I must discuss with you at length." He cleared his throat twice.

Duchil must have been commanded to come in because he took off his shoes and put them beneath the ledge, and then he quietly opened the door to the master's room and went in. After that, his voice could not be heard in the yard in front of the mule mill.

Ssangne's heart pounded in her chest. A terrible foreboding that something awful would happen soon writhed in her heart like a snake. She hurried in through the central gate and went into the kitchen by the master's room. This was the kitchen where fodder was boiled and the fires were stoked to heat the floor of the master's room. But she could hear no voices from within the room here, either. Not only was there a thick wall between the kitchen and the room, but there was no door in that wall. Like one possessed, she rushed into the kitchen. She took down a brass bowl from a cabinet, ladled some scorched-rice water into it, and went back out to the master's room. There was no one in the kitchen, and the wife of her master's second son, Bobu, was washing her hair in lye. She turned to look at Ssangne for a moment as she left, her hair still in the brass basin, wondering when there had been a command to bring scorched-rice water to the master's room.

Ssangne stood outside the door to the master's room with the bowl in hand and listened.

"Well, if that's how you feel, then I don't really have anything to say, but do you have any friends who have worked in road construction? Your family may be small, but, still, many have been enticed by the words of others, taken their families with them, and come to ruin." These were the measured words of Assistant Curator Bak.

"Something urgent has come up that has forced me to leave this area, and so I have made up my mind to go see for myself."

"Well, if that's the case then there is nothing for it, but I will have to find someone to take on the farming that you do, so if it can be helped at all you should stay at least through the Dano Festival. I don't know how far the newly constructed road has progressed, but you and your wife have done much since you came to my house. So if you stay until then, I will see that you are not disappointed. Leave after the Dano Festival."

Assistant Curator Bak did not ask him what this urgent matter was that made it necessary for Duchil to leave this area, perhaps because he had his own suspicions, and he graciously granted Duchil's request to leave this household and head off to Wonsan to become a road construction worker.

Ssangne did not need to hear any more. She did not even consider bringing the scorched-rice water she was holding into the room but instead carried it back into the kitchen. She put the bowl on the stone table, avoided Bobu's gaze, and went out the back alone. She crouched down in grief in front of the peony bulbs as big as chestnuts, not knowing what to do about the tears that flowed down her face.

Bobu had taken her hair out of the lye and was rinsing it in clear water when Ssangne passed through the kitchen in a flurry of skirts, and seeing her strange expression and behavior, not to mention the fact that she came back in carrying the bowl she had just carried out, it was clear that something was wrong. She had heard a rumor from her eldest sister-in-law that her younger brother-in-law from Dumutgol had gone into Ssangne's room, and she wondered if something had not happened as a result of this. She dried her hair off with a towel, twisted it haphazardly and stuck a hairpin in it, and then glanced out the back door of the kitchen at Ssangne. She saw the simple shrine made of bound straw, and beyond the irises growing thick and lively, behind the laundry line, Ssangne sat facing the peony bulbs, her shoulders heaving. It was clear that she was crying. Bobu felt sorry for her, and she watched her for a little while longer with her hand on the doorpost, but then she stepped forward and went to Ssangne's side. Even though she stood right behind her, Ssangne did not turn around. She might not know she was there — so Bobu took a step forward to stand beside her and put her right hand on her shoulder.

Ssangne did not look round, seeming to know whose hand it was that had been placed on her shoulder, and quietly stood up.

"Why are you crying? Did something happen?" Bobu asked gently, and Ssangne swallowed back her sobs and walked into the cellar. Below was the earthen pit, and above was the dark storage room. Rice cake steamers, wooden bowls, bamboo baskets, sieves, warp beams, gourd dippers, sieve stands, and mesh frames for growing bean sprouts — these were scattered here and there, but that was all there was in the hollow, dusky room. The shrine to the spirits sat

on a shelf beneath the joists, and beneath that sheets of white paper flapped and waved in the wind that blew in between the bars
in the window. Bobu followed her in. She could tell that Ssangne
wanted to unburden herself in a quiet place, and that touched Bobu's young heart.

Ssangne tossed an old straw mat onto the floor, sat down on
it without taking her shoes off, and crouched there quietly in the
center of the room. She stared off into space with her elbows on her
knees and then let out a long sigh. Bobu was using a towel to blot
the water that still dripped from her hair, and she leaned over next
to Ssangne.

"Whatever will I do about this?" Ssangne said, and sighed
again.

At this, Bobu squinted slightly and sat down beside her.
"Well let's hear what it is that has happened first. Not that hearing about it will make it better, of course." She furrowed her brow.

"I can no longer stay here with you but must go far away."

When one starts talking, it is only natural that sorrow and
sighs will lessen for a while. As if her story were someone else's, she
became intoxicated by the bitter, plaintive taste of the tale. Bobu
also felt a devastating grief welling up inside her as she listened, and
it felt as if she might be swept away by the pitiable melody. Bobu
was younger than Ssangne, but she found Ssangne's emotions as she
pleaded like a child adorable and pitiable.

"Why should I have to live in a frightening world, deep in
the mountains where only boorish workers live and there is no joy
to life?"

For a moment, Bobu did not understand what Ssangne was
talking about. "What? This is the first I have heard of this . . . you
must explain to me more clearly what has happened," she gently
urged in a quiet voice.

"He heard a rumor somewhere . . ." At this Ssangne stopped
for a moment and, as if she were touching upon some great secret,
lowered her voice even further. "The eldest young master, unable to
satisfy his urges with me, went off and tattled for no reason at all,
and now we must leave this area. If it were with someone I was fond
of, then it wouldn't matter whether we went to the mountains or

under water, but how am I to live such a lonely life with someone who is not my destiny? That horrible man sticks to me like a leech, suffocating me! When I am here with you or the mistress, at least it takes my mind off things and makes life bearable, but now we must leave, just the two of us alone, and I must spend endless days looking at his ugly face. How am I to go on living?"

"But what else can you do if this is your destiny, and you are bound to your husband, for when the needles goes, the thread cannot simply choose not to follow, can it? You have tempered your heart and survived this long, so why would you suddenly not be able to live any longer?"

"No, that is not it all. I have set off down the wrong road, and my bond with my husband is not my destiny. He is the wrong man for me."

"Then has some other relationship suddenly sprung up, is that what you are saying?"

Ssangne said nothing in reply to this. When Bobu saw her lower her head and sit there dumbly, she suddenly thought of the young master from Dumutgol. Perhaps Ssangne wanted to say that the young master from Dumutgol was the spouse determined for her by the heavens. She thought about what Ssangne had said so far and of the rumor she had heard from her sister-in-law previously, and she realized that without a doubt Ssangne's sudden hesitation after speaking so freely meant that she cherished the young master from Dumutgol in her heart.

But although Bobu had realized this much, she could not open her mouth and say anything about it. From what she had heard from her mother-in-law this morning, plans had been made for the young master's marriage the night before. The girl was from the Gangneung Choe family in Namjeon, and although originally a distinguished yangban, they were now impoverished, so they had agreed to a marriage with the son of a concubine. With the marriage planned, the household now had to rush to send off letters, prepare the gifts, and perform the wedding. It was a belated marriage, and who knew what would happen if the young master were left to his own devices, so it was safe to rush things, her mother-in-law had told her without hesitation. Thus she wanted to reason with Ssangne, telling her what had happened, advising her not to entertain vain hopes, and persuading her that it was only proper that she should cultivate the virtue of being submissive to her husband, but she could not easily say these words, not necessarily because they were harsh, but because they sounded to her like they came from an impure jealousy.

In truth, though Bobu seemed fine now, and even if she was the only one who knew about it — and, after all, nothing had actually happened — the truth was that there was still the faintest thread of her heart that reached out to her brother-in-law from Dumutgol. Was it not Hyeonggeol who first opened her tightly closed heart and stirred up waves in what had once been calm waters when she had mistakenly replaced her husband Hyeongseon with her brother-in-law Hyeonggeol? Late last winter, until the day she married Hyeongseon, she had longed for Hyeonggeol in her heart, and even when she realized that her new husband was to be Hyeongseon and not Hyeonggeol, though she made no sign of her displeasure or foresaw any misfortune, she could not deny the fact that she felt sad, lonely, and guilty. And she suspected that the tall young man who had thrown the large rock onto the wooden ledge was Hyeonggeol as well. Even after she was married and came to live in this house, she did not see much of Hyeonggeol, and he never went out of his way to greet her. If she was the wife of his elder brother, shouldn't he show her courtesy as such? But even if he sometimes came into the inner yard, he pretended not to see her. Every time this happened, Bobu was cut to the quick with shame over her feelings toward Hyeonggeol.

When she heard from her elder sister-in-law that Hyeonggeol had visited the room of Duchil's wife Ssangne, at first she did not believe it. Had there been nothing between her and Hyeonggeol, she would have at least told her husband as they lay in bed at night, "I have heard this about the Little One from Dumutgol," and in the kitchen this morning she would have joked about having heard it from her elder sister-in-law, but Bobu let the rumor slip in through one ear and out the other and did not tell anyone else about it.

As she sat there in the dark storehouse and listened to this ardent, tearful confession from Ssangne's lips now, she felt a strange emotion in her heart.

Even if it were true that her brother-in-law from Dumutgol had gone into Ssangne's room, and even if he and Ssangne had made some pact between the two of them, she did not think that he intended to spend the rest of his life with Ssangne. It was clear that he had just followed where his feet had led him in his drunkenness. It just so happened that this truth became known, leading to this state of affairs. And yet no matter how lowly Ssangne might be, Bobu could not deny that there was something violent and cowardly about Hyeonggeol's actions as well. As suspicious as this all might be, though, Bobu had no intention of finding fault with what her brother-in-law Hyeonggeol had done. She just could not think of him as an improper young man who behaved in whatever way suited him. Her elder sister-in-law had pouted about Hyeonggeol's inappropriate behavior because he was the son of a concubine, but even when she heard that, Bobu simply could not agree with her. Did that mean that there was still a small part of her that harbored a heartbreaking longing for her brother-in-law from Dumutgol? But even thinking about that was wrong, impure, and inappropriate. She shook her head. Just as Bobu herself had become someone with no connection to Hyeonggeol at all, so would Ssangne, who had mingled flesh with him, become a stranger who had absolutely no connection to him.

As these vague thoughts passed through her mind, she said, "The young master from Dumutgol has boasted that he will not get married, but it looks like he will have no choice in the matter. He can't go against his parents' decision, after all. You've served your husband this far, so you can't just suddenly do something like this."

As she said these things, Bobu felt an unexpected sense of pleasure. She watched quietly as Ssangne's face grew darker at her words, and her pleasure seemed to grow. She did not understand where this pleasure came from. But when she realized that it came not from her cruel nature, but from that last thread of jealousy she felt over Hyeonggeol, Bobu was shocked at herself, and she discovered that her face was hot and blushing.

She was disgusted by her cold-heartedness, and she got up suddenly, as if trying to shake it off. "Come, if someone were to see us, what would they think? Let us go outside. This is not something you can solve by thinking about it. The world will be as it is. Come, let us go outside."

Bobu led the way out into the bright, piercing sunlight of early summer and repeated to herself, 'Hyeonggeol from Dumutgol is my brother-in-law.'

15

The Dano Festival had arrived. In celebration of Dano, and to make the most of the festival, the village bustled with a new liveliness. At long last, the peonies and cattails were in season and, along with the fresh irises, bloomed in all their glory.

Inside Visiting Immortal Gate, Bak Rigyun, using his house as collateral, had borrowed four hundred nyang at six percent interest and completely renovated his house. He had closed his noodle shop, divided the place into many rooms, and opened up a new-style inn. The name of the inn, "Dongmyeong Inn," with the words "Owner, Bak Rigyun" beneath that, were resplendent on the wooden signboard, the smell of ink still fresh. The wood had been whitened with a coating of chalk, and on that the letters were written in dark ink in a semi-calligraphic style. His brother, Bak Seonggyun, had also fixed up the aging parts of his house and taken over Rigyun's noodle business, starting on an ambitious scale and running it alongside his inn and stable. He anticipated that the wrestlers who would flock to this area for the Dano Festival, as well as the students who would gather for the athletics meet, would come to the noodle shop. Once the athletics meet was over, though, no one could say whether the customers would keep coming. But at least the launching of the business was splendid.

The cartload of miscellaneous merchandise that the sharp-witted Nakanishi had had delivered before Dano had mostly been sold, so he had nearly another cartload of merchandise for the athletics meet brought from Pyeongyang. There was not a house without a kerosene lantern, and the young man who did not wear socks was rare. The farmer's hats made from wood shavings had sold out in a flash, and the several cases of cigarettes he had brought in flew out of the store as if on wings and landed in the pockets of people everywhere.

Kim Yonggu, who lived below Assistant Curator Bak, did not have the capital that others did to open up a busy store, but he had his own way of making a profit, and he got himself an A-frame carrier and fixed shelves onto it so that he could carry loads on the bottom and on the top. He planned to load this A-frame full of walnut taffy, ice cream, ice lollies, sesame taffy, dried Solomon's seal root, and assorted fruits, and sell these at the wrestling grounds and in the hills where the women of the village went. The plan didn't require much investment, so he hoped to make a gradual profit.

Then there was Yi Chilseong, the grocer who had become popular thanks to the bicycle he had bought and the stylish new wife, who followed all the new Western fashions, that he had brought home from Pyeongyang. He thought of all sorts of ways to take advantage of this opportunity, such as opening a dry goods store, but then again there were already five or six large dry goods stores in the area, so it would be hard to compete against them to earn a profit, so he then considered opening up a general store, but seeing Nakanishi's success, he abandoned that idea as well, at last settling on opening up a small store with only a few types of goods with which he could compete with the other stores. So he got on his bicycle and sped back and forth between Pyeongyang and other manufacturing centers, buying up several rolls each of fabrics that would be in demand during the Dano Festival and that he could sell cheaply, such as raw Chinese silk, patternless silk, thin summer silk, ramie, and rough summer silk, and for general goods he sold things like kerosene, farmer's hats, socks, and matches at dirt-cheap prices that were just high enough for him to not lose money. This tactic of selling at low prices made him very popular. Thanks to this, his grocery, which mainly dealt in things like rice, seaweed, salt, fresh pollack, and herrings, thrived as well.

Rice cake sellers, noodle sellers, vegetable griddle cake sellers, acorn jelly sellers, liquor sellers — these food vendors also drew on all their resources to earn their share of the market, and a few inn- and stable-owners, though they could not transform themselves into new-style inns like Bak Rigyun, still fixed up their facilities so that they could accommodate respectable guests.

So it was that a magnificent Dano Festival, more opulent than any seen before in this area, was held under dry and clear skies.

The festivities began on the third day of the fifth month according to the lunar calender, and on the first day the women climbed up the hills of Mount Geum and played on the swings, and on this day there were also the lion and crane dances, while on the next day, the fourth day of the month, in addition to the women's entertainments, wrestling was held in the field known as Soujeon outside Visiting Immortal Gate. The wrestlers flocked from many other regions, such as Yangdeok, Gangdong, and Samdeung, so the schedule was changed to allow two days for wrestling. The large numbers of wrestlers gathering here was due to the athletics meet also being held in this village this year. The prize was at first a calf, but when participants took pains to gather from all over, the orga- nizers declared that they needed to raise the stakes to avoid embar- rassment, and they made the calf second prize and put up a fattened cow as first. After two days of wrestling, on the day after Dano it- self, the last day of the festival, this region's first athletics meet was held in the wide, freshly swept schoolyard of Dongmyeong School, for which a third of the grounds of the Confucian school had been dug up to make level.

The games played by the women who went up into the hills — the first day on Mount Geum, the second day on the twelve peaks, and the third day in the pine grove of the Confucian school — were held separately from the men's wrestling, but an order was issued that no other meetings were to be held on the day the athletics meet began. Wrestling was the men's sport, and there were no wom- en spectators, but the athletics meet was an enlightened gathering and thought to be different from something like wrestling, so even if young girls, maidens, and newly married women could not at- tend, the day was chosen and widely advertised so that at least married women over the age of thirty in their hooded coats, as well as old women and gisaeng, could attend. In particular, Dongmyeong School teachers Mun Useong and Jeong Yeonggeun did not forget that the reason for having the athletics meet was to take this opportunity to propagate among the women the need for physical education and the promotion of health, and to encourage women to take the lead in sending their children to school to study the new learning. Thus, right next to the headquarters of the advisory staff for the athletics meet, in the quietest spot, awning-covered seats for the women were specially prepared in order to make it more convenient for them to attend. The president of the athletics meet, who was also the governor of the county, was Principal Gang Munpil of Dongmyeong School. He attended the athletics meet in his black swallow-tailed coat and lustrous bowler hat with its wide brim, and in the front of his suit he wore a large flower as a boutonniere.

In attendance at the athletics meet were ten students each from Daeseong School and Ilsin School in Pyeongyang, five or six students each from the southern regions of Yonggang, Gangseo, and Yeongyu, ten students each from the nearby towns of Eunsan and Jasan (none came from Suncheon), nearly all the students from the schools in the local villages of Daedeuri, Gaenggoji, and Namjeon, and finally the students from Dongmyeong School, making well over two hundred fifty in total. Among the students from Dongmyeong School there were still those who had not cut their hair, and these did not participate in the athletics meet, and even those who did participate were not consistent in their uniforms, but the students from Pyeongyang and the southern regions were all dressed in black cotton, Western-style uniforms and, although their shoes were made of either hemp or straw, looked well-mannered enough in their white gaiters. There were even a few buglers among them, so in their attire, marching, and carriage they looked just like an army. They had gathered early in the morning a day or so before the athletics meet, on the fourth or fifth day of the month. One group followed the road from Pyeongyang to Visiting Immortal Gate, another group came from the west and crossed the Biryu River over Ascending Immortal Bridge, while yet another group came around the mountains on the northern road, and these were all welcomed by the residents and the students of Dongmyeong School, who had gone out to greet them; the visitors entered the village with the bright ringing of bugles before dispersing to their various lodgings. Large, festive pine-branch arches were erected, not only at the entrance to the Confucian school alley that led to the Dongmyeong School yard, but also here and there around the village, and the wooden signboards hanging from these arches had the words "Congratulations" or "Welcome" spelled out with buckwheat or millet grains, adding to the festive mood. Straw ropes were tied around the edge of the schoolyard, and on these were hung the flags of all nations with their brilliant colors. On one side an awning had been raised, and the ordinary seats outside this awning were lined with straw mats. When morning came, everyone ate breakfast and then came out to watch the processions of students as they went from every house to the schoolyard, men and women, young and old alike standing outside the front gates of their homes, and even the women who had to stay at home stopped their dish-washing and stared at the sight through the cracks in their front gates or fences. The students formed groups depending on where they were staying and went up the narrow alley by the Confucian school, followed by crowds of residents going out to watch the athletics meet like a flock of white birds flying beak to tail. With the exception of maidens from those households that strictly believed in keeping men and women apart, every house in this village on that day was as empty as if it had been deserted.

On this brilliant, splendid, and exciting day, Bak Seonggwon, that is, Assistant Curator Bak, was far more cheerful than anyone else. He was content, as if he had reached the heavens for the first time in his life or had finally made his mark in the world at the age of forty. It might have been because he had donated five hundred nyang to the athletics meet and two hundred nyang to the wrestling matches, but he was given the title of vice-president of the athletics meet and thus allowed to wear a large red flower on his chest. There were many who had titles such as licentiate, head clerk, and assistant curator, or who had experience as petty officials, but to the honorarily titled Assistant Curator Bak Seonggwon, being award-ed the honorary office of vice-president was of course proof that the times had changed greatly, but it was also a silent witness to the power of money. At any rate, Bak Seonggwon—Assistant Curator Bak—had been made vice-president of the athletics meet, selected by the people of the village and recognized by the government of-fice, and now was second only to Governor Gang. It was thus not without reason that he had been exceptionally cheerful that morn-ing and greeted the new day gladly.

Whatever the case, he had sent off the letter regarding the marriage of the troublesome Hyeonggeol, so now it was all but set-tled. He had searched high and low, unable to find a proper girl, but then he unexpectedly stumbled upon a good bride. It was the daughter of a Gangneung Choe family, who, though poor due to declining fortunes, were from an illustrious line. He had no designs on their fortune or wealth, so what did it matter if they were poor? The couple were compatible according to the fortune-tellers, and Hyeonggeol's mother, Lady Yun, had ridden a palanquin and visit-ed the family in person to arrange the marriage, so he thought the girl would be flawless in appearance as well. Even the problem with Duchil's wife, Ssangne—although there was nothing there to call a problem in the first place—had turned out well in the end, as Duchil had decided to leave this region and take his wife far away. Everything was falling into place, and with the title of vice-president of the athletics meet fallen into his lap like a ripe pumpkin, he was secretly satisfied that his luck had been as good as he could expect. He had heard that Hyeonggeol had protested to his mother that he was not going to marry anyone, but it was nothing more than the grumbling of a young heart that had set off down the wrong road. He murmured to himself, everything is going well, everything is go-ing well.

The president of the athletics meet, Governor Gang, had gathered the students and given his opening speech to start the meet, and he had only sat in the president's seat to hand out awards before going back to the government office shortly before noon, so now, after lunch, Vice-President Assistant Curator Bak was sitting there with dignified mien as the president's representative. Next to him were those who held government posts, sitting side-by-side with the leaders of the community, and they all watched with interest the contest currently at its peak in the schoolyard, a tug-of-war. All of the students had been divided into two groups, and each of these was again divided into two teams, and two teams lined up at either end of a long, thick rope. When one side dug in and shouted, "Pull!" with all their might, the other side clenched their teeth and yelled "Pull!" to counter this, and the thick cable didn't even think of budging. For some time, all they heard were cries of "Pull!" but then one side, whose feet had been planted in the earth, began to falter forward before finally collapsing in a rush, and the rope was pulled to the other side in an instant, followed by a great roaring shout and the sound of applause like thunder from the spectators' seats, so loud that it seemed it would shake the heavens. Only when the two other teams took to the field and prepared to begin their match could the sound of chatting and talking be heard in the spectators' seats.

A large horsehair hat sat neatly on Assistant Curator Bak's head, and as he turned his strong, masculine face with its high cheekbones toward the schoolyard, a princely smile played at the corners of his lips. Beneath his crisply pressed ramie overcoat, his light, raw silk trousers were bloused out above the hemp socks he wore under his white leather shoes. After some time he took out a large folding fan and waved it a few times at himself before turning to his in-law, Head Clerk Jeong to ask, "It appears this custom is still present in the southern regions."

Head Clerk Jeong replied, "It seems to still be alive and well in the south, along with something they call 'rat fires,' but seeing it reformed as an enlightened sport, it is quite fun to watch."

But then they were swept up again in the shouts rising from the schoolyard, and they stopped talking and looked ahead.

When the tug-of-war was finished, the winning sides lined up in long rows as their representatives received their prizes of two pencils for each team member, but then, from another part of the schoolyard, a bugle fanfare was played to draw the attention of the crowd, and once this was done it was announced that the next contest would be a mock cavalry battle, and the contestants were called forth.

"A mock cavalry battle? So do they fight on horseback?" someone asked.

Someone else replied, "That's just what they call it—but they will probably have some students be the horses and some be the riders."

The command "All rise!" was given, followed by "Attention!" then "Dress right, dress!" and at last "Count, off!" after which the two groups of students followed their leaders into the center of the schoolyard.

Assistant Curator Bak looked over the parade of students with a gentle smile on his face, unable to clearly distinguish one student from another, but then he discovered Hyeonggeol at the head of the team on his right with a red ribbon around his head, and he watched him carefully for a moment. Hyeonggeol had taken off his outer jacket and was wearing only his white inner jacket, and as he patted his "horse" of three other students, he was smiling broadly and in high spirits.

'Seeing him out there like that, I am certain that no one can match him in looks,' thought Assistant Curator Bak, and he looked on his son with satisfaction. Someone shouted out a sharp command and both teams of riders strolled over to their horses and climbed up into the saddles. One strong boy stood in front, and behind him two boys stood side by side, locking their hands onto the other's shoulders to form the saddle. Hyeonggeol leaped up into the saddle at once, just as he did with their white horse at home. With his right hand he tousled the hair of the boy in front, then finally raised his arm high to the heavens. Each side consisted of ten horses and riders. The twenty horses and riders, divided into red and white teams, would engage in close-quarters combat. Their teacher, Jeong Yeonggeun, stood in the middle of the field, looking back and forth between the two sides, and when the students had finished their preparations and the field had fallen silent, he blew his whistle and shouted so loudly that the heavens rang, "Begin the battle!" At this the riders lifted up their hands and, with shouts from both sides, slowly advanced toward each other.

With this shout given by the young people, Assistant Curator Bak felt something boil up inside of him. He quietly savored the pounding in his chest and sought out Hyeonggeol. At the head of the red team, he sat straight in his saddle with practiced movements, raised his right hand high, and stormed toward the enemy's position. At that moment, the leader of the other side came forward to engage in close combat. Hyeonggeol tapped the shoulder of his horse with his left hand and gave him some command, and the horse rounded about and attacked the enemy on the flank. The white team rider reached out with both hands to grab Hyeonggeol by the chest, but Hyeonggeol twisted away and brought his right hand up, grabbed the enemy rider by the arm, and pulled him forward. The white rider flailed about on his horse in an effort not to fall off, but when Hyeonggeol grabbed him by the collar and pushed once more, he lost his balance and fell from the collapsing saddle. Anyone who fell from their horse or lost the ribbon around their head was counted as killed in battle. Having felled one opponent, Hyeonggeol righted himself in his saddle and prepared to fly into the center of the fray, where horses and riders fought like angry bees in a hive. He tapped the boy in front on the shoulder, as one would pat a horse on the head, to turn him about, when an enemy rider swooped in from behind like a swallow. He did not intend to engage Hyeonggeol, but simply intended to sweep by to the side, and as he did so he reached out like an arrow and tried to snatch the ribbon from Hyeonggeol's head, as a falcon plucks a pheasant from the air. Hyeonggeol nearly lost his ribbon, but he skillfully turned his body and grabbed the hands of his opponent, and they ended up grappling in close combat. Hyeonggeol struggled at first with his upper body twisted around to his rear, but then his horse managed to turn around, allowing him to fight head-to-head.

Assistant Curator Bak watched with interest as the battle between these two riders took place near the edge of the yard, away from the frantic melée in the center. Hyeonggeol seemed to have not thought much of downing one rider with ease, but now, having barely escaped a thrilling close call, as he struggled to regain his balance, strangely enough, Assistant Curator clenched both of his fists.

Hyeonggeol straightened up, but he must have been the weaker of the riders, as he seemed to be constantly leaning toward one side of the horse as he avoided the hands of his opponent. The two students who made up the saddle kept bracing their arms, using every last bit of their strength to prevent Hyeonggeol from falling off the horse, but the student in front kept faltering and trembling like an aspen. This went on for some time, and Assistant Curator Bak let out a deep breath and relaxed the hands he had clenched into fists.

'Am I this nervous because he is my child?'

It made him laugh to think of it. He thought his bias was childish and undignified, so he tried to look elsewhere, but his eyes kept going back to Hyeonggeol.

Hyeonggeol had always been a skilled rider. Though he slipped from the back of the horse and clung to the side, he did not fall to the ground. He grabbed the shoulder of the student who stood in front and pulled hard, and in a moment he shot upright in the saddle again. Having nearly fallen off, when he righted himself again his right hand came down on his opponent's head and pushed him down. Not only did he lose the ribbon wound around his head to Hyeonggeol, he was also overpowered by the hand on his head, and he leaned back, his hands flailing about in the air, and finally lost his seat and fell to the ground.

Having watched Hyeonggeol's leopard-like exploits, moving as fast as lightning over the course of only a few seconds, Assistant Curator Bak nearly slapped his knee. He stopped his hand in midair and then quietly placed it back on his knee so no one would notice, but then there was a loud cry from the ladies' seats next to him, and that cry sounded just like the sound of his hand slapping his knee. What lady could have been watching so nervously and at last let out an unashamed cry of admiration . . . there was no doubt that she had been watching Hyeonggeol's brilliant struggle and then let out a shout without even thinking, but even if Bak, as Hyeonggeol's father, did something like that, he could not help but think it odd that someone in the ladies' seats beneath the awning had been watching Hyeonggeol so closely.

Elated by his defeat of two enemy riders, Hyeonggeol went into the heart of the enemy camp. There were already a good many casualties who had been dislodged from their horses and were sitting on the ground. About five or six riders remained, but before these five or six could face off against each other, the whistle sounded to call a ceasefire. The white army had won by one rider. With a hurrah, the general of the defeated army, Hyeonggeol, rode into his camp. Assistant Curator Bak was satisfied. And it seemed as if his own life at around the age of twenty had appeared before his eyes.

The applause of all assembled swept across the broad field like the sound of a raging tempest, and Assistant Curator Bak felt the passion of youth rising in his heart. He even thought that the blood coursing through his body had sped up. Youth: when he thought about it, it seemed that at the age of forty he had already lost all of the joy it brings.

He looked around the seats and saw the dignified gentlemen of high standing whispering to each other and quietly watching the games, and it seemed that there was no one in whose body or on whose face appeared the flush of excitement that he felt. Assistant Curator Bak suddenly felt melancholy, as if a cold autumn breeze had passed through his heart.

He saw himself with new eyes, someone who had thrown away all his youth and delight in the twenty years during which he had amassed his fortune.

As the games went on, the three-legged race gave way to the finals of the footrace around the perimeter of the schoolyard. It was a race contested by eight runners who had been selected through heats from the students who had come from all over, and from the students from Dongmyeong School. Among them was Hyeonggeol. Hyeongseon was a good runner as well, but he did not make it to the finals. Daebong had been eliminated as well, and only two students from this village, Hyeonggeol and one other, had made it, with the rest of the runners being students from other areas. There was no reason, of course, for the students of this village to fall behind in terms of strength or spirit, but in footraces they were no match for the students from Pyeongyang or the southern regions, who had been trained properly in running. Still, at least two of their students had made the cut, and everyone hoped that they would win.

"Your son is a man of many talents," someone said from behind.

"I am merely thankful that he is healthy," Assistant Curator Bak replied.

The eight runners all put their left feet on the chalk line drawn in the schoolyard and waited for the sound of the whistle. They clenched their fists, tightened their Achilles' tendons, and stared piercingly at the ground. Their ears were attuned to the slightest sound.

"One!" shouted Jeong Yeonggeun in a thundering voice as he raised his hand, and the eyes of the audience all turned to him.

"Two!"

Then he blew the whistle. A deep thrumming sound was heard, as if someone nearby were fulling cloth — beating it with paddles on a wooden block. The eight runners raced across the yard. They ran like arrows shot from a bow between the two straw ropes on either side, curving around the yard. As they flew around the first corner, Hyeonggeol was in the lead. Seeing this, the crowd sent up a cheer. Assistant Curator Bak shouted along with everyone else, but then he regained his senses and stopped. But there was another runner coming up fast on Hyeonggeol's heels. He ran at a leisurely pace, putting one foot ahead of the other without too much effort. About three or four feet behind him, the remaining six runners vied for third place.

At last the two runners raced across the finish line. But Assistant Curator Bak could not see them clearly from where he sat. It seemed that they both crossed the line at the same time. The crowd cheered and shouted, clapping their hands and making quite a racket. Shouts could be heard from the ladies' seats as well.

"Who came in first?" people asked from here and there, but no one knew for certain and the only reply was, "I don't know." But when it came time to receive the prize, it was the student from Pyeongyang who claimed first place. Hyeonggeol had fallen into second place right before the finish line. Hyeonggeol took second prize and then walked toward his father, smiling broadly as he held a red flag.

Assistant Curator Bak gave the prize to the first-place student and said, "You have done well!" but when he glanced at Hyeonggeol as he stood behind the student, he saw that his son was looking off to the ladies' seats.

Having received their prizes, the athletes returned to their places amidst the sound of applause. Assistant Curator Bak slowly turned his head and looked toward the ladies' seats. Because the awning slanted down toward the front he could not see them clearly, but he could catch a glimpse of those at the very front. Amid the middle-aged and old women, a young, pretty woman caught his eye. She did not wear a hooded coat, and seeing as how her hair was oiled and combed, it was clear that she was a gisaeng.

Bak quickly turned his eyes away and pretended to look off at the far end of the schoolyard, but then he glanced back at the ladies' seats once more. The gisaeng just happened to be looking his way. Their eyes met, and the gisaeng turned her face away in embarrassment. He could not remember ever having seen this gisaeng.

Bak looked back at the schoolyard. In preparation for the obstacle race, nets, ladders, ropes, and other impediments were being arranged here and there around the schoolyard. But the face of the gisaeng he had just seen in the seats next to him hovered before his eyes. He stole another furtive glance in her direction, making sure that no one saw him, but there was no sign of the beautiful young woman. Where could she have gone? He wondered if she had become aware of his gaze and hidden herself somewhere. If that were the case, then had there been a strange look in his eyes? Was it the gaze of a wolf eying his prey, or perhaps the eyes of a baby pleading for milk? Did she know who he was, and where had she come from, anyway — Bak thought it both odd and embarrassing that these questions were boring their way into his soul. His many children were all grown up, and he even had a grandson, a wife, and a concubine . . . how embarrassing it was that his heart was aflutter from casting sidelong glances at the ladies' seats, where Hyeonggeol had just been looking, and how much more embarrassing it would be if anyone found out.

'When did I grow this old?' But the sound of the whistle in the schoolyard brought him back to his senses, and he said to himself. 'But I am still only forty, aren't I?'

16

When the athletics meet was over, the bustling village streets were suddenly desolate, as if after a long, heavy rain. The wrestlers and students that had gathered from across the land scattered to their hometowns, and the young and old that had flocked from nearby farming villages to watch the events were gone within a day; all that was left were forlorn streets cluttered with dirty scraps of paper, sawdust, and trash. The pine branch arches, yellowed with age, stood gloomily here and there with their wooden signs ready to fall off, and the wrestling ground, the schoolyard, the hills, and the mountains were a mess of trampled grass and scattered trash. After the festivities were over, the sleepy streets of this village flowed full of melancholy as early summer approached.

It was the eighth day of the fifth month, already three days after the athletics meet had ended.

Ssangne did not eat dinner, but sat in the back yard and watched dispiritedly as the crescent moon, thin as a thread, climbed briefly above Mou Peak and then dropped behind it again.

After packing up their meager belongings, Duchil had just gone out to have one last drink with his friends before he left them.

Ssangne realized that the moment of decision had come, and she sat there by herself in the dark yard, calmly contemplating what she should do. After receiving permission from Assistant Curator Bak and passing his work in the fields and rice paddies to another, Duchil was prepared to leave on the road to Wonsan before dawn the next morning.

Should she follow Duchil toward Wonsan, or should she escape from his grasp and establish a new life of her own? She had not forgotten the fortune that the old woman had read for her and even now was pondering it. She had placed her hope in that fortune, so even at this moment, in the predicament that she was in, she felt that she was on the brink of some miracle and yearned desperately for that fortune to come true.

She sunk so deep into despair that she did not know what to do, and after considering everything she could think of she was still no nearer to making a decision, but as she chose her final path and hastened through the dark night toward a deep abyss, she still desperately believed that there would be some miracle — no, something even more extraordinary — a sudden light appearing or, as in the storybooks of old, a wizened old man appearing as if in a dream to show her the way, or, if that was too absurd, that the young master from Dumutgol, knowing that she was to leave for a far-off place the next day with her husband, would come up with some plan to save her and even now be racing toward her, around the mulberry grove by the river and toward the bramble hedge. It seemed as if it would happen. It seemed as if it must happen. And when she thought of it that way, it seemed as if such an extraordinary event was occurring right now. She listened closely. She shot up from where she sat. Did she not hear the rough sound of a man's footsteps at the head of the mulberry grove? It was dark, so she could not see, but had not the young master secretly come to the bramble hedge to study her face? Might he not have been standing there for some time and, seeing her lost in quiet thought, given up and decided to turn back? As these distressing thoughts came to her, she became convinced that this had happened, that this was indeed what had taken place.

Ssangne leaped down from the stone step in her bare feet. She ran to the gate in the bramble hedge. She opened the gate. She waved her hands back and forth in the air, but she felt nothing.

"Hello?" she called, but there was no reply. Her breathing was loud in her ears. "Is anyone there?" she called again, but the only breathing creature there was Ssangne herself. There was no one.

There was nothing. Had everything been a lie?

She let out a deep sigh and, with her hand on the gate, sank into a gloomy despair.

'It was all a dream, all a lie after all. When the old fortune-teller said that Hyeonggeol and I were meant to be together, that was a false fortune, too. The husband determined for me by the heavens and granted by the high spirits is that ugly, loathsome, shameless, dull-as-an-ox, oozing-as-pine-resin Duchil. The young master from Dumutgol has a respectable new bride waiting for him. A pretty, young, fair, slim, noble, and learned woman — it was always going to be that sort of woman who would find herself in the arms of a young master from a yangban family. The young master would never think twice about this tavern he merely visited in passing.'

Ssangne went back up onto the stone step and sat down. 'In the end, I must follow Duchil.'

She reasoned with herself in this way, telling herself that this was the most proper course of action. What made her think she could hold her head up like that and give her heart to the young master? It was just a daydream. It was no more than a ride on a rainbow, a risky yet brilliant, once-in-a-lifetime ride. The rainbow was already gone, and she was left sitting next to Duchil. How could she wait for that rainbow to appear again, and even if it did stretch out again, how could someone like her expect to sit on it once more?

'Duchil is my husband, and there is nothing I can do about that. He is the most suitable partner for me, one that I cannot — that I must not — disobey.'

She forced herself to think this way and then waited patiently for the affection to well up inside of her. She focused all her efforts on kindling a fire in her heart, a warmth that then spread to her fingers and breasts, a peaceful glow that settled on her lips. But then, with her heart properly filled with this affection, when she thought of embracing that loathsome Duchil, who reeked of old dishcloths, she felt her gorge rise in her mouth, her eyes grow dizzy, and her stomach grow nauseous, and there was nothing she could do about it.

'There is nothing to be done. Whatever else I might do, I cannot force myself to feel that.'

With her head in her hands, she shivered and stood up. It was strange how she had been able to go to sleep next to him all this time. It was odd how she had been able to share her bed with him all this time. It was uncanny how she could have given her body over to his caresses all this time.

She followed where her feet led her, walked out of the hedge gate, and ran through the darkness in haste. Tears flowed hot down her cheeks.

After running for some time as if mad, she stopped and found herself standing before Dumutgol. If she walked over the stepping stones in the stream and then approached where the zelkova tree stood, she would be at the Dumutgol house. She hesitated and looked all around her. The broad plain was filled with only a black darkness, but it was still only twilight, and she saw a rare lamplight flickering in a window here and there.

But Ssangne did not stay in that place for long. She made her way down a small, familiar road to the stream and then hopped lightly over the stepping stones. The gravel crunched beneath her feet. A dog barked at the sound. But Ssangne paid no attention to the barking and walked to the zelkova tree. Only when she stood in front of the main gate that led to the yard of the men's quarters of Assistant Curator Bak's house did she stop walking.

The master's room was dark. Was Assistant Curator Bak already asleep? It was still early in the evening, and it wouldn't have been long since he had dinner, so there was no way he would already be asleep . . . but then she suddenly remembered that Assistant Curator Bak was attending a banquet that evening at Descending Immortal Pavilion at the invitation of Governor Gang, and that he had left for the banquet without eating dinner. He obviously had not returned from Descending Immortal Pavilion yet. So only the servant, the errand boy, Lady Yun, and the young master would be home. Would the young master be lying alone in his room, or perhaps sitting there reading a book—while she was thinking these things she stepped up onto the threshold.

Now she would hear from him one last time, or if not, at least see his face, and then go her own way. What was she afraid of, and what was there to fear? Ssangne steeled herself and entered the main gate. But as soon as she stepped inside she stopped. Had the dog barked she would have scolded it and then walked in confidently, but the dog must have been hiding somewhere, and the light was bright in Lady Yun's room and in the young master's room as well, so her feet refused to take her forward. Which door would she approach, and whom would she seek out? There was nothing stopping her from going to the women's quarters and calling the mistress, telling her that she had come to say goodbye before leaving tomorrow. But her purpose here was to somehow see the young master. If she could, she wanted to share at least a word with him. And if she could have what she desired, the reason she had run all the way here was because she wanted to ask the young master what he intended to do about her, and to hear his reply. But if she called on the mistress, how would she then be able to see the young master? So she could not stride across the yard and go to the mistress's room. Yet it was an even more difficult thing to go straight to the young master's room, was it not? As she hesitated there for a moment, the light in the young master's room swept out into the yard like a broom, and she heard the sound of the door opening. Without even thinking, Ssangne crossed back over the threshold and stood outside the main gate. Then she hid next to the gate and listened. She heard the sound of shoes, and then she clearly heard the young master's voice.

"Mother, I am going to visit Mr. Mun."

Then came the sound of the door to the mistress's room opening. Lady Yun replied, "Your father has not come home yet . . . you should not be long."

The sound of the door closing again. Then the sound of leather shoes drawing closer to the main gate. The sound of footsteps approaching. The footsteps reached the main gate. They crossed the threshold. Finally, an inscrutable black silhouette sliced through the air before Ssangne. Ssangne peeled her body away from the gate where she had been standing.

After the Dano Festival, Dongmyeong School had a temporary recess of one week. Hyeonggeol only went out briefly every time a group from another area left after the athletics meet was finished, and the rest of the time he stayed shut up at home, thinking about his marriage, which had already been decided. They said the bride was the daughter of a Gangneung Choe family living in Namjeon, but he had no way of knowing what she looked like or what her character was. His mother had told him that she had ridden a palanquin there with Assistant Curator Bak's first wife to arrange the marriage, and that the bride was everything they could have wished for; but the way they saw things and the way they thought would of course never coincide with the way young Hyeonggeol thought, and even if their thinking somehow did coincide, like a blind man being lucky enough to stumble onto the door latch, there were a few reasons why Hyeonggeol could not simply go along with his parents' decision.

He did not give too much thought to Duchil's wife, Ssangne. He had put her behind him, suspecting that she would not give him much thought, either. He was annoyed by his older brother, Hyeongjun, going about and sticking his nose into things, and to tell the truth, having experienced the refined beauty of someone like Buyong, it was only natural that the passion he had once felt for Ssangne would take second place in his heart. But his reasons for not wanting to marry did not end with his promise to Buyong. At the end of the day, Buyong was a gisaeng. She was a flower that stood by the road beneath the willow and the wall, a flower that anyone could pluck. Though they had tattooed each other with needles and sworn that they would never forget the love they had shared, even Buyong would understand that this had nothing to do with Hyeonggeol's marriage. When Buyong first met Hyeonggeol, even when she had him imprint his affection on her arm and swore an oath, she thought that Hyeonggeol was already the husband of another, a man with a wife and children. Seeing this, Hyeonggeol could believe that Buyong's affection would remain unchanged, even if he married or took a bride. But now that the time had come, Hyeonggeol found that Buyong's affection held him back not a little. He did not know what Buyong thought, but he didn't think he could forget her. At the same time, he also had no idea what he would have to do for them to enjoy a proper married life together.

Besides this, though he had not spoken a promise aloud to Mun Useong, as he listened to his teacher explain in detail about the philosophy of early marriage, he resolved within himself that he, being yet unmarried, would not be sacrificed to this stubborn custom, at least until he had decided upon his goals in life. He did not want to see this resolution, which he had made firmly to himself and not even told Mr. Mun about, be washed away so easily.

And yet, as he contemplated making these thoughts a reality, he also feared that the road ahead would not be an easy one. Even Son Daebong, who had made such a fuss about how he did not want to marry, was to be married to Geumne from Bak Seonggyun's family on the fifteenth of the month. The more he heard about such things, the more nervous he grew about what lay before him.

It did not seem to be wrong at all to confess all these things to Mr. Mun or even Buyong and seek their advice. He thought that only by finding a solution that caused the least trouble, or by somehow escaping from this difficulty, even if he had to call on their aid, could he save himself from this first sacrifice that he was about to suffer. Whatever happened, he thought it would be no problem to confess his relationship with Buyong to Mr. Mun.

So he had eaten dinner and, unable to wait any longer for his father to return from the banquet held at Descending Immortal Pavilion for those involved in the athletics meet, left his room, and he was now passing through the front gate. He had crossed the yard and stepped over the threshold of the front gate, having received permission from his mother. Once over the threshold, he did not cross the stepping stones but strolled along the bank of the stream, enjoying the cool darkness beneath the willow trees and the zelkova tree by the well, when he thought he heard footsteps behind him. He doubted his ears and paused in his steps.

"Master, it is me."

The soft, trembling voice was without a doubt Ssangne's. Hyeonggeol felt a hot flame race down his spine. He could never have expected this. But when the voice came again from behind him, "Master, it is me," he turned his face. Though it was truly unexpected, when he thought back on everything, he could not say that Ssangne had no reason for coming to see him. Was she not going far away tomorrow, leaving with Duchil to find work on the way to Wonsan? When he heard that she was leaving, he thought that his relationship with Ssangne would thus be hidden away in a corner of his youth like a brief vignette, and that for Ssangne it would be a single spot of color in her hapless existence before she flowed back into her normal life. He thought that it might even be like the waters of the great Biryu River. The waters swirled in eddies for a long time, but eventually they would be swept away in the rapids. If there was a small rock in the way, the waters would smash into it, shedding bright beads as they were torn and parted, but once beyond the rock they would flow in their course to the Daedong River and on to the Yellow Sea. For Hyeonggeol and Ssangne, those two nights they spent wrapped in passion as their emotions overflowed were in the end the same as waters meeting a small rock. Just as the great river gave no thought to rocks or pebbles it met along the way as it flowed toward the sea, neither Ssangne nor Hyeonggeol thought they would cherish those brief memories for long. And yet this same Ssangne, the night before a momentous day, had come to see Hyeonggeol. Hyeonggeol's heart brimmed with a regret mixed with remorse and guilt. But with no need, and indeed no time, to think back on all those things, although no one could see him in the darkness, a blush of confusion passed across his face.

When Hyeonggeol turned around, Ssangne's faintly visible body moved a few calm steps forward. But Hyeonggeol could not move — it was as if he had turned to stone — and merely stood there speechless. Ssangne stopped only one step away from him. She was overwhelmed and thought that if his hand brushed even her skirt or the hem of her clothes, she would give herself over to him or surrender to her flaming passions with a desire that could only be sated if she threw her arms around his body, but she just stood there, only barely managing to suppress this desire. As soon as Hyeonggeol's reply fell from his lips, Ssangne thought that she would give no thought to anything else but give her body to him to do with as he pleased. Her heart was bursting with a hot, suffocating tempest. But Hyeonggeol said nothing. Was he unaware of her desire and passion? He could see neither her face nor her body. But could not Hyeonggeol's youthful skin feel the dark, early summer air reverberating with her blossoming, trembling flesh as she held back the fierce passion that flared up like a flame?

"Master, it is me," she repeated, but she could no longer keep her heart in check, quickly threw herself toward Hyeonggeol's bosom, and sobbed until her shoulders shook. Her arms wrapped around Hyeonggeol's body, and she rubbed her burning face violently in his bosom as the hot tears ran down her cheeks.

Hyeonggeol was quite shaken. But he lifted his arms and held Ssangne as she rushed toward him like a wave. Then his hands found Ssangne's shoulders and his lips found her tearful eyes. He cradled her head in his bosom again, but he remained dispassionate even as he tried to comfort her.

"What if someone were to see us on the road? Come, step aside now."

Ssangne pressed her body against his like a baby, but at last she stepped back. They moved a few steps off the road toward the ridge at the edge of the field. They stood there wordlessly for a moment. The sweet smell of the grass crossed the road on the early summer wind and spread out over the plains. The wind caressed them and then crossed over the stream in the dark night and whispered through the willows and the zelkova tree.

As the wind blew across her once-hot face, Ssangne's eyes grew dry. She savored the passion she had just tasted, now quiet and cool, and she wondered why she had come to see the young master. There was no doubt that she had come to see him one last time, and to hear his last words. But what had she planned to do after she had seen him? Had she come to demand that he run off with her, or to somehow rescue her from Duchil's clutches? That was not quite what she had thought at first. Now that she stood in front of him, though, wrapped in this curtain of pitch black, feeling his body heat in her flesh and savoring it in her heart, she did indeed feel such a quiet desire steal up on her. The old woman's fortune crossed her mind.

And yet, even after she had embraced the body of a man as she pleased, she could not help but feel that there was some distance between them. That their two bodies would become one, or that their two hearts would become one — even in this flush of intense and heightened emotions, she felt nothing like this, and she realized that there was something about this man that made it impossible for her to serve him as a husband. Is it because we are of different blood? Ssangne grew forlorn again. Duchil's face appeared clearly before her eyes.

"What has brought you here this night?" These were the words he said to Ssangne. But they were exceedingly reserved words. Hyeonggeol had asked her what had brought her here this night. How could he not know why she had come? Ssangne did not answer. There was nothing to say in reply. There was no need to reply. Ssangne raised her head, as if she had suddenly come to her senses. It felt as if a cool breeze was whistling through her hair.

"Do you not know the reason?"

She had never before uttered such sharp words in her life. She barely managed to spit them out, and then she stood there trembling. Her body and her heart trembled like aspens, so fiercely that she could no longer stand there. She whirled around where she stood. She went back down onto the road and strode through the darkness. Hyeonggeol had severed the thin anchor line of hope she had held out to him. That one phrase was not something one who loved her would have ever said.

'Whatever made me seek him out, with no shame and no fear, and come to meet him like this in the night?'

"Hey . . . hey!"

She heard Hyeonggeol's voice calling her. But there was no need to listen.

"At least hear what I have to say. Don't be like this."

He followed her and then stopped in the middle of the road, murmuring after her pitifully. But Ssangne stopped up her ears with her hands and ran through her tears down the road that led to Nine Dragons Bridge. She did not turn onto the road that led to her home but instead went toward the embankment by the Biryu River.

Long after even midnight had passed, in the room where Duchil waited, Ssangne was nowhere to be found.

Hyeonggeol called after Ssangne as she raced off into that dark curtain, but at last he fell silent and stood there on the road, and he thought for a moment that the woman he had just met was not Ssangne, but someone else. Yet there was no doubt she was Ssangne.

His head ached as if it had been struck by something. An incident that he had thought little of and pushed aside as not a problem suddenly and unexpectedly sprang up like a bolt out of the blue, lashed out at his head, and then ran off again. Only then did he feel an agonizing responsibility for what he had done. It was the first time he had ever experienced anything like it in his life. He now had no choice but to think about Ssangne. But what good would his thinking do her? At a single utterance from him she had come to her senses and run off. Tomorrow morning she would bid a final farewell to everyone and to this village, and then, whether she liked it or not, leave to establish a new life. At this point, what happiness could he give to Ssangne? Yet in some small corner of his heart there lay a twisted lump like lead, and he could not be at ease.

He wanted to tell someone everything, and to confess all of his wrongdoings.

He began to walk. He could indeed do nothing but meet Mr. Mun. The problem of his marriage, the problem of Ssangne, and the problem of Buyong, where the unbreakable roots of affection had taken hold — there was no one from whom he could seek counsel about these but his teacher, Mun Useong. But on the way to the church he would pass by Buyong's house, and he naturally felt the desire to see her first. His young heart believed that the one who could cleanse the head that had been struck by Ssangne, the one who could heal all the wounds of his heart, was first and foremost Buyong. He hesitated for a long while at the entrance of the alley before at last turning his steps toward Buyong's house. It had been quite some time since he had seen her. He couldn't see her because of the preparations for the athletics meet, and then on the day of the athletics meet he merely looked from afar on her smiling face as he stood in the schoolyard, but he had not been able to meet her. As he imagined Buyong sitting all alone inside this house that lay before his eyes, lost in thought as she recited the love poems of her namesake, he could not continue on his way to Mr. Mun's house.

He passed down the alley and went to the front gate. The gate was not closed but ajar, as if someone had just come out or just gone in. So he did not call out for the mistress, but stood there before the gate for a moment and listened, and he heard the sound of talking coming from Buyong's room. It must be a guest, and if so he would have no choice but to go visit Mr. Mun first, and as he thought these things he looked toward the brightly lit room once more.

Yet in that moment Hyeonggeol pulled his face back from the main gate and doubted his ears. The voice coming from within the room was very familiar. No, it was not just familiar — it was the voice of his father, Assistant Curator Bak! In a flash, before he even knew what he was doing, he hid himself in the shadows and barely managed to begin breathing again. What was his father doing here at this house? Had he heard about Hyeonggeol's relationship with Buyong from someone and come to tell her to be careful in the future? Yet he could not imagine his father taking such a vulgar approach. Surely he had been coming back from Descending Immortal Pavilion with Buyong, who would have been called to the banquet, and stopped by briefly on his way. Only with this thought was Hyeonggeol able to catch his breath. And then a faint smile played at the corners of his lips. Led by his curiosity, he leaned forward to listen again.

"So, you despise me that much?"

When Hyeonggeol heard that voice, so unlike his father's, the blood rushed to his face. His father was quite drunk. Buyong's voice could not be heard clearly. She began replying in a friendly tone, but before she could even finish, his father's slurring voice cut her off. "Then what should we do, if you won't listen to me like this, hmm?" The voice was lecherous. Once again, Hyeonggeol could not hear any reply from Buyong. But what was taking place in that room kept appearing so clearly before his eyes that he could no longer stand it.

What was Buyong doing as she sat there? Crouching down and paying no mind to his father's demands, parrying them with courteous words. And what was his father doing as he sat there? With his horsehair hat on his head, heavily drunk on liquor, lust burning in his eyes and in his face, his two hands . . . Hyeonggeol took his face away from the door and straightened up. He could not stand the strange passion that boiled up in his heart.

"Ah . . . Father is drunk. He has passed out."

He mumbled this to himself, but his heart was not calmed. Yet there was nothing he could do, was there? Unable to either come or go, he lingered by the main gate, when suddenly a coquettish laugh from Buyong was heard. Hyeonggeol was rather displeased by that laugh, and the coquetry that was so unlike Buyong.

"Sir, have you gone quite mad? Please, stop that and have a drink."

"Ha ha, I am tired of liquor now. But how impertinent of you to call me mad! You are right, I am mad. Indeed, I am mad about you."

He stopped talking. Hyeonggeol did not try to hear any more of their talk. But in that lull in the conversation, what was going on in that room? It was too horrifying a prospect to think about. He listened again, and sure enough he heard low voices continue to speak.

"Explain what you mean." His father's voice grew distinct, so even though he spoke quietly he could be clearly heard. "Go on, explain what you mean. I'm not going to be angry with you, am I?"

There was a long, heavy silence, and then, in a flustered tone, "Why are you crying and not talking?"

When he heard this, Hyeonggeol grew nervous. His body stiffened like a rock and was rooted fast to the earth, and then, without even realizing it, he leaned forward to listen again, and heard Buyong say a few words between her tears, followed by, "What?!" His father's sudden, surprised outburst rang through the paper doors.

"You would violate the law of heaven?!" The massive shadow of Assistant Curator Bak shot up behind the paper doors. That shadow suddenly grew larger, and then the sound of the door opening was heard.

"Sir, please don't be angry." This from the long-skirted shadow that followed behind him. But Assistant Curator Bak had already stepped down into the yard and was pulling on his leather shoes.

Without thinking, Hyeonggeol hid himself in the dark shadows. The main gate flew open and Assistant Curator Bak stepped out, panting like an enraged animal. His hat shaking, he passed out into the alley and out of sight, still unable to contain his fury. Even after his father was gone, Hyeonggeol still could not work up the courage to step out of the shadows and into the light. For some time he stayed buried in the shadows, holding his breath. Buyong crossed the yard and came to the front gate. She glanced in the direction that Assistant Curator Bak had gone, then put her hand on the gatepost and let out a long sigh.

Hyeonggeol studied Buyong's face. The tears streaking down her tired face glistened in the distant light. Hyeonggeol wanted to quietly walk up behind her, put his arms around her, and caress her back. He thought he could see some virtue in her face. But his feet remained planted on the ground.

At last, Buyong shut the gate, crossed the yard, and returned to her room. Hyeonggeol waited for her to shut the door, then he stepped out to stand before the gate. Beneath the planks in the gate he could see a gentle light from her room. For a moment, he felt something religious, something spiritual in that light. He simply stood there like that for some time.

He wanted to see her, he wanted to see her and say nothing, but simply stare at her beautiful face, but he realized deep in his heart that he could not call on her, nor could he go into her room.

Struck by this heartrending thought, he turned his eyes once more to Buyong's room, and at last he worked up the courage to move his feet.

He stood in the middle of the road and felt a hush all around him. A cool breeze blew across the road. Where should he go? But there was no need to think twice, as the answer was obvious. He reminded himself that he had been on his way to the church to see Mun Useong. His heart suddenly felt lighter.

Let us go to Mr. Mun! Yet his reason for visiting Mr. Mun was completely different from what it had been before. He was not going to discuss a solution and receive comfort because he did not know what to do; he was going to see him as the first step in carrying out his new resolution. Teacher Mun was no longer an evangelist above him, he was a patron beside him who would aid him in his cause.

This resolution Hyeonggeol had arrived at in his heart may

have been vague, but, whether he left this village tonight for Pyeongyang or somewhere even farther off, he meant to strike out on a new path. Imagining himself walking out of Visiting Immortal Gate along the newly constructed road toward the Pyeongyang-Wonsan road, he marched along surefooted as a soldier toward the church where Mr. Mun was staying.